48 Hours,
Then She Dies

Harry Fisher

Cover Image: Victoria Swing Bridge, Leith Docks (built 1874)

email:	harry.fisher.writer@gmail.com
web:	www.harryfisherwriter.com
Amazon Author Page:	https://amzn.to/3CkR6GL
FB:	facebook.com/harryfisherwriter/
Twitter / X	https://x.com/HFwritesCrime
Bookbub	https://bit.ly/3fx6rLV

Dear Reader,

As a small contribution to help the environment, not all chapters in this book begin with a fresh page. An unusual approach, perhaps, but it has saved 16 sheets of paper plus the related resources. This translates into an equivalent saving of ten books for every 100 printed.

For my sister,

Karen

Chapter 1

1966
Friday 28th January – 23:50

Given his hard-earned reputation as the most powerful and ruthless businessman in the port of Leith, Alessandro De Luca was probably entitled to believe he was invincible. But that miserable night, in January 1966, he was about ten minutes shy of being abruptly and violently disabused of that notion.

Standing there, just inside the East Gate to Leith Docks and swaying dangerously close to tipping point, he pondered the old wives' tale he'd heard trotted out often enough: "It's when you step outside and the fresh air hits you".

Alessandro had always reckoned the adage was simply an excuse for men who imagined they were still sober as they breezed out of a pub, but miraculously became sozzled the second their feet hit the pavement. Thing is, he'd never given any credence to such nonsense. He knew damn fine he didn't feel so drunk because it was kicking on for midnight, in Scotland, at the arse end of January. No, it was because he'd been daft enough to go drink for drink with a gang of dockers, most of whom were half his age and thought getting paralytic on a Friday night was mandatory for any working man worth his salt. Plus, the occasion had involved a head-wetting, meaning the disaster potential automatically increased tenfold.

Steadying himself, he took a bold step but caught the toe of his highly polished black brogue on a shard of broken slab and almost went over. As he pitched forwards, the sooty brick wall of the gatehouse loomed directly in front of him. He stuck out a hand to arrest his fall but misjudged it, and the elbow of his dark blue Crombie coat dragged across the pebbledash. He sensed, rather than heard, the cloth ripping. He was in for it now; his son had bought him the coat for Christmas and tonight was only the second time it had been on his back. Alessandro swung his other arm round and pushed himself upright. *Not good*, he muttered to himself. *Not good at all.*

1

If he hadn't been so pissed, he'd have kicked himself up the backside. He should never have accepted that last dram, but the new father had insisted, vehemently, as only highly intoxicated men do. *There'll be hell to pay when I get home*, he thought. *She'll go ballistic. And no doubt remind me I'm sixty-five, not twenty five.* He sighed and leaned on the wall; his coat was ruined, so an extra smear of soot mattered not a jot.

He made a vain attempt to summon an air of sobriety before setting off again. A few yards further on, he had to jink smartly off to the side to skirt an oily puddle that barred his way. He stuck his tongue out at it, felt his feet were beginning to get ahead of him, so pulled up short. He stood, swaying like a spinning top on its last few revolutions then, resolute, he scuffed his palms together before staggering on.

Earlier, when he'd arrived at the working men's pub on a scruffy side street near the docks, he'd intended to spend no more than an hour or so celebrating with the new father. Two beers at the most and conduct the odd piece of business. Word had reached his ears that a couple of his men were moaning about their lot but nothing that couldn't be smoothed over with a quiet word and a wee backhander. Turning the final corner, even if he'd been stone deaf, the menacing rumble that reverberated from the pub would have guided him in. He hesitated on the pavement outside. The half door crashed open and two men wearing overalls and donkey jackets tumbled out. They joined arms but set off in opposite directions and both of them hit the deck. One sprang to his feet, rolled his mate into the gutter, and ran away, cackling like a demented baboon.

Alessandro hesitated but decided he might as well join the fray. He pushed at the door and the noise hit him like a factory chimney being pulled down. This was a party that had gone a few stages past full swing. Any quiet words he'd planned to have would need to be yelled in an ear from point blank range, and the chances of them being remembered were lower than a snake's belly in a wagon wheel rut. As for the smoke, the revellers were visible but only as ethereal images waving arms and slopping beer.

'Fuck this for a game of soldiers,' he said.

His legs were still processing the *Let's get out of here* command when a meaty paw clamped onto his arm and hauled him inside. 'Hey, boys! Look what the cat dragged in.' This was Charlie Kinnear, Alessandro's closest friend. If Charlie said Alessandro was going nowhere, well, that was that.

The booze-fuelled racket hit a new crescendo if that were possible. A short man wearing a cloth cap back to front tottered past bearing a tray of drinks at head height. The glasses contained liquids of every hue, from coal black to clear. There was neither a soft drink nor a cube of ice in sight. In this establishment, a lager shandy was akin to a cocktail.

Charlie swiped two beers off the tray and thrust one in Alessandro's direction. He shouted something unintelligible at three worthies slouched over a table. They retaliated with a volley of insults, but shuffled over to let the two men slide in beside them.

"Time gentlemen please" was at ten, the theory being fifteen minutes drinking-up time before everyone was heaved out. The reality was that lesser known faces were *encouraged* to vacate, the lights would go down, shutters banged closed, and the double doors bolted from the inside. Even if a policeman did wander past and wonder if a lock-in was taking place, he'd keep walking if he knew what was good for him. And if he did report it, his superiors who sanctioned these transgressions would inform him in single-syllable words that he must have been mistaken.

By the time Alessandro eventually left, the Sabbath was fast approaching. As a younger man, he could sink a skinful and make it all the way home without stopping. These days, he made sure his last port of call before hitting the street was a visit to the gents'. Such a pity he'd forgotten tonight. So it was his bladder that determined the route, and the docks provided a multitude of dark corners for a man caught short. Instead of heading back to the pale orange lighting on Salamander Street, a warehouse lined road that bordered Leith Docks, he'd managed to negotiate his way through the wicket door set into the main gates, which were chained shut to prevent illegal access. And perhaps more importantly, egress.

The Scottish word that best represented the weather that Friday night was dreich. If the moisture level in the heavy mist had risen by one percentage point, it would have turned to rain. Apart from a few shafts of light spilling from a nearby hangar where a night shift was working, there were only a few underpowered lamps scattered about. But the saturated air meant that any illumination hardly radiated more than a few feet from its source.

As inebriated as he was, Alessandro's internal compass was locked on home. Portable cranes shifted their positions daily, boats berthed and sailed, but the buildings, harbours and dry docks were a permanent presence. So despite the weather rendering the skyline invisible, he weaved along, altering direction from time to time. It didn't cross his mind he might be vulnerable; there was little chance he'd meet anyone at that godforsaken hour and, after all, most of the dock workers knew him by sight. He wouldn't come to any harm.

All he had to do was watch his step. He'd replace the coat without his wife knowing but he'd inherit a world of hassle if he tumbled and landed on his face.

It wasn't long before his route bisected one of the multitude of railway tracks that interlaced the docks. The main line arrowed in from the east before splitting into dozens of spurs. All bar a few deposited their freight at various points inside the docks but the greasy rails he was negotiating like a toddler who'd only recently discovered the status known as upright, ran straight through the heart of the area, over the Victoria Swing Bridge, and headed off for satellite harbours like Newhaven and Granton. That was Alessandro's route home, but necessity dictated he'd need to make a stop before crossing the bridge.

Now clear of the lines, Alessandro stumbled into the centre of a crossroads. The atmosphere stank of ingrained diesel and filthy water. Albert Dock, the smallest of three on that side of the harbour, brooded silently off to his right, and a night watchman's hut stood in an open area between him and the dock. Beneath a ramshackle lean-to, a brazier sheltered, and below that, a cat, black as the darkest of nights. By degrees, it flattened its belly against the damp ground, claws dug in and primed to scarper at the merest hint of danger. But when

4

Alessandro lurched to a halt in front of the brazier, the animal held its position. He had no idea it was there.

He stretched his arm out above the coals, palm down. They retained some residual heat, but any glow had long since subsided. Had he been sober, he'd have noticed the coals had been carefully banked so the fire could be brought back to life with minimum fuss. The door to the hut was ajar, but there was no light inside. He jabbed his toe into the rotting wood at the bottom. The door scraped across the flagstones but stopped after a few inches. 'You skiving little bastard.'

Said *little bastard* was a spotty thirteen-year-old named Paul, who Alessandro paid to keep an eye on what went on. The real night watchman was an old family friend whose remaining time on this earth numbered in weeks, not months. The man was no longer able to work but the family was desperate for money so Alessandro had fixed it so the docks' supervisor knew the old man wouldn't be at work but as long as Alessandro paid for a replacement, he'd turn a blind eye and keep the wages coming. But Paul had deserted his post, and the brazier suggested it hadn't been recently.

'I'll tan his arse tomorrow.' Alessandro swung round, corrected a minor wobble, and staggered behind the hut to relieve himself. The mercury had dropped, and the billowing sheets of fog changed to a heavy drizzle. He pulled his overcoat closed and set off again. Then he stopped.

A pair of insipid headlamps was trundling towards him. Shallow pools of light failed to penetrate the rain, rebounding off the white sparks now falling in earnest. The wiper blades alternately squeaked and thunked against the base of the Commer van's windscreen. It drove a few yards nearer then puttered to a halt, engine idling. The rattles suggested it had been round the block a few times. One of the headlamps began popping off and on, in tune with the engine.

Alessandro held his hand across his forehead, trying, and failing, to make out the driver. The passenger door creaked open, and the engine wheezed on for a few beats before falling silent. The wipers stopped too, vertically on the windscreen. A gull wheeled and banked overhead, screeching and yipping at nothing in particular.

A black Chelsea boot crunched into the ground beneath the door and a voice sang out. 'Hello, Sandro. Had a good night?' The man strolled out from behind the door and Alessandro recognised him instantly. He was dressed like a carbon copy of the influential pop groups of the times. Styled collar-length hair, and cream turtleneck jumper beneath a houndstooth sports coat.

Alessandro blinked. His eyes refused to focus. 'Aye. Just wending my weary way home, Speedy.'

The man's eyebrows dropped. 'It's Edward, as I'm sure I've told you before.'

Alessandro didn't react. *Speedy*: a nickname after the cartoon character, Speedy Gonzales, a Mexican mouse who sported an enormous yellow sombrero, and scorched around the desert lightning-fast, righting wrongs and scattering dust and pebbles in his wake. The man who insisted on being called Edward had attracted the moniker because he was the slowest runner Leith had ever produced. He possessed no knee or ankle flex and moved like he was on stilts. Edward Tweed – Speedy Tweedy.

Alessandro was sobering up rapidly. 'Does mummy know you're out so late?' His voice was clear, no slur at all. 'And you're slumming it a bit down here, aren't you?'

A metallic screech sounded from the rear of the van then there was movement behind Speedy. Two men sauntered into view and a second pair appeared from the other side. The driver stayed where he was, both hands visible on the top of the steering wheel. Alessandro studied the men as if they were exhibits in an anthropology museum. All four were light on their feet, axe handles swung easily from their grips, the polished wood catching the wan light from the headlamps.

Alessandro didn't need anyone to draw him a picture. He faced up to the man in front of him, straightened and leaned forward on the balls of his feet. Eyeballed him. 'No, Speedy. No.' There wasn't a chance he'd call him Edward. It was far too late for that. 'What are you playing at, son? You're only what: twenty? Way too young to dream about taking over. You don't know how things work. Haven't served your time. You won't last five minutes.'

'Served my time?' Speedy rocked on his heels and made a pretence of laughing uproariously. The rain prevented it from echoing. 'I'm not waiting till all you old bastards start falling to bits, or worse, hand the businesses over to your spawn.' He hawked a gob of phlegm onto the ground. 'Dead men's shoes, that is. Ha! Life's too flamin' short. Haven't you heard; this is the swinging sixties. And about time you realised we're a lot smarter than you ever were.' He tugged at his lapel, smoothed the flat of his hand down the lambswool jumper. 'In more ways than one.'

Alessandro blinked against the drizzle. He was faltering. The adrenaline had faded fast, the alcohol in his system had regained the upper hand. Outnumbered five to one, with only his fists to call on. He who fights and runs away, and all that.

So he turned, tried to accelerate, but his legs moved like he was wading through treacle in divers' boots. The rain began teeming down. But he'd lost his bearings, he was moving away from the Victoria Bridge, and away from the rails that gleamed in a curve off to his left. Speedy strode alongside him, hands jammed in his pockets, coat tails flapping. Two of his henchmen flanked Alessandro on the other side. The others walked along behind; they didn't need to break into a trot. Try as he might, Alessandro couldn't bring up a head of steam. *Have to get rid of this damned coat. Weighs a bloody ton.*

He'd just shrugged off the garment when Speedy signalled, and the man closest to Alessandro poked his axe handle deftly in between the old man's ankles. He was never going to stay upright, and he was too slow to bring his hands up to break his fall. His face smacked into the stones, and he grunted in surprise.

Speedy stopped. Eyeballed the gang. 'Remember, boys, he'd been drinking. A tragic accident, right?' He ambled off in the direction of the Commer.

Alessandro pushed himself up on one elbow. Rising to his feet was beyond him. 'People will come looking for you, you bastard.'

The young man paused. Smirked. 'I doubt it.' He carried on walking and shouted over his shoulder. 'But even if they do, I'll be ready.'

An axe handle was raised, just as the cloud base cracked open. Alessandro registered a flash as the polished wood slashed across the surface of the moon.

And then, nothing.

A couple of minutes later, there was a scraping sound followed by a dull splash. The four men trotted towards the headlamps. Doors slammed, the engine kicked into life, tyres crunched on gravel as it made a wide U-turn. Only one of the tail lights was working. Within seconds, the van had vanished.

The cat was still under the brazier, glassy green eyes glinting in the moonlight. A few seconds later it lost interest and wandered off.

Leaving only one pair of eyes focussed on the scene. And they didn't belong to an animal.

Chapter 2

The Present Day
October 2023 – Tuesday 22:30

Marlon Stevenson gazed through the van's windscreen onto Commercial Street in Leith, a wide poker-straight thoroughfare linking The Shore and Ocean Terminal. Retail outlets and small business premises lined the left side of the street but further along these changed to apartment buildings that had replaced derelict tenements razed to the ground in the 70s. The opposite side, the right, was formed by a run of former whisky bonds converted to expensive flats. His view was of the rear of the buildings; their frontages faced onto Victoria Quay, home to what was the Scottish Office, and no more than a lusty "Land ahoy" from the Royal Yacht *Britannia*. The extension to Edinburgh's tram system passed nearby, the construction of which had been the bane of everyday life in the city for fifteen interminable years.

It was a Tuesday night, not long after half ten so there weren't too many people about. A couple of teenagers sauntered by, heading towards The Shore. Hoodies, hunched shoulders, eyes glued to phones. Two parallel beings, locked into their own little worlds.

A couple, Marlon imagined they were in their twenties, strolled past, arm in arm. They were laughing, and every now and again they bounced off each other. Merrily pissed, he decided.

By and large, it was a quiet night. Leith as an entity still had its dodgy elements, and that would never change, but since the turn of the century this area had been revitalised and then some. The pavement on his side of the road was wide, with bright lighting. There wasn't a free parking space in sight, and every 80 metres or so, the pavement extended a car's width into the road to accommodate communal wheely bins. Gentrified area or not, people still jammed them till they were well past capacity, a bizarre form of rubbish Jenga. So Marlon had reversed the van up onto the pavement, squeezed in between a bin and a Kawasaki motorbike that had been slotted into the last remaining square foot of legitimate parking.

He wouldn't be staying long so wasn't concerned at all about being badly parked. Throughout Leith, drivers parked illegally and every street resembled chicane central because of those who double-parked. Everyone was guilty, so no one batted an eyelid.

A young woman appeared, framed in his door mirror, walking along from the direction of The Shore, a strip of waterfront cafés, bars and restaurants bisected by Commercial Street. She was wearing trainers, a short skirt, and a fleece with the zip undone. As he watched, she skipped forwards a few steps and booted a discarded coffee cup off the pavement and under a car. She shot her arms into the air and danced a jig, as if she'd netted the winner in the Champions League Final.

Marlon smiled. If he'd been out on the pavement he might have applauded. He glanced behind him at a cardboard box filled with mixed recycling, including several wine bottles. He climbed out of the van, slid open the side door and lifted the box. He shuffled backwards away from the opening, switched the box to one hand and raised a knee to support it. His grip on the box was precarious and it began to slip to the side.

His reactions were slow. The box toppled and the bottles began sliding out. In the still evening air they clinked and clattered as they hit the stone paving. The young woman, now almost in line with the van, slowed her pace. Two of the bottles bounced under her feet and she stopped dead in her tracks. Marlon dropped the box and rushed towards her. 'Oh my God. I'm so sorry.'

He bent down, scrabbling around, trying to scoop them up. 'So sorry. So sorry.'

She stopped a green tinted wine bottle with the sole of her shoe then stepped off to the side. 'Look. It's okay. Don't worry—'

Marlon shot upright and grabbed her. Before she could react, in one action he lifted her and swung her towards the van's side door. As he propelled her into the vehicle, her right hip clattered into the leading edge of the floor and her cheek scraped along the ribbed metal. He hoisted her legs in behind her then jumped in, sliding the door shut at the same time. He reached into a rack, grabbed a flashlight, and shone it straight in her face, knocking out her vision. Then he threw a heavy sack over her head, flipped her on her stomach, wrenched her hands behind her and zip tied her wrists.

The young woman didn't resist when he hauled her ankles together so forcibly, the bones on the insides clashed together. Then he used another cable tie to immobilise her feet.

He grabbed her hair through the sack, jerked her head back, and snarled in her ear. 'Shut up, girl. Do not move. Do not struggle. You can't break free, and no one will hear you. Understand?' Seconds later, deafeningly loud rock music reverberated around the insides of the van. His aim had been to shock and disorient her, and it had worked because while all that had been going on she hadn't uttered a sound.

The engine clattered to life, and as the van drove away, she was propelled sideways across the floor. She yelped as her knee banged into the wheel arch.

Then she screamed. And carried on screaming. Until she almost choked.

Chapter 3

The Following Day
Wednesday 09:15

I'm hightailing it down the stairs. All my boss had said on the phone was, "Come down to Interview One quick, Mel. This is a strange one".

Mel. That's me. Detective Inspector Mel – short for Melissa – Cooper. If anyone apart from my mother uses my full name, I'm probably in bother. I'd just turned fourteen when I announced the new cool abbreviated monicker. Dad was predictably relaxed about the whole thing and has been to this day. Mother, equally predictably, was not, and gave us both an earful.

My colleague, Detective Constable Tobias Hartmann is trailing behind me. Tobias is German and specialises in crime data analysis. He joined my team permanently from Cologne after a secondment with us a year or so ago and fits in perfectly. If he even hints at returning home to Germany, I'll chain him to a desk. I speak over my shoulder as we push through corridor traffic. 'It's not like Jeff to be so abrupt, so whatever it is, it's urgent.'

We arrive outside the door, I knock, and we march straight in.

The building that houses Leith police HQ, being kind, is in a constant state of flux. You'd need at least double my twenty years of service to remember when there wasn't refurbishment work on the go. But every time there's a suggestion that we relocate to Police Scotland's shiny new building, two miles across town, it never happens. Truth is, I don't care, and I doubt many of my fellow inhabitants do either. The crime happens here or hereabouts, so this is where we should be. Centralised resource, or whatever's the latest buzz phrase, can go take a hike as far as I'm concerned.

The interview room is shabby, with zero in the way of chic. Painted walls the colour of seagull puke, a persistent aroma that defies every detergent known to woman, and the standard table and four chairs that will be older than me. My boss, Detective Chief Inspector Jeff Hunter, has moved his chair to the end of the table that's furthest away from the door.

When I'm standing talking to Jeff, I have to be careful that the top of my spine doesn't seize up. Even sitting down, it's obvious he's a head taller than everyone else in the room. His features can only be described as angular, with a benign gaze that many a dumb criminal has misinterpreted. To their cost.

A laptop sits there, lid open a crack like a silent black clam on the lookout for tasty titbits. Flashing LEDs on the side broadcast its "on" status. Lying next to it is an evidence bag. Poking out the top are three items: a plain white envelope, and a sheet of A4 inside a clear plastic wallet. The paper contains lines of typed text.

A chap has one side of the table to himself, facing the remaining two chairs. I guess he's the reason we've been summoned here at a fast lick. I slide into the first chair, leaving Tobias to walk round me and drop his comfortably-sized backside into the one next to our boss. Whoever this man is, I want to sit opposite so he can experience my most penetrating interrogator's expression, should I feel the need to call upon it.

When I take a closer look I realise that's not likely to be necessary. This gentleman is smartly dressed, probably around seventy, and the impression he's transmitting is that his next smile will be his first one of the day. There's a light sheen to his face, and a distinct tremor to his bottom lip. Not quite ventriloquist dummy level but getting there. I don't know who this man is yet but he's not a crook, or even a suspected crook; the way Jeff's laid out the seating plan makes that clear.

Tobias and I speak at the same time. 'Boss?'

Jeff nods and flaps out his left hand. 'This is Hugo Emerson. Retired Detective Inspector Hugo Emerson, to be more precise.'

I introduce myself and let Tobias do likewise. Emerson restates his name, then does so a second time. I come to the rapid conclusion that the man is a wreck, and I'm curious to understand why. I signal that I have a question, but Jeff holds a hand up. 'Best just listen for now, Mel.' Then, to the retired DI, 'Run through your story again, Hugo.'

Hugo Emerson's eyes are twitching around. He appears to be struggling to open up, and clearly decides the best way to overcome that is to go straight for the punchline. 'My granddaughter, Natasha, she's been kidnapped. Last night, we think. We know she was out, but we don't know where, or who she was with.'

That was succinct. But given the context, not much point in beating about the bush, is there? 'Have you tried contacting her?' I ask.

'Of course we have.' His gaze drops to the table. 'Sorry. Yes, we've all tried. Calls go straight to voicemail.' I don't respond, figuring that would just upset him more. It's obvious we need him on an even keel for as long as possible.

There's a light tap on the door and a bloke who's about Tobias's age strides in. I recognise him as a tech from our Computer Crime Unit. He hands Jeff an evidence bag. Jeff delves into his inside jacket pocket, pulls out a pair of latex gloves and snaps them on. He tilts the bag and lets a plain black USB key slide out onto his palm. He twirls it round, reads the logo, then places it to the side. 'It's clean,' says the tech. 'You can use it in any device.' He hovers, waiting for a critical procedural step to take place.

Jeff looks over the table at Tobias. 'If you would do the honours, please?'

My colleague uses his phone to scan a Quick Response, or "QR" code on the evidence bag. Instantaneously, the phone beeps twice signifying that he has now accepted formal responsibility for the USB key, which might turn out to be an important piece of evidence. The tech throws out the briefest of smiles and exits as quickly as he arrived. In the olden days, someone would have quipped, "Who *was* that masked man?"

Jeff plucks the plastic wallet from the other bag, holding it between thumb and forefinger as if he were in danger of catching something nasty. He lays it on the table, spins it through 180 degrees and prods it towards me. Tobias and I lean forward to read it, keeping our hands folded in our laps.

It says, "This is about Natasha. I have kidnapped her. If you want to see her alive again I suggest you follow my instructions TO THE LETTER. Take the USB to Leith police station. Ask for DCI Jeff Hunter, no one else. I know he's in the station today so DO NOT take no for an answer. Your granddaughter's life depends on it. Plug the USB into a laptop that has an internet connection and a camera. Everything you need to know is on there".

Hugo points at the white envelope. His hand quivers like he's been on a three-day bender. 'Our doorbell rang at about 08:45 this morning. Found this lying on the mat. I opened the front door but there was no one there, and no one in sight. As soon as I realised what was inside, and I can't really explain why, I went straight through to the kitchen and put on the wife's Marigolds. Not particularly scientific but the best I could do.' He aims for a smile but doesn't come close. 'I didn't touch the USB, and it was me who put the letter in the plastic thing.'

'Do you have a doorbell camera?' I say.

He shakes his head. 'Nor CCTV.'

Jeff picks up the USB. 'Let's find out what's on this.' He turns to Hugo. 'Technically speaking, I should ask you to leave, but …'

Natasha's grandfather doesn't reply but the glare makes it clear he's staying put unless my boss throws him out.

'Hugo,' I say. 'You can give me full details later but tell me a bit more about Natasha. How old is she? What does she do for a living?' I'm about to ask Tobias to take notes but he's ahead of me, already tapping into his iPad. Good man.

Hugo wipes at his eyes. When he blinks the tears fall, but his voice is steady. 'She's only nineteen. A student.'

'Studying?'

'Electrical and mechanical engineering. Not long started second year.'

'How's that going?'

'She's doing well. Enjoys it. She teases us about the wild time she's having but that's all it is. We know how hard she works.'

'Where does she live?'

'A flat on Commercial Street, near Ocean Terminal.'

'On her own?'

'She shares with the woman who owns it. She's a bit older. A nurse, I think.'

'Her name?'

He takes a second. 'Robyn? Yes, that's it. Robyn. Sorry. Don't know her surname.'

I say to Hugo, 'What number on Commercial Street, please?' Then I indicate Tobias. 'My colleague will arrange for Robyn to be interviewed.' Tobias jots down the address, turns away to the side and murmurs into his phone.

'Is Natasha in a relationship?' I don't mention boyfriend, or girlfriend. Times are vastly different to when I was footloose and fancy free.

'Not as far as we know.' The tears flow again. 'Detective Cooper?'

I raise my eyebrows.

'She's my only grandchild.'

I stretch over and lay my hand on the back of his. I don't make stupid promises that we'll find her; that's the realm of the TV cop. I simply nod and offer him the tiniest smile I possess in my repertoire.

* * *

Jeff lifts the laptop lid, and the screen pops on. The USB jams as he tries to slide it into the port, so he flips it over; this time it goes in. He lifts an HDMI cable off the floor, connects it to the laptop and picks up a TV remote. The two devices form an immediate connection, and the computer's display is replicated on a wall-mounted TV with at least a 40-inch screen. On the laptop, Jeff navigates to the "G" drive, identified as the USB. He double-clicks the only folder; it's been named *Natasha*. This contains a Microsoft Word document, also named *Natasha*. Jeff opens it. There's only one page, with a URL. He sighs, copies the URL, pastes it into the browser, and hits *Enter*. A new window appears with a video icon.

I read the kidnapper's instructions again. 'Wonder why he's so specific about the laptop's capability. Internet ready, and a camera?' Nobody questions my assumption the kidnapper is male. We've yet to find out, but I'll be stunned if it's a woman. And it's worth pointing out I'm only dealing in binary. It's a bugger finding the right box to tick if it's one of the other options.

'Don't know,' says Jeff. 'We'll find out soon enough, I suppose.'

He moves the mouse over the *Play* icon, but I hold up a hand. 'Hang on a minute, Boss. We don't know how long the link will be live, so we should record it. Just in case.'

'Good thinking, Mel.' He brings up the Windows Apps menu on the left of the screen, scrolls down till he finds a media app, clicks a couple of icons and sits back. A small black rectangle pops up: "The screen is recording". He presses *Play*.

The film reveals a man, sitting on a chair, his back to a blank wall. The carved black spindle poking out above his left shoulder suggests it's a dining chair. He's wearing sunglasses. One of the first steps we take in these circumstances is to show the video to an in-house expert on body language. Non-verbal communication, to give it its proper title. They can learn a lot from the eyes, so that's one avenue closed down. I notice he's keeping his hands out of sight too, below the foot of the screen. Clever. But still, his voice and his posture might give clues away.

He puts me in mind of an ageing boxer. Welterweight, or similar. Probably late fifties, slender, narrow frame. Shaved grey hair, bald on top. White tee shirt, plain silver chain round his throat. He looks like a man under pressure; hardly surprising, to be fair.

From the angle of his body, one shoulder slightly further forward than the other, he might be filming himself with a phone on a selfie stick. Yet the screen is steady, as if to prove me wrong.

Jeff maximises the window and we all nudge our chairs round to face the TV.

The man takes a breath, hesitates, then speaks. 'Mr Emerson. You know your granddaughter, Natasha, has been kidnapped. That was me. She's safe. Unharmed. That's all you need to know.' His voice is hoarse, shaky in parts. He drinks from a bottle of water. It's clear plastic, with one of those click-open drinking tops. The label's been ripped off, leaving patches of white glue residue. He could have bought it anywhere. He lays it down, off screen, then rubs his sternum with the ball of his thumb before dropping his hand away. It was his left hand, which may or may not be significant. 'I sincerely hope for her sake, and yours too, that you've followed my instructions and you're watching this in the police station with DCI Hunter. But I'll find that out in a minute or two. However, if you are not, it'll be profoundly bad news for Natasha. Or Tash. Because that's what you all call her, isn't it? Except her grandmother of course, she would never use *Tash*. Always Natasha.'

I shiver. Instantly think of my own mother.

He takes another swig, speaking more smoothly now. He's settled into his spiel. 'So, DCI Hunter. I'll cut right to the chase. My name is Marlon Stevenson.'

Marlon? What the hell kind of name is that?

'On the 29th of January 1966, my grandfather, Sandro De Luca was brutally murdered —'

Hugo gives out a huge gasp, a mixture of groan, wail and rage. 'Oh, please no. Not this again. Not after all these years.' He rises half out of his chair, palms on the table. He yells at the TV. 'Let her go, you bastard.' But as soon as he realises we only have one-way communication, his emotion flatlines.

Jeff clicks the *Pause* button, about to say something to Hugo. But Stevenson is still talking, so Jeff clicks *Pause* again. But still the video plays on, so this time he taps the *Space* bar. Normally that would do the trick but still the film runs on. We have no choice but to turn back to the TV. Later, we'll have to quiz Hugo on his reaction because clearly the murder of Stevenson's grandfather has a significant meaning to him.

We zone in on the kidnapper. '… and it wasn't that they failed to solve the case; no, they didn't even try. And if they did, it was nowhere near hard enough, not by a long chalk.' While he's talking I hear Jeff tapping the keyboard a few more times but somehow this video file is stuck on transmit. The laptop can't break in, so we're forced to listen to Stevenson. '… eventually, years later in fact, I was tipped the wink. The investigation was deliberately suppressed.'

Now Hugo has his elbows on the table, head in his hands, moaning like his appendix has spontaneously perforated.

'So here's the bottom line,' says Stevenson. 'If you don't reopen the investigation and get working on it – to my complete satisfaction, I might add – it is possible that today or tomorrow, Mr Emerson, your granddaughter will die.'

Hugo is sobbing, thumping his fists on the table. Tobias doesn't have to be asked. He stands up, grips the older man gently by the arm, supports him out of his seat and guides him out into the corridor. I call after him. 'Tobias. Find someone to look after Mr Emerson and come straight back.'

'I will, Boss.'

'Now,' says Stevenson. 'You'll want proof I'm serious, and you'll have that in a minute. I also imagine that you've tried to pause or rewind the film and discovered that's not possible.' I recoil as if I've been slapped. Why has he brought this to our attention? But I can't focus on these thoughts just now because he's still talking. '... I do not want you to misinterpret, disregard or even worse, forget my next three statements. One: this is not a hostage situation, not in the normal sense. Two: and listen carefully, I will not negotiate, nor leave myself open to negotiation. I'm sure you'll bring in experts, that's entirely your prerogative, but I will only talk to you. Either you meet all my demands, without discussion or debate, or Natasha Emerson dies. And, finally, number three: you will have no means of contacting me. I will contact you, every six hours if not sooner, and if you haven't followed my instructions precisely, and met the objectives I have set, then you will be responsible for putting Natasha's life in danger. Not me. You.'

He stops speaking, and I wonder if he's finished. He hasn't.

'I promised you a demonstration. Keep watching.'

* * *

Momentarily, the screen turns black, then a washed-out cream bathed in a harsh unnatural light. The image is of a room, and just off centre in that room is a young woman. She is sitting on the floor with her back against a blank wall, her legs folded beneath her in the lotus position. She's slender. We know she's still in her teens. That could be my daughter sitting there. I kick that thought into touch. She is dressed as if it were a Sunday, and she's taken root on the sofa. A pale grey hoodie, darker coloured shorts, bare feet. A redhead, with a spiky cut. Her complexion is pale, but I don't know if that's her skin tone or a trick of the light. Doubtless she's petrified.

She's being filmed in wide angle from a point high up to her left. She's not looking at the camera so either she doesn't know it exists or she's avoiding making eye contact. My eyes narrow as I spot a livid bruise on her right cheek and, as I watch, she adjusts her position to massage her right hip. She stretches out that limb, wiggles her toes, curls it back into place. She hugs herself, but that doesn't stop her shoulders shaking. There's no way of telling if it's cold in the room or not.

I hear a click, then a footfall; Tobias slips in beside me. 'Natasha,' he says. It wasn't a question, but I nod anyway.

I study the room. At first glance it appears to have no angles but once I can tune out the lighting I begin to pick them out. There are no skirtings, no doors or windows, nothing on the walls. The floor might be vinyl, pale blue or grey. Industrial perhaps. The surface is smooth, continuous, no obvious joins. The only area that's not covered by the camera is the wall immediately beneath it. The ceiling stretches out ahead; no lights hanging down but two brighter areas in a direct line suggest downlighters. Otherwise, nothing else protrudes.

Jeff says, 'There's no sound.' Again I nod. We're watching a silent movie; there's a vacant space where noise should be.

To Natasha's right is a low table with pale wooden legs. The surface is white, it reflects the light. It can't be more than half a metre high. It strikes me there's something weird about it. On closer inspection it's a standard rectangular kitchen table for four but the legs have been cut down. On the top is a flat clear plastic storage box with a clip-on lid. A larger version of the type I use to store food in the fridge. From what I can make out, it's jammed full of stuff. Packets of nuts or dried fruit, towels, what could be travel-sized bottles of liquid soap or sanitiser. There's also a round object, which might be an apple but it's hard to tell. Standing next to the box is a sizeable translucent sports bottle with a green top. Not in the first flush of youth, by the look of it.

In the space between the table and Natasha is a red plastic bin. One half of the top has what appears to be a colander set into it. I walk over to the TV and point. 'Is that one of those old-fashioned pails that comes with a floor mop?'

Jeff says, 'I'd say so. My mum still has one. Ancient old thing, made out of galvanised metal.'

My German colleague screws up his face. 'Pail?'

'Another name for a bucket,' I say.

'Ah,' is the full extent of his reply.

I realise I'm experiencing a dreadful fascination as I observe from afar. This is heightened by the harsh lighting, similar to a sci-fi movie that's been over-exposed for effect.

Natasha jumps to her feet and rubs her cheeks briskly. She lifts the bucket to the side, leans down and stares at the point where the floor meets the wall. She drops to her knees, folds her feet beneath her bottom. She reaches out, runs her fingertips from side to side, and shuffles along the full width of the wall. 'She's trying to find a join,' I say. She rises up on one knee, places the flat of her hand against the wall. Quickly, she works in the opposite direction, rising to her feet as she moves, examining the entire wall by sight and touch.

While she's conducting her search I study the whole space. 'The walls are totally smooth; not even a light switch.'

'Could the door be on this wall, below the camera?' says Tobias.

'If there was a door there,' says Jeff, 'surely she'd check that first. The room can't be sealed, he got her in there somehow.' He peers at the TV. 'Maybe through a hatch but I can't see one.'

Now Natasha is working her way along the longer wall, to our right. I scan the space again. 'Is she in a basement, do you think?'

'That would be my guess,' says Jeff. 'If it is sealed, I can't imagine how you could easily do that with an outhouse or a lockup.'

'It might be possible if the garage was integral to a house,' says Tobias. He scratches at his scalp with the fingernails of both hands, pauses, then makes a grab for the laptop and hits a combination of keys. He marches over to a whiteboard on the far wall, plucks something off the frame and rushes back, rubbing his thumb and forefinger together. He jams his thumb on the laptop's screen, top and centre. Blu Tack. He puts a finger to his lips, grabs a piece of paper and begins scribbling. He spins the paper on the table and pushes it into a space between Jeff and me. "If he can control film, can he see us thru cam? – mike is off now". Now it's clear why Stevenson specified a camera.

Jeff nods. Takes the pen and writes, "Keep quiet till laptop off".

I fix them both with my best line in quizzical looks. I have to say it's all a bit *Mission Impossible*, but these guys are normally sharper than me on this sort of stuff, so I play along.

We all turn our attention to the TV. The lack of meaningful perspective makes it difficult to gauge the size of the room, but by my guess it's easily three metres by five. Or ten feet by sixteen in old money. Now Natasha's about half way along the wall.

A term Jeff mentioned a minute ago begins nibbling at my gut: "sealed". A belt of adrenaline hits me. Is there an air supply? Might she suffocate? I can't see her face because she's kneeling, but apart from being a bit pale and having suffered knocks to her face and hip, she'd looked healthy enough.

I'm still processing all this when Natasha whips round and gawps at the opposite wall, into the corner to our left. She rushes across, her hands flying to her face, and stares up into the corner. It takes a moment before we realise what's grabbed her attention.

A flow of water has appeared, falling down from the ceiling. Like from a tap that's been left on but would take a couple of minutes to fill a sink.

But one thing's for sure – we don't need audio to tell us this young woman is screaming her head off.

Chapter 4

Wednesday 09:30

Natasha crouches down, clenches her fists and jams them into her eyes. She forces herself to relax and again, stares up at the flow. She stands, stretches her arm as high as she can but she's well over a foot short of the ceiling. She lifts the bucket over to the corner and tries to stand on it. But she rushes it. Her foot slips and she tumbles over onto the same hip she was rubbing earlier. She cries out, once more in silence, and slaps her hand over her mouth. I cannot begin to imagine her distress.

Now the water is advancing across the floor, and it ebbs against her hand. She snatches it away as if she's been scalded, but there's no steam so I assume it's cold. She struggles to her feet, tests out the leg, and limps to the bucket. She snatches it off the floor, screams at it then hurls it away, smacking it off the wall. It bounces on the floor and twirls round a couple of times before coming to rest on its side.

Now she's at the table but we groan when she hauls at the top and it stays put. We lean in closer to study the image and only then do we notice all four legs are fitted with right-angled metal brackets. Jeff murmurs out of the side of his mouth. 'Bugger. He's bolted it to the floor.'

Natasha whirls round. Scans the space again. But there's nothing else for her to stand on. She returns to the table, heaves at it, but still it doesn't budge. Her back is to the camera but she's screaming at the room, her body bouncing with energy. Her terror is palpable.

My stomach heaves. I rip the Blu Tack away from the laptop's camera and scrabble at the keys to switch the mike on. I yell at the TV, 'Turn that fucking water off, you evil bastard!'

My words are still bouncing off the walls when the water stops flowing. I stare at the screen in disbelief.

The film fades out and Marlon Stevenson reappears. He speaks in an even, calm tone. 'I could say my wish is your command, DI Cooper, but as it happens, I was about to turn it off anyway.'

* * *

I gawp at the screen. How the hell does he know my name? And when he made the recording of himself, how could he have known I would be here, watching.

But then, blinding realisation, he's spoken to us, so now he's on live transmission. Both Jeff and I start to speak but Stevenson holds up a palm. 'Be quiet, both of you, and listen. From this point on, if you interrupt me, or displease me in any way, this situation will escalate. So I strongly recommend that you take me seriously.' His expression is deadly. 'Have I made myself clear?'

He sits up straight. 'Some facts for you. The room that holds Natasha Emerson has a capacity of 33 cubic metres. The rate of flow you've witnessed is 694 litres per hour. When I turn the tap on again, at that rate the room will fill with water in approximately 48 hours. And 48 hours, DCI Hunter, is precisely how long you have to find out who killed my grandfather back in 1966. And if you don't, Natasha Emerson's fate is inevitable: she will drown.'

No one speaks. And even if I wanted to, I couldn't. The horror of the situation facing this desperate young woman is unimaginable. But we catch a break; Stevenson interprets our silence as acquiescence and picks up. 'I've stated the deadline is 48 hours, but your first target must be achieved in six. At that point you will show me documented proof that my grandfather's case has officially been reopened and that your investigation is under way. I will provide you with an email address and if you don't scan and email me the proof within five minutes of receiving it, you will have failed. And the penalty for failure is I will double the rate of flow for a period of one hour. For the avoidance of doubt, that will fill the room at double the rate, meaning you will lose one hour off your target time every time you fail to do as I say.' He pauses. 'At least one hour.'

We're stunned, unable to grasp the enormity of the task he's setting us, or envisage such a dreadful, tragic outcome, should we fail.

Stevenson continues. 'Now, despite all this, and I doubt you will come even close to believing me, I am not an unreasonable man. You will have questions. So ask.' He pauses again, deliberately it seems. 'And if I deem your questions to be – how can I put it – fit and proper, I will answer them.'

I can't stop myself, I'm first in. 'This is an enormous shock as you can imagine. We will have lots of questions so can we negotiate some time to gather our thoughts and speak to you in, say, an hour?'

He sighs. Angles his face towards the ceiling. 'I've heard about you, DI Cooper—'

'Mel is fine. You don't—'

Stevenson bounces forward in his seat, goes all bug-eyed. '*You interrupted me*. Have you forgotten already that I stated explicitly you should not do that. Or are you not taking me seriously?' He falls silent. His lips tighten. The blood drains away. 'I strongly suggest you all give me your undivided attention. I have already said this is *not* a standard hostage situation. I will *not* negotiate. I will *not* leave myself open to negotiation. And I will *not* be side-tracked. At all. So don't think about using any of the hostage negotiation tactics you've been trained in because my immediate response will be to open that pipe. *Understand*? You follow my rules. You do exactly as I command. You meet all my demands. On time, and to the letter. Comply, and Natasha Emerson survives. Fail, and she does not.' His tone had been rising throughout that tirade but, with no small amount of visible effort, he brings himself under control. 'You can believe this if you like, I really don't give a toss, but I do not want this young woman to die. However, if she has to die, she most certainly will.'

He slugs at the bottle again. 'So, I will only address you by your official titles, and you will address me as Mr Stevenson. You will not get close to me. I will not leave myself open to manipulation. Have I made myself clear?'

'Yes,' says Jeff. 'You have. But I too must be clear. I will move heaven and earth to save Ms Emerson's life and to help me do that I would like to ask three questions if I may.'

Stevenson smiles. 'If you'd started by reminding me I had claimed to be a reasonable man, I'd have turned you down flat. But you catch on quick so ask your questions.'

'Before I do that, you've set us a deadline of 48 hours. But your grandfather's murder will be classified as inactive and I cannot re-examine the case without signed authority from my superiors, which will, unavoidably, take time.'

'Don't treat me like an idiot, DCI Hunter. You don't have to seek authority. An officer of your rank can make that decision.'

'Mr Stevenson, if this conversation had taken place three, maybe four years ago, you'd have been correct. But the protocols were changed because too many cold cases were being reopened with little or no evidence to support them. For example, the murder of a grandmother in Ayrshire back in the 50s. As a result, the level of authority required was increased to Detective Chief Superintendent. I'm reasonably confident I will get that authority, but I would be a fool to describe it as a certainty.'

Stevenson doesn't answer, he remains fixed on the camera as if he were looking Jeff in the eye. My boss doesn't wait, he carries right on. 'You've stated we have six hours to meet our first target, but from when? When does the clock start ticking?'

The response is immediate. 'As soon as I'm finished here, DCI Hunter, the tap goes on and the clock, to use your words, starts ticking. There will be no delay.' He glances down. 'And, to be clear, the current time is 09:32.'

Jeff moves straight on without saying thank you. 'To secure Natasha's release, you want us to solve your grandfather's murder that happened, what, 57 years ago, and has been a cold case since 1980?'

'That's correct.'

At that, Tobias rises from the table and heads for the door. Stevenson points off screen as if he were following Tobias's path. 'I don't know where that detective's going but if he imagines he can trace the source of this transmission, tell him not to bother. Unless, that is, he's on first name terms with criminals who run proxy servers in nasty little places like

Albania.' He puts on a superior expression. I'd sell my granny to be given the chance to slap it off his face.

I'd scribbled Jeff a note, so he leaves the third question to me. I choose my words carefully, desperate not to sound like I'm trying to bring him onside, or get inside his head, or use any police-speak bullshit. 'Mr Stevenson. No matter how this pans out, it cannot end positively for you. You will go to prison for a long time and your life will be wasted. As DCI Hunter said, this case was closed in 1980 so why have you taken this action now, after all this time?'

'You're quite correct, DI Cooper, I know that I'll end up in prison, almost certainly for the rest of my life. But I don't care, my life has been ruined already. You see, I was born the same day my grandfather was murdered, the 29th of January 1966. My mother was already in labour, and he died not knowing his first grandson had been born. I was about seven or eight before I realised that all my birthdays had been crap. Not the same as other kids. No parties. No going to the pictures. Nothing like that. Because every year, on that date, my mother, my grandma, my aunties – all miserable, all crying. Oh yes, they were full of the best intentions. But every birthday, every single one of them, was overshadowed by the bloody great elephant in the room. After the case was closed, my mother became a basket case, and ever since, thirty-odd years, I've had to look after her. She's eighty-nine now, and she has cancer. She won't see ninety. She made me swear to keep fighting but legally, there's nothing I can do. All avenues are closed. So, before she dies, she needs to know who murdered her dad, and why. Maybe then she'll be at peace. And as for what happens to me, like I said before, I'm well past caring. And that makes me dangerous, as you can imagine.

'Now, I assume you'll investigate me. I wouldn't bother. There's nothing to find. You'll discover that everything I've told you is true. What I will say is every minute you spend investigating me is a minute you could have been solving my grandfather's murder. And you need to do that to save Natasha Emerson's life. So you'd better get on with it because that tap is going on at 09:35, not a minute later, and in 48 hours that room will be full of water. Your first deadline will be in six hours – at 15:35. And let me emphasise, I will not repeat myself,

26

you know what you have to do. I'll be in touch. Six hours. No extensions.'

I leap out of my chair, slap both hands on the table. We're about to lose all control of this. I look straight into the camera. 'Mr Stevenson, if we don't solve your grandfather's murder and this poor young woman does drowns, you will be caught and tried for her murder. Do you really want your mother to know her son is a killer and take that to her grave? I'm a mother too, and I know that would destroy me.'

As I'm finishing my sentence I realise I've let my maternal emotions get the better of me and I've screwed up. Big style. I eyeball Stevenson and despite the sunglasses, I know he's glaring right back. My eyes are already watering, and his image blurs. But my ears tell me everything I need to know.

His voice changes to flint. 'I warned you, Cooper. I bloody *warned* you in terms that I thought even an imbecile would understand. But clearly not. However, just to remind you, I told you I would not leave myself open to manipulation, and you would not get close to me.'

'Mr Stevenson –'

He throws his palm directly in front of the camera. 'No, Detective Inspector Cooper. Enough. That was a ham-fisted attempt to manipulate me by bringing my mother into it. And I'm not having that. You need another demonstration.'

The screen switches to the room. Natasha had moved away from the corner, but now she takes a couple of hesitant steps towards the flow inlet. She gazes up at it as if she can't believe it's stopped. I sense rather than see her muscles contracting and her expression changing.

She leaps away as the water flows again, this time with significantly higher force. She grabs handfuls of her hair and bends forward at the waist. I open my mouth, but Jeff grips my forearm. He squeezes tight, twice, before releasing his hold. Natasha moves like a zombie to the diagonally opposite corner and comes to a stop. For half a beat she remains perfectly still. Then someone flicks a switch. She throws her head back, glares up at the ceiling and screams at it. I watch, horrified, as she waves her arms above her head. Her whole body is quivering uncontrollably. It's as if she's at a rave.

She's completely ignoring the water, which is washing across the floor. I'm hauling the table out of my way. Screaming at the TV. From a distance I hear, 'Mel! Mel!', and I wonder why Jeff is calling me from the bottom of a deep dark well, when he's sitting right across the table.

I turn to ask him.

But I don't make it.

Chapter 5

When DC Steph Zanetti hit the buzzer for number 7/23 Commercial Street, she had to wait a while before Natasha's flatmate opened the door. Not only did Robyn Russell have to cope with being dragged out of her bed less than an hour after finishing a particularly shitty night shift, she was also hit with the shocking news that her young friend had been kidnapped. Steph didn't share any details, only that Natasha was alive but her whereabouts were unknown.

'Tell me about last night, Robyn,' said Steph. 'Did anything unusual happen before Natasha went out?'

They were sitting at the kitchen table. Robyn was leaning slightly forward over a crossed leg, clutching her robe like she'd just been rescued from a blizzard. Her foot tapped in midair. 'No. She was floating about, doing bits and bobs, chatting to me while I was getting ready for work.'

'What time was this?'

'I left here at about 19:30.'

'What do you do?'

'I'm a nurse. At the Western. Haematology. I start at eight and it's only ten minutes to the hospital at that time in the evening. I like to arrive a wee bit early so I can take the handover in plenty of time. The nurses going off shift are always desperate to escape.'

'So Natasha wasn't dressed and ready to go out?'

'Good God, no. Tash is always last minute.' Her voice caught and she steadied herself. 'She takes everything right to the wire but she's never late for anything. Exam deadlines, leaving for an appointment, going off on hols, the lot. She's always totally relaxed about it, but it drives everybody else nuts. Me included.' She snagged a tissue from her pocket and blew her nose. Dragged her sleeve across her eyes. 'I'm a lot older than her but we rub along just fine.'

'Do you know who she was meeting?'

'All she said was two of her chums from uni.'

'Names?'

The answer comes right off the bat. 'No. Sorry.'

'In her class? Her year?'

'I imagine so. She's possibly a bit early in uni life to make friends in other years. Or even other disciplines. From my experience, anyway.'

'You went to uni.'

She nodded. 'Yes. I have a degree in economics, but I realised too late that I would have hated working in that environment. I finished the course; the degree might come in useful for passing a paper sift or something.'

Steph tilted her head a little. Her ponytail brushed against her collar. 'So, if she wasn't ready to go out, would I be correct in saying you don't know what she was wearing?'

'No. I don't.'

'Would you know what might be missing from her wardrobe?'

Robyn snorted. 'Tell you what. You go and look in her room and you'll know the answer to that one.' Then she burst into tears.

Steph had no choice but to wait till the woman settled down and as soon as she did, the detective jumped straight in with her next question. 'Where were they going?'

'Along to The Shore, see what was going on. I expect they'd have had a few drinks, maybe some live music. They meet most Tuesday nights because the pubs have deals running.'

'Do they go out to eat?'

'Nah. Too expensive along there. But anyway, she had pasta for tea.'

'Any favourite place we should check first.'

Robyn chewed on her lip. 'They'd have probably picked whichever one was the liveliest.'

She paused there. Her eyes glisten. 'Dear Lord, I hope you find her. I don't know what I'll do if …'

As she pulled the apartment door closed behind her, Steph had a little moment to herself. But she recovered quickly; in her job, sentiment was a luxury she couldn't afford. She called the office. 'Tobias. I'll be back in five.'

Chapter 6

I open my eyes. Jeez, it's bright in here.

I close them again. Try opening one this time. That helps but I don't understand why someone is shining a square ceiling light directly into my face. I blink but that doesn't help so I lift an arm to shield my eyes. Or at least my brain sends instructions to my muscles. My arm stays put.

I really don't get this at all.

I hear a voice I know well. 'Glad you're back with us, Mel.' It's Jeff. 'You gave us a big scare.'

He moves, and his head blocks most of the glare. I'm pleased about that.

But he's a tad too close, I have to say. We've worked together for over ten years and our faces have never been this close. I don't seem able to pull away but eventually I get it. The floor. I'm flat on my back. *This is highly embarrassing*. I know what's happened. I've fainted. So I try to bluster my way out of it. 'Boss.'

'Yes?'

I smile. I've worked it out. The immovable arm thing. 'Are you holding my hand?'

Some of his features shift around so I assume he's smiling too. 'I am indeed holding your hand.'

Another head enters from stage left. 'Is she okay?' This voice has a German accent.

'Yes, DC Hartmann,' I say. 'She's fine.'

'There's your answer, Tobias,' says Jeff. 'Let's get her into a chair and hopefully, she will enlighten us on what that was all about.'

Effortlessly, and miraculously, I levitate. My feet hardly touch the floor and I'm deposited on my rear end into the chair I'd been occupying right up until this unfortunate incident.

Fainted. What a girlie thing to do.

And then I remember. Hugo Emerson, his granddaughter, and a stark bright room filling with water. I groan, put my hand to my forehead.

'Would you like a drink, Boss?' says Tobias.

The feeling I was about to throw up has subsided. A drink's probably a sensible idea so I accept. After a few sips I notice the laptop's lid is down. 'Did he sign off?'

'He did,' says Jeff.

'Why do I sense there's a "but" heading in my direction?'

My boss obliges. 'But … before he signed off he told me the water would flow into the room at the higher rate for an hour, so –'

'So, after that hour, we'll only have 46 hours left.'

Jeff nods, and I say, 'Fuck!'

'He posted a website URL,' says Jeff. 'We know it's a live stream from the room where he's holding Natasha but I've no intention of watching it from here.' He glances up. Tobias pats me gently on the shoulder, grabs the laptop and the evidence bags and rushes out. 'We can't afford to hang about, so he's away to get things moving. I've asked him to take the laptop downstairs to Bob. We need the video footage and the live feed on a secure server so we can watch it without fear of Stevenson hacking in.'

Bob. Short for Roberta, but you'll get the sharp edge of her tongue if you call her that. She's a civilian, one of my best mates, and my IT go-to person. What she doesn't know about the subject wouldn't sell for free on eBay. Bob is a denizen of the deep, the sub-basement of this building, referred to by all and sundry as "Downstairs". There are precious few cases where I don't call on her technical expertise and boy does she know it.

Jeff moves to his own chair and sits down. Stretches out his legs – his shoes appear on my side of the table – and clasps his hands in his lap. He gives me the gimlet look. 'I know we're on a ridiculous deadline, but I need to call timeout. You've always been rock solid, Mel, so I need to know what happened there.'

I puff out my cheeks and tell him the whole story.

Shock, horror – I'm terrified of water. When I was a kid, eight or nine, my mum took me and my younger sister on holiday to Northumberland. It was Easter but the weather was sparkling. The coastline comprises a series of outstanding beaches, most of which are connected by clifftop paths. We'd taken a bus to a village about four miles away from our B&B and had intended to spend the day walking back. Paddling in the sea, searching for crabs, picnic lunch; all that good stuff. Wandering along one of these paths, I wasn't paying attention and strayed too close to the edge. I must have only weighed about three stones, but it was enough to collapse the ground underneath me. I slid down, arse over tit as they say, amongst a pile of earth, stones and grass, and fell into the sea. It wasn't deep, only up to my chest but after a couple of waves had splashed me in the face I completely lost it. Trouble was, the angle of the slope meant my mum couldn't see me. I was hidden by a slab of overhanging rock.

I could swim, but not without armbands, and certainly not in the North Sea in April. My mum panicked. Should she jump in after me and leave my four-year-old sister alone on the path, or what? But she was in luck. A local couple walking their dog heard her screaming and came running. She flung my sister at them, scrambled down the slope, and dropped into the sea beside me. I'd managed to keep my head more or less above water, but it was choppy, and I'd swallowed more of the salty stuff than was good for me.

Long story short, I held on to her like a Velcro limpet and, several hours later, two men shinned down and helped us out.

'Several hours?' says Jeff.

'Okay, Mr Nitpicker. Minutes.' My gaze falls to the floor. 'And now I can't even let the shower run down my face.' I giggle, but then I feel dreadful considering a young woman might drown in the next couple of days. I blame the shock.

He gives me a quizzical look. 'What?'

'I'd been dating Callum for a few months. We were still teenagers, long before we lived together, and we went to Ayia Napa on a Club 18-30 holiday. Hedonism and chips for fourteen straight days. One night – we were both rat-arsed – he suggested we go skinny dipping. I told him I'd happily do the skinny, but as far as dipping was concerned he was on his own.'

Jeff smiles. He and Callum get on like a house on fire; they'll probably have a laugh at my expense next time they're out for a pint. 'But here's what I don't get,' he says. 'You're a police officer in a port, we're practically surrounded by water, and I know for a fact that you've been involved in cases where bodies have been dragged out from under bridges and God knows where else. So how did you avoid coming up close and personal with the wet stuff?'

I shrug. 'Well, Andrew knows, and he's bailed me out a few times. But sometimes I just had to grit my teeth and get on with it.' Andrew, or Detective Sergeant Young to give him his proper title, is my long-time sidekick. We've worked together for going on five years. I'd trust him with my credit card, never mind my life.

Jeff glances at his wrist and instantly turns serious. 'Okay. You've presented me with a problem, which I'll deal with later if I have to. But in the meantime, Stevenson's bloody deadline is counting down.' He stands up and pushes his chair under the table top. I do likewise. 'Time's marching on so let's walk and talk,' he says. 'We need to get the team moving, and pronto. We'll have to treat this as two different investigations: Stevenson's grandfather's murder in '66 and, because it falls under the crime in action policy, Natasha Emerson's kidnapping.'

Crime in Action. Where the crime actually occurs whilst the investigation is ongoing, meaning the situation is dynamic and we are constantly reassessing in reaction to whatever's happening. 'Policy states I'll need to fire it up the line to the Chief Super,' he says. 'Of course, under normal circumstances I'd step aside and let you manage both investigations, but that poor woman will be on live feed, and as time goes by, and more water flows into the room, there's a fair chance your phobia will kick in again. I'm sorry, but that must impact on your ability to run that investigation, so we'll work together on it, and I'll trust you to step back whenever Natasha is centre stage.'

Shit. I knew that was coming. My boss is not one for mealy-mouthed evasiveness and, as expected, he's hit me right between the eyes. But the trouble is, damn him to hell and back, he's right. As much as I might want to be fully involved in finding Natasha, I'm all too aware I could throw a wobbler any time I'm watching her. That's how I feel when I see a body of water, never mind a body in water. Even imagining it sends a shiver sprinting up and down my spine. But I know as well as he does, I'm not his only problem. And by his expression, that's next on his agenda.

'It'll have to be me,' he says. 'I don't have another DI spare.'

Jeff might be a relatively new DCI but he's in charge of four Major Investigation Teams, or MITs, which cover the city of Edinburgh. The teams are headed up by DIs, and it's an unusual day if we're not running multiple investigations in parallel. Our complement of DIs should be six, but we have one off following a near breakdown, while another is recuperating after being stabbed in the side when a dawn raid on a drug dealer's gaff went tits up. The four of us are up against it – escalating caseloads, shrinking budgets, and recruitment *challenges* all conspire to make our working lives hell on earth. Any time I meet my colleagues they look, quite frankly, like shit. Mind you, I'll wager they think the same about me.

I know of police departments where resource management has been driven by internal politics. And that's resulted in them having far too many generals, while the infantry are thin on the ground. My boss's problem is the opposite. A young woman's life is in grave danger so he can pull in uniformed support till we're knee deep, but experienced DIs and DSs with spare capacity are about as common as fish in the desert. How Jeff will balance conflicting priorities is anybody's guess. I would say that's his problem, not mine, but that would be grossly unfair especially as my phobia has complicated the issue.

Into the bargain, my team and I are running on empty. We've closed two cases in the last week, one of them in the early hours of this morning, and we desperately need a break. We're only here today to tidy up loose ends; we'd all agreed we don't even have the energy for a celebratory boozy lunch.

And now this. A new investigation, with potential stress and exhaustion levels I'm not prepared to contemplate. I'm already dreading breaking the news to my team, but I realise Tobias will already have done that, and his colleagues will likely have given him both barrels. Never mind, the lad's broad shouldered.

I wait while Jeff works things through in his head. He takes a pen from his inside jacket pocket and fiddles with it. It's fancy, a *Mont Blanc* bearing his initials. But instead of "JDH" – Jeff Daniel Hunter – it reads "DJH". He told me about it once, apparently he goes by his middle name. I know a few people who are the same, so hardly a big deal.

Jeff jots down a couple of notes then says precisely what I expect. 'I want you to work both halves of the investigation but keep your eyes off that live feed. Take a step back and leave it to one of your team.' He holds my gaze for a second but leaves the warning unsaid. 'I'll tell Stevenson I'm taking the lead, which might help keep him onside. The head honcho's on the case and all that.'

I don't argue; he'll tell me it's not up for debate. 'On that,' I say. 'Stevenson made sure Hugo brought this straight to you – do you know why? Have you ever met the guy?'

He holds the door open for me and we set off for my office, two flights up to the rear of the building. I practically have to jog to keep up, not my strong suit. I really should make some use of the gym membership my darling husband gave me last Christmas. Bloody sadist.

'His face rings no bells,' says Jeff. 'Unless he knows I head up the MITs. That information wouldn't be hard to find.'

'The murder case, do you remember it?'

He smiles. 'Cheeky bugger, I wasn't even born. I only know about it through folklore. The grandfather, Sandro De Luca, was a powerful man – in Leith terms at any rate. Mind you, I'm told he kicked arses in other parts of the city when he needed to. Story goes, back in 1966 he left a head-wetting in a pub down by the docks late one night but never made it home. I worked with Hugo for a wee while not long after I joined the service in '96. From memory, he retired in 2001, 2002, but he was well past his sell-by date and had been for a while.'

'Why was that?'

'Because he was the DI who was handling the investigation when the higher-ups pulled the plug. They sent him to tell the De Luca family, which really cut him up. He felt he'd failed them. He stuck the job out for a while, probably hoping new evidence would come to light and the case would be reopened.'

'But it wasn't?'

'Not as far as I know.' On the landing outside the operations room he says, 'Who have you got on duty?'

I rattle off my colleagues' names, but Jeff won't need any introductions, he knows them all personally. He's that sort of manager, happy to get his hands dirty and would never ask us to do anything he wouldn't be willing to do himself.

We walk through the door. The ops area is in bright sunshine. My office is off this room, but I spend great chunks of my time out here with my team. I was only promoted to DI a couple of years ago and I still prefer to be in the thick of it.

Our HQ on Queen Charlotte Street is a fantastic three-storey ashlar sandstone building with a basement and sub-basement. Nearly two centuries old, it was originally designed as Leith Town Hall. Later incarnations included a prison block, a courtroom, and for as long as I can remember, a cop shop. Until recently our offices were dotted around the building, which still boasts a grand central staircase and ceremonial meeting rooms. If we sold tickets on *Doors Open Day* we'd make a mint. A number of years ago, the bean counters authorised additional capital investment and bolted a huge extension onto the rear; a glass and steel monstrosity immediately christened the *Fish Tank*. Thankfully it has snazzy solar control glazing, so we aren't boiled alive while we go about our detecting. It's a terrific place to work which confirms my desire to remain, literally, in sunny Leith and my reluctance to emigrate to Police Scotland Central or whatever it's called this week.

Other teams share this space but it's remarkably quiet today. A scattering of officers at desks around the room, but none of my team are in sight. Steph's out interviewing Natasha's flatmate and Tobias must still be downstairs talking to Bob about the video files. Jeff starts tapping his phone. 'I'm going to check in with your colleagues. Only be a minute.'

He moves off to the side, but only manages one call before Tobias appears and makes a beeline in our direction. He's out of puff but to be fair he's just climbed four flights of stairs. Looking at him, it's difficult to tell whether he's in good nick or not. To put it mildly, Tobias is a bit of a scruff, and the complete antithesis of the stereotypical German. Being specific, he's black, could do with losing at least ten kilos, and even if he does shave in the morning, he'll be sporting a five o'clock shadow by lunchtime at the latest. The creaky black leather jacket he's wearing is on his back come rain, hail or shine; it would be a kindness to describe it as wrecked.

'I have been speaking to Bob,' he says. 'She has uploaded the film to our server in a secure area that she guarantees can't be hacked. She will email me a link and a password. She said security was tighter than … I apologise, Boss, I didn't catch what she said, and I didn't want to ask her to repeat it in case she thought I was stupid.' He gives his earlobe a couple of healthy tugs. 'But it was something to do with a camel.'

Bob is a redhead, early sixties if she's a day, and glam with it. She gets her kicks out of razzing up male colleagues, and the younger the better. But she's not stupidly inappropriate, she only does this with selected favourites, and Tobias and Andrew are right up there. So I'm guessing that when she told Tobias the security was tighter than a camel's arse in a sandstorm, she'll have been tickled pink at his reaction. Poor lad. I could have a word with her, but I'd get more change out of a parking meter. 'Don't worry about it, Tobias. I know what she means. Now, what did she say about tracing the source of the transmission?'

'That she'll try but she doesn't hold out much hope. It would have been routed through proxy servers.'

'Yeah, that's what Stevenson said. Talking about him, he must have Natasha's phone. Ask Hugo who her provider is, and get onto them, please.'

'Will do.'

'Tobias,' says Jeff. 'What about me being unable to pause the video file?'

'Bob wasn't sure about that. One possibility is, while it was playing, the file was transmitting a constant stream of data that prevented the laptop from interacting with the file. Commands like *Pause* weren't getting through. The problem is she can't prove that without analysing the original video file. And we don't have it.'

I jot down some notes. 'Can she enhance the quality of the video?'

'She said it's already high resolution.' He rakes about in his jacket. Searches every pocket at least twice. 'But she did copy it for us.' Eventually he hands me two USB drives sporting Police Scotland logos. 'I've logged the original back into the Productions Store,' he says.

The white envelope, including its contents, which landed on Hugo's doormat are all items of physical evidence – *exhibits* or *productions* relating to our case. With any production, it's vital we can accurately state who had it in their possession at any point from when it was discovered until when it's brought to court as part of the prosecution's case against the defendant. If the item is unaccounted for at any point, the defence would argue it could have been tampered with and its veracity will be questioned. For example, could the prosecution confidently state the accused's DNA was already on the bloody knife when it was pulled from the victim's back? Therefore, our first task after discovery of an item is to log it into our Productions Store, managed and controlled by dedicated officers.

When Hugo handed Jeff the envelope containing the USB, the plastic wallet and the sheet of paper with Stevenson's instructions, Jeff knew the Computer Crime Unit would scan the USB before allowing it to be mated with a laptop. So he booked it into the store immediately. He reasoned we could read whatever was on the sheet of paper while it was still in the wallet, and book both items in later. At that point we'll copy the paper, meaning we won't ever have to handle the original.

The *ownership* of the USB can now be traced through Jeff, the store, the tech, and Tobias, who was last to accept responsibility for it. When he scanned the QR code, the app conversed with a server in the Productions Store, and the server recognised that Tobias was now in possession of the USB key and recorded it against his profile. But because he didn't relinquish responsibility to Bob, and we now have copies of it, he booked the USB back in to the Production Store. This tightly controlled process is known as the *Chain of Evidence*, or CoE. In days gone by, this meant completing a small woodland of paper forms, but Police Scotland now operates this shiny new electronic system with QR codes on all evidence bags.

Tobias's phone pings. 'That's the link from Bob. Will I forward it to you?'

I'm just about to say, "yes", when Steph bursts in. She flings her coat in the general direction of her chair and marches over, yawning as if her jaw has been disconnected. DC Zanetti is a chirpy blonde, what you might describe as petite but powerful. Nothing fazes her, and she normally bops around the place like Tigger on Duracells. But today even she looks a tad washed out. And little wonder because when she left me at 03:00 after a twenty-one-hour shift, she was heading home for a quick kip before her regular weekday spin class at six. Then hot yoga, whatever that is. Finally her favourite café down by Newhaven harbour where doubtless she packed away a breakfast that would floor a navvy. After that, she came in here to help tidy up all the relevant paperwork from last night's case. So between Tobias, Steph and me, we can probably summon up enough energy to light a camping stove and I've no idea how we're going to manage through the next 40-odd hours.

We all move closer to listen to what she has to say. 'Natasha's flatmate is Robyn Russell, she's a nurse at the Western. Poor woman was just off a night shift when I dragged her out of the land of nod. She said Natasha was heading for The Shore – a five minute walk as we know - to meet a couple of her uni pals. Robyn doesn't know who she was with, or what she was wearing to go out because she went off to work before Natasha left the flat. I contacted the uni and spoke to their admin, hoping they'd put me in touch with her classmates, but I struck out there too. Wednesday's not a lecture day so none of them are in.'

'Tuesday is a funny night to go out, even for a student,' says Jeff. 'But I guess that's maybe why.'

'That's definitely part of it but according to Robyn they often meet on a Tuesday. Lots of deals on, apparently.'

'Okay, Steph. Thanks,' I say. 'Folks, give me two minutes. I want to bring Dave Devlin in on this. We'll need his lads to canvass the bars and restaurants along The Shore.'

* * *

PC Dave Devlin. Top bloke, top cop, and top of my list of people to call. Dave's a senior PC with no intention or desire to move up the command chain. Part of his role is to coordinate uniformed support through our Area Control Room, known to us all as *the Control*. I call their number and find my old pal, Police Sergeant Ronnie Cockburn, is running the show today. Ronnie laughs when I explain I'm looking for Dave. 'He's working his way through a couple of "CBT" modules this morning, Mel, so I expect he'll be absolutely delighted when I tell him there's real work on offer.'

"CBT": *Computer Based Training* modules. I tell Ronnie there's a better than even chance Dave would rather burn his own eyes out with a soldering iron than sit at a PC for more than five minutes, and he laughs some more. 'The training is out of office, so I'll give him a shout. Send him straight to you,' he says.

'Thanks, Ronnie. I owe you one.'

A chortle comes trundling down the line. 'My dear Melissa, if memory serves me right, you owe me more favours than a horse could shit. But as you've never paid up yet, I don't plan on holding my breath.'

I finish the call to find Jeff's on his phone again. Steph and Tobias have their chairs jammed together while they stare at a monitor. I walk over and stand behind it, figuring they're watching the film of Natasha. Tobias already knows what's coming but Steph doesn't, and I'd rather be a few feet away when she finds out. We could be talking Vesuvius on a bad day.

Jeff comes over to join me, but they don't drag their gazes away. I cough. 'Pause it there, please, Tobias. I need to set some hares running.'

We wheel a couple of chairs in to form a rough circle. I steal a glance at my two colleagues and wonder if they're as exhausted as I am. We were all out in the middle of the night, waiting to pounce on our murder suspect. Intelligence strongly suggested he was heading for his estranged wife's flat, where he planned to hole up. And that's where we caught him. Talk about an ex-marriage of convenience?

But my ponderings are interrupted when Jeff says, 'I know the three of you must be absolutely knackered. You've been stretched to the limit over the past three or four months, and well beyond it at some stages. I could butter you up by saying I know you'll give it your best, but I couldn't handle the grief you'd fire at me. Despite the seriousness of this case and the urgency attached to it, I'll be upfront with you – I have zero spare resources at my disposal, so it's unlikely the cavalry will be riding over the hill any time soon.'

'Aw, that's a shame,' says Steph. 'Men in uniform make me go all wobbly at the knees.'

Once the titters die down I say, 'Speaking of resources, where is the bold hero?' Everybody knows I mean Andrew, the only Detective Sergeant on my team. I should have two but see earlier statement about resource challenges. I check the time. 'I did say he could come in late, but this is pushing it.'

What's making me wonder is Andrew's never late, he's genetically programmed to be punctual. If he had an appointment on the moon for the next day, he'd show up with enough spare time to have a coffee. Tobias wanders over to a window that overlooks the car park, four floors below. Forehead to the glass, he gazes down then glances at Steph and makes a face. She sends one straight back.

The vibes aren't difficult to spot. They're as thick as thieves, this pair. 'Right you two, spill the beans or it's thumbscrews time.' I glare at Tobias first, he'll cave long before that little minx.

He walks away from the window. 'Andrew's just been dropped off, Boss.'

Dropped off? That's weird. My sidekick's a fitness fanatic so he always cycles or runs to work. 'By whom?'

'It's a small car, a Fiat 500. I believe it belongs to his mother.'

'His mother? I thought he had a hot date last night.'

Andrew's been working as long hours as the rest of us, but he tied up his part in our murder case the night before last. He'd had about as much, or as little, sleep as we have so he'd knocked off yesterday lunchtime. He was planning to spend some quality time with his new squeeze; they've been virtual strangers since he took up with her a couple of months ago. Don't mean to sound inappropriate but I hope he made the most of it.

Because no one in my team is going to get much in the way of beauty sleep in the next couple of days.

Chapter 7

A full five minutes passes before the door to the incident room bumps open. And even then, it stops halfway. We watch as Andrew backs in. When he first became a detective, his snappy line in suits and ties earned him the nickname *Pretty Boy*. But today I'm more than a tad dumbfounded to witness him in a training top and loose jogging bottoms. I'm about to despatch a bollocking in his direction when he swings a pair of crutches into the room. He hops round, grimaces, then realises every eye in the place is on him. It's impossible to miss the royal blue airboot on his right leg.

'Em, hi,' he says, stopping in the middle of the floor and leaning on the crutches.

'What the bloody hell happened to you?' I say.

Bright pink patches flood his cheeks. 'Regrettably, I have a badly bruised coccyx and a knackered ankle. Result of a fall, I'm afraid.'

Andrew doesn't drink much so I doubt alcohol was the cause and I'm about to interrogate him when Steph pipes up. 'Weren't you going to your new girlfriend's flat for dinner last night?'

Now four pairs of eyes are more sharply focussed. 'I was, as you well know. And I can imagine what you're thinking, but you're wrong.'

Steph is grinning. She folds her arms tightly and drops her head off to the side. 'Go on, then.'

Andrew glowers at her then turns to me. 'Well, the thing is, she asked me to replace a downlighter in her kitchen. But she didn't have a ladder, so I stood on a chair.' He studies the airboot. 'And it collapsed under me.'

'Elf and safety, my boy,' says Jeff, in his best George Carter from *The Sweeney* accent.

'I hope you're not signed off,' I say.

'Not yet,' says Andrew. 'But I can't sit down for long, and the doc's advised me to move about as little as possible. It's only twisted, nothing broken, but I can't really walk.'

Tobias holds a hand up, bless him. 'Andrew. What is the coccyx?'

'His tail bone,' says Steph. Then like some music hall comedian, she slaps her thigh. 'We've always known our Andrew was a right royal pain in the arse and now he's gone and proved it.'

Andrew treats that like water off a duck's back, then he glances round. We don't normally have Jeff in our midst. 'I take it something's up,' he says.

We all sit down, except the invalid of course, who perches uncomfortably on one bum cheek while Jeff dishes out the potted version.

I finish off with, 'So we're up against it big time. There might not be any resources to pull out of the hat. And …' I glower at Andrew, 'I'm one officer down. Shit!'

* * *

The investigation will accelerate from this point on, so we've decanted from the ops area into one of four incident rooms that were included in the spec for the fish tank, the super hi-tec extension they stuck on the rear of our HQ. These rooms, one for each MIT, are kitted out with technology that initially filled me with terror on the three-day training course. I was set to hand in my badge and become a reiki practitioner but instead, I burned my Luddite tee shirt, and now I'm forever banging on about the benefits these gadgets bring to modern policing. Much to the amusement of my better half, Callum.

The focal point of the room is a wall-to-wall interactive whiteboard, which duets with a Smart Table, a futuristic wonder with a surface like a giant iPad, two metres by one. Using it as the interface I can project objects like maps, photos and documents onto the whiteboard then move them around, resize, annotate them, and draw connecting lines in whatever colour or style takes my fancy. We can use electronic flipchart pens to add notes, which are translated by the whiteboard and added to the file. Beats ending up with blue and red ink marks all over your best skirt, I can tell you. And I can pull up interviews and statements that we've uploaded from our PDAs. For most operational police officers out in the field, notebooks have gone the way of hobnailed boots and truncheons; we now use Personal Data Assistants. I could never be described as an early adopter of technology but boy, am I a convert.

If there were only two or three of us, we'd work at the Smart Table, but it'll be easier if I use the whiteboard. I tap the iPad a few times; the lights in the room dim and the whiteboard illuminates. On our left is a glass wall that gazes out over the rooftops; it would be a stretch to call it a window. It runs the width of the room and virtually floor to ceiling. The bottom four feet are protected by a burnished steel banister, topped by a pale wooden handrail. Another tap on the iPad and, as if by magic, the glass becomes tinted. I could sit and watch it doing that all day long, but we have a kidnap victim to save. And, on that, Tobias has already logged onto one of the many PCs and is monitoring the live feed. Ever the gentleman, he's angled the screen away, but my feelings are secondary, and I need an update. 'Tobias, what's happening?'

'No change to the water flow. Still on high, and it's beginning to cover the floor. Natasha is sitting on the table. Staring down. Not moving.' He reminds me of a sonar operator in a submarine movie, his eyes glued to his display, providing a sitrep to the captain. He catches my eye. I don't comment, just nod.

I start by pulling two photos onto the whiteboard and highlight each in turn. 'This is Natasha Emerson, our kidnap victim. Aged nineteen, a second-year student and granddaughter of retired DI Hugo Emerson.' The image is a head and shoulders shot of Natasha smiling at the photographer. Fresh faced, happy, not a care in the world. Until now.

'And this is Marlon Stevenson, her kidnapper. This is a screenshot taken from our conversation online this morning, where he stated his demands. Obviously it doesn't cast him in a particularly positive light, but that's how I'd rather present him. He's fifty-seven, single, Edinburgh born, but so far we don't know much else about him. His motivation for snatching

Natasha relates back to an unsolved case, the murder of his grandfather, Alessandro – known as Sandro – De Luca, in 1966. Hugo Emerson was a DI working that investigation, and it was Hugo who had the unenviable task of telling the De Luca family that the case had been closed. I'll be visiting Stevenson's mother as soon as I'm clear here.'

While I'm letting that all sink in, I type the initials of the five people present: Mel, Jeff, Andrew, Steph and Tobias, tap a couple of icons, and the initials appear down the right-hand side of the whiteboard. 'Right, everyone, brainstorm everything we need to do to find this woman, ideally well within the next 46 hours. You all know the rules. Throw up suggestions as they occur to you, anything goes at this stage, and no questioning or debating. I want as many ideas up there as possible. We'll delete duplicates and unsuitable items later.' I look around the group. 'Ready? Then go.'

Within a few minutes, I've listed seventeen key tasks, plus another half a dozen that are less urgent and might be subsumed by higher level tasks. I tap an icon from an array of options on the right side of the board, and an information window pops up. "Screen contents saved". This is one of the real benefits of this technology. At any point I can save what's up there and recall it, if and when I need it. So this is version one of our list of tasks, and if we make a material change to the list I'll save it as a new version.

Now it's time to start allocating tasks so we can really get shifting.

Chapter 8

Wednesday 10:00

Natasha forced herself to sit on the cut down table, in her lotus position. She was shivering, beginning to lose it, so she dropped her eyelids and called up a mantra that always came to her rescue when her nerves threatened to run riot. *Be calm, Natasha. There are worse things in life. Be calm, Natasha. There are worse things in life.*

It only took a few intonations before the tremors died down and she was able to think rationally. She'd been through it several times already, but she went back down the same road. Was she the victim of mistaken identity? Had he seized the wrong woman? She sensed the pain in her right cheek, lifted her hand, gently massaged her face.

She relived the horrifying sequence of events in her mind.

After Stevenson had thrown her in the van, throughout the journey Natasha had been propelled around on the metal floor desperately trying to use her feet to brace herself against any panel she came into contact with. So when the van slewed to the left and decelerated abruptly, once more she slid in the opposite direction and thudded painfully into the wheel arch. This time her right knee bore the brunt. She howled in pain but between the heavy cloth hood and the rock music, even if someone had been right beside her it wouldn't have registered.

The van tilted to the right and hardly any time passed before it tilted again. She felt the engine revving before the van shot off. It took her a few seconds to figure out the driver had climbed out and back in. She couldn't imagine why, and she was in such a state, neither did she care. She was completely disoriented.

There were more abrupt stops, fast starts, and changes of direction before it decelerated rapidly, veering sharply to the right at the same time. The van heaved and this time she thought she detected something trundling and screeching across the ground outside. After a brief pause, the van jolted forward, and all four wheels bumped over an obstacle. The motion was similar to crossing a speed bump diagonally. The vehicle stopped almost immediately, another heave, more trundling, followed by silence as the music was switched off. That was no small mercy. It had been Led Zeppelin's *Whole Lotta Love,* a section played on a loop that lasted less than a minute before repeating, and it included some of Robert Plant's most strident vocals. They'd have swamped Natasha's screams. Ironically, she knew the song inside out. Her grandad was a huge fan of the band and perversely, so was she. Hugo had often proudly announced that excellent taste in music had skipped a generation in their family.

But music enjoyment was nowhere on her list of priorities. Between pain, lack of mobility, and being rendered blind and nearly deaf, her other senses were battling against each other to provide her with any form of equilibrium. So, when the van doors were hauled open, she didn't notice until her captor grabbed her ankles and dragged her until her legs were clear of the lip of the van and waving in fresh air. Natasha was wearing a short denim skirt that had ridden up to her waist. And there was a huge gap of cold skin between that and her tee shirt and fleece. She was powerless to preserve her modesty but was shocked when rough hands hauled about at her clothing, all in the right direction.

Sensing she wouldn't be outside for much longer, she tensed up to scream but he grabbed the back of the makeshift hood and twisted the material and her hair in his fist. 'Even if you do scream, no one will hear you.' Her hands were still fastened behind her, and he tugged on her pinkies. 'But make any noise at all and I will break both of these. So don't test me. You hear? Do *not* test me.'

She nodded furiously inside the bag but wasn't sure it had moved. In not much more than a whisper, she croaked, 'Yes, yes, I hear you. Please don't hurt me. Please.' That last syllable was long and drawn out.

The next tug was at her feet. 'I've freed your legs. You will be walking, but not far.'

Inside the hood, the tears were coursing down her cheeks. 'Who are you? Where are you taking me? Please, why are you doing this. I haven't done anything.'

'I know you haven't. But that's not the point. Now shut up. I warned you.' He hauled her torso out of the van by the waistband of her skirt, his knuckles rough against her belly. He manhandled her upright, twisted her round, grabbed her wrists with one hand, her left shoulder with the other, and shoved her forward. 'Move. Walk straight ahead.' He guided her across a hard flat surface. She sensed it was cold, concrete probably. After about a dozen steps, he turned her to her right. 'Lift your foot. Take a step up.'

Although some artificial light seeped in from the bottom of the hood, essentially, she was still blind. She waved a foot in front of her, made contact. He kept the pressure on. 'Now, forward.' As she brought the other foot up, she stubbed her trainer on the edge of the step, but he kept her upright and moving ahead.

She took about twenty paces before he stopped her. 'There are stairs in front of you. I've got a hold of you, so keep going up.' Once they were on the first step and she'd moved up to the next one she found it straightforward. The surface felt like gridded metal; she could sense the pattern through her soles. But the steps were unsteady, they seemed to give, and she heard them creaking every time she moved. At one point they lurched to the right, and she yelped. Her wrists were still tied together so she couldn't maintain her own balance.

He was right behind her, their bodies touching. She tried to move further forward, away from him, but he kept hold of her. 'You're coming to the last step, then we're turning right.' They did so and her waist pushed up against a bar. It was cold, flat, squared.

'Don't move,' he said. She felt him twisting away. She heard a click. Whining from an electric motor. A chain rattled; links slid down her back. She cried out. He gripped her right pinkie. 'What did I say? No noise. You do not speak unless I speak to you. Got it?'

She nodded furiously, the sack irritating the skin below her hairline.

A few seconds later the motor stopped. His body was still tight to hers. She flinched. He moved closer, spoke directly into her ear. 'That's one thing you don't have to worry about. I'm not remotely interested in you sexually, so pack it in.'

He shook her, and her attention snapped back on him.

'I'm going to untie your hands soon,' he said. 'Don't ask why but I need you to change clothes. I'll tell you what I'm going to do, so make sure you listen.'

She tensed up, made herself smaller. If her hands had been free, she would have hugged herself, folded her arms over her front for protection. 'Stand still,' he said. 'I'm going to undress you, but I won't untie your hands till I'm ready.' She felt a tug at the hem of her fleece and the unmistakeable sound of scissors cutting. She started to scream but he was ready. He jammed a hand across her mouth. 'For fuck's sake, stand bloody still. Because the more you struggle the longer it will take. And if these scissors cut you, it'll be your fault not mine.'

His tone became softer. 'You got a fright when I cut your clothes. I get that. But be quiet. If I touch your body, it'll be an accident. This is not a sex thing.' He tugged again, more cutting, all the way up and through her collar. She felt her fleece dropping away, but he hadn't cut the arms, so it stopped at her elbows. He repeated the process with her tee shirt. He was still behind her, so she felt slightly less vulnerable. He tugged open the popper on the waistband of her skirt and pulled her zip down. The skirt dropped to her feet. She drew her knees and thighs in tight. There was a pause and he pulled something over her head, on top of the sack. A soft material rested around her neck.

He held her at the wrists. She heard a snick, and her hands were free. Her fleece dropped away. 'I've pulled a hoodie over your head. Take your tee shirt off and put the hoodie on properly.' She did that, then he handed her some material. Small, light, with a synthetic feel. 'Kick your trainers off and put these tennis shorts on.' She tried to obey too quickly and got her foot all caught up. She overbalanced but he steadied her. He was being kind, gentle when he could be. Her confidence was rising. She didn't feel anything like safe, but she wasn't so scared. She wondered if and when that would change.

She heard rustling. He was gathering up her clothes. A part of him bumped against her thigh. His shoulder, she imagined. She didn't flinch that time.

'Now,' he said. 'One last thing. And you'll be okay with it because I know you've been on a climbing wall.'

'How do you —'

'Quiet! No questions. Just, quiet.' He shook her again, more vigorously this time. 'I'm going to put you in a body harness. I'll be lowering you about ten feet. You can't see, so I know you'll be scared, but trust the harness like you were taught on the wall. Got it?'

She nodded. She'd only been to the university climbing club a few times and she'd enjoyed it. But then she was taken on an outing to a range of crags north of Stirling and the weather had been awful. The difference between climbing indoors in shorts and tee shirt compared to wearing outdoor gear and battling the cold and rain helped her decide the sport wasn't for her. But now the harness was on and tightened, and although it felt completely different to a waist harness, she sensed the similarity.

She was still wondering how he knew she'd been a member of the club when the motor whined, and the chain pulled taut.

This time he didn't warn her what he was about to do. He pushed her in between her shoulder blades, and she was left dangling in midair. She screamed, he didn't complain, the motor and the chains were at it again and she dropped like a stone. Then it braked, and her feet landed on the ground. She was standing on a more solid floor although the new surface seemed to give a little. And it felt warmer. She was shaking and if the harness hadn't been taut, she'd have fallen over.

He called down. 'Unbuckle the harness.'

Her fingers were numb, she couldn't coordinate them but eventually after much fumbling she released it at her waist and stepped out of it. The chain and the harness scraped against her. Up and away.

'Right,' he said. 'Last thing. You can take that hood off soon but first, I want you to count to a hundred, slowly, and out loud so I can hear you.'

She could hardly speak but managed to squeeze the words out. 'A hundred?'

'Yes. But slow and steady, like it was your pulse.'

She breathed out. 'Okay. One, two, three …'

She heard a metallic sound, a gentle whoosh, along with a soft rush of air. But she didn't dare stop counting.

'… 98, 99, 100.'

She hesitated. Remained motionless.

Total silence.

She lifted her hands, took hold of the bottom of the sack and teased it out from under the neck of the hoodie.

Then quickly, before she lost her nerve, she whipped it up, forward, and down off her face.

Chapter 9

'Right, Andrew,' I say. 'What with you being a passenger —'

'A passenger? Oh, come on, Boss —'

'Come on, Boss, nothing. If you'd told me you'd hurt yourself chopping firewood or some other manly activity, I might be sympathetic. But falling off a chair while you were fixing a lightbulb for a damsel in distress? Now be quiet and take it like a man.' I glare at him, dare him to answer back. 'Okay, the quickest way to bring you up to speed is if you go through the videos. A word of warning though, the one showing Natasha is not an easy watch. Apparently they're already in high resolution so Bob doesn't think she can enhance them. Tobias will tell you where the files are stored. I want you to study them, end to end. You know the timescales we're working to, so a full report, please. Stevenson, where he's talking from, the room Natasha's in, the works.'

'Understood.'

'Also, talk to Forensic Services. Ask them to review the videos of both Stevenson and Natasha. For him, body language. What can it tell us? And for her, Linguistics. I've absolutely no idea if using a lipreader for Natasha is worthwhile but I'm keen to find out. And before you talk to Edinburgh forensics, give the Scottish Crime Campus over in Gartcosh a call first. They might have a wider view.' I drum my fingers on the table. 'Oh, yes. Talk to the multimedia unit. I need sound technicians to analyse the Stevenson audio. Ask if they're able to identify any background noises that might fix his location or, at least, give us a steer. I have my doubts, but you never know.'

As I've been rattling items off, Andrew's been typing them into the system and his initials have several actions against them. He looks at me expectantly. 'Anything else?'

'Yes. When the rest of us are out and about, the live feed will need to be constantly monitored so I have to leave that with you. But I'll be bringing in support, so bear with me. Oh, and one more thing. As the clock is running down, make sure we're always aware of the time remaining.' I close my eyes. This is horrific. A young woman's life is literally ticking away, and hour by hour we'll be reminded of that. But none of us can dwell on it, our job is to find her. *Move on, Mel.*

'Now, Tobias,' I say. 'Someone, possibly Marlon, put that envelope through Hugo Emerson's letterbox at 08:45. Check if there's municipal CCTV near his house that might identify who it was, but if you strike out I'll arrange a canvass of the immediate area. And while we're on that, Dave Devlin will also be canvassing venues at The Shore to ask if they remember Natasha and her friends. If any CCTV comes out of that, he'll pass it to you. And last question for now, confirm their movements at and around The Shore last night. If she set out to walk home, her route would have been directly along Commercial Street. I can't imagine she jumped on a bus, it's only two stops. Stevenson must have snatched her somewhere along there, and he didn't stick her in his back pocket so we're looking for a vehicle. My money's on a van of some sort. So, get cracking on CCTV.'

'Okay, Boss. Will do.'

'Next. Jeff will be interviewing Hugo as soon as we finish here, so that'll give us background on his granddaughter. But we'll need more detail, so whether Hugo likes it or not I'll be sending in a Family Liaison Officer. He might say no, but ...' I jerk my thumb in Jeff's direction. 'I'll be relying on the big bad wolf here to talk him round.'

A police Family Liaison Officer, or "FLO", is specially trained to support families in circumstances like we have with the Emersons. Their primary function is investigator, to gather evidence and preserve the integrity of the investigation while balancing those against the family's needs. As well as those, they advise on aspects like legal and police procedures. They keep the family up to date with progress, and, contrary to how the FLO is often portrayed in TV dramas, they're not there to spy, and neither is their role confined to making endless cups of tea.

'I'll need to bring in a FLO and I've got a particular person in mind. But in the meantime, Steph, I want you to talk to Natasha's parents. I need an insight into her personality, her character, understand how she might behave as a kidnap victim.' I look at my boss. 'How much do we tell the parents about Natasha's circumstances? The room, the water, the deadline.'

'Hmmm. Tricky.' Jeff lets his gaze bounce around the team. 'I would simply state that the kidnapper has her, she's unharmed, he's made his demands, and that we'll do our best to meet them. And, as Hugo would expect as an ex-copper, we're already trying to find out where he's holding her.'

'Threat to life?'

'We don't believe she's in imminent danger.' He meets my eye. 'Which is true.'

'Only technically.'

He hitches up his right shoulder an inch or two, then drops it. 'As you say. But I'm not going to bullshit Hugo. He'll see right through me.'

'There's not a lot we can do about that.'

Steph puts a hand up. 'Boss, with other kidnappings we've made appeals through the media. Will we be doing that this time?'

Jeff does the shoulder thing again. 'I'll run it past the media guys, but for my money, would broadcasting an appeal be appropriate?'

He's the master of the rhetorical question, is Jeff. I move on. 'Despite what Stevenson said about it being a waste of time checking him out, we can't possibly ignore him.' I start ticking items off our list of tasks. 'Andrew. First up, I'll go and visit his family. I intend to appeal to his mother, hopefully find out where he recorded the films, and if she knows where he might be holding Natasha. So, get me an address. An octogenarian woman with terminal cancer and a son called Marlon. Can't be too many of them about.'

I log Andrew's initials against that item and scan the list. 'I'll ask about relatives and friends, and what he does for a living. Safe to say he's not at work today.'

Tobias is next up, but before I can speak he says, 'His phone, his email, social media if I am able to find any, and his bank accounts. *Ja?*'

I smile as I'm adding his initials to those points. 'It's true what they say about you Germans being efficient, isn't it?'

Andrew signals with his pen. 'Boss. Something's occurred to me about the water in that room. If Natasha does end up submerged, even partially, how long can she survive? Like you said earlier, she's not in imminent danger because she can stand on the table but eventually, it might well happen.'

We all fall silent while we consider the implications. Steph begins waving her iPad around. 'I'd been thinking about that too. I've found a marine site that contains hypothermia charts. They list how long a person can survive in water, depending on the temperature.' She glances at her screen. 'Anything from less than fifteen minutes to indefinitely, but that's not much use if we don't know the temperature of the water flowing in.'

'Send me the link, Steph, and I'll take a look,' says Andrew.

Tobias pipes up. 'I apologise for being blunt, but Stevenson intends her to survive for up to 48 hours and then she will drown. Therefore the water cannot be cold.' He scratches at his chin; it rasps like heavy duty sandpaper. 'So if it is heated, it means it is likely she is being held inside a building, which may help us narrow down our search parameters.'

'Excellent point, Tobias,' I say. Then, 'Andrew. Get in touch with the city council. Go in at high level and tell them we need someone at our beck and call who has the authority to pull people in when we need them, even if it's in the middle of the night. I imagine they'll have a disaster emergency team we can hook in to. Talk to the planning department. I'd be surprised if Stevenson went through the proper channels for something he only needed short-term, he's definitely been planning this for a while, so you never know.'

Andrew is typing while I speak. 'I'll get straight onto them.'

'Next. He's already demonstrated he can adjust the flow, but can he regulate the temperature too? It could be he's in an adjacent room but if not, he's controlling them remotely. Another one for you, Andrew. Speak to our facilities management people, I need to know how he would do that.'

Steph raises a finger. 'I doubt Stevenson will be anywhere near his own house, and ditto with his car if he has one. He's bound to be broadcasting from somewhere else. So, in the meantime, do we break into his place?'

'Well, we can't just ignore it.' I turn to Jeff. 'What do you think?'

'What's the chances of you finding anything that'll help us?' he says. I don't reply. 'Well, there's your answer. It's a question of risk and reward. If we don't believe a search would produce tangible results, then no. We can't pussyfoot around him, but there's no earthly point in antagonising him any more than we have to.' He stretches his arms above his head, scratches at his dome. 'While I'm on the subject of risk, I've already had a couple of discussions with the Chief Super, and she's stressed how vital it is that we follow the kidnapping protocols covered by our policy documents. If, God forbid, Natasha Emerson doesn't come through this, I want to be able to demonstrate we've done everything properly and correctly. As with all kidnappings, this will be fluid throughout, and I may have to make decisions quickly. But I will not allow Marlon Stevenson to influence those decisions. I won't bend to his every whim, which means I will have to take calculated risks. And yes, taking those risks could piss him off. He might increase the water flow like he did earlier, putting poor Natasha in even more jeopardy. Eventually I might have to answer for those decisions, which means they have to be correct, but above all they must follow policy.' He takes a pause. 'Going back to what I said earlier about the kidnapping falling under crime in action, I'll be keeping in touch with my boss, and we will constantly review what we're doing based on the current position with Natasha.'

This is Jeff to a tee, and if it were possible to back him with more than one hundred per cent, I'd do it in a heartbeat, and so would everyone else in my team. 'On that,' I say, 'I want a full run-down on Stevenson but first things first, where does he live, and does he drive a car? Does he have a record? Have we come into contact with him for any reason, not necessarily related to abduction. Wherever he's holding her, does he own it? Could it be rented, or borrowed? So check land registry, leasing agents, the works.'

'Mel,' says Jeff. 'I'm thinking about how Stevenson behaved. Cool. Calm. Chilled. No sane person would do this, no matter their motivation, so we need to examine his medical records for mental health issues.'

'That'll need a warrant.'

He lifts his phone. 'I'll speak to the Chief Super. We might need her clout.'

'Andrew.' I point at an already extensive array of items up on the board. 'That list is only going to get longer so talk to Ronnie, he needs to put resources on this.'

My poor wounded soldier shuffles around on his seat, stretches his leg out. 'Sure. I'll sort all my actions into priority order and farm some of them out.'

I spot Tobias checking his screen. 'What's the latest?' I say.'

'Nothing has changed. She hasn't moved.'

I find myself in a real quandary. I have to keep this woman uppermost in my mind, but I can't dwell too heavily on her situation. And even that word "situation" seems far too insipid to describe what's happening to her. My gut starts churning but I swallow the tension down. Jeff's right, I need to leave this to my team to manage. I don't want to be a liability.

I glance at the bottom right of the board. *Jeez, the time's flashing by*. 'Have I missed anything.' Shaking heads all round. 'In that case, let's crack on, folks. And no matter where we are or what we're doing I want everyone back here, or reporting in on video, for a full review at, let's say, one o'clock. Keep in touch and call in with in any developments – positive or negative.'

Tobias gets his head down and Steph grabs her coat, while I eyeball Andrew. 'Right, my man. All joking aside, I hurt my coccyx skiing off a jump I shouldn't have gone anywhere near, so I know how sore it is. I know you'll be a big brave lad, but while you're talking to facilities management, sort out whatever you need to allow you to work comfortably. Although God only knows how you're going to manage that when you can't sit down, and you can't stand up. But this could be a blessing in disguise as it means you can act as a central liaison point for everything on our task list.'

He screws up his face. 'A blessing in disguise?'

I ignore him. We talk it through and summarise the list. Liaise with Ronnie in the Control; talk to Forensic Services, Linguistics, and Edinburgh City Council; act as focal point for updates and reports from the other departments; keep me and Jeff posted when we're out and about; and monitor the live feed with support from the others. But not from me, obviously. I leave him to create a table with actions against all of us, pick a desk and get straight on the phone.

* * *

I need reinforcements, but halfway through the morning is hardly the best time to be going out cap in hand. The officers I want will almost certainly be knee deep in their own investigations. So I'll have to flutter my eyelashes. Not easy over the phone, I grant you … but let's give it a go.

My first call is to the Area Resource Manager. I'm hoping he can reassign a couple of Detective Constables from the shared MIT pool. In truth, I'll take anyone, but my first choices are Ella Jackson and Crissi Banerjee. They've worked with us before. They're smart, capable, and they're a good fit for the way we work. Plus, I know Crissi has recently been through her FLO training and accreditation, so fingers crossed. I'm only halfway through my tale of woe to the resources guy when he cuts in. 'Jeez, Mel. The tears I'm shedding here are watering down my coffee.' He asks for half an hour, tops, for the two DCs to tidy up and handover and he'll send them straight up.

Next stop, a Crime Scene Manager, Greg Brodie. He's relatively new to Police Scotland but we've worked together a few times, and we get on well. Helps that we went to primary school together, although it took me a while to place him. Turned out his mother had remarried, so he'd changed his name. I don't need his services yet because there isn't a crime scene, so this is merely a standby call. I also drop an email to a pathologist; a Polish woman named Klaudia. She's definitely a bit odd. For a while we struggled to build a relationship, but we eventually found some happy middle ground. What I haven't yet mastered is how to pronounce her surname. Naturally, all my team can, meaning they will drop it into conversation whenever they spot an opportunity to wind me up. *Smartarses.* Similarly, I won't need her unless we end up with a cadaver, the avoidance of which is the point of the exercise. Still, it does no harm to warm her up, as it were.

In between calls I start pulling together the names of specialists from a range of departments; the list could stretch to the other side of China.

* * *

I've just hung up when Jeff finishes tapping at his phone. I say, 'You told Stevenson that a particular case had altered the protocols for reactivating closed investigations. A grandmother murdered in Ayrshire. Doesn't ring any bells.'

His mouth ticks up at the corners. 'I'm not surprised. That was a complete fabrication on my part.'

'You sneaky bugger.'

He lays his hand on the centre of his chest and makes big eyes. 'Mercy me, I'm cut to the quick.' Then he shrugs. 'Just needed to buy some time. Erode his belief that he's totally in control.' He leans sideways to look past me. 'Andrew.'

'Yes, Boss.'

'Can you find an official form on the system and mock it up to look like a request to reopen a cold case. Put spaces for two signatories at the bottom – mine, and the Chief Super's. I'll ring her and explain what we're up to.'

Andrew begins typing, a smile on his face. 'Will do.'

Chapter 10

'I was only eighteen,' said Hugo Emerson. 'Fresh out of college, and no more than a warm breathing body as far as experience went. Apart from traipsing around Leith supposedly being mentored by a sergeant or a more senior PC, I can't really remember anything I did prior to the night of Sandro De Luca's murder.'

Jeff was interviewing Hugo in his office. The DCI had taken pity on the older man and whisked him away from public view. Word had spread at twice the speed of light about who he was and why he was there. But even those few who were still around from Hugo's day had no idea what to say to him, especially those with granddaughters or daughters.

Jeff knew that as soon as the interview was over, he'd send his old colleague home to his family. The former DI was already making noises about *helping* with the investigation, but Jeff wouldn't countenance that. Even if Hugo was still a serving police officer he wouldn't be involved. Conflict of interest trumps all.

Jeff hadn't told Hugo about his granddaughter's circumstances: the room, the water, nothing. He and his family were in enough pain. Jeff simply said there was video evidence that proved she was alive but as yet, her whereabouts were unknown. Hugo understood this but knew the DCI was duty bound to inform them of any significant events. But as far as that was concerned, Jeff did have some latitude around the word "significant".

'Talk me through that night,' said Jeff.

Hugo drew in a deep breath and closed his eyes as he recalled the scene. 'It's been going through my mind all morning. It had been a terrible winter. Bloody Baltic. High 30s, low 40s at best, and measured in Fahrenheit of course, so only a few degrees centigrade. Storms, blizzards, snow and ice on the ground for weeks at a time it seemed. But the weather was different in those days, or is that just me? I do remember that night wasn't too bad. Yeah, it was cold, approaching one in the morning in late January after all. It was drizzling, rather than chucking it down, but I was still chilled to the bone by the time my shift ended.'

'And you were one of the first on the scene?'

'That's right. You'll know the docks as they are now, of course, but back in the 60s they were huge. Safety and security legislation were virtually non-existent. Bordering on lawless in some areas, I'd have to say. You can probably imagine how we operated. Although we did set up a cordon, it was more about defining the area we'd be searching for evidence, rather than protecting it. No such thing as crime scene management. Blundering about in our size tens obliterating evidence right, left and centre, waiting for authority to be dragged out of their beds. A total shambles, and that was on a good day.

'Of course, this was easily fifteen years before HOLMES.' Hugo was talking about Home Office Large Major Enquiry System, which eventually replaced the archaic manual card index the police utilised to store crime related information. Everything pertinent to a case was written on index cards then filed, stored, and reviewed as necessary. Names of suspects and witnesses; statements, fingerprints, addresses and phone numbers; dates, times and locations; vehicle registration numbers; articles of evidence both physical and forensic. Add to that, information provided by the all too prevalent weirdos and attention seekers who responded to appeals and phoned in with their sightings, suspicions and, regrettably, their fairy tales. Usually concerning ex-wives and husbands. Or neighbours whose only crime was they didn't take their share of sweeping the stairwell. All of these had to be followed up, no matter how unlikely.

And with all this, it's easy to imagine how human errors crept in, like duplication, omissions, or simple misfiling. Examples were legendary of both suspects and witnesses interviewed more than once or missed entirely. More than one serial killer of comparatively recent times wasn't caught early enough due to simple mistakes like these. As a result, victims were injured, brutalised, and tragically some were killed when they need never have been in danger.

The DCI could only imagine how difficult, if not impossible, it must have been for detectives struggling to manage all the data generated by a murder investigation.

'Who actually found the body?' said Jeff.

'A night watchman on his rounds. Like most watchies, he was already long past retirement age, but unfortunately the old man died while we were still investigating.' Hugo paused there. 'But, at that stage it wasn't a body. Sandro was still alive. The watchie went to a hangar nearby. A team of welders working the night shift lifted Sandro onto a flatbed barrow, got him inside and phoned for an ambulance.'

'Ah. So did he die in hospital?'

'No. The ambulance was still on its way out of the docks when they had to pull over. But they couldn't save him. He died right outside the pub he'd been in earlier.'

Chapter 11

1966
Saturday 29th January – 00:40

Paul Taylor hadn't long turned thirteen and legally, was way too young to be working as a night watchman in Leith Docks. The key word was "legally", but these were the 60s, so the concept was rather loose. He was paid cash-in-hand, and no record of his name appeared on any document related to employment.

Paul had felt guilty about deserting his post just before Friday clicked over into Saturday, but he reasoned that a late January night in piss poor weather was as good a time as any to slip away for a couple of hours. Plus, his mother needed him. She'd gone downhill recently, and when Paul had set out for his shift his waste-of-space older brother still hadn't come home from whichever party he'd gate-crashed.

He hadn't told his mother that once the late shift were well clear, he'd sneak home to make sure she was okay, but when he arrived at their flat, he discovered she'd been sick again. So, he helped her to clean up, cycled over to his auntie Jean's house and walked back with her. She'd offered to pay for a taxi but the telephone number for Leith Cabs' despatch office was permanently engaged. Or more likely off the hook while the despatcher gossiped with the drivers. Jean was a hugely capable woman so immediately they arrived at the flat she assumed command and sent him packing.

Cycling through the docks within striking distance of his hut, he'd spotted the lights on the stationary van. Instinctively, he hung back. If it was dodgy, the type of men involved were not the sort a thirteen-year-old would dream of challenging. And, when it came down to it, whatever they were stealing didn't belong to him.

He heard muffled voices, the sounds of several men moving away from him towards the Albert Dock. There was a boat moored there, he could hardly make it out, but he knew it had arrived in port the day before. It was scheduled for the dry dock on Monday, so it would remain berthed over the weekend. He heard a scuffle. Grunts, more voices, the sound of something being dragged. The moon peeked out through a gap in the clouds and a minute or two later he picked out four men jogging towards the van. It took him a few beats to figure out what all four were carrying. Axe handles.

He dropped to one knee. Carefully, silently, he laid his bike down. The van drove away and the single tail light receded into the gloom. But Paul didn't move from his position. *This is none of my business*, he thought, and wheeled his bike in the direction of the watchman's hut. Earlier, he'd banked up the coals in the brazier, so it didn't take long to come alive. He stood there for a few minutes, rubbing his hands together above the heat.

He kept glancing back towards the dock, senses on high alert. What had the men been doing there? They hadn't been carrying anything, apart from … Maybe they hadn't been stealing. He began adjusting the coals, then stopped. *Was that*

63

a splash? There's no wind, so definitely not waves. He concentrated, still staring in the same direction. And when he heard a groan he couldn't put it off any longer. He made his way hesitantly towards the dock.

He arrived at the point on the dockside where he'd seen the four men. Thin cloud was wafting back and forth across the moon, so the light was inconsistent. But his night vision was improving and, scanning around, he spotted what appeared to be a crumpled bundle lying on the ground a short distance away. It was close to the railway line, about twenty yards from the dockside.

When Paul cycled to work, his route took him through areas of Leith at a time of night when a squad of paras would be ideal company: pub chucking out time. Drunks, both local and seafaring, were ten a penny, and fistfights were hardly worth commenting on. But these were hard men, and most of the time they dragged themselves upright and staggered away. Even for his tender years, Paul had seen more than his fair share of comatose bodies and he reckoned that's what was in front of him.

Approaching the bundle, he kicked something. It didn't feel particularly solid, but it didn't tumble or roll across the asphalt. Rather, it skidded away from him. It was a shoe, and an expensive shoe at that. A highly polished black brogue. He dropped it faster than if it had been molten steel, straight from the forge. He stared at the bundle, then leaned down and brushed his fingers against the material. Soft, rich, damp. He picked it up and turned it till the collar was uppermost. As he did that, an object slipped out of a pocket and bounced off his foot. It was a notebook, black with a hard cover.

Forgetting about the coat, he stood up, twisted this way and that, searching through the mist. In these docks, probably only one man could afford shoes and a coat like these. But the notebook sealed it. On several occasions, he'd witnessed Sandro De Luca writing in what he called his "journal". Paul didn't know what was inside, but he knew it was important to Sandro so would make sure to return it.

He looked up, scanned around. In the lee of the boat, he picked out a larger, darker form. He ran over and gently touched the nearest part with both hands. It was a man's shoulder. And it was saturated in a stinking oily film.

'Mister De Luca! Mister De Luca!'

But Sandro didn't respond. Paul gave that shoulder a damn good shake but all that happened was his employer rolled onto his back. The movement made a squelching sound.

'Oh, Jesus. Mister De Luca, wake up!' But he didn't. Paul slumped to his knees, held his head in both hands, and tried to scream. Nothing came out.

He sprinted to the hut, snatched his bike away from the wall and cycled away as if the hounds of hell were snapping at his back wheel.

Chapter 12

The Present Day
10:30

'Tell me about Alessandro De Luca,' said Jeff.

Hugo shifted around in his seat before answering. 'The story goes that Sandro was born in Naples on New Year's Day 1900. The family emigrated to Scotland and settled in Leith. A number of their relatives were already here, and others joined them as time went by.'

'How many kids?'

'Unusually for an Italian family there were only three. Sandro had two older sisters, but I heard the eldest was only about four when their mother died. His father brought the kids up himself, never remarried. Then tragically, he was killed in a mining accident at Newtongrange Colliery when Sandro was about ten. The kids were taken in by relatives. Sandro was always a bit of a lad, apparently, and had to grow up fast, not having a dad and all. But clearly he was smart enough to turn things to his advantage and he began to make decent money.'

'Was he legit?'

'From what I learned Sandro was a crook, no doubt about it. But nothing heavy. We didn't have drugs-running on a major scale, and prostitution was more or less restricted to brothels run by a few local madams and almost exclusively for the benefit of sailors and dockworkers. He was involved in smuggling, unregistered shipments that disappeared in trucks and vans, some loan sharking, strongarming. Minor stuff. But volume: he had fingers in so many pies. So yeah, he was a crook but in kind of an old-fashioned way. Like Fagin but on a much grander scale.' He changed position in his seat and hooked an ankle across his other knee. 'But having said all that, you wouldn't have wanted to cross him. He had men in key positions all over the port – inside the docks and out. They were intensely loyal to him, and they mobilised themselves to find out who was responsible. But they had no leader, so it wasn't long before they ran out of steam.'

'Were they just looking for revenge, or were they trying to make sure no one else muscled in?'

Hugo waggled his hand from side to side. 'We suspected it was for revenge at first. But, like us, his men couldn't find anyone to blame. Then reality began to bite. Through Sandro, they earned extra cash off the books. Backhanders, unofficial bonuses here and there. But that all vanished and they were left with a basic wage. Despite their loyalties, the golden goose was dead and buried. Not by his family, as you would expect. They never stopped badgering us; trying to keep the case alive.'

Jeff sat back. 'Speaking of the family, did De Luca not have a number two? A son, or a deputy? Someone to step in and keep the organisation going if they had to.'

'Not in the family; he only had one daughter, Isobel. And no brothers. He did have a staunch ally, guy called Charlie Kinnear –'

'I noticed that name in the file.'

'You would have done. They grew up together, met during the first world war. You've maybe heard about this but sometime in 1916, two German Zeppelins cruised in from the

Forth Estuary and started dropping bombs over Leith and parts of Edinburgh. There were no air defences so they couldn't be shot down. Sandro and Charlie were two young lads out on the make and when the bombs started falling, they dived over the same wall for cover. Apparently, a warehouse belonging to a fruit and veg wholesaler took a hit, a loading bay door blew out, and a pile of fresh food landed in the boys' laps. They piled as much as they could on wheelbarrows and flogged the whole lot on the cheap to Sandro's neighbours. And that was that. Partners in crime from then on in.'

'I'm guessing Sandro was the brains?'

Hugo nodded. 'Kinnear was tough, with a reputation of being more enforcer than smart, so definitely a number two, not a leader. Sandro didn't appear to rely on anyone else. We wondered if he simply hadn't foreseen the day coming, when he might want to step aside.'

'This guy, Kinnear. Was he interviewed?'

'Yes. He'd been at the head-wetting too and had really tied one on. Went on a bender, finally showed up for work on the Tuesday morning and that was when he found out about Sandro. Charged about threatening people but, same as everybody else, he fizzled out like a damp squib.'

'With Sandro gone, did someone make a move on his business? That would have given you a motive.'

Hugo sat back and folded his arms. 'As far as we could tell, no one did. Well, not at first anyway. A few of Sandro's men were quite resourceful in their own way, but like I said, it didn't last. Rival gangs started picking up the slack, and eventually everything settled down again. Weird, because whoever killed him didn't do it to take over his patch. Or it didn't seem like it, anyway.'

Jeff pondered that for a moment. Hugo was right, that was weird. He picked up the case file and began to flick through it, but Hugo shot to his feet and threw his arms out. 'Come on, Jeff, this is taking too bloody long. All the time we're talking, my granddaughter is still missing.'

'Hugo, I know it must appear as though we're not doing much, but leaving me aside, DI Cooper already has her whole team plus officers from other departments working on it and she'll be pulling in ancillary resources from wherever she can get them. And every officer she calls on will have this as their top priority. We can't afford to start running about like headless chickens so we're gathering data to help us make the best decisions straight from the off, so we don't go up any blind alleys.'

Hugo was only slightly mollified by the DCI's explanation but no matter how sorry Jeff felt for his former colleague, he didn't have time to sit and hold his hand.

Jeff stabbed his finger on a sheet of paper. 'The pathologist suggested time of death was between midnight and three.'

Hugo shrugged. 'It was the best guess at the time.'

'How did that fit in with when he was supposed to have left the pub?'

'Ah. That's all a bit shaky. The men had been drinking since they'd finished work on the Friday afternoon, including those who were due on shift the following morning. The pub shut at ten as they did in those days, but then they had a lock-in. When we spoke to the ones we could find over the weekend, they could hardly remember their own names, never mind what time one person, even Sandro, left the pub.'

'But surely the barmen?'

Hugo snorted. 'They might have started drinking later than the punters but they were just as bad. They don't stand behind the bar polishing glasses during a lock-in, you know.'

'And the cause of death?'

Hugo made a face. 'He'd suffered a terrible beating. Massive damage to his internal organs.' He hesitated.

'But?'

'But his body was discovered right next to the dock, and he'd been in the water. So either he fell in while attempting to escape his attackers, or he was pushed.'

Jeff blinked. Natasha's prison, and the water flowing in, now made sense, but he had no intention of sharing that with the older man. 'Go on.'

'The pathologist didn't believe Sandro's internal injuries were caused by the fall, most likely he was attacked with highly polished axe handles. No splinters, you see. His attackers were incredibly careful. He'd fallen, or he was pushed, into the gap between the hull of a boat and the dockside but his injuries, plus forensic evidence like oil and algae all over his hands and clothes, suggested he'd somehow managed to climb up the anchor chain. There's no doubt he did sustain injuries by falling in, so death was caused by a combination of the attack, the fall, and the amount of water he ingested. Which would have been foul as you can imagine.'

Jeff showed Hugo a list of potential suspects from the files. The older man shook his head. 'Jeez. The names on there don't half bring back bad memories.'

'So they were all in the frame to one degree or another, but nothing stuck?'

Hugo studied the list. 'Almost all of these guys were at Sandro's funeral. St Mary's was jam-packed. But I don't think whoever killed him would have dared to show his face. People talked about who could have done it, but it was all conjecture, all gossip. We followed up on everything, but we drew a blank on every lead.' Hugo scowled. 'If you could call them leads.'

'The investigation,' said the DCI. 'Tell me about that.'

The older man sighed. 'The trail literally went cold straight from the off. No witnesses, no suspects, nothing to go on. It was a violent assault, but no blood. Most probably by design.'

Jeff rooted around in his paperwork. Andrew had called the archive store and asked them to courier the summary file relating to the case. He'd discovered a map of the docks as they were then and marked where De Luca's body was found. Jeff spun it round on his desk and pointed. 'This is definitely the right location, yeah?'

Hugo nodded. 'There weren't many proper roads in the docks back then. Vehicles often shared the same routes as the trains because, apart from the major lines, the rails were set into the ground.' He pointed on the map at a road that meandered alongside the Water of Leith. It led down to The Shore. 'Sandro lived here, Coburg Street, so it's reasonable to assume, even if he was pissed, he was taking a logical route that took him from the pub, through the docks, over the Victoria Swing Bridge, and from there he's only about five minutes from his house.'

'But if he was that pissed, wouldn't someone have suggested that walking through the docks at that time of night might not be the safest route home?'

Hugo flicked a glance in Jeff's direction. 'Have you ever tried telling a drunk that he's pissed?'

Jeff studied the map too. 'It would definitely have been quicker if he'd gone straight along Salamander Street, parallel to the docks.'

'Of course it would. But all we could imagine was Sandro needed to talk to some of his men who were working that night.'

'On night shift, do you mean?'

'Possibly. But nightwatchmen too. Guaranteed they were on his payroll. He'd have greased their palms to keep an eye on what was going on.'

'And you spoke to them?'

'As many as we could find. But records of who was working, or was meant to be working, were … let's say, not particularly accurate. It was a three monkeys situation.'

Jeff smiled. See no evil, hear no evil, and definitely speak no evil. And certainly not to the cops. 'Forensics on the ground; anything useful?'

Hugo pointed at the documents. 'It'll all be in there, but as far as the murder scene was concerned, nothing. You have to remember these were working docks at the height of their powers. Hundreds of men wearing similar work boots, vehicles of all sizes moving about, leaking fuel and oil like nobody's business. The terrain didn't help. Gravel, broken slabs, dirt and rubbish everywhere. We would have checked for soil samples, tyre tracks, footprints, but given the fact it had been pissing down for most of the Friday it's hardly a surprise we never found a single useful print. Although forensics were basic, the scientists were as diligent then as people are now. It's just they had a lot less to work with. And effective crime scene management was a thing of the future.'

Jeff was beginning to feel dispirited that he and his officers were trying to investigate a murder that had happened the guts of six decades earlier, with no more evidence than the first time around. He consoled himself with the thought that at least they'd be able to bring modern techniques and technology to bear, but how on earth would he persuade Stevenson they were making progress? 'Okay,' he said, 'you were getting nowhere fast. Did that ever change?'

Hugo put on a glum face. 'I'd be lying if I said it did. We had nothing to go on and nobody was talking to us. As time went on and I moved up the ranks, the importance of the investigation headed in the opposite direction. Yes, a man died, but Sandro De Luca wasn't exactly Snow White.'

Jeff glanced at his wrist; time was marching on. 'In your heart of hearts, do you believe it was investigated properly?'

'I know I tried my best, and so did my boss. But he died in '79, so there aren't many of us left who were around at the time. Plus, in the late 60s and 70s, Leith was becoming a bit hairy, local gang culture was beginning to develop right across the city, so we had a lot on our plates.'

'Local gangs? What, like the "YLT"? Were they not just a bunch of kids?'

'Ah, the *Young Leith Team*.' Hugo lifted both hands, and arranged his fingers and one thumb in a symbol that broadly illustrated the letters "YLT".

Jeff peered at Hugo until he got it, then said, 'Well, that's a new one on me.'

Hugo stared at him in disbelief. 'How long have you been a cop in Leith? And no, they weren't just kids. Some of them were right vicious bastards, who thought nothing of beating rival gang members half to death.'

Jeff didn't like asking his next question, but he had no choice. 'Is it possible that police corruption meant the case was pushed down the lists?' He'd hesitated to ask that in case it was a bit close to home, but Hugo took it in his stride.

'No sensible person would deny there were bent coppers kicking about. But, honestly, it was all about casual backhanders, free meals, bottles of booze at Christmas. Nothing heavy, and certainly too low level to influence how a murder was investigated. But remember, I'm talking about Leith because this is where I worked all my days. Take Edinburgh as a whole and it might have been different, but I wouldn't have known about that.'

Momentarily, Jeff recalled that old British TV comedy drama *Life on Mars*, set in 1973, which starred Philip Glenister as Gene Hunt, a sexist, racist and homophobic DCI for whom rules and procedures were there to be ignored. And mocked. Hunt would have choked on his whisky if anyone had been fool enough to set him straight. Jeff mused that the depiction of Hunt and his misogynist colleagues was probably far closer to real life than the police services would like to admit. On balance, he was pleased Hugo had come out with a straight answer, but thought, *Damn it. It would have been much better if he'd given me something to go on.*

He checked his notes. 'And you informed the family the case was closed?'

'I did.'

'That strikes me as a bit odd. Why you? A comparatively junior DI. Why not a more senior officer?'

For the first time that morning Hugo smiled. 'Ah, that was down to old Mama De Luca, Sandro's missus. She was a total harridan. Everyone was scared shitless of her, so I was landed.'

Jeff smiled too. He could picture it. 'What age would she have been?'

'She was Sandro's second wife. The first one died in childbirth. Sadly, the kid didn't make it either. So he was a lot older than her, making her mid to late sixties. But she looked ancient. Or at least she did to me.'

'What was their reaction when you told them it was closed?'

'They went bananas, particularly her. I was lucky to get out the house alive, we both were.'

'Both?'

'Yes. There was a young policewoman … sorry, police officer. Tracey … No, Theresa. Sorry, I can't remember her surname.'

'Thanks. We'll find her.' Jeff took a note. 'I've read the family wouldn't let it go.'

'No, they bloody wouldn't. They tried campaigning, got their MP involved, some local news coverage but not much. After a couple of years, which would have been early '82, they were already beginning to run out of steam. And then the Falklands war happened, and IRA bombings in London, and the media wasn't interested. Eventually nobody was listening to them, and that was that, as they say in the business.'

'Was Marlon Stevenson involved at the time?'

Hugo placed his face in his hands and peered at Jeff through his fingers. 'Marlon. What the hell was his mother thinking? Nobody pronounced it "Mar-*lon*". All he got was "Mar-*lyn*", poor lad. Even the papers spelled it wrong. You know he was born on the day Sandro was murdered?'

Jeff nodded. 'I'm guessing she must have had a Brando fixation.'

'She must have. Anyway, the boy was only fourteen when we officially closed the case. Only sixteen when it was all fizzling out.'

Jeff began tidying up his paperwork. Clipped his *Mont Blanc* pen into his inside jacket pocket. Hugo caught sight of it. 'Clearly the stationery budget's a bit more generous these days,' he said.

'It was a gift. From my aunt.'

Both men stood up. 'One thing I can't get my head around,' said Hugo. 'His grandfather was murdered nearly sixty years ago. Why's he done this now? It's so extreme.'

Jeff sighed. 'His mother, Sandro's daughter, is terminally ill. And he's promised her he'd find her father's killer. What's tragic is the way he's chosen to do it.'

Chapter 13

I'm on hold when DC Ella Jackson strides into the incident room. She gives me a quick wave, so I hang up and beckon her over. Ella's mid-thirties but you'd never guess. She's tall and rangy, and fit as a butcher's dog. She told me once she's a fell runner in her spare time, the concept of which I'd rather not imagine. When I said it sounded like the ultimate form of masochism to me, she had the good grace not to look me up and down.

We exchange brief greetings then she says, 'I've been asked to let you know Crissi Banerjee is on her way.'

I bring her up to speed and tell her about the deadlines. That opens her eyes, but otherwise she doesn't respond. She's got a sensible head on her shoulders, this one.

'I want you to work with Andrew to start with. He's reviewing a couple of videos; two with the kidnapper, and one with his victim. He'll explain what we're looking for. I should also warn you that the content might be distressing but it needs to be done. I want the live feed monitored full time, but I'm afraid you'll have to timeshare that with other stuff. That's why the two of you are on it. If one of you needs— no, make that *when* one of you needs a break, the other one can take over.'

Just at that, a young man in a navy-blue polo shirt bashes his way through the door. I'm about to bollock him for barging in without so much as a by-your-leave but he has a package under his arm. It's about two feet square and wrapped in polythene. Andrew is hobbling across from the whiteboard on his crutches. The bloke spots him and calls out, 'DS Young?' Andrew stops and looks over. 'This is for you.' He rips the polythene off, and hands it over.

Andrew switches both crutches to one hand and glowers at it. 'A cushion? I asked for an ergonomic chair.'

The younger man twists the polythene and ties it in a knot. 'Sorry. We don't carry them in stock, it's a five-day lead time. Besides, your message said you had trouble sitting, a broken whatsit.' He pretends to check out Andrew's bum then points at the cushion. 'That'll do the trick.'

And with that, he spins on his heel and disappears faster than he arrived, leaving Andrew still holding the offending article.

I try not to crack up but I'm struggling. 'Lucky for you,' I chortle, 'that Steph's not here.'

He doesn't reply but slings me a murderous scowl that says more than any number of words.

* * *

Earlier, Marlon Stevenson had told us there was no point searching his house, social media accounts, computers, phones. "I wouldn't bother. There's nothing to find". Smug bastard.

Okay, Marlon, thanks for the heads up. We won't, then. Yeah, that'll be right. I can hear the pronouncement of the chair at my Professional Standards hearing. "So, DI Cooper, you didn't go to Mr Stevenson's house, or scrutinise his social media or finances. Could you explain to us why not?"

"Oh, that's an easy one. He told us we wouldn't find anything".

"I see. Well, I think that's fair enough. Off you trot. Sorry to have bothered you".

In my dreams.

I glance up to find DC Crissi Banerjee crossing the room. She and Ella are starkly different in nature. Where Ella is confident and engaging, Crissi, perhaps because she's a few years younger, is more reserved and more of a listener. Or it could be her upbringing or culture is the reason she's quieter. Her family is from Bangladesh; it was her grandparents who emigrated to Scotland in the 60s. I met her mother and her grandmother once, when I was picking Crissi up from their house. Despite Crissi's protestations they insisted I went in for a cup of tea. The cooking aromas in the house were mouth-watering, I must have put on a couple of pounds just sitting there. When we left, Crissi's grandmother insisted I take a jar of their homemade chutney away with me. Our family are real curry buffs, and we demolished the delicious relish in a couple of sittings. They told me I should pick her up from home more often.

Crissi's standing in front of my desk, her jacket folded over her hands which are clasped in front of her. I smile up at her; the woman has eyes you could swim in. 'Good to see you, Crissi.'

'And you, DI –' I give her a look with a smile attached. She blushes and her skin deepens to a fabulous mulberry colour. 'Sorry. Mel.'

I wave a hand to say *No matter*. 'I've asked for you because there's a family I need to place you with. Pull up a chair and I'll tell you all about it.'

* * *

Not long after Crissi set off for Hugo Emerson's house, I hear a familiar voice. I spin my chair round slowly. 'Morning, PC Devlin,' I say. 'How's my favourite man in uniform?'

He places the tip of his index finger on his lower lip. 'I don't know, Detective. Tell me his name and I'll find out for you.'

'Hmmm. I'll rephrase that. How's my favourite man in uniform with a baldy head and a dodgy Hitler moustache?'

That gets a belly laugh. 'He's fine. How may I help you, ma'am.'

Bugger. He knows calling me "ma'am" winds me up something awful, so I say, 'Park your arse and pin back your lugs.'

Once I've related the whole sorry tale I rattle out what I need him for. 'Liaise with Tobias and the Control. I need officers to canvass in two different areas. First, trawl all the venues down at The Shore that were open last night. Find out if Natasha and her pals were in any of them. If anyone recognises her, go through their CCTV and find out when she left their premises. That might help us narrow down the times she was on the street. If you strike out, collect CCTV anyway and send it to Tobias. Secondly, we've checked cameras near Hugo's house for Stevenson or anyone else for that matter, posting the envelope through Hugo's door but we drew a blank, so I want officers going round his neighbours. Ask if they saw anything. And also ask for household CCTV while you're at it.'

Dave gives me a cheeky salute and heads off.

Andrew catches my attention. 'Couple of things, Boss. Been checking out the link Steph found about survival rates in water. According to this marine website, for Natasha to survive indefinitely, the temperature will have to be 75 to 80 degrees Fahrenheit. Minimum. And I spoke to our facilities management guys. When I told them the camera lens isn't fogging they reckon there'll be extractor fans running.'

'If he's planning to heat that amount of water, he must have a boiler running flat out.' I wonder briefly if we could trace him through his energy consumption but immediately file the idea under the *behave yourself, Mel* category. 'You said a couple of things …'

'Yeah. Spoke to the council. You were right, there is a disaster reaction team. I spoke to the woman who heads it up. Posh Scottish accent, sounds super-efficient. Says it doesn't matter who I need to speak to, she'll have them on the phone to me within half an hour at the latest.' He pauses. Smiles. 'A guy from the planning department called me less than five minutes later. You won't be surprised to hear Stevenson hasn't made any planning applications.'

My colleague is correct. I'm not in the least surprised. That would have been a stupid thing to do, and, however I might describe him, stupid wouldn't be high on my list.

Chapter 14

It was 10:30 and in three minutes time, Marlon Stevenson would reduce the flow of water into Natasha's chamber back to normal.

Marlon couldn't understand why, but he became noticeably nervous whenever he watched Natasha on the live feed.

I mean, I kidnapped her, imprisoned her, sent Hugo Emerson to the police, and put the water up to high when that stupid cow DI Cooper tried to manipulate me. I stood firm. I carried out my threat and I acted immediately.

Therefore, I have the upper hand. Still in control of the game. And that's how I see it – a game. A game where I'll keep my opponents under pressure, so I have momentum throughout. I will not allow them to strike back. I will stay in control.

He flipped open his laptop and entered the password. Sixteen digits, containing the full range of alpha, numeric, and special characters, in lower and upper cases. He was utterly confident that if the laptop fell into the police's possession, even their software would take at least a day to crack it. He hit *Enter* and Natasha appeared, static, until he pressed *Play*.

She was on the table, still in the lotus position, elbows on her knees, hands covering her ears, and by the angle of her head, eyes focussed on a point just in front of her feet. At least he assumed her eyes were open; from this angle he couldn't tell. For all he knew they could have been tight shut.

Marlon was sitting at a card table he'd set up in the spare bedroom of the house he was using, a refurbished Samsung in his hand. The phone had no network SIM, he'd uninstalled all unnecessary apps and disabled the GPS, and although he felt secure accessing the house's Wi-Fi because no one knew where he was hiding out, he kept the phone switched off when he wasn't using it. He tapped the screen to reconnect Bluetooth and launched an app he'd installed.

He'd studied several YouTube videos to devise a cheap facsimile of a proprietary central heating control that normally cost a couple of hundred pounds. His version wasn't programmable, so he had to change the settings manually, but as he'd only be altering them a few times that didn't concern him.

Near the top of the display was a slider marked *Power Off / On*. It was set to *On*. In the centre was a dial with a marking on each side and another at the top. The marking on the left was annotated with the word "Closed". At the top it read "Half", and on the right was "Full". The dial was currently set to the right, meaning the tap feeding water to Natasha's prison was fully open.

He glanced at the time: 10:32. One hour since he'd opened the tap fully. He set the screen timeout to five minutes to make sure it stayed on and kept his eye on the time. The instant it changed to 10:33, he tapped the dial at the top, reducing the flow of water by fifty per cent.

It was a few seconds before Natasha reacted. First, she dropped her hands away from her ears and raised her head. She looked up to her right, where the water still flowed in. Now the flow was similar to when it first started running. She stretched out her legs, eased slowly to her feet, her eyes still fixed on the water falling down from the corner of the ceiling. Her gaze travelled to the floor. She went down on one knee and poked her fingers, all four together, into the water until the middle one touched the floor. She studied her hand, withdrew it from the water and studied it again.

Marlon switched his phone off, closed the laptop's lid, and walked out of the bedroom.

The time was 10:34.

Chapter 15

As the morning wore on, Dave Devlin called in with progress updates for Tobias.

"Sorry, my man, but as you might expect, most of Hugo Emerson's neighbours aren't at home just now. We've only been able to speak to five householders; two were out running the kids to school, and none of the other three witnessed Marlon Stevenson or persons unknown posting the envelope through Mr Emerson's letterbox. We've left the usual "Please Contact Us" letters. If necessary, we'll follow up later in the evening".

* * *

Dave's next call brought better news. "Looks like we've struck lucky. It wasn't particularly busy down at The Shore last night, and we have two definite sightings. In both places, the bar staff didn't know Ms Emerson personally, but they did recognise her from the photo. The second sighting was at 21:18, where the three of them were heading towards Fishers Bistro. It's the last place on The Shore before you fall into the harbour and although it's primarily a restaurant, they have a few tables that double up as a bar when they're not busy with diners".

* * *

Not long after that, Dave was back on. "Two of my lads are in Fishers Bistro now. The staff who were on last night aren't in yet, but their CCTV shows the women leaving at 22:20. They were walking towards the junction of Commercial Street and The Shore".

* * *

Finally, Dave dropped the last piece into the jigsaw. "There's only one bus stop on that stretch. It's right outside a café, so we looked up their CCTV for the time Natasha and her pals left

Fishers. They waited at the stop for a shade over five minutes till 22:28. A bus appeared, and her two friends got on. I've checked the timetables. It would have been a number 16".

* * *

I walk in as Tobias is relaying Dave's canvassing results on to Andrew. I loiter beside them, so they don't have to repeat themselves.

'I'll ask Lothian Buses for video footage,' says Andrew. 'As soon as I have it, I'll get right on to the university and hopefully identify her friends.' I'm about to leave him to it when he stops me. 'Two more updates for you. I've sent the films to the multimedia unit; they'll examine them immediately. Plus, I've spoken to a team lead in Forensics Services about lipreading. They would have to bring in a professional lipreader, and they're few and far between. The team lead will look into it for us, but she doesn't believe we'll get much value, especially given the situation Natasha's in.'

'How come?' I wonder uncharitably if this woman is making excuses to avoid spending her budget.

'According to her, common consensus is that only about thirty per cent of lipreading is accurate because there are too many influences that affect the lip pattern. For example, the person's accent, or if they're shouting, or crying, or in distress.'

'Which, if you're describing Natasha Emerson, is bang on the money.'

'It does. And the other main factor is that the lipreader's results are more likely to be accurate if their subject is facing them directly. And Natasha has her head down most of the time.'

I throw all that around in my head and come to a decision. 'Okay. Leave it for now. If we change our minds, we'll revisit.'

Chapter 16

Wednesday 10:35

Natasha had tried facing away from the water flowing down from the ceiling but found it impossible. She'd freaked when it had first started, and her panic level had shot through the roof when the flow rate increased. But once it had returned to the lower rate she'd been able to rationalise. She reckoned that given the size of the room there was a long way to go before it became critical, but still felt more secure if she kept an eye on it. She stayed immobile and attempted, once again, to work through her situation without falling apart.

'Right, Tash. Get a grip.' She didn't really understand why, but speaking out loud immediately made her feel better. She mulled that over, gave one precise nod, and carried on talking.

'Okay, who is this effer, and why has he done this?' She smiled. It went nowhere near her eyes, but her spirits rose further. Not by much, maybe just a notch, but that was plenty. Now she had a name for him. The Effer. It originated from an old Billy Connolly joke about city kids on an outing to the countryside for the day. They were shown all sorts of animals including cows they promptly named "fuckers". The punchline was, "The teacher told us they were effers, but we knew what she meant". So that became Natasha's name for her kidnapper: The Effer.

She repeated the term, tried it on for size and decided whoever he was, it suited him. To a tee. And her mother would approve because, although *she* swore like a trooper, she would practically keelhaul her daughter if she uttered even the mildest curse. A serious case of "Don't do as I do …"

But the thought of her mother immediately derailed her; the shakes kicked in again, and her eyes brimmed. She called up her mantra again. *Be calm, Natasha. There are worse things in life. Be calm, Natasha. There are worse things in life.*

Like before, it took only a couple of repetitions before she felt the strain easing and was able to concentrate. 'Okay. The Effer. Who is he?' That was a simple one; she hadn't a clue. She was easy-going, laid back. Rarely, if ever, did she upset people or fall out with them. Stumped, she shook her head for what seemed like the hundredth time.

She gazed down at the water without it actually registering. It wasn't quite ankle depth and as the flow splashed in, it created tiny ripples that rolled out diagonally across the surface. 'I'm not scared, you know,' she said in her normal voice, although even she could detect the quaver. She upped the volume. 'If you can hear me, I *said* I'm not bloody scared.'

You fucker. This time under her breath.

It's possible he can hear me. I wonder if there's a mike somewhere.

But she'd already scrutinised the whole space, over and over. Blank walls, not an interruption anywhere. No doors or windows; no light switches, alarms or smoke detectors; no shelves or pictures. Nothing. Set into the ceiling, close to the corners, were aluminium airflow vents similar to those that are installed above internal doors. She couldn't see through and had given up shouting at them hours earlier. Three downlighters were set diagonally in the ceiling although the one in the far corner had stopped working. After she'd pulled the hood off and her vision had adjusted, she'd looked around, taken in her surroundings. The light had definitely been on. But a few minutes later, it flickered and went off.

She continued to feel more positive when she spoke to herself out loud. 'So, I'm gonna keep talking, okay? And if you want to hear what I've got to say then why don't you come in here and we can discuss it.' She'd been going to add the *you fucker* bit, but decided that might antagonise, so she didn't. *Certain things are better left unsaid.*

Natasha watched the water falling, while feeling strangely indifferent about it. Earlier, it started off running slowly, faster for, what, less than a minute, then slowly again. She didn't know why. 'Maybe he turned the tap the wrong way.' She ran that through her mind. 'That'll be it. But when it was on full blast, it was on for ages. Now it's back to a trickle.'

She couldn't make head nor tail of it so pushed it to the back of her mind.

Not long after she had found herself imprisoned, and once she'd stopped weeping, she'd checked out the contents of the plastic box and immediately christened it her "survival kit". It was 15 centimetres high, 25 wide, and 40 long. The contents were jammed in. Packs of nuts and dried fruit, high energy cereal bars, and a bag of four red apples. There was a small bottle of liquid soap, another of sanitiser, a bundle of white terry facecloths and two hand towels. Briefly, she considered eating something, but her stomach had been replaced by a churning void. She couldn't imagine anything going over her throat and staying down.

She remembered a lecture she'd attended in her first term. It was about presenting to an audience, and the trainer, an older bloke with greying hair, had critiqued a short talk she'd given to the class. When he'd asked if she'd been nervous, she laughed and replied, 'God, yes. Total butterflies.' But he told her that she neither looked nor sounded nervous so, even if she were, it hadn't come across and she should take confidence from that.

Right then, she reflected on the trainer's advice. *Inside, I'm not exactly a wreck but I'm not far off. But my voice sounds fine and I'm not shaking like a leaf so if The Effer is watching or listening, there's no way he can tell how I'm feeling.* That was yet another boost to her morale, so she chalked it up as one more point for Natasha.

She coughed into her palm, cleared her throat, tilted her head to stare at the ceiling. 'I want to ask you a question. I'm only nineteen. I've never done anything to harm anyone.' She pointed at the floor. 'So why are you doing this?' The panic resurfaced and she called upon her mantra once more. *Be calm, Natasha. There are worse things in life.*

The panic subsided. It hadn't vanished, but it had become manageable.

'This!' She flapped an arm at the water flowing down. 'This is barbaric. Do you hear me? Barbaric.'

Chapter 17

Tobias calls me over and shows me footage on his screen. This end of Commercial Street is only about five minutes' walk from here and I recognise it at once. He clicks *Play* and uses the mouse pointer to show me what he's found. 'Here is Natasha approaching Commercial Street from the bus stop and turning left towards her flat,' he says.

It's a clear night so the quality of the film is excellent. I see a young woman dressed in a short denim skirt just above the knee, a fleece, and casual shoes. Converse, or similar. Natasha isn't carrying a bag but if she's anything like my daughter, Lily, pretty much all she needs is her phone, tissues and some lippy. She's walking steadily along the left side of the street. She's not in a hurry but neither is she dawdling. Tobias pauses that film and switches to another window. She passes below this camera. It's a zip-up fleece she's wearing, with a tee shirt underneath.

'So,' I say. 'We know for certain that when Stevenson put her in that room, he made her change into the hoodie and shorts. Why would he do that?'

Tobias rocks his head from side to side. 'Perhaps it was to change how she feels about herself, make it less familiar. What she is wearing now is like a prison uniform.'

'Hmmm. You could be right. Where is this camera?'

'An Italian restaurant on the corner of Sandport Street. Domenico's.'

I'm steeling myself because I know what's about to happen to her. I lean forward and tap the space bar to restart the film, but Natasha only takes a few more steps before she moves out of view. I wait for Tobias to switch to another window, but I wait in vain. 'Is that it?'

'I'm afraid so. The next camera on this side of the street is beyond where she lives but the angle of the lens doesn't give us a view all the way back to her flat.'

'Nothing on the other side?' I'm talking about a long line of converted whisky bonds that face onto Victoria Quay.

'There isn't, no.' He rewinds the film taken from above the Italian restaurant and manages to pick up part of the pavement on the opposite side. A couple of teenagers are meandering along in the opposite direction, but one glance tells me we don't have a cat's chance in hell of identifying them.

'Bloody hoodies,' I say with feeling. 'Should be outlawed.'

I yawn. It's the first one today and I've been waiting for it. My head feels a bit woozy, like there's a wee aeroplane buzzing about in there. Not a good sign. Coffee is looming but I'll need to be careful with my intake. I clamp my eyes shut and try to concentrate. 'Right,' I say, with more gusto than I'm feeling. 'We know Natasha was heading home along Commercial Street, but she didn't make it. Stevenson snatched her somewhere between the Italian restaurant and her flat but unless we can turn up domestic CCTV we'll have no footage. 'So, where does that leave us?'

'I agree with what you said earlier about him taking her in a van. We shouldn't rule out that he used a car, but it's unlikely. So, I'm concentrating on vans first.'

'Hang on a minute, did we find out if he owns a car?'

My colleague smiles. 'He does. A red Volvo Estate, nine years old. Andrew put a call out, it's on his driveway and we have uniforms watching it until we decide what to do.'

I recall Jeff's point about risk and reward. What are the chances we'd find anything helpful inside Stevenson's house or his car? Probably nil. But we have no choice. We must investigate him, his family and all of his connections because if we don't we'd be in dereliction of duty, and we wouldn't be following policy. That might piss him off and he might retaliate by increasing the water flow for longer. Or it might not, he might accept that we have to do our jobs properly. Unfortunately we won't know until we test him. On balance, it doesn't seem sensible to test him on something that won't help us. Again, I reach a decision, lean back, and speak to Andrew. 'Call off the watch on Stevenson's car, it's a waste of resources. But ask Ronnie to keep an eye on it whenever he's got uniforms in the area.' He waves an acknowledgement and I return to the screen.

Tobias clicks another window, and a map of the area appears. Commercial Street bisects it horizontally, running more or less east to west. There are CCTV annotations in red at each end, and more to the south. 'I've downloaded footage from the time period in question, from The Shore, and from Ocean Terminal. To the north, the only exits lead into residents' car parks, and to the south there are only two routes that give access to other parts of Leith.'

I peer at the map. 'Only two? But I can count … seven.'

He clicks again and the mouse changes from a pointer to a red marker pen. Tobias uses that to put crosses through five of my seven. 'Two of these only provide access to commercial properties or apartments, and the other three turn into walkways that are too narrow to accommodate a vehicle.'

'Any point in taking a look at these properties first?'

'Only if we don't find a van that exited Commercial Street from either end, or via these two routes: Prince Regent Street or Dock Street. I would be surprised if Stevenson was holding her somewhere so close to where he snatched her. And, practically on our doorstep.'

'Fair comment.' I study the map. As Tobias said, the section of Commercial Street where it's likely Natasha was taken is only a few minutes away from HQ. When I was a DC, I was familiar with the area, but I need a refresher. I study the two streets that offer easy escape. 'No question. If he drove up either of these, he's free and clear.' I stand up, give my spine a good stretch. 'I'll let you crack on.'

I feel another yawn about to hit, jam my hand across my mouth till I bring it under control. Tobias smirks. 'Your face goes all funny when you do that.'

'Thank you for pointing that out.' I pretend I'm serious – but fail miserably. 'Have to say, though, if this goes the distance I'm going to struggle.'

'I think we all will.' His accompanying sigh is heartfelt.

Chapter 18

Tobias leans back, catches my attention. 'We're ready, Boss.'

As I'm dragging my chair to his desk I notice how warm it is in the room, yet he's still wearing his black leather jacket. I wonder if it's to save him ironing his shirts. I manoeuvre myself alongside him and Ella.

There's a video icon on the screen, ready to play. 'I think I have something,' he says. He points at a sheet of A4 on his desk. It contains a list with three columns: vehicle colours, make and model, registration. All bar one are highlighted in yellow. 'Excluding heavier commercial vehicles and couriers, only seven vans were on Commercial Street between 20:30 and 22:45 last night. Five were driven in from the west, two from the east. Six of them drove straight through and out the other end. One stopped and parked near the junction with Dock Street. It's still there so all seven are accounted for.'

'Does that mean he didn't use a van?'

'No. He did, and here is why. If you remember, Natasha's flatmate told Steph that Tuesday was a regular date, so perhaps he knew that and had been watching her. But he couldn't possibly have known when the women would call it a night so he couldn't simply turn up and hope to intercept her. He had to be in position early, and ready to act. I said only two vans were driven in from the east during the time window, but I've discovered *three* vans exited to the west. I was able to pick up the registration numbers for all three, so I tracked back in time for that extra van arriving. I eventually found it, driving in from the west at 19:52, and returning the same way at 22.36. After, I suppose, Stevenson snatched Natasha.'

I run my finger down Tobias's list of vehicles. 'A silver VW Transporter.' I look up. 'Registered to?'

He doesn't miss a beat. 'I can't answer, I'm afraid. It was displaying stolen plates. Taken from a black VW van overnight on Monday. I've spoken to the owner; he hadn't noticed the plates had been switched.'

I give that some thought. 'Whether they're genuine or not doesn't matter, we should still be able to track the van using that registration. Do you know where on Commercial Street it stopped?'

'Not precisely. It passed the camera opposite the entrance to Ocean terminal but didn't appear on the next one at Café Domenico. So, somewhere in between.'

I nod. Satisfied. We have a vehicle description and a registration number, almost certainly the kidnapper's van, and the times it arrived at and left Commercial Street. Now for the key question. 'Have you tracked its route to Commercial Street or where it went after he snatched Natasha?'

'Not yet. But I have the search parameters all set up and ready to go.' He checks his watch. 'Ella will help me, and we hope to have results within the hour.'

I turn to Andrew. 'Natasha?'

'A lot of the time she's deep in thought, taking stock, maybe. But she's also talking aloud. That could be to keep her spirits up, but we do get the impression that whatever she's saying is directed at him. Maybe she knows she's being filmed.'

'Any idea what she's saying?'

'No. But now I understand what they meant about lipreading success, because she's rarely face on to the camera for very long.'

'That's a bummer. Hopefully Steph will learn something from talking to Natasha's parents.' I glance at the clock. 'Where the hell is she? I was expecting to have heard from her by now.'

Chapter 19

1966
Saturday 29th January – 01:20

Paul Taylor closed the front door to his mother's flat to find his Auntie Jean framed in the living room doorway. Behind her, blankets were draped over a wing chair. A white pillow was jammed into the angle between the arm and the back.

'What are you doing home, Paul?' she said. 'I told you I had everything under control here.' But as he moved forward into the light, she read his expression. 'What's wrong, lad? You look like you've lost a pound and found a shilling.'

Paul swallowed. 'Nothing. There's nothing wrong.'

'Then why are you home so early? Your shift's nowhere near finished yet.' She glanced at the pendulum clock on the wall. 'It's only just after one o'clock.'

His lower lip began to wobble. 'It's … em …' He burst into tears. Jean rushed towards her nephew, gripped his upper arms.

A door opened by their side. Paul's mother, Patsy, poked her head out, her hand on the door jamb. She was wearing a nightgown beneath an open robe, the ends of the belt hanging down by her legs. She stepped out into the hall, unsteady on her feet. 'Paul? What's happened?' She peered up into his face. 'Why are you crying, Son? That's not like you.'

Paul hesitated, then it all came tumbling out like a rug unrolling. He finished with, 'What am I going to do, Mum?'

She stood a little taller. 'First things first, and it's a hell of a cliché but let's have a cup of tea.' She nudged Jean in the ribs. 'And a slice of toast, please. I'm famished.'

Jean smiled, reached out and laid a hand on her sister's forearm. 'Feeling better, are we?'

'Much.' Patsy winked, but Paul was oblivious.

Jean raised an eyebrow but stayed quiet.

* * *

Paul's mother pushed toast crumbs around her plate with her forefinger, then licked the tip. She clanked her cup down into the saucer. 'You have to go back, Son. Doesn't he, Jean?'

His aunt nodded. 'You're sure it was him, Paul? Mr De Luca?'

Paul nodded, produced the black notebook. 'This is his. He writes stuff in it all the time.'

Jean took it from him. Opened it. Read a few lines then slapped it shut. 'Are you certain he was dead?'

Her nephew concentrated for a second. 'Pretty sure, yeah.'

'If you're only "pretty sure", that's why you have to go back. Because if he's not dead, we have to help him because Sandro De Luca has helped so many people over the years. Perhaps it's our turn now.' Jean paused. 'Assuming no one else has found him, that is.' She leaned forward in her chair. 'You said there were no injuries, no blood.'

Paul shook his head twice, and quickly. 'But what if he is dead? What'll I do?' He stared down at the table. 'Oh, God. I'm in so much shit.'

His mother's brow dropped; her eyes narrowed. 'Paul! I know it's a terrible situation but please don't take the Lord's name in vain.' She stretched out and rested her hand on his shoulder.

'Sorry, Mum.' His eyelids fluttered but he didn't look up.

Jean spoke. 'This isn't your fault, Paul. Remember that. Now, your watchman's hut, how close is it to the Albert Dock, where you found Mr De Luca?'

Now he did raise his head. 'I don't know. Not far. Fifty yards?'

'And when you're working, doing your rounds or whatever you call it, would you normally go past that dock?'

He turned to his aunt. 'I could, but I don't have to. There's a big warehouse to the left of where …' His eyes brimmed, but he drew in a deep breath. 'To the left of where he is. The doors are at the far end, and I have to check them.' The boy glanced off to the side. 'So if I'd walked round the other way, I wouldn't have seen him.' Paul's voice was stronger, the sniffles had subsided down to the occasional hiccup. He looked at Patsy, then Jean. Shivered. 'But I really don't know if I can go back.'

'I'll come with you,' said Jean. She used the table to pull herself upright then straightened the cloth. 'Now, go and find us a bag. A holdall, or something like that. We'll need to take blankets and first aid with us. And bring your bike. You might need to go and fetch help.'

Chapter 20

The Present Day
11:10

Steph eventually phones as I'm about to head out to speak to Marlon Stevenson's mother. 'How did you get on with Natasha's parents?' I say.

'They're in a helluva mess as you can imagine, Boss. Crissi's got her work cut out for her.'

In conversation with Hugo earlier, I'd offered him the assistance of a Family Liaison Officer and he'd agreed straight off. He understands the value a perceptive, sensitive "FLO" can bring, and that's why I'd lined Crissi up. He told us his daughter and son-in-law would probably have refused but he reckoned they'd need someone. I have two kids who are similar ages to their daughter, and I can't begin to imagine what they're going through.

'One question before you start, Steph, do her parents know who Natasha was out with last night?'

'Sadly, no. They haven't met any of her uni pals.'

'Okay, never mind. Andrew's searching for video footage from the bus they caught in Leith. If it's useable, he'll contact the university and hopefully we can identify them. Now, what have you found out that we didn't know already?'

'Natasha's nineteen, five foot three, slender, a little over eight stones. Short hair dyed dark red, and spiky when she pays attention to it. Which isn't all that often; they say she's not hung up on her appearance. Single: last boyfriend was in sixth year. According to her dad, she's not interested at the moment. Her studies come first.'

'And according to her mum?'

'Natasha's year is full of engineering nerds and the older students are too far up themselves.'

I smile. My daughter's made similar comments in the past. In our family, the straight-talking gene runs down the female side. 'Gay?'

'Her mum's asked her that before, but Natasha laughed and said no.'

'What strikes me as odd, is why does she choose to live way down here in Leith instead of nearer the uni? Like Marchmont; student party central, and staggering home distance from all the dives they frequent.'

'Seems her pals are always pulling her leg about that. Natasha tells them Leith's home, she shares a fabulous flat with a professional woman ten years older than her, and not in a crappy let surrounded by a thousand other students. But she has admitted her flat's within easy walking distance of her mum's house, so she can go home to be fed.'

'Makes a lot of sense,' I say. 'Had they ever heard of Marlon Stevenson?'

'No.'

'Any siblings?'

'Nope. Maybe it's come up already, but her parents didn't marry till she was twelve. Her mum didn't change her name so neither did she. Hence Natasha Emerson. The wedding was during the summer holidays, and she didn't want to show up for her first year at secondary school with a new name. "That would have been, like, totally weird."'

'Sounds like your average pre-teen to me,' I say. 'How did they describe her personality? Her character.'

'It seems that not much bothers her. Never gets too excited or too down about stuff. Dad said tough, mum said resolute. Described her as logical, practical, not airy fairy in any way. They reckoned she'd be scared, obviously, but she would be trying her best to keep it hidden from him. They also said that wherever he's holding her, she'll be thinking about escaping. In fact, she'll see it as a challenge.'

'Why so sure?'

'Apparently she went through a phase a couple of years ago, obsessed with escape room games. Even went as far as designing one at school.'

'Might she be a bit naïve about the danger she's in? Nothing can really prepare a person, especially a young woman, for being kidnapped.'

'Ah, well, they both fell to bits at that point, but Crissi did a sterling job picking them back up. The mother said no, Natasha wouldn't be naïve. She'd be realistic. Overall, they thought she'd be positive, optimistic, expecting everything would turn out okay in the end.'

Now I wonder if the parents are the naïve ones because, sadly, kidnappings don't always work out like that. Maybe they were simply trying to put a brave face on. 'What about her health?'

'No issues.'

'Her fitness? Does she take exercise?'

'I asked about that. She runs occasionally, but she's not a fanatic. Not keen on rain and wind. The gym is the same, she has a student membership. They did say a few months ago she was talking about joining the university climbing club, but she packed it in after she got soaked halfway up a cliff. She practices yoga but, a bit like me, for flexibility and stretching, not meditation.'

'Can she swim?'

'Her dad told me she's been able to swim since she was tiny, both he and Hugo took her to the pool. But she never mentions going swimming, so she's probably comfortable in water but not exactly a water baby.' Steph stops there. Says, 'And that's about it.'

'Okay. One more thing. Did they ask about a TV appeal?'

'Yeah. Her mum said they'd do it in a shot. I told them we didn't think it was appropriate in the circs. They didn't push it.'

'Okay, Steph. That's all good. Tell Crissi I know she'll keep in touch but if she needs anything from me, she should holler. And, instead of coming here, can you meet me at old

Mrs Stevenson's house. I think it'll be an … em, interesting visit and I could do with you riding shotgun.'

I'm about to stand up when Tobias waves an arm at me. He rolls his chair back a couple of feet. 'I've spoken to Natasha's mobile provider. Until we get a warrant, they'll provide location data and not much more, although they were willing to confirm she doesn't make or receive many calls. The last one being to her mother on Monday evening at 21:23, the day before she was taken. On Tuesday evening, location data follows her through Leith, mainly along The Shore, but it ceases on Commercial Street when she is on her way home.' He pauses while I express my disappointment, using a selection of colourful vocabulary from my extensive repertoire. He blinks before continuing. 'She doesn't text, which is not surprising. More likely WhatsApp or Instagram.'

That she doesn't make many calls and never texts is, I would say, fairly standard behaviour from a nineteen-year-old, so what Tobias has done is rule out a few lines of enquiry. We know she wasn't in contact with Stevenson either, so that helps. But the electronic investigation door has been nailed shut as far as WhatsApp, Instagram and Facebook are concerned. *Meta* owns all three social media platforms and contacting them would be a waste of time. They're based in the USA and even if we could convince them that Natasha's life is under threat, which it surely is, they may still decline our request for vital information like message logs. We'd certainly become embroiled in international bureaucracy between our Crown Office and their equivalent, and however long that process would take, it would be far in excess of the 45 hours we have remaining. Once we find Natasha's friends we can ask them what platform they used to make their meeting arrangements but likely it will tell us nothing.

I thank Tobias and change tack. 'Andrew. Anything new?'

His face is grim. 'No. She's been fairly static. And still talking a lot. We're becoming more and more convinced she's trying to communicate directly with him.'

There's nothing I can add, so I leave it there and grab my coat. *Right, Mrs Isobel Stevenson. Get the kettle on. I'm heading over to tell you that your son's an evil bastard.*

Chapter 21

1966
Saturday 29th January – 02:00

Paul stopped dead in his tracks, let the crossbar of his bike rest against his hip. The drizzle had let up, but it was still a murky night. Only two lights were in view, both in the middle distance, but the heavy moisture in the air prevented any illumination from spreading.

'What is it?' said Jean.

He pointed towards an oddly shaped patch of grey that was a slightly darker shade than the rest of the world. 'That's the Albert Dock, there's a boat berthed there till Monday. I found Mr De Luca in front of it.'

His aunt patted him on the arm. 'Come on. We need to go and take a look.' But Paul didn't move. Jean gripped his cuff. 'It's nearly over. The worst bit's past.' She tugged gently but insistently at his jacket. 'Now or never, Paul.'

They walked on more slowly towards the dock, stopping a few yards away. Paul kept his hands on the handlebars. He squinted into the gloom then wheeled his bike through ninety degrees and faced in that direction. He turned this way and that, to confirm his position in relation to the dock and the watchman's hut.

'He's not here.' He leaned forward on the handlebars. 'He was lying over there. He must be okay. Oh, God. Thank f—' Paul spoke over his shoulder. 'Sorry, Auntie Jean.'

She smiled. 'It's alright, Paul. Considering the circumstances, I would say "thank fuck" is a fairly appropriate comment.'

Paul gawped at her. None of the women in his family ever swore. He scanned the ground a few feet further on. He took a few steps, let his bike fall on its side and picked something off the ground. He held it up. 'His shoe. He didn't take it with him.' He checked to left and right. 'His coat was here – a Crombie – but now it's gone.'

Jean eased one handle of the holdall off the bike's saddle, dug about inside and pulled out a towel. Then she guddled about further down in the bag and produced a bottle of water. She unscrewed the cap and sloshed some on the material. She used the other end of the towel to take the shoe from her nephew, rubbed it vigorously all over with the wet part, and dropped the shoe on the ground without handling it herself.

Paul stared at her. 'Fingerprints,' she said. 'You've handled the shoe.'

He blinked. 'But the polis don't have my fingerprints. I've never been in trouble.'

Jean appeared amused. 'No. And I don't know much about this sort of stuff because, believe it or not, they don't have my prints either. But I do watch *Dixon of Dock Green* and sometimes the detectives fingerprint witnesses just to rule them out. So let's not take any chances, eh?'

Paul chuckled. She was a case, his Auntie Jean. 'Can we go home now?'

'Well, I can. But not you.'

'But —'

'But nothing.' She dropped the bottle into the bag and stuffed the towel in on top of it. 'Go to your hut, finish off your shift, then straight home. I'll wait with your mum till you get there.'

'But what if the polis turn up, asking questions?'

She shrugged. 'Why should they? Mr De Luca can't have been as badly hurt as you first thought, and he's got up and walked off home. That's why his coat's not here.'

'But what about his shoe? He wouldn't walk away wearing only one shoe, would he?'

Jean stood on her tiptoes and took a tight grip of Paul's lapels, pulling him towards her. 'I don't know, do I? It was dark, he was injured, maybe he looked for it and couldn't find it. So, forget the shoe. The most important thing is if anyone does ask, you saw nothing.' She tugged on his jacket, twice. 'Nothing. Got it?'

Paul nodded. Once again, the tears weren't far away. 'Thanks, Auntie Jean.' He glanced back the way they'd come. 'But will you be okay walking home yourself?'

'Me? Of course I will, silly boy.' She flapped a hand at him. 'Go. I'll see you just after eight. Now remember?'

'Yes. I saw nothing.'

'Good lad.' Jean lifted the bag and walked off into the night.

At the hut, Paul began to relax. He'd relight the brazier, warm up a bit, see out the end of his shift. Then home, a bite to eat, and sleep for Scotland.

But no sooner had his plan settled in his head when the shouting began.

And the nightmare kicked off all over again.

Chapter 22

The Present Day
11:30

'Mrs Stevenson,' I say, wondering if it's acceptable to grab a cancer-ridden eighty-nine-year-old by the throat, and rattle her till her remaining teeth fall out and bounce across the laminated floor. 'Do you not get it? Your son has kidnapped a nineteen-year-old woman and is threatening to murder her in a way I can only describe as vile.'

Marlon's mother lives in Cables Wynd House, a 1960s concrete monstrosity known since day one as the Banana Flats, due to the building having a serious kink halfway along its length. In those days, slum tenements abounded throughout Leith and this building was one that the locals were decanted to. Like many other architectural hen coops, the concept was of social living in a vertical concrete community. I don't know how many years that lasted but in time, the good people moved on, and the local council replaced them with less desirable citizens.

Isobel Stevenson's days are numbered, we both know that, but you wouldn't know it by the fire in her eyes. If looks could kill, as they say. Her daughter had taken us into what was the living room, but now doubles as a medical centre and her mother's bedroom. Then she left us, closing the door with enough of a slam to make it clear that Steph and I are about as welcome as a turd in a tuna sandwich. Isobel glares at us from the depths of half-a-dozen pillows, and in a tone that is chilling and calm in equal measure, says, 'Well, he must have had good reason.'

I don't dignify that with a response. Instead, and I'm probably wasting my time, I try to appeal to her better nature, assuming one is lurking in there somewhere. 'Natasha Emerson is only nineteen. Completely innocent of any wrongdoing in relation to your family. I'm pleading with you, please, help me find out where your son is holding her.'

She stays silent for a few seconds. Studies me with a completely blank expression. She spreads her arms wide. She's wearing an ancient cotton short-sleeved nightie; flaps of loose skin around wasted triceps wave like bedsheets on a washing line. 'I would. But as you can see, I'm kinda busy right now.' She coughs, once, but that kicks off a series of rolling hacks that easily last a minute.

Steph takes a couple of steps to a bedside cabinet, offers Mrs Stevenson a tumbler of water. The old woman hesitates, then accepts it, takes a couple of sips and hands it back. She doesn't say thank you. Steph turns away, catches my eye and mouths the words "old cow".

I don't have time for this crap. 'Mrs Stevenson, this young woman, Natasha, has a mother too. If she dies, two mothers will lose their children because your son will go to prison for the rest of his life. Do you want that? Your only son? Locked up? Forever?'

She swallows, and momentarily I think I might have her. But no. She slings another acidic glare in my direction. 'Marlon told me you'd come out with something like that. Play with my mind. So, I'll tell you, you're right. It would be an awful thing for me to live with. But …' The glare morphs into a smile – a smile with evil dripping off both ends. 'I ain't going to be around for much longer so it's up to him. This is the way he's chosen to finally have my dad's case reopened. He makes his own decisions, and that's fine by me.'

I pull a couple of sheets of A4 from my bag and smooth them out. 'We've been analysing your phone records –'

'What? You've got no bloody right to do that without my permission.'

'The *Investigatory Powers Act* of 2016 states otherwise, Mrs Stevenson. Now, you've received three calls during the past two days from this number.' I point out the highlighted entries on the paper. 'Who were they from?'

She stares at the wall facing her bed. Shrugs. 'Cold calls. I never answer them.'

I read out how long each one lasted, none were less than six minutes. 'Like to try again, Isobel?'

'No.'

This old bat really is a piece of work, but I'm stuck. The calls are from an unregistered mobile, a burner. It would be a shock if they weren't from Marlon, but there's no way of proving it.

I stand up. Steph follows suit and says, 'I'll go and have a word with her daughter.'

Isobel Stevenson pushes herself half upright on pipe cleaner arms. 'You'll do no such thing, you bitch. And anyway, she doesn't know anything.'

As Steph marches out the door she calls over her shoulder. 'She will once I've finished speaking to her.'

'Oi, you!'

'Yes, Mrs Stevenson?' I say.

'Stop her. Right now.'

I pick up my bag. 'I will, if you tell me where Marlon is.'

She folds arms, tight. 'No way.'

I turn away. 'In that case, so long, Mrs Stevenson.' And I am so tempted to sign off with something nasty, but I just can't bring myself to do that.

But when she shouts, 'Fuck off out of my house, you pig bitch,' I wish I hadn't been so nice. So I half turn and blow her a kiss instead. She has an expression like thunder but to paraphrase the tree falling in the forest, nobody saw me, so it didn't happen.

'Are you winding me up?' says Marlon Stevenson's sister, Florence. Steph's told her what her brother has done.

'We're not in the habit of making things up,' says Steph. 'I'm deadly serious and he's put a deadline on us of 48 hours, less than that now obviously, so we desperately need to find out where he might be holding her.'

Florence is late fifties, no wedding ring, a couple of years older than Marlon but she's wearing well for her age. I reckon she spends a fair amount of time in the fresh air. We know there's an older sister, so Steph asks if Marlon could be hiding out at her house.

'Oh, I doubt that. We haven't spoken in years.' She slumps down at the kitchen table, stares at it, in a trance. 'I'm sorry, but I wouldn't have a clue where to look for him.' She gazes up at me, eyes wide. 'Mum?'

'She says she doesn't know but even if she did, she's got absolutely no intention of telling us.'

Florence sighs, as if she suspected as much. 'I'm sorry. I really am. But please believe me, if I knew where he was there's no way I'd keep it to myself.'

Steph sits down opposite Florence, and I position myself at the diagonal. In the main, my role here is to give Florence encouraging looks and adopt a plaintive expression. 'Okay,' says Steph. 'There are two locations we're interested in. Does your brother own a second house?'

'Are you kidding? He's a blacksmith in a dead-end business over at Granton, where would he get the money for another house? He lives in a two-bedroom terraced, and he put himself well in hock for that.'

'Who's his employer?'

'Wallace Fabrication, but I've no idea of the address.'

'We'll find it. Anyone else in the family Marlon might confide in?'

She ponders that for a few moments. 'Nobody springs to mind. We're quite a small family, and I don't have kids. None of us do, in fact. And I don't think he's close with any of our relatives.'

Steph tries again. 'Your sister?'

Her spine straightens at that. 'I told you we don't speak. Ever. And I meant it.'

'May I ask why?' I say.

She turns to me. 'I doubt that the fact my stuck-up bitch of a sister refuses to speak to her family, even although her mother's dying, has anything to do with what my brother's done. So no, you may not ask.'

I open my mouth to try another tack, but she barks, 'It's private.'

Steph opens her iPad. Taps it. Clicks on a JPEG. 'He sent us a video. I can't show it to you, but would you look at this image?' She keeps the screen facing towards her, says, 'Your brother is in the photo, but you'll see he's been blurred out.'

Florence swallows. Nods. Reaches out to take the tablet. 'There's not much to see,' says Steph. 'But do you recognise this room? We're wondering if he's communicating with us from a house belonging to a friend or relative.'

Marlon's sister only glances at it. 'It's a blank wall. What's there to recognise?'

Steph pulls a face. A long shot, but she had to ask.

Florence peers through the door into the hall, stands up and gently nudges the kitchen door to. 'Let me tell you about Marlon and my mother. You know he's the primary carer for her, has been since you lot closed my grandfather's case?'

'Yes, he told us.'

'I bet he did. Okay, prior to her cancer, which was diagnosed about eighteen months ago, health-wise there was nothing wrong with my mother. Mentally, she was in a hell of a state back in the 90s, so Marlon moved in with her; precisely what she was angling for. But, over time, she sorted herself out and he went home. She wasn't happy about that, so she played the grieving woman card so strongly that although he didn't move in, he was round here every other day. It eventually reached the point where, week in, week out, he was spending more time here than at his own house. When we, that is my sister and I, offered to give him some respite, he refused.' She pauses, 'Actually, refused is a bit too strong. He declined, politely but firmly, told us he was "fine". "No worries, sis", and all that crap. Before long he was expert carer-in-chief, no one could look after Mum like he could, so apart from work, his whole life centred around her.'

I wonder if that's why the sister fell out with them. She didn't like how Marlon was monopolising Isobel's affections, and that her mother had no time left for her girls. Or perhaps Florence tried to defend the situation – who knows? When I speak to the older sister, I'll ask.

But Florence is off on one. 'And that suited her right down to the ground. Her wee boy back under her roof, despite the fact she was perfectly fine and quite capable of looking after herself. Don't get me wrong, I love my mother and my brother, but she doesn't have much love left for me once she's lavished it all on him. But what can I do, she's still my mum. You can't choose your family can you?'

She appears confused for a moment before continuing. 'Now, where was I going with that? Oh yes, has Marlon got any friends.' She glances at Steph and me in turn. 'Do I need to say any more?'

Seems not. 'That does leave me with a question, though,' I say. 'Marlon always looks after your mother, but you're here now. So when did he ask you to step in and what reason did he give?'

Her face suggests this is the first time she's considered that in the context of our visit. 'About a month ago he told me he was on the waiting list for an op on his hand. He's had this wonky finger for a while. Like this.' She bends her ring finger till it's a right angle. 'Can't remember the name but I think it's French, named after whoever first diagnosed it, I suppose. Then he rang me last night, said he'd been offered a cancellation. Told me he'd be in overnight as it was a complicated operation, and his hand would be really sore for a few days. The op was scheduled for first thing this morning so could I cover him till Monday, give him the rest of the week to recover. Of course, Mum needs a lot more support now, so I didn't think anything of it. Injured hand and all that.' She looks up. 'He's not been in hospital at all, has he?'

Nobody needs to answer her. 'Do you have contact details for your sister? Oh, and what's her name?'

Florence looks troubled. 'Denise. I'm not supposed to have her number, but I do.' She moves to the worktop, searches through her phone and scribbles on the back of an envelope. Hands it to Steph.

'And do you or your mother have keys to his house?'

'No. Never have. He always comes here.'

As we're leaving, Florence promises that if Isobel gives anything away, she'll contact me immediately.

* * *

An hour later she's on the line. 'It's no use. All Mum will say is she knows nothing about it, or where my brother is.' I hear a catch in her voice. 'It breaks my heart, but I don't believe her. If anything changes I'll be in touch.'

What's that old saying about hell freezing over?

Chapter 23

Wednesday 12:30

Fed up sitting on the table, and frustrated by doing nothing, Natasha concentrated her mind on escape. She'd already scrutinised the room and everything in it, so now she was trying to find possibilities she'd missed. In different circumstances, it would have been a fun mental exercise, but this was deadly serious. Clearly the room was designed to be escape-proof, but she was encouraged by the fact that people had broken free from all sorts of places which fit that description.

She was talking aloud again; it definitely boosted her mood. 'Just like an engineering problem, all I have to do is find the solution.' She dropped into tutorial-speak. 'First, define the problem.' She pondered for a few seconds. 'I need to escape from this room. Simple as that. But, if I can't escape, at least not straight away, then possibly the bigger problem is how to save myself from drowning.' She considered that but refused to add the caveat: *for as long as possible.* 'And to do that, I have to find a way to stop the water flowing in. But how? Worry about that later, Tash. Let's see if I can shift this table first because I'll have to stand on it to reach the inlet. And if I can't move it, that'll change the plan.'

The water was lapping at her shins so although she couldn't avoid getting wet, she preferred to remain dry whenever possible. So, she stayed on the table while she studied it. 'Right, I know it's fixed to the floor, but screws can be undone. So, how far do they go in? Maybe they're too long for the floorboards and they go right through.' She brightened at the thought. 'If they do, and I can loosen them, the water will drain away.' She leaned over and peered underneath the table, was able to make out the screwheads through the water. 'I'll have to move quickly; all I need is something to use as a screwdriver.' She leaned further down; the ripples weren't helping. 'Are they crosshead? They won't be slotted; nobody uses them now.' She lay down on the table, rubbed her fingertip across the screw. 'Yes, crosshead. Without a proper screwdriver it'll be a bit more difficult, but not impossible.'

Natasha had been far from a typical teenage girl. All her life she'd spent lots of time with her grandad, who'd retired the year before she was born. Hugo was always tinkering; usually had a DIY project on the go and he was never done repairing his car. Whenever she visited her grandparents' house, after a quick hug with Grandma, whom she adored, she scooted straight out to the garden, the garage, or the shed -- wherever Hugo was working. For her eighth birthday, he bought her a pair of dungarees and a tartan overshirt and called her his "little workie". He taught her the names of every tool in his extensive collection, and she kicked off her apprenticeship by handing him whatever he asked for. The following Christmas, he refurbished one of his old toolboxes and kitted it out with a selection of brightly coloured, hard plastic screwdrivers, spanners, and assorted tools. One day, after she'd gone home, he was tidying up when he noticed that his rack of screwdrivers contained a pair of blue-handled ones. When he checked Natasha's toolbox, he discovered his two missing drivers stored neatly in their new home. He laughed, took the hint, and gradually replaced her toy tools with decent quality alternatives.

Over time she held things steady for him and helped him move heavier items around although it took her a while to figure out he bore all of the weight. It wasn't long before she graduated to loosening and tightening nuts, bolts and screws, and when she bashed in her first nail and made her first cut with a saw, her world was complete. By the time she was in secondary school, she could put many a husband to shame with what she could achieve with domestic chores and tasks. To the total exclusion of anything from her grandma's domain, it had to be said.

So, when she announced at the age of sixteen she'd be pursuing a career in engineering, no one in her family was in the slightest surprised. Grandad, naturally, was the proudest man in Leith.

Natasha manoeuvred herself carefully to face into the room. 'Apart from the table, the box, and the sports bottle, all that's left is the bucket.' It was still floating in the corner where she'd thrown it during her temper tantrum earlier on. 'Bugger. No choice. I'll have to get wet now.' She splashed over, flipped it upside down, and emptied it.

Back on the table, she snapped open the plastic box, lifted out a white terry facecloth and dried her feet. As she rubbed at her toes she thought, *last thing I want is athlete's foot*. She shook her head at the sheer incongruity of the idea.

She examined the underside of the bucket. It had three castors set into the base, held in place by metal plates secured by rivets. They were set out in a triangle to allow it to be rolled in any direction by the person wielding the mop. 'Are you expecting me to pee in this, or what?' Up until that moment, such a prosaic issue hadn't occurred to her but at that precise second, she felt the need. She willed it to go away. 'I'll have to delay that as long as possible. I'll— Enough, Tash. *Enough*!' She held it up, waved it in front of her, shouted into the air, 'What bloody use is this, you muppet? Wheels on a flooded floor! And where the hell do I empty it?' *Joined-up thinking – or what?*

She rotated the bucket in her hands. It had an arched metal handle with lugs that fitted through holes in the sides. 'This might come in handy as a tool. Or a weapon.' As she twisted the handle to disconnect it from the body of the bucket, she was distracted, wondering, *is he watching me*? Even the possibility made her spin round and check the room, this time for a hidden camera.

After a cursory search, she stopped. *Problem is, I don't have the foggiest notion what a camera looks like. I mean, they're tiny, aren't they? And why would he be watching me, anyway? It's not as if I can go anywhere, is it*? The answer hit her like a skidding truck. *You're a kidnap victim, Tash. He hasn't kidnapped you for the good of his health, he's done it because he wants to trade you for something. But what, money? No, don't be daft, we haven't got any money. But if not that, what else is there? Or has he mistaken me for someone else, some foreign student whose family is loaded*? She made an effort to clear her head, but The Effer wasn't done messing with it yet. *Basically, you're his prisoner and he needs to keep an eye on you. But mainly he's filming you so he can show it to the police. Or the family. To prove you're still alive, otherwise he'll have no leverage.*

Having worked that through, Natasha decided to err on the side of caution and expect she was being watched. As for the bucket handle, she satisfied herself by confirming she could easily and quickly remove it, ready to use.

She examined the castors again. Each one was secured to the underside by four rivets through a chromed metal baseplate, approximately three centimetres by two. There were scratches and scuffs all over the external surfaces of the bucket. Clearly it had been well used, and it was far from new. The plastic seemed rigid; she imagined it would be brittle. She spoke softly. 'What if I smash it, use one of the baseplates to try to loosen the table?' Then, 'Wait a minute. The table. How is it constructed?'

The items laid out on the top meant it was awkward for her to lie flat on her stomach, but she was naturally extremely flexible and yoga classes helped her maintain that. So, she switched to her knees, tucked her feet underneath and stretched her body out over her thighs; a comfortable position she could hold for as long as she needed to. She dropped her head and studied the table's design. Four wooden legs, fixed to right-angled metal brackets, and fastened to the top by heavy bolts with hexagonal heads. She tested all four bolts but there was no play in any of them. She thumped the heel of her hand on one of the joins. Once. 'Damn. That hurt.' She massaged the soft tissue. 'I suppose it was bound to be solid, or the legs would wobble.' She glanced at the bucket. 'One of those baseplates needs to come off.'

She reverted to her lotus position. Wondered yet again if she was being watched and, if so, what difference would it make? *If I start smashing that bucket to pieces, will he come in to stop me? Or will he leave me to it because he knows I can't get out of here? Okay, Tash. What are you going to do?*

Her brain was churning, always returning to the same answer. *I have to keep working at it. If he doesn't show up, I'll keep going, see if I can loosen the table. But if he does, I'll be ready for him.* She remembered how easily he'd overpowered her and heaved her into the van. *But I wasn't expecting that, so no wonder I couldn't fight back. This time I'll be ready for him.* She smiled. *The Effer.*

If he appears, I'll grab the metal handle. But where will I hide it? On me? She looked down. *But where? Inside my shorts. Or is that too obvious?*

All these questions and self-doubts began to swamp her, and she feared that if she did have to face him, she'd freeze. But she concentrated, forced herself to be positive, trust her instincts would take over. But what instincts? How would she use the handle? If push came to shove, could she use it as a weapon? Hurt him? How? Where?

She was reluctant to admit it, but she already knew the answers. She'd attended self-defence demonstrations at uni, put on especially for women who were in the habit of walking home at night whether that was from the library or the pub. The point had been well made. You're not setting out to seriously injure a person but if you're in danger of being assaulted or raped, or if your life is under threat, don't hesitate. Go for the soft areas. Balls. Face. And the place that a hooked piece of metal would do most damage: his eyes.

Her mind was made up. She'd do it. She didn't have a choice.

Once more, she worked out the steps. *Simple, really. If he makes an appearance it won't be as if by magic. He'll make some sort of a sound. I'll know he's coming. I'll grab the bucket, take the handle off, and hide it in my shorts.*

Then I'll face up to him. Ready to attack. Ready to hurt. Ready to escape.

Ready.

Chapter 24

When Steph and I arrive back in the incident room, Jeff introduces us to a pair of DCs he's drafted in from his other teams. We're more than a bit baffled when he says everyone calls them the Thompson Twins, meaning the pair of bumbling detectives from *Tintin*, not their musical counterparts. They were actually an 80s pop band, and there were three of them to boot.

They are alike, these two, down to their crumpled white shirts and narrow black ties. When I ask, they explain that an old boss had christened them the Thompson Twins and it had stuck. They say it doesn't bother them at all, in fact we should just call them Tom 1 and Tom 2. Although I imagine it might take me a while to figure out which one's which. Seems they should have been on their days off but they're enormously enthusiastic and have readily agreed to help. In fact they've already completed their first task; they've come back from the archive store with a pile of case notes and evidence relating to the De Luca murder. In a corner of the room are enough boxes to fill a Transit van. Police Scotland is working through a programme of digitisation but hasn't yet reached as far back as 1980.

Jeff had told them to stack the boxes high and take photos. He plans to show them to Stevenson to demonstrate the futility of trying to analyse the case notes in any detail apart from the summaries. Even cross-checking the boxes' contents against the inventory within his timescale will be a huge ask.

I listen as Jeff lays out what he needs them to do, then I leave them to it. With a task like this it's easy to be distracted by something juicy, but they're under strict instructions: find summaries, skim them to get the gist, log them, flag up anything vital to Andrew and move swiftly on.

This will be an enormous task and given the ridiculous deadline we've been set, I'm far from certain they have any chance of unearthing information we'll need to convince Stevenson to release Natasha in time.

* * *

I was heading for my desk, but I take a sharp right to join Andrew and Ella. I sit facing the backs of their monitors so I can't see what's on that damned feed. 'Sorry you're landed with this, can't be the most pleasant of tasks.'

'No, Boss,' says Ella. 'It's not. But it's a damn sight worse for that poor girl.'

That's typical of Ella, and one of the main reasons I asked for her. I settle myself in. 'What's the score, Andrew?'

He doesn't beat about the bush, simply states the fact. '44 hours remaining.' He doesn't wait to let that sink in, he moves on. 'She's a remarkable young woman.' Ella is nodding along enthusiastically. 'Since you went out she's been doing a fair amount of thinking, but she's been on the move quite a bit too. She's been examining the table. We think she's trying to dislodge it, although it does appear to be solid. She had a good look at the bucket too, took the handle off it. We were wondering if she was thinking about using it as a tool.'

'I'd be working out how I could hurt the bastard with it,' says Ella.

I'm about to ask how deep the water is, but I don't. It won't help. 'Talk to me about the films.'

There are two monitors on their desk. Andrew aims a pen at the one to his left. 'I'm recording the live feed so, if we need to, we can go back to it later.'

'How long has it been running?'

He runs a finger down his notes. 'Just over three hours.'

'Anything important I need to see?' He folds his arms, tilts his head. I hold my hands up. 'I know, I know.'

Andrew winces, adjusts his position. 'A linguistics bod from forensic services has been in touch to say they've viewed both films in conjunction with a body language specialist. They've made it clear this is only a preliminary report because of the urgency. They'll examine them more closely and get back to us if necessary. Unsurprisingly the stressors in Stevenson's voice spiked in the early stages of both the recorded video and when he was speaking to you live. There were several obvious indicators. For example, licking his lips, voice cracking, tone fluctuating, taking more frequent sips from his bottle. The tremors when he lifted his hand were noticeable. All that sort of stuff. They thought he was clever to give us very few opportunities to assess the veracity of his statements, and possibly his state of mind.'

'The sunglasses?'

'Yeah. Plus keeping his hands out of sight and maintaining a similar posture throughout. They all meant it was virtually impossible to interpret gestures and eye movements or differentiate between true or genuine statements versus untrue or disingenuous ones. They did note specific changes to his general expression, like his forehead and around his mouth, which may have determined truth versus untruth. But these were only indications, nothing more solid.'

I need to hear all this but actually, it tells me nothing. It's all moot because Stevenson's freely admitted to what he's done; that he has abducted Natasha, and why. All we can do is possibly gauge whether he intends to carry out his ultimate threat. It might be easier to measure that once we have a second film from this afternoon's call to compare with. And that's assuming he's live and not recorded.

'The recorded element,' I say. 'Filmed in one take, or edited?'

'Definitely edited. The techs said it was obvious where it had been spliced. They reckoned he couldn't have done a worse job if he'd spliced it with an axe. And a blunt one at that.'

'Any location data attributed to the file? You know, like we can get from a photo?'

'That would have been too much to hope for, Boss,' says Ella.

'True,' I say. 'What about his surroundings, any clues there?'

This time Ella leans forward and angles her monitor so I can see. She pulls up a window displaying a still showing Stevenson and the wall behind him, the same one we showed his sister, Florence. 'It's blank, as you can see. Matte emulsion is our best guess, off-white or a pale shade. At first, the fact that's there's nothing on the wall struck me as strange but then I realised he'd have removed anything that might give away his location. I mean, even if that was my wall I couldn't identify it. But you can make out a few blemishes – here, and here for example – that suggest dust marks left by pictures. And these two wee holes close together, probably a double picture hook.'

Andrew comes in. 'We'd be surprised if he filmed himself in his own house because he practically challenged us to go there. And we can't imagine it belongs to anyone he knows unless the person is on holiday, or away on business.'

My two colleagues wait while I take some time. 'We could be on a wild goose chase. That room could be in an Airbnb, a dingy hotel, anywhere. Is it worth the effort to track it down?' I drum my fingers on the desk. *Make a decision, Mel.* 'Right. This is really getting on my wick, but we have less than two days, and I can't justify the time to trace his movements, especially as we've got bugger all to go on. I'd rather find out where he is now and, much more importantly, where he's holding Natasha. And for your info, no way his mother's giving him up. But his sister, Florence? She might.' I point at the screen. 'What else is there, Ella?'

She hits fast-forward and the film stops automatically where they've set a marker. 'The only visible part of the chair is the left-hand side of the high back, which suggests it's a dining chair or an occasional chair. And the only other object in the room is the bottle he's drinking from but it's generic, could have been bought in any retail outlet. Nothing visible that gives the location away.'

'Background noises?'

'The sound techs have taken a first pass at it and nothing obvious jumped out,' says Andrew. 'But they'll examine it again in finer detail. They've promised a report within the hour.'

I glance at my watch. *An hour? Jeez, that's like, forever.*

Chapter 25

Wednesday 13:30

Natasha stepped down into the water, searching out the floor with her toes. She lifted the bucket; her plan was to remove a baseplate and use it as a tool. So, she held it by the rim, adjusted her grip, and began smashing it against the wall. At the same time, she was primed to move if there was any sign of The Effer entering the room.

She wasn't prepared for the racket she was making but after fewer than half a dozen smashes, she was wheezing like an asthmatic donkey and was forced to rest. Despite the noise and activity, there was no sign of him. 'Does this mean he isn't watching me at all? Or is he sitting somewhere, having a bloody good laugh at my expense.' That pissed her off and drove her on.

After a few more hits a jagged crack appeared on the underside, running between two of the baseplates. On the next smash a rivet popped out and flew into the water. The wheel on that baseplate came loose and she hauled it off, making the crack significantly wider and longer. She dropped the bucket on the table and tried to pull the plastic apart, but the edge nicked her hand. She sucked at the blood; it welled up but didn't drip. She picked up two of the facecloths, wrapped them round her hands and instantly felt more confident. She grabbed the bucket, pulled one way, pushed the other. She was right about the plastic being brittle, it split across the base from one side to the other.

The loose baseplate was still held on by the remaining three rivets. She turned the bucket, looked inside, and discovered the bottom was still intact. There were two skins of plastic to accommodate the castors and give the rivets a stronger fixing. She felt like flinging the bucket at the wall again but regained her composure.

She focussed her attention back onto the baseplate and discovered some play at one end. On closer inspection, the rivet at that corner was sheared almost through. She worked away at it till it eventually snapped. It only took her a few minutes more to break out the other two and lift out the baseplate.

'Now, loosen the screws.' She scrunched up her face. 'I'll have to kneel on the floor.' She touched the front of the hoodie. 'And these clothes are going to get wet.'

She looked down at the water. It was obvious she'd have to lean right down but she wanted to avoid the hoodie becoming soaked, so she rolled up the sleeves until they were high on her biceps then tightened the drawcord at the waist and folded it over until it formed a wide band just below her breasts.

But she didn't want the tennis shorts getting wet either. She thought for a second then didn't hesitate in case she chickened out. She put one hand on the wall to steady herself, climbed to her feet, hooked her thumbs into the waistband and yanked them down. She stepped out of them and dropped them into the box. She wasn't particularly happy about being in her underwear but had reconciled herself to the idea that in the stay-alive-versus-preserve-modesty game, survival had to win hands down. And wearing cold wet clothes wouldn't help with that. *Tough shit if he is an old perv*, was another thought she kept to herself.

As time passed, frustration began to overwhelm her. Trying to loosen the screws holding the table legs to the floor by using the baseplate as a stand-in screwdriver had been a total failure. A combination of wet hands, peering through moving water, and the corners of the baseplate being slightly bevelled meant she couldn't get decent purchase and it kept slipping off the screwheads. After she'd banged her hand several times and made zero progress she gave up. She glared at the piece of metal as if it was at fault and flung it in the box. She rested back on her heels to reconsider and to force herself to calm down. Sitting in the water had been an unpleasant sensation at first but she'd become used to it.

'Oh, wait a minute. What the hell am I thinking about? Why did I go straight for the floor screws?' It had dawned on her that the two screws holding the brackets to the foot of each leg were fixed into soft wood so might come out easier. But no. Her temper flaring, she grabbed each of the legs in case rocking them might do the trick. The front left one did move slightly so she attacked it with renewed vigour, but the movement didn't increase.

She turned her attention back to the screws holding the table to the floor. If I can free them, will the water drain away through the holes in the floor? Because even if the volume that goes out is less than what comes in, that'll give me longer.' She couldn't prevent the words "stay of execution" entering her head but no way was she going to say them out loud.

Having expended significant amounts of emotional and physical energy, she began to feel light-headed and realised she hadn't eaten or taken on fluids since she'd been imprisoned. For the umpteenth time, she pulled herself onto the table. She faced into the wall and used cloths to dry the lower half of her body before dressing. Apart from a few splashes on the hoodie she'd managed to stay dry but had made zero progress. She tried to drink straight from the sports bottle but misjudged it, sending more water onto the floor. 'Jeez! Ironic, or what?'

She took more care the second time and managed a long drink. She demolished a ginger and dark chocolate cereal bar, which made her feel a bit better so followed that up with a few nuts. *Salted*. Not her preference, so she put them back and clicked the lid tight.

Sitting there, she drew her knees up to her chin and hugged her shins. Her initial burst of enthusiasm and confidence had evaporated, and she felt worse than she did before. Much worse. Images and sounds flashed into her head. Walking along the beach with her dad. Her mum snuggled in close on the sofa while they watched a trashy film. Her grandad helping her to drill her first hole in a plank of wood. This time, even her mantra didn't come to her rescue.

Minutes later, she was still sobbing when she heard a mechanical sound behind her, but her reactions were non-existent and by the time she remembered about the bucket handle and how she planned to use it as a weapon, it was too late.

Far too late.

Chapter 26

'That's the report in from the sound technicians on the Stevenson video,' says Andrew. 'Bottom line is there's nothing in the background to determine where he was talking from. They're fairly certain he's in a residential area. And they're sorry, they know that's inconclusive.'

"Bottom line". My team all know to hit me with the punchline early and I'll ask questions if necessary. As we're still in the early stages, I do ask for more.

Andrew reads from an email. 'No TV, radio or music. Mild traffic noise, no sirens or car alarms, nothing to suggest buses or heavy vehicles, one instance of a vehicle door slamming. No examples of children playing, but the live video was during the school day. Dogs barking, twice, possibly three times. No sounds of property maintenance like electrical tools or building works. One instance of a hedge trimmer. So, excellent chance it's a building in a residential area.'

I nod my thanks and watch as he amends the actions list on the whiteboard. Then he moves on to explain that Lothian Buses have supplied footage from the number 16 that

Natasha's friends boarded. Although some students can be distinctive in the way they dress -- it goes with the territory -- these two were relatively conservative. But Andrew provided enough of a description for the university admin team to identify them. He called them both, and once they'd recovered from the shock, they confirmed they'd made all their arrangements through WhatsApp, and sent him the content. As expected, a pile of nonsensical chat spread over dozens of messages that told us nothing new. Pressed further, they both said they hadn't noticed anything or anyone suspicious either last night or during their previous evenings down at The Shore.

'That's unfortunate,' I say. 'But not exactly a surprise.' If my daughter, Lily, was deep "in convo" with her pals, the Band of the Royal Scots Dragoon Guards could march through the pub, and she'd be oblivious. I take a breath to disguise my disappointment before moving on. 'Tobias. Social media?'

'I can find no references to Marlon Stevenson on Facebook, Twitter or Instagram,' he says. 'But that means nothing as he could easily be using an alias. I asked Crissi to question Natasha's parents about her social media usage, and I've cross-checked with her university friends. Everyone agrees she's not a heavy user, and doesn't share much, usually only amusing posts. They all say she is intensely critical of people who reply to posts that are obviously phishing and data trawling. Apparently that drives her bananas.' He glances up, as if to confirm his use of the word "bananas" was correct in that context.

None of us react, so he carries on. 'I've searched Natasha's accounts to try to establish if she's being followed by anyone that could be Stevenson but again, many people use aliases and avatars, so it is entirely possible he has been watching her from a disguised profile.'

We come to the quick conclusion that social media is a non-starter so Andrew ticks it off.

I ask about the university climbing club. Andrew says, 'Crissi made that call. Natasha attended club sessions at the indoor wall a few times, went on a couple of trips but didn't keep it up.'

I ask, 'Anything crop up on Stevenson's email or phone?'

'Nothing so far,' says Tobias. 'But we'll keep searching.'

'Bank account?'

'Also nothing.'

'Okay. Tell me if you find anything but I'll assume not – unless I hear otherwise.'

It's Steph's turn. 'I spoke to his employer, Wallace Fabrication. A small company. Apart from the owner, Stevenson is the only employee. Worked there since he was a young man, over thirty years. Mr Wallace says there have been no changes in his behaviour recently. Apparently he's quiet, industrious, gets on with his job. Never causes any bother. He asked for time off a couple of weeks ago, short notice but he mentioned tying it in with a pal's holidays. Stevenson only confirmed on Friday that he wanted this week off, but it wasn't an issue as they rarely have tight deadlines, their customers are usually flexible. So his boss didn't give it any thought and was expecting him back at work on Monday.' Steph makes big eyes. 'Well, that's not happening, is it?'

'Andrew. Criminal record?'

'No.'

'Is he registered anywhere as a tenant? Or as a recent property purchaser?'

'No to both. So wherever he's holding her, he's borrowed it. Because he can't have broken in and created a sealed unit in someone's premises, can he?'

'Only if they've gone to New Zealand for six months.'

At that point I need to know so I ask the dreaded question.

It's Ella who answers. '43 hours remaining.'

Chapter 27

It's approaching two in the afternoon. We're all gathered round, ready for Jeff to give us the latest update when I hold my hand up. 'Andrew. Before we start, anything happening with Natasha.'

It's no exaggeration to say we're shocked when he says, 'She smashed up the bucket. Battered it off the wall.'

'Temper?'

'Don't think so. She was purposeful, deliberate. At first we couldn't figure out why, but it appears she managed to break out a baseplate. She hurt her hand, but nothing serious by the look of it.'

'A baseplate? What the hell for?'

'We can't be certain because she's working underwater but it could be she's trying to free the table leg.'

'But surely it's bolted in tight?'

No one points out I'd made a statement of the bleeding obvious. I don't dwell on it, just say to Jeff, 'The floor's yours, Boss.'

Jeff opens an A4 notepad. 'Right, everyone, listen up. I'm going to start with what we know already that can be corroborated from the summary documents written back in '66.'

He leans forward on the table and taps his pen on a sheaf of papers. 'Before I do, I want to emphasise I understand how difficult a case this is.' He eyeballs each of us, one at a time. His gaze is benign. 'If any of you feel like you're beginning to struggle, talk to me. Easy for me to say but try not to let it get to you.' We give him nods and murmurs in return and I know the team appreciate the sentiment. Jeff doesn't throw stuff out like that without meaning it.

'Andrew,' he says. 'While I'm going through all this can you act as scribe?' My colleague nods and taps on his iPad.

Jeff holds up a sheaf of papers. 'These documents reflect what Hugo told me during our interview this morning. The pathologist, long deceased of course, reported Sandro De Luca had a small amount of seawater in his lungs, so formally he drowned. Meaning his grandson's MO for Natasha Emerson's appalling predicament makes some sense, horrific though it is. De Luca also had injuries consistent with him falling in between the quayside and the hull of a boat, and the abrasions on his hands and arms suggested he managed to pull himself out of the dock by an anchor chain.'

He looks up. 'Although quite how he managed that, at his age and with his injuries, I have no idea. Anyway, the pathologist discovered oval bruises on his chest, abdomen, and the front parts of his shoulders. He concluded that the bruises were caused by a hardwood implement, and the oval shape suggested an axe handle. But he didn't ever confirm that.'

'So he was pushed in backwards, Boss' I say. 'Any other marks on him that might identify how he died?'

Jeff shakes his head. 'The PM stated that was inconclusive. The picture was confused by injuries caused by the fall, hitting both the dock wall and the boat, plus his attempts to climb out. The occasional bash about the head or body was considered to be incidental.'

'Was the boat manned?' says Andrew.

'No. It was due to stay there till a dry dock became available. No one aboard.'

'Anyone important still alive?' I say.

'The watchie who raised the alarm died during the investigation. To still be around today people couldn't have been much older than twenties or possibly thirties at the time. Hugo Emerson was eighteen, now he's seventy-five, so that gives you an idea.' He turns to the Thompson Twins. 'Task for you lads is to find out who was part of the investigation and track down any who are still alive.'

'And preferably with all their marbles intact,' I say.

Jeff closes his eyes at that one before continuing. 'Hugo's already mentioned one person we definitely want to speak to. Her name's Theresa. Don't know her surname, but she was a young PC who went with Hugo to the De Luca house to inform the family the case was formally closed. She'll only be mid-sixties now.'

Ella jots a note. 'I'll take that one.'

'What about men from the pub?' says Steph. 'I've said men because it doesn't sound like the sort of place women would have frequented.'

Jeff smiles and points at the pile of boxes. 'We don't have that info to hand, but it could be in there.' He addresses the Thompson Twins again. 'Lads, can you work with Andrew on that.' They both nod and smile enthusiastically. They don't say much, but I don't think I've ever met a happier pair of police officers. They don't half cheer me up.

Jeff slaps his notebook closed. 'And that's all I have. Anything else we need to know?'

Tobias says to me. 'Boss, while you were out I walked along Commercial Street. I found a mess of recycling scattered around the bins at a wide part of the pavement. It might be nothing, but I arranged for the area to be taped off. I contacted Greg Brodie and he's gone along to examine the area as a potential crime scene. I'm not all that hopeful as people will have been walking along there all day. But we're canvassing nearby too, just in case.'

Not all that hopeful. Hopeless, more like. Perhaps I'll keep that to myself.

Jeff checks his wrist. 'Less than an hour till the six hours is up. Andrew, got that so-called cold case form for me?'

'Scanned and in the system. I'll send you a link.'

'Thanks.' He glances over at the pile of evidence boxes and paperwork scattered about all over the place. The impression is there's tons of it. 'We've got photos of all that for Stevenson, plus redacted scans of the case note summaries. Unless we video Mel running about like a blue-arsed fly, that'll have to do him. I dare say we'll find out soon enough what hoops he wants us to jump through next.'

Jeff's distracted by Ella knocking seven bells out of her keyboard. She hammers the spacebar several times, jiggles her mouse and rattles a few more keys. She glares at her screen. 'What's wrong, Ella?' says Jeff.

She's still concentrating on her monitor but there's no light reflecting onto her face. 'The live feed's gone down.'

'Shit,' I say. 'I was about to ask how Natasha was doing. Could it just be a glitch?'

'I can't tell. I'm constantly refreshing, tried a few things, but all I have is a blank screen.'

Andrew rolls his chair over and sits beside her. He watches what she's doing but doesn't interfere. Ella performs a few more actions then shrugs and pushes her mouse away. It's telling that Andrew still doesn't take over. He turns to me. 'I'll ring Bob. Ask her to check it out.'

I say to Jeff, 'We're going to have to ask the bugger if this is down to him, aren't we?'

I glance up at the wall. The feed might have stopped but the clock hasn't.

42 hours remaining.

Chapter 28

Wednesday 15:35

Absentmindedly, Natasha rubbed at the dark stain on the waistband of her hoodie. Totally confused, she didn't know what to think, how to react, what to do next. *Is it worth waiting to see if what just happened will have a bearing on how all this will end up? Or should I ignore it and carry on with what I was doing?*

Sitting on the table, trying to work things out, she became mesmerised by the water falling from the inlet. Two different battles were raging inside her head: the crucial one being the possibility of her drowning. But as soon as any notion of succumbing to the inevitable entered her orbit, she hounded it till it disappeared without leaving so much as a vapour trail.

She considered the other aspect to be eminently solvable and that was to stop the water flowing in, so it didn't ever rise to a level where she could no longer survive. She did allow this one mental houseroom. She wasn't stupid, she was as far away from the solution as she'd been since it became the centre of her world. But she refused to accept that a solution didn't exist. *Blind faith, maybe, but at least I've got some.*

Measuring the depth of the water accurately was impossible. All she could do was gauge it against her own body or the tabletop. And it was the latter that was in sharp focus because the water was lapping against the underside. The legs had been cut down, so the water still wasn't particularly deep; just below her knee or, by her reckoning, 35 to 40 centimetres. By the same measure, the room was something like fifteen per cent full. A long way from critical, but still.

So, despite her fascination with the water, she forced herself to refocus on the table. If she couldn't move it away from the wall, the inlet might as well be on Mars as far as reaching it was concerned.

She smiled again but this one had a hint of malice attached. 'Like it or not, table, you're helping me get out of here.' She stepped down into the water. And this time she didn't give a toss about getting wet.

* * *

Most of the time she'd been imprisoned Natasha had either been sitting on the table or standing, facing it side on. She wondered if a different perspective might help so she moved round to the left and off at an angle. The inlet was behind her.

'Your mission, should you choose to accept it, is to free this bloody table.' She gazed at the legs, mulling over the problem. 'The floor covering is some sort of heavy vinyl, like in the toilets at uni. So, the screws go through it, then into the subfloor. Ah. Wait a minute. I wonder how thick the vinyl is.' She made a gap between her thumb and forefinger. Moved them together and apart, trying to judge what might be realistic. 'Maybe five mils?' She worked an idea through in her head. *If I can get rid of the flooring between the bottom of the leg and the subfloor, that should leave a 5-mil gap. And that might make the leg unstable.*

Thinking about the subfloor, for the first time she considered what might be beyond her little world. Accepted, she was in a space lined with vinyl, but he'd dropped her in from above. A basement? No, he'd escorted her up a flight of steps. *So, a garage, then. Or an outbuilding.* She recalled how, after he pulled her from the van, he'd walked her across a level surface. She was sure that had been concrete. *Does that mean the subfloor is concrete too? Or am I in an internal space, with wooden floorboards?*

She felt the tension rising again. She was turning herself inside out and getting nowhere. 'This is pointless, Tash. Move on.'

She placed one hand on the edge of the table to support herself while she studied the leg more closely. 'I'll have to cut the vinyl away, but with what? The only metal things in here are the baseplate and the handle. And the baseplate's rounded, so it's no use.' She picked up the bucket, unhooked the handle and examined the ends. 'Bugger. They're smooth too.' She hefted it in her hand. 'But it might be sharp if I broke it.' She had a go at bending the metal, but it laughed at her. 'What can I lever it against?' The table was the only option, so she checked between it and the wall. There was a tiny gap that looked wide enough to accept the handle. She jammed it into the space and tried to bend it towards her but only succeeded in shearing off a shard of the table's laminated surface. Attached to it was a jagged splinter of composite wood, clearly a cheap piece of furniture.

She switched her attention to a stronger part of the table; at a corner, behind one of the legs. She slid the handle down the side of the leg and, by trial and error, discovered the sweet spot where it was held securely, but not so tight there was no chance of it bending.

She levered it in all different directions, changing the angle continually as she fought to weaken the metal. As she persevered, the tender parts of her hand began to throb. She grabbed a facecloth, but the handle slid about inside it, so she soaked it. That gave her a far more secure grip. Using both hands, she worked it furiously back and forth. She had to stop every few seconds, but eventually the metal gave. The handle bent. Only slightly, but all the same, she felt like cheering.

Invigorated, she attacked the metal which was beginning to make a groove in the wood. She was on the point of switching to the back leg at the other end of the table when the handle ran up the white flag and bent in half. She grabbed it in both hands and flexed it until eventually it snapped.

Now she was grinning. She touched the broken ends. They were sharp. 'Well, if The Effer is watching, I expect he'll come in and take these from me. But now I'm armed, and I'm in no mood for any crap.'

The burst of activity made her realise yet again how hungry she was. So, she climbed onto the table, dried herself off then drank some water and crammed a handful of nuts into her mouth. She knew she needed the protein and the salt. She polished off a cereal bar and a pack of dried fruit, washing the whole lot down with more water. 'Right, no time to waste, let's get shifting. Vinyl, you're next.'

Chapter 29

'So you reckon you've made progress,' says Marlon Stevenson. 'Reopened my grandfather's case and dragged a pile of boxes out of your archives. But in reality, those things mean nothing. I want you to tell me what you're going to do next. Apart from hassling my family, that is.'

I wonder who told him. His mother? His sister? Which one? My bet's on the mother, no way on earth has the blue-eyed boy disappeared from sight and Isobel doesn't know where he is.

'I told you you'd be wasting your time,' he says. 'I don't know what you hoped to achieve but you're drawing resources away from what you should be doing.'

We're in the incident room but only Jeff and I are visible to Marlon. The rest of the team are scattered around, hunched over their monitors. Andrew is on an open call to the body language expert from Forensic Services. We've sent him the link. He'll give us live input and Andrew will message me with anything vital. Plus, we've patched in the sound technicians. But Stevenson isn't stupid, he'll have figured out what we'd be up to.

My boss doesn't respond to Marlon's sniping. We'd agreed this earlier. Jeff won't be making excuses. Snivelling is way down his list of preferred behaviours. He'll be patient, try to draw Stevenson out. But we agreed I'd keep silent; we need him to believe Jeff is front and centre on this, massage the man's ego.

Stevenson's in the same room as earlier, being filmed from the same angle, and in the same chair. I'm pleased he's not moving about from place to place, might make it easier to trace him. But he's still wearing the sunglasses, still sitting on his hands.

Jeff speaks without preamble. 'Mr Stevenson, the live feed you sent me has dropped out.'

'Has it?' The tone is flat.

'It has. Was that deliberate?'

All he does is shrug.

So it was *deliberate; I wonder what he's hiding from us.*

'Progress, DCI Hunter,' he says. 'That's what we're here to talk about. Everything else is irrelevant.'

Jeff draws himself up as if he's going to sigh. But he stops himself. 'I'm stating facts here, Mr Stevenson. As you can see, the evidence on Mr De Luca's case is extensive to say the least. I emailed photos to you, to illustrate precisely what we're dealing with. As you will be perfectly well aware, in the 70s and 80s everything was manually compiled so we don't have any shortcuts at our disposal.'

'My heart bleeds. Pull in more resources. You've got the clout.'

'Resources are, regrettably, finite. But I have made several high priority requests, and I'm waiting for answers. I'll know one way or the other by our next call. Which is why I must make it clear that, professionally, I would be in dereliction of my duty if I didn't ask if there is some other way we can resolve this situation.'

Jeff's deliberately avoided mentioning that Stevenson stated he wouldn't negotiate. If he brings it up, that's up to him. But if Jeff decides to mention it, he'll need to pick his time carefully. Statements or answers from Jeff will be as direct as possible. He'll be concise. He won't make long-winded speeches or attempt to browbeat Stevenson into submission. He'll ask questions, make suggestions, hopefully our kidnapper will bite. We still have time on our side. Natasha's life is not in imminent danger although we are incredibly aware of the potential damage to her mental health and wellbeing. We continue to hope she remains strong.

'No,' says Marlon. 'There isn't another way. No other choices. Find out who killed my grandfather, and why.' He looks as though he might be about to smirk in some sort of triumph, but Jeff stops him dead.

'In that case, Mr Stevenson, I'll sign off. We have fewer than 41 hours remaining, and we have too much to do to spend time on this call.'

'You what?' Stevenson half rises out of his chair, bends forward to stay on camera. 'No way you're ending the call. I decide that, not you.' He presses his fingertips into his upper abdomen for a second or two then sits down. Our Marlon is becoming a trifle agitated; time will tell if that's a good thing.

Jeff doesn't respond. That was simply a wee cage-rattler. But he follows it up with, 'Of course, Mr Stevenson. Was there something else you wanted to say?' His tone is flat too, mimicking Marlon from earlier. Not a hint of smarm or condescension. Keeping the man onside, but only just.

Our kidnapper has been caught on the hop, and it takes him a few seconds to regain his equilibrium. 'I don't want to *say* anything. I have questions, and I want answers.'

After the briefest of pauses, Jeff says, 'Go ahead.' Which I'm sure was his intention all along. Nice one.

'How many people are working on the case?'

'I don't know, offhand. As many as I could grab from competing investigations.'

'Answer, damn you. How many?'

Jeff knows he's treading a fine line here. He does want to keep Marlon on edge, but we don't want him so annoyed that he increases the water flow. Jeff makes a play of ticking off fingers. 'A dozen, at least. With other specialist teams standing by if I need them.'

Marlon leans forward as if he's going to develop that but changes tack. 'Are you going to stop bothering my family?'

'We have no intention of speaking to your mother or your sister again.'

'I have two sisters.'

'So I understand, but as you're not in touch with Denise, we don't see any need to contact her.'

Above the sunglasses, Stevenson's brow furrows but he lets that go. Is that because we don't actually need to talk to the woman, or is he secretly pleased we're not going to?

'Who have you managed to trace?' he says.

Jeff opens his notebook and flicks through the pages as if he's searching for something. Fortunately, Marlon doesn't know they're blank. Jeff runs his forefinger down to the middle of a page then glances up at the camera. 'You will understand that most parties from that time are deceased. And sadly, a few are no longer in good health. So, the answer to your question is none.' He sends a level stare in the camera's direction. 'Thus far.' He checks his watch. 'But we are only a little more than six hours in.'

The silence between the two of them reminds me of that old childhood game, "Who Blinks First?"

Turns out it's Marlon. 'One final question, and I want the answer to this by your next deadline, six hours away at 21:35. Have you found out why your predecessors closed the case down in the first place? Because that's what I need to know. And if you don't have the answer by then, I will increase the flow rate.' He leans forward to stare at the camera. 'And it will stay like that until you do have the answer. You have six hours, not a minute more. Then every hour that Natasha has left before she drowns, becomes half an hour.'

He stretches an arm out and the screen turns black.

'Shit!'

My boss doesn't often swear but when he does, you know it's justified. He swivels his chair. 'Andrew. Body language tell us anything?'

'Only two comments. One, when you said Stevenson wasn't in touch with Denise, his brow furrowed. He might have been surprised you knew about her, or he might be worried we'll talk to her. Impossible to tell.'

'And the other?'

'When you told him you were ending the call he rose out of his chair, his voice increased in volume, and his tone became harsher. At the same time, he displayed signs of discomfort when he pressed his fingers into his abdomen for a second or two before sitting down again. That could have been nervous tension, plain old indigestion, or something more significant. The suggestion is we talk to his GP, but we're still waiting for the warrant.'

Andrew reads from his screen. "But predominantly, our man is following the same strategy as earlier. Hands out of sight, eyes concealed, facing directly into the camera. Sitting straight, staying upright". He looks up. 'Not a lot to go on, is it?'

'Perhaps not,' I say. 'But if Stevenson is becoming agitated he might make a mistake.'

'Bank error in our favour?' says Jeff. 'We can only hope.'

Chapter 30

Wednesday 16:00

Now Natasha faced a more serious problem because the water was touching her knees. She would have to crouch down to gouge her way through the vinyl with the broken handle, so she had zero chance of keeping her top layer dry. However, she'd broken this barrier before and was far more intent on protecting her life rather than her modesty. She stripped down to her underwear, jammed her clothes in the box and knelt in the water.

Then an idea hit her, smack between the eyes. 'Tash. Are you stupid, or what? Use the handle to gouge holes in the wall so the water can drain out.' She couldn't believe that had never occurred to her. Immediately she targeted an area of wall at the waterline. The sharp end cut straight through the vinyl but came up short against a solid layer. She tried her hardest but couldn't put a dent in it. She moved to her left. Same result. Then she moved to the opposite wall. No matter what she did, the layer beneath the vinyl defied her efforts.

She thought about trying again but realised all she'd managed to do was waste precious time and annoy herself. She was back to her original plan; get those screws out.

Down on the floor again, hacking at the vinyl was creating waves and she was struggling to see what she was doing. The handle was slippery and even holding it through a facecloth her hand was beginning to bruise. Nevertheless, she soldiered on. 'When I get out of here, if all I've got to worry about is a sore hand, that'll be a result.'

She battled away until she'd scored a groove all the way round the bottom of the leg, on the outside of the bracket. The floor below the vinyl felt solid, impenetrable. 'But the screws went into it so surely the surface can't be that hard, unless the holes were drilled.'

She carried on. But working at arm's length was exhausting, and if she stopped for a break, the water would only get deeper. Even if she could free that leg, the task for the other three would be harder than ever. 'Keep going, Tash. Keep going.'

To give her hand a break, every few minutes she stood up and tested the table leg for movement. Threw her full body weight against it. Nothing.

Now she'd cut a channel about an inch wide in a rough oval round the bracket. She was gouging and ripping at the vinyl as best she could when suddenly, she yelped and stared at her index fingernail. It had split, vertically, and was bleeding. She stuck it in her mouth, which took her straight back to her childhood. This time she couldn't run to her mother for comfort. And that brought waves of emotion that engulfed her.

She wept. Floods. Huge great gulping sobs followed by a ridiculous temper tantrum. She hauled herself upright, grabbed the edge of the table, and heaved it around. Up. Left. Towards her. Every direction possible. Away from the wall, and up from the floor.

She felt, rather than heard the snap. The left front leg had sprung from its bracket.

Broken nail forgotten, she grabbed the leg with both hands and hauled at it. It wobbled. Not much, but it definitely wobbled.

'You little beauty!'

Then she broke down.

Chapter 31

Once he'd ended the call, Marlon moved to the bedroom window and peered down through the Venetian blinds into the back gardens. Only one was remotely tidy. The others were choked with weeds and rubbish, including the space directly below the window. Definitely not a part of town he'd choose to live in.

Standing there, hands in pockets, he wondered who else had been in the background during the call, watching and listening. *A shrink? Or an expert checking out my body language? Maybe they've brought in a hostage negotiator, although I expect Hunter's got some experience in that line.*

Hunter. Give him his due, he's impressive. Calm, measured, firm. Not a guy to be messed with.

Apart from what he'd gleaned from watching TV documentaries, Marlon knew precious little about being a police officer, but he felt that the DCI's bearing, what he'd said, and the way he'd said it were all bang on. In different circumstances Marlon would have admired him.

And that thing about the volume of paperwork. What he said was true, there would be mountains of it. No computers in those days. And I get it that resources are finite, I'm not bloody stupid.

But threatening to sign off before I was ready? What a flamin' cheek.

Marlon pondered if the DCI really would have shut it down. *Or was he bluffing, attempting to regain control. I nearly lost it there, showed them part of the real me. Think I managed to pull it back in time, but I'll need to be more careful in future. Maintain discipline, stay focussed, don't give anything away.*

He glanced around the room. It was tiny, no space for much more than a single bed and a chest of drawers. *They'll be trying to figure out where I'm talking from. But they've got no chance. The old dear doesn't know and even if she did, she wouldn't shop me.* He laughed, but it sounded more like a short, harsh bark. *Bitter and twisted, that's Mum. Right to the end.*

Marlon tried to recall events from 40-odd years earlier when the police had closed the case. He didn't blame Hugo Emerson. *He was only the messenger, the poor sucker who was landed with telling Granny De Luca and the rest of them.* Marlon had stayed in his bedroom, left them to it. He'd only been about fourteen, and a bit screwed up himself. *The family were an angry bunch. Wouldn't let it go. Mum still hasn't.*

Many years later, he'd spent time in Leith Library poring through newspapers and scanning microfiche. It didn't take a genius to work out if there's no evidence, no suspects, no witnesses – basically, you're screwed.

Marlon shook himself out of his downward spiral. 'Stop it,' he said, and left the room. Downstairs he drank from his water bottle, munched on a biscuit, which he didn't lay down. The worktops were covered in crumbs and stains that might have been there for weeks. No way would he prepare food in this kitchen, so he'd bought sandwiches and salads from the supermarket.

He thought back to the call, remembered the DCI asking if he'd taken the feed down. *Of course I did, I can shut it down whenever I like. There are things I can't let you see, need to keep you bastards on your toes.* He clenched his fist. *Because I'm in charge, I decide what happens. I shout, you jump. And I tell you how high.*

He'd demanded they stop bothering his family, but that was only for show. *Florence is completely in the dark and Mum would rather rip out her own tongue than talk to the cops.* He'd often wondered how his eldest sister, Denise, was getting on. They'd met up for a coffee a few weeks after the big fallout, but it hadn't gone well. *Another one that's bitter and twisted, but not for the same reasons.*

So all he could do was wait. *Will they track me down? Will I have to increase the flow again? Or will Hunter give me the name of the bastard who deliberately suppressed the investigation?*

At this stage, there were no answers. It could all turn out to be a dead end. Literally.

If they don't give me a name, I'll have a real decision to make. And however that pans out, well, I'll just have to live with it. Won't I?

Chapter 32

'The next call's at 21:35,' I say. 'Same six-hour gap.' We're in front of the whiteboard, discussing if items can be ticked off. 'Okay, folks. What did we get out of that? Anyone spot anything we can use?'

Andrew was first in. 'Do we go back to his family? Apply more pressure?'

'I'm pretty sure his mother knows more than she's letting on, but she's got nothing to gain by giving him up. She knows she's on her way out so, strangely, she has nothing to lose either.'

'And you don't think the sister's in on it?'

'Florence? No, I don't. What about you, Steph?'

'No,' she says. 'She actually told us she didn't believe her mother. Thought the old bat was lying without actually saying as much.'

'I'm listening to what you've been saying about his mother,' says Jeff. 'But if I'm going to play hardball with anyone, she's my first choice. Ask her to come in.'

Well, I didn't see that coming. 'I know you've already spoken about taking risks that could piss Stevenson off,' I say. 'But is that not pushing it?'

'Do you think she knows where he is?'

'I'm certain she does.'

'In that case it's a risk I'm prepared to take. If she does agree to come in, maybe it'll ramp up the pressure. You never know, she might give something away. And, while we're at it, find the other sister too. What's her name again?'

'Denise,' I say. 'Yeah, she's a definite possibility. Andrew, it would be handy if I could talk to her before the next call. We should bring Hugo back in too. He'll be able to give us more in-depth info on why the case was closed. Although we will have to be careful, we can't give him more details about Natasha. Not yet, at any rate. He's already being a bit snippy with us and we've got enough on our plate.' I pause while

Andrew takes a note then ask Tobias, 'Any joy tracking down that van yet?'

'Not conclusively. I have traced its route, travelling west, heading away from Commercial Street. But it didn't stay on the main road, it cut off at The Old Chain Pier.' Tobias is talking about a popular watering hole near Newhaven Harbour. 'I've plotted all the CCTV cameras in a 270-degree arc, ahead of where he cut off, but the van doesn't appear on any of them. Not so far. And I don't believe he doubled back because he wouldn't have got far before hitting a main artery and being picked up.'

'What are the chances he's still in Trinity?'

Trinity. Almost exclusively residential, and probably the poshest area in Leith. A conservation area, stone-built homes, and therefore expensive. And although there are wide tree-lined avenues with sizeable properties, it also possesses its fair share of tight streets with rows of terraced houses. 'It is possible he stopped in there somewhere,' says Tobias. 'But I think it's unlikely. I've contacted Dave Devlin, and he will send teams to pick up any domestic CCTV, but I asked him to wait until I spoke to you. Such a search would be resource hungry, and I'm highly conscious of how long it would take and how much it would cost.'

Budgets, regrettably, are a harsh fact of police life these days and have been for a while. But Jeff says, 'This can't be driven by cost, or not yet anyway. So tell Dave to go for it, but you should work out a plan first. Choose the streets he should concentrate on, based on how likely it is that Stevenson would take a van along there, even a small one, and whether they are dead ends or not.'

'Let me give you a hand with that once we're finished here, Tobias,' says Steph. 'Some of the narrower streets down there are jam-packed with cars on both sides, and they don't give a toss about yellow lines. Loads of people double-park so we should be able to rule out the routes that would be impassable to a van.'

Tobias smiles a *thank you*, and jots down a couple of notes.

'Ah hah!' says Andrew, and we all turn round. 'The feed's back up.'

'What the hell's Stevenson playing at?' I say. 'It goes down before the call then it's restored after we ask him about it.'

'Maybe he didn't know it had gone down, and he fixed it as soon as he killed the call.'

'Nah. I don't believe that for a second. He's up to something. Anyway, what's Natasha doing?'

Andrew's silent while he studies the screen. 'I think she's still trying to move the table, but she isn't having much success.' He leans in closer. 'Sorry, her body's in the way. I'll keep watching.'

'Okay,' I say. 'Who's next?'

It's Ella. 'I've managed to track down the PC who was with Hugo when the case was closed. Name's Theresa. She's married, surname Green. Left the job in 1983, only served four years.'

'That's great. What's her address, we need to interview her.'

'I doubt we'll be doing that in person, Boss. She moved. Lives in a place called Ness.'

'Inverness? Bloody hell. Okay, never mind, get her into the local cop shop, we can set up a video link.'

'Ah, no, not Inverness. Just Ness. It's a village at the most northernly point of the Outer Hebrides. Closest manned station is Stornoway, about an hour away.'

I look at Ella as if it's her fault this woman has decided to live at the arse end of nowhere. 'Okay, get her on the line. I assume they do have phones up there, yes?'

Ella grins and turns away. She's getting used to my tantrums by now. Thankfully.

'What about posting on social media?' says Andrew.

'That's a tricky one,' says Jeff. 'But it's a no. We'll use up too many resources managing the calls, especially with the deadlines we're working to. Plus, if Stevenson's monitoring our feeds, that might annoy him. So, on a risk versus reward basis, let's leave it for the moment.'

Andrew's phone pings. 'That's the warrant granted to examine Stevenson's medical records.'

'Brilliant,' I say. 'Steph. Here's your chance to grill a doctor.'

She smiles as she's rising from her chair. 'Hope he's fit.'

'It might be a she.'

This time she winks. 'Don't knock it, Boss.'

She's halfway out the door and I'm still shaking my head.

* * *

Less than an hour later Steph phones in. No banter about handsome doctors, she cuts right to the chase. 'Stevenson's own GP wasn't working today but one of his colleagues talked me through his records. Mental health, all fine. Physically, for several years he's been treated for high cholesterol, high blood pressure and associated issues, but is always strangely reticent about following the doc's recommendations. He uses the practice's e-Consult system to report all manner of minor ailments but then he cancels the appointments or doesn't show up, even when they send out text reminders. I get the distinct impression the practice think he's a hypochondriac and they're fed up with him. So, I've been wondering …'

I perk up at the tone she's applied to that last word "wondering". 'Go on then, Steph. What have you been wondering?'

She spends a few minutes talking me through her theory. At first, I think it's off the wall. But the more I think about it, I realise it might, just might, put a completely different complexion on things.

Chapter 33

Natasha wiped her face with a cloth. She seemed to have done that dozens of times lately. Both her hands ached, and she was fast running out of energy, despite taking on more food and water.

By constantly rocking the front left table leg she'd eventually sheared it from the bracket holding it to the floor. She'd then turned her attention to the front right but, with both legs on that side still fixed in place, it wouldn't budge. Next, she tried the back left leg, tight against the wall, and found that to be as secure. Once more, her emotions escalated, partly because progress had halted. But also, a memory of her grandad had materialised. She'd heard him complaining several times about the DIY truism that declares, "If there are six bolts or screws to be loosened, five will come out like a dream. But the last one will always be a bugger".

She smiled through her tears. *It's the other way round this time, Grandad. I've got one free, it's the other three that are being a bugger.* He'd always maintained that whichever method had worked on the others, there was no chance it would work with the stubborn one. So, you have to try something different. Yet again she stood back to consider her options.

The table top was underwater, and the box, the sports bottle and the bucket were floating around free range, bumping against the walls and each other like miniature waterborne dodgem cars. Cutting the vinyl was no longer a possibility, the water was too deep.

Using the facecloths to grip the slippery surface, she tugged at the table to test what she might do. 'This end has one point of contact to the floor; the other end has two. That seals it, I have to work from here.' She moved around, testing as she went. 'Problem is, it's too close to the wall so I can't rock it.'

The shard of laminate she'd broken off earlier was floating nearby. She lifted it from the water, rolled it in her fingers. The bucket was in the corner. She waded across and lifted out one half of the broken handle, weighed it and the laminate in each hand then moved to the corner of the table above the back left leg. She smiled. 'This table's cheap as chips. Let's see if I can do it some damage.' She began hacking at the edge that butted against the wall. It took a while, but she created a gap wide enough to accept her fingers. She put two hands to the corner and began jerking it around. This time it did move.

She padded her hands with the cloths, took a deep breath and set to work. After nearly half an hour including rests, food, and multiple mops of her brow, eventually she felt it give. She whooped. Both legs at her end of the table were free. She did a double fist pump, not caring a hoot if there was a camera running.

Chapter 34

Steph appears at my desk. 'Isobel Stevenson's refusing to leave her house. She's playing the sick old woman card.'

'Well, she wasn't bloody sick when she was shouting and swearing at us earlier on.' I rock my head from side to side a couple of times while I think. Annoyingly, although Isobel can be classed as a significant, and probably hostile witness in this investigation, she hasn't committed a crime, she's not suspected of anything, so we can't compel her to attend.

'In that case, my dear Steph, we'll have to pay her another visit. Although we won't be stopping on the way to buy her a bunch of grapes.'

* * *

Marlon Stevenson's mother is indignation personified. 'I'm not bloody talking to you without a brief,' she says. 'And you have no flamin' right to keep turning up at my door.'

This old battle-axe might be terminally ill, but no one's mentioned that to her eyes. She hits me with a stare that would cut through a strongroom wall. But I'm not having it. It kills me to smile sweetly at her, but I do it anyway. I tell her about being a significant witness and she doesn't need a solicitor. I indicate Florence, who's sitting on her left. 'And your daughter's here, so she can act as your responsible adult, and report me to High Command if I step out of line.'

Poor Florence is so on edge she looks like she's about to have root canal treatment without anaesthetic. I do feel for her because I don't think she's involved. But I can't prove that yet, so I press on with Isobel. 'If through later questioning we discover you do know where your son is, and you fail to disclose it, you will be classed as an accessory and you will be tried the same as him.'

She attempts a forced guffaw, but it morphs into a hacking cough. I'm surprised her lungs don't flop out and land on the table. Florence reaches out, but Isobel slaps her hand away. 'Is that the best you've got, copper? I'll have popped my clogs while the lawyers are still arguing.'

'Mum,' says Florence, tears in her eyes. 'Please. Don't.'

'Don't what? Grass up my own flesh and blood? Too bloody right I won't.'

'Mum! I can't believe this. You know where he is, don't you?'

Isobel gives her daughter the full treatment. Stony silence. Folds her arms so tightly I'm surprised she can draw breath.

In my head, I'm yelling, *Go, Florence*! Such a pity it has to stay there.

I stand up. 'Might be a good idea to listen to your daughter, Isobel. Think on that, and we'll be back in fifteen minutes.'

Hopefully that'll be long enough.

* * *

It isn't.

Isobel's arms remain resolutely folded and her gaze is fixed on the wall. Florence catches my eye and motions towards the door. We step outside to the tune of, 'Don't say anything you'll regret, Florence. Just keep your gob shut.'

Florence pulls the door closed and turns to face us. She's obviously been working herself up to this, so doesn't hesitate. 'My grandad, that was such a long time ago. And even if you did find out who killed him, there's a good chance they're dead too.' Florence inclines her head towards the door. 'But trust me, she won't budge, even with something as serious as this. Truth is, and I know she's my mum, but she's changed so much over the years and there's no point in trying to appeal to her conscience because she doesn't have one. Or, at least, she doesn't now.' She puffs out a long breath. 'I've done my best and got nowhere but you're welcome to keep trying.'

But Florence had called it right. Isobel tells her daughter she doesn't want her in the room, practically throws her out, then proceeds to give up the square root of bugger all. And that's precisely what I have left open to me as far as this old cow is concerned: bugger all.

We drive back to the office. I'm in a foul mood.

Steph keeps quiet. She's not daft.

Chapter 35

To stand any chance of finding people who might have been bent, back in the day, we're working through the chain of command in Hugo's Division at the time. I'd passed this on to Andrew who's looking more uncomfortable as the day wears on. The poor dear can't sit for long and standing up isn't much easier for him. At one point, he was stretched out on the floor conducting a conversation with Ella, who'll probably end up with a crick in her neck as a result.

It takes a while, but eventually with the help of the Thompson Twins, Andrew unearths organisation charts for the period in question. Those were different times. My mum worked in a typing pool, and she's forever regaling me with tales of how primitive things were in her day. Forms and the like were typed first before being run through a manual duplicator to churn out copies. These old machines, Gestetners, took up half a room and spewed ink all over the floor. The copies came out a funny purple-black colour and off-straight; enough to make you look twice. Seeing one now, I remember Mum explaining how she used the underscore key to draw horizontal lines, before rotating the paper through ninety degrees for the vertical lines. Apparently the design process was so complicated, it became part of the secretarial exam.

The format too is strange. No first names are listed, and nearly all have more than one initial. Some have three or four. It could be his parents were keeping family politics in harmony, but I have to say "D Insp W. E. P. Farquharson" is a belter. I imagine a gentlemen sporting flowing whiskers, monocle jammed in one eye, resplendent in a three-piece suit with a silver pocket watch dangling from its chain.

The charts and their contents mean nothing to me, so I hand the bundle back to Andrew. 'See what you can find out, my boy.' He throws me a look of distaste.

'Ah, well,' I say. 'It's not as if you're planning to go out clubbing, is it?'

* * *

Andrew's been on the trail of Stevenson's other sister, Denise Lithgow. 'Long story short,' he says, 'she's not answering the mobile number we got from Florence. She doesn't live at the address we have, but eventually I got one from the solicitor who conducted the sale of the house. Apparently she doesn't have a landline, which is more and more common these days. The Control sent their nearest car round. Upshot is, she wasn't in, but a neighbour did have a number for her. So I've left a message.'

I blink at him. 'And that was the abridged version?'

* * *

The sound techs provided a second report from the afternoon call with Stevenson, and Andrew paraphrases it for us. 'This time they did detect a radio or TV broadcast – voice not music. Traffic noise moderate but still nothing to suggest heavy commercial vehicles. Many instances of children shrieking and shouting, but the schools had just disgorged their contents. Low background noises most likely caused by gardening equipment or possibly domestic works. Nothing else of significance.' He looks up. 'Their opinion has strengthened that he's in a building in a residential area.'

We all agree the report tells us nothing, so we arrange for support to be on hand for the evening call, three hours hence.

* * *

'Boss,' says Ella, holding up a handset. 'Denise Lithgow for you.'

It takes me a second. 'Ah, Marlon's other sister.'

The conversation doesn't last long. As I explain to Ella, Denise wants nothing to do with any of them. Eventually she'd become sick fed up with her mother living a life that was stuck in 1966, at a point when Denise was starting school. Also fed up with Florence for allowing their mother to wallow in it. And *totally* fed up with a brother who was a doormat. I asked if she was shocked at what Marlon had done. She said she certainly was. 'Didn't think he had it in him.'

Ella is stunned. 'A young woman's life is in danger, and that's all she can come up with?'

'Yeah. I made that point forcefully enough but I'm not sure she got it.'

'Dead end?'

'Looks like it.'

Chapter 36

Andrew and Ella have posted the first positive news about Natasha in hours; she's managed to loosen the table from the floor.

We bombard them with questions, so they explain that while Steph and I were wasting our time with Isobel Stevenson, Natasha was hacking away at the wall behind the table with the broken handle. They couldn't figure out what she was trying to achieve but eventually, all became clear.

They didn't require the skills of a lipreader to recognise the whoop she gave out when she lifted up the end of the table, meaning both legs on that side were free. As my colleagues describe Natasha's efforts, I am genuinely in awe of this young woman for the guts and resourcefulness she's displaying. But if I think about her too deeply I choke up. And I can't have that. She needs and deserves all of us to remain utterly professional, including me, so when my emotions do begin to bubble up I trample them into the ground.

We're boosted by Natasha's achievements, but we don't have the luxury of sitting down to watch, so Ella will maintain a vigil while I ask for updates on how the other aspects of the investigation are going. I pull up subject headings on the whiteboard so we can talk through them.

I relate a call I took from Greg Brodie, our Crime Scene Manager. "Sorry, Mel, but if the pavement on Commercial Street by the recycling bins was indeed a crime scene, it's totally compromised. The surface is lock-block, not exactly clean as a new pin, but there's no mud or earth to pick up footprints or tyre tracks. However, I suppose that's a moot point if you find the van. You could canvass that section of the street, but I'm not sure how much you'll get from it. The scene is directly outside an outdoor activities retailer, but that wall of the store is a series of plate glass windows covered in adverts. The posh apartments opposite are converted whisky bonds, but the windows facing onto the street are tiny. They're paying for the view out the front, onto Victoria Quay".

Andrew has an update on this one. 'Although Greig's made a fair point about those apartments, Dave's canvass did produce one woman who'd been sitting by her window, reading. She heard what sounded like bottles breaking, assumed it was someone dumping their recycling in the bin, and didn't bother to check. A pity she wasn't a curtain twitcher, usually they're worth their weight in gold. Result is, we have no one who saw the van either arriving or leaving.'

'Okay. Another long shot. Next, Tobias?'

My German colleague looks a bit glum. 'We had to abandon the search for Stevenson's van with those number plates once we discovered they were stolen. And despite trawling through CCTV at points in an arc south and west of Trinity we were not able to capture a decent quality facial image that might be him. It appears as though he made it through undetected, and the question is, how far did he drive to hide her. Steph, could you show that map again, please?'

She brings it up on the board, while Tobias picks up a laser pointer and shines its green light on the map. 'We know he turned into Trinity at The Old Chain Pier,' he says. 'It's reasonable to assume he switched plates soon after. If he did that, he might have been blasé about driving along main roads or perhaps he went the whole hog and changed to a second set of stolen plates.'

'That seems a bit overkill,' I say. 'Did you confirm if there were any other reports of VW plates being nicked?'

Tobias nods. 'We did. Nothing.'

'In that case, draw a wider arc round Trinity and check cameras at every main junction and every set of traffic lights. Identify all silver VWs that passed during the time frame. It will be one of them, and then you'll have the new registration number.'

I explain to Jeff that Isobel gave us nothing but I'm expecting Stevenson to know we've spoken to her again. And while we're on the family, I confirm the oldest sister, Denise Lithgow, is a dead end. She hasn't been in touch with her family for years.

'Did we get anything from the "Please Contact Us" letters at our canvassing sites?' he asks.

'Zilch, so far,' I say. 'Which is hardly a surprise. Help the polis? In your dreams!'

'Same as it ever was.' He turns to Andrew, who is becoming paler by the hour. 'How are you feeling?'

Andrew grins ruefully. 'I daren't tell you I'm feeling crap, Boss. I'll get pelters from this lot.'

I adopt an air of mock indignation. 'Too right you will.' Then, 'Oh, by the way, Boss, Steph learned something interesting from talking to Stevenson's doctors.' I begin to explain but when he doesn't appear all that enthusiastic I run out of steam.

He fiddles with his ear lobe. 'I'm sorry. It could be me, but why is that interesting?'

'Well, on that first call this morning he said he knew he'd end up inside for a long time, but he didn't care because his life had been ruined already. He told us it was all related to his grandfather being murdered on the day he was born, but I'm not sure I buy that.'

'And what do you buy?'

'Without using these exact words, the GP practice think he's a hypochondriac who's forever reporting health issues. Specifically, for over a year he's been complaining about chest and abdominal pains but he either cancels the appointments and doesn't reschedule, or he's a no-show. And whenever he does actually see the doc, he doesn't follow up on the recommended treatment. So Steph and I are wondering if all these issues, chest pains, high blood pressure, and all that, have convinced him he's about to pop his clogs. That's why he's in such a hurry to appease his mother, and why he's not daunted by the possibility of a long jail sentence.'

As I was explaining my theory, it was beginning to sound a bit desperate even to me, and the vibes around the room suggest I'm right. I glance at Steph for support, but even she looks doubtful now. My boss keeps his gaze fixed on me but stays silent.

'You think that's tenuous, don't you?' I say.

'Sorry, Mel. I'm afraid I do. And anyway, even if it isn't, what can we do with it?'

Annoyingly, I don't have an answer to that.

So, we break off and, slightly dispirited, I wander off to the loo. On my way back, I hear Steph talking on her mobile. The tail end of a conversation; one of those curious snippets that makes you think, *what the hell was that all about*?

'That's right,' she says. 'It's in the garage. And definitely not the blue one. It has to be the pink one. Give me a shout when you get closer to the station, and I'll meet you at the front door.' Then a pause before, 'Thanks, honey. See you soon.'

I catch her eye as she ends the call, give her the eyebrow. 'What are you up to?'

She doesn't reply. Just taps one finger against the side of her nose.

Chapter 37

Tobias and Steph have been working on the routes Marlon could have driven through the residential streets of Trinity and out the other side. We're fairly certain he avoided main roads and the resultant cameras. Our last sighting was when he passed The Old Chain Pier. If he did switch plates, he did it somewhere in Trinity. Likely, they'd have been stuck on with tape or Blu Tack, so a few seconds' work.

We sit round a map printed on a sheet of A2, it resembles one of those mazes published in the fun sections of the Sunday papers. All over the map, there are streets marked as dead ends, cul-de-sacs, and some that appear to continue but in reality they morph into lanes and paths that are unsuitable for vehicles. They've also highlighted a few narrow roads that Steph, who knows the area well, reckons are usually crammed with parked cars on both sides.

Tobias points at three routes marked in green. 'We have assumed he is not still in this area because it is almost entirely residential. Too risky to stop while he transferred Natasha from the van into a house. Naturally, we can't be certain, but on the balance of probability it is unlikely. We have already established that there are no ANPR cameras on these green routes.

Tobias is referring principally to the original Automatic Number Plate Recognition or ANPR network; the blue ones that were installed on all the trunk routes in the UK. But there are other cameras that read number plates such as local authority CCTV, garage forecourts, supermarkets and average speed cameras. ANPR gathers traffic data from these and many others besides.

Tobias continues. 'So, we're gathering footage from main roads or junctions that Stevenson may have crossed. We've stopped searching for the registration, we're concentrating on capturing the driver's face.' He swirls the tip of his pen across the surrounding districts to the west and south. 'I hope we can pick him up because if he has crossed into, for example, Granton, we will have a much wider area to search.'

There's little point in me sounding positive about all that. He and I both know that if Stevenson jammed a cap on his head, or wrapped a scarf around his face, we're screwed. I rub my eyes. 'I agree with you about the wider area, and especially with all the new construction down by Granton harbour. What other options do we have?'

'I've been in touch with Dave Devlin, and he is running house to house on all these routes, starting from the far end. Stevenson drove through there late in the evening so our chances of finding anyone who saw the van are remote. But perhaps CCTV on a house will pick something up.'

'You're right. The chances are remote but it's worth a try.'

I struggle to suppress a yawn. But the yawn wins, hands down.

Chapter 38

Wednesday 19:00

At last, Natasha was able to lift the left end of the table. Despite being submerged, the table's own weight acted as a fulcrum, and it took no more than a few lifts and twists before it was off the floor and away from the wall. Waves slapped against the sides of the room, while the items in the water bobbed around.

As soon as the table was free, she towed it to the corner diagonally opposite the inlet, beneath the hatch her kidnapper had dropped her through. She grabbed the box and clambered onto the table. Her weight kept it solidly in position. It was the first time she'd been up close and personal with the hatch, and after a brief inspection she began thumping the box into it. After a few hits, she stopped. The hatch didn't budge or even rattle, suggesting it was battened tight. She pulled the box to her chest, hugged it. 'Well, I didn't think it would spring open at the gentlest touch, but hell, I'd hoped for something a bit more encouraging than that.'

She didn't waste any more energy on it, she slipped off the table, floated it to the opposite corner and positioned it to one side of the inlet.

Standing on the floor, the water had been above her knees. Still holding the box, she climbed up on the table again. Her heart sank. Even standing up there, she was ankle deep. And then some.

Being on the table had bought her some time but things were becoming serious, and she fought to keep her emotions suppressed. She failed.

* * *

She dried herself as best she could and pulled on her top and shorts. All the activity of the past couple of hours had left her underwear damp, but not yet so uncomfortable that she felt the need to take anything off, although she knew the time might come. She glanced at the ceiling, as if her captor was some

149

heavenly deity. 'That's the end of the show for now. Or are you gay? And that's why you're not bothered that I've been parading around half naked.' She wasn't sure if The Effer being gay was a thing. And, in truth, she didn't care.

She fished out another cereal bar and an apple, sat on the box and devoured them. She'd rather have stayed standing, but she needed to rest, if only for a few minutes. She hadn't slept in ages; she had no idea what time it was. The last time she'd tried to assess how much water was in the room, it had been up to her knees, so she'd guessed fifteen per cent full. *But now it's up to my bum, so not quite double. Twenty-five per cent, maybe?* The wall was so featureless she couldn't begin to gauge the depth accurately. *But then, I don't know what time it is, or how long I've been in here.*

She snorted. 'Pack it in, Tash,' she said aloud. 'You're wasting energy. Let's just say you've got plenty of time and leave it at that.'

Chapter 39

It's not long gone 19:00 when the phone rings. It's Dave. 'This is a bad news/good news call,' he says.

'Leave the good news till last, Dave. Then things can only get better.'

I can practically hear him smiling. 'Nothing showed up on the domestic CCTV we checked. Most cameras are trained on the owner's house or driveway, not on the street. But …' He leaves the tiniest of pauses. 'On house to house, we spoke to a chap who had to jump out of the way of a van travelling too fast along his road.' Dave gives me the address.

I grab the map and mark the location, while he continues. 'It was a light-coloured VW, heading west. The bloke said it flew past and he didn't catch the registration, but it turned south at the end of his street, towards Ferry Road, so that should give you something to work with.'

'Great, Dave, thanks. Tell your guys to take a break while Tobias figures out where you should go next, and he'll get back to you.'

I look up. Tobias and Steph bump shoulders as they squeeze through the door, munching fruit and carrying drinks. I paraphrase what Dave told me. 'So, if that was our VW, and the timings do fit, we can jump ahead of him. Hopefully you'll manage to pick up an image of the driver.'

* * *

The next caller at my desk is Ella. 'I've managed to contact Theresa Green in Ness. She's happy to talk to you by Zoom. Despite being the next stop past the back of beyond she's got a decent connection. And she works from home, so any time suits her.'

'Thanks. Can you set that up for me? And right away if you can.'

* * *

A quick movement catches my eye. Steph is marching across the room carrying a bright pink contraption that, when she unfolds it, turns out to be a garden lounger. Unfortunately she gets all tangled up in it. Ella leaps out of her chair, her running shoes squeak on the tiled floor. Between the two of them, they get it set up. Steph slings Andrew's chair in the direction of another desk, and just in the nick of time.

I watch as Andrew hirples through the door and makes his way towards his desk. Even if the floor was covered in foam we'd all hear the pin drop. Ella is frozen solid, staring at her monitor. Steph is aiming for an excess degree of nonchalance but looks more like a kid waiting to be told Santa has been.

Andrew's pace is slow, and his stride is affected by the airboot. But, for all that, he maintains it all the way across the floor. When he reaches the lounger, he leans down, manoeuvres his hip onto it and swings his legs up. He's flat out with his eyes closed, and none of us have moved a muscle.

A smile creeps across his face. 'Cheers, Steph. Much appreciated. Oh, and FYI, I love the colour. Doesn't half match your coupon.'

Then he raises a middle finger and casually aims it in her direction.

She leans forward and bumps her forehead on her desk. Several times.

Chapter 40

The lighting in Theresa Green's home office isn't the best, so her image is grainy. And she's looming over whatever device she's talking on, so the angle means her face is illuminated from below. Therefore I have a wonderful view up her nose, tiny silver filaments and all.

Once I explain why we've tracked her down, Theresa nods and tells her story. 'Yes, I remember going with Hugo to visit the De Luca family. I think he was hoping that if I was there, they might go easy on him. Or us, I suppose.'

'Did you imagine they were expecting the case to be closed down, or did it come out of the blue?'

She doesn't hesitate. 'I'm pretty sure they were expecting it. On the way there, Hugo explained how it had all been gradually fizzling out over the years. He told me there really was nowhere else to go unless new evidence emerged, or witnesses came forward.'

'And the family's reaction?'

'You've maybe already heard this, but old Mrs De Luca went absolutely nuts. Full-on Italian, I called it.

Understandable, of course, it was her husband. The rest of the family had to calm her down.'

'Were they not angry too?'

'They were, but I'm pretty sure they saw it coming. It made no sense to keep their hopes up for any longer. Honestly, it was kinder in a way.'

I'm beginning to suspect this is another dead end, but then I ask her about whether the case might have been deliberately suppressed. I don't know if it's because I used the word "corruption", but her response doesn't half spark my eyes open.

Chapter 41

Wednesday 20:00

Natasha was exhausted. She couldn't get her legs into a comfortable position, no matter how she arranged them. She had to rest, but how?

She hauled the broken bucket onto the table and tested if it would bear her weight. She tried to stand on it, but the base was too slippery, and the broken parts creaked alarmingly. *No, this is way too dangerous.* She figured if the bucket did shatter while she was on it, a jagged piece of plastic could easily slice an artery in her leg. She grimaced. *Didn't think about that when you were battering the bloody thing off the wall, did you?*

But by combining it and the box, she constructed a makeshift seat, although she lowered herself onto it with great care. She jammed her feet in the bucket, but trying to keep it from floating away placed undue stress on her muscles and they cramped up like there was no tomorrow. All the way through she'd done her best to stay dry, but she had no choice but to accept her feet would be wet from that point on, and she didn't know or care what effect that would have on her skin.

When Natasha was about seven or eight, she'd been present at a family gathering when her mum had told a story about a university research trip to the jungles of Borneo. One of her colleagues had ignored health and welfare instructions, and the poor woman had developed trench foot. Natasha remembered one of her aunties throwing up her hands in horror, "Oh no, not trench foot!" Natasha had been too scared to ask what it was, but she reckoned it wasn't good, and now she wondered briefly if she was likely to contract this clearly horrendous disease. Being a practical soul, she chose not to worry about something she couldn't control and promptly banished it from her mind.

Sitting there, tense and immobile, she could neither stop the shivers nor the questions. 'The water's warm: how come?' Like most people, she knew plenty about air temperatures but precious little about the liquid equivalent, apart from freezing and boiling points. 'Is it heated to make sure I survive? Is this room lined with vinyl to insulate it, or to keep the water in, or both? Or is it to make sure I don't die of hypothermia before something happens?' Of the many phrases she'd refused to think about too deeply, *Outlive my usefulness* was added to her list.

All questions she couldn't answer, but one thing was guaranteed: her grandad would be all over his ex-police colleagues, desperately trying to find her. But how? She took herself back in time. *Okay, Robyn didn't know where I was going but the cops will have tracked the girls down. They'll say what time I left them, and that I would go home along Commercial Street. But did anyone see The Effer grabbing me and chucking me in the van? Were there people ahead of me, further along the street? Shit, I can't remember.*

She'd gone over those points a dozen times, and they left her with some hope. *That's positive, isn't it? Hope. Means I'm not in a hope-less situation.* That cheered her up a touch, but then another thought struck her. *My phone. What's he done with it?* She grinned. *Because the cops can track phones. There's all sorts of stuff they can do these days. CCTV. Car registrations. Facial recognition*. She paused. *Or did I make the last one up?* She nodded. *It'll be okay. They'll find me. Definitely*.

She stretched her neck, stared up at the inlet. *But it would be much better if I rescued myself.*

And, despite being excruciatingly uncomfortable, Natasha drifted off to sleep.

Chapter 42

'It's funny, you know,' says Theresa, 'but in those days no one used the word "corruption". It was almost … how can I put it … just the way of things. Little favours for turning a blind eye or *forgetting* to complete the paperwork. But nobody was making a fortune.' She hesitates. 'Well, apart from one guy.'

'And who was that?'

'Hugo Emerson's gaffer, Detective Inspector Fraser bloody Anderson.'

I smile. That knocked the scab off a fresh wound. 'Tell me more, Theresa.'

She puts on a sour expression. 'Fraser Anderson. So-called Christian and man of the church. My arse. I don't normally speak ill of the dead, but in his case I'll happily make an exception. That man was a complete sleazeball, especially with younger … no, make that *any* female officers. And especially newbie PCs.' She shuffles around in her seat; her voice takes on a harder edge. 'It wasn't only in the force he had that reputation. I heard stories about him in his private life, including the church, so it was nowt to do with him being a copper.'

I sit back. 'Did Hugo and his colleagues know?'

Theresa rubs her eyes. 'Look. I liked Hugo, a lot. But for some strange reason he and all his mates thought the sun shone out of Anderson's backside. They were totally blinkered, couldn't see what was perched on the ends of their noses. And they called themselves detectives.'

I was with her on that. I could quote similar examples from earlier in my career, DIs and DCIs who couldn't find their arses with both hands, or whatever. It was as plain as day to the rank and file, but the hierarchy always seemed completely oblivious. Thankfully it's not something I could ever pin on Jeff. 'Did you or anyone else complain?'

'I didn't. Far too young. But I knew one PC who did. Anderson had her transferred out of there faster than you could say "knife". I just kept schtum and made sure I was never alone with him. He was definitely on the take, and more than most, although in public he always banged on about how he was dead against any form of dishonesty and how he expected his officers to be squeaky.'

'Theresa, you'll understand I need to corroborate anything we turn up, especially after all this time. That PC, do you remember her name, or where she was transferred out to?'

'Wilma. Same as my mum.' There's a brief pause. 'Surname was Knight. And as far as where she was transferred to … Edinburgh West, as I recall. Is there an area out there called Baberton Mains?'

'There is.'

'I thought so. Edinburgh West it was, then.'

'Thanks.' I check my notes. 'Going back to Anderson for a minute, was that not a strange attitude? If he was on the take wouldn't it have been better to keep a low profile?'

Now it's Theresa who's smirking. 'I should also add arrogant to the list of things I could accuse him of.'

'Was it just him, or were other officers involved?'

'A few, not Hugo I should emphasise, were at it to one degree or another. But Anderson was by far the worst. Him and another DI. Or he might have been a DS. The two of them were joined at the hip.' She snaps her fingers. 'I can't remember the man's name, but everybody referred to him by his nickname.' She stops to think. 'Oh, bloody hell. I can't remember that either. But it was a very long time and several careers ago.'

I throw that around in my head before saying, 'So, to one extent or another, Anderson and a couple of others were corrupt. But were they corrupt enough to close the case down and stop it being investigated further?'

She waggles a hand. 'Anderson was potted by then, so it couldn't have been him. So maybe it was the other guy.' She throws her arms in the air. 'Bugger. What was his bloody name?'

'Okay, Theresa. Thanks for your time. If that name comes back to you, let me know. But it might help if you speak to my colleague, he's trawling through old organisation charts. I'll ask him to call you.'

* * *

Unlike in modern day policing, in those times staffing levels were bloated, so it transpires there were dozens of DIs and DSs, and the organisational charts didn't always show individual names. "DS x 6" for example. Andrew's research often showed the charts were correct when they were printed, but not for much longer. And, of course, they didn't include nicknames. More's the pity.

Then it dawns on me – do I have one?

I look around the team. If I did, none of those buggers would admit it. I catch sight of Ella. She's new, she'll tell me. I stroll across to her desk.

Turns out I misjudged her. Bollocks!

* * *

It doesn't take long for Andrew to track down the woman who spoke up against Fraser Anderson. He has her on the line.

I pick up. 'Wilma, this is DI Mel Cooper. Thanks for talking to me.'

'Your colleague said it was urgent. What can I do for you?'

'Theresa Green has told me you would remember a DI, back in the late 70s, early 80s. Chap called Fraser Anderson. I understand you were part of his team until — '

'Until he tried to feel me up, and I kneed him in the balls. And while he was rolling about on the floor, I told him I wanted transferred out of there in five minutes flat or I'd resign and take my story to the *News Of The World*.' She pauses for breath. 'Total sleazeball.'

I'm doing my best not to crack up. 'Funnily enough, that's what Theresa called him.'

'Did she, indeed? Great minds, eh?'

'So now I have the right man, and I know he died a long time ago, but apart from the unwanted advances, are there any other aspects of his behaviour that might have concerned me, had I been investigating him?'

'You mean the fact he was as bent as a nine-bob note, to coin an old saying.'

'Precisely that, Wilma. Second question, do you remember a sidekick he had, another DI or maybe a DS? Theresa reckoned they were joined at the hip.'

There's silence on the line for a few seconds. 'I hadn't actually been on the team all that long before I got out of there, but I can only remember one other DI. And maybe two or three DSs …'

After I close the call, I pass the names over to Andrew. Hopefully one of them is the guy we're searching for.

* * *

Andrew and I are reviewing the outstanding items on the actions list when Jeff ambles over and slumps into a chair by the side of my desk. 'Any joy tracing Fraser Anderson's mysterious sidekick?' he says.

'Not so far.' Andrew indicates the corner where the Thompson Twins have their heads down. 'We've been digging through the case papers and staffing info from the time, but we're talking forty years ago and we've no idea what might be missing. Plus, it doesn't help that everything quotes initials instead of first names so we've no way of knowing who's male and who's female. Although I don't imagine there would have been too many female officers around. I've spoken to Theresa Green again, but she still can't remember the man's name. She's promised to phone if it comes back to her.'

'Okay,' says Jeff. 'We're about to reinterview Hugo, so I'll ask him. If the chap was a DS at the time –'

'Or a DI,' I say.

Jeff nods. 'Either way, I'd expect Hugo to remember.' He pauses there. Taps his finger on the table a couple of times. 'I have to say, though, a case that's not investigated fully, and we're wondering if it's because of bent coppers? Is that not a cliché from a rubbishy TV drama or a second-rate crime thriller?'

What a man he is for rhetorical questions.

* * *

We're interrupted by Andrew yelling, 'Oh, brilliant!'

In tandem, Ella screams, 'Go, Natasha! What a star!'

We all fly out of our seats and rush over. 'What?' I say. 'What?'

They're both grinning. 'It's taken her ages, but she's only gone and broken the table away from the wall,' says Andrew. Then he and Ella high five.

'Wow! What's she doing with it?'

'You know how we thought there must be a hatch? We're now fairly certain it's in the corner diagonally opposite the inlet. She floated the table over –'

Too late, Andrew realises the implication of what he's said.

My world does seem to rock and roll for a few seconds while images of a prison cell half full of water threaten to overwhelm me, but I shut my eyes till the feeling subsides and wave him to continue. 'She, eh, thumped the box into the ceiling and yelled at it a few times but nothing happened so she moved the table again. To beneath the flow.'

I wonder if I should risk watching her, but common sense prevails. Most unlike me.

Ella pipes up. 'It's also worth pointing out that, during all of this, she has been eating and drinking so she's been looking after herself. And she's been changing in and out of her clothes, trying to keep her top layer dry. Which must be a boost for her morale, Boss. Yeah?'

Dear God, I hope so. With all my heart, I hope so.

159

Chapter 43

'Look, Jeff,' says Hugo. 'You have to let me help. My experience could be invaluable.'

Not fifteen minutes earlier, Tobias had called the retired DI and asked him to come in to meet with Jeff and me. Hugo had turned up at reception so quickly, we joked he must have been sitting in his car with the engine running.

Jeff's expression is impassive. 'You know as well as I do, it's too much of a conflict of interest. There's no way your judgement on any aspect of this case could be impartial. Plus, you're a civilian. I'd have to jump through God knows how many hoops to ratify your involvement, and that would take forever. And time is one resource we're desperately short of.' The older man moves to argue but Jeff speaks right across the top of him. 'Out of the question, Hugo. It's not happening.' My boss doesn't state that's his final word on the subject but it sure as hell is.

'Well in that case you need to put more pressure on his family. That old battle-axe of a mother, she must know where he is.'

'We've visited her. Twice. We're certain she does know, but she's not giving him up.'

'Well lean on her, for fuck's sake.'

'Lean on her, Hugo? The woman is eighty-nine. She has terminal cancer. She's not a suspect. We have no evidence she has colluded with her son. We've pushed her as hard as we can and unless something changes, I won't push any harder.'

Hugo's moves his head from side to side, slowly, deliberately. 'You bloody snowflake. This would never have happened back in—'

'Your day? This isn't your day any more, Hugo. Times have changed, and for the better. So, let me put it to you straight. I have to balance how hard we can push Stevenson and his family, with the wellbeing of your granddaughter. If I put too much pressure on him, the likelihood of a positive outcome diminishes.'

'Jesus. Will you listen to yourself, man. "The likelihood of a positive outcome?"' He snorts so hard that tiny globules of spit spray out of his mouth and nose. I recoil. COVID has left lots of legacies, some of which may never disappear. Hugo continues his rant. 'You mean the chances of her not dying, that's what you're really saying.'

'Hugo. I'm going to stop you there. When we finish here, please go home. Leave it to us. You'll have to trust me on this.'

'Trust you? I'm supposed to trust you when my Natasha's life's in danger and you're making sure you cover your arse. That *will* be fucking right.'

He stands up and kicks his chair from underneath him. It scrapes across the floor, and he hooks his jacket off the back.

'Hugo,' says Jeff. 'You're distraught. I can't possibly imagine what you and your family are going through, but I need you to compose yourself and answer our questions. Now, please, sit down.'

Hugo Emerson is not a happy man. He starts to speak, stops, then hits us with a look that says, *Have it your own way.* And slumps into his chair.

Jeff jumps right in. 'This morning, I asked if you believed Sandro De Luca's murder was investigated properly. You said you did. I also asked if it was possible the case was pushed down the lists because of police corruption. Although you admitted there were bent coppers kicking about, you said it was small fry.'

'What are you suggesting?'

Jeff sits back, tilts his head to the side. 'Why do you think I'm suggesting anything?'

Now this is interesting. Why has Hugo gone so far onto the defensive? I watch him closely.

Hugo draws in a deep breath, makes the time out signal. 'Sorry. Sorry. Didn't mean that. I'm up to high doh. We all are. Completely on edge.'

Hmmm. Nice recovery, retired Detective Inspector Emerson. But I'm still watching you.

Jeff holds his hands up. 'Understandable, Hugo. But I need to get to the bottom of this. Was the case investigated properly?'

Hugo takes an age to spit out an answer. 'At the time, as a wet-behind-the-ears plod, I didn't really understand what was going on. For the following couple of days, we threw everything at it but got nowhere fast. Then, a few days later, there was another murder and the focus switched immediately to that. But I'd picked up a serious dose of the flu and I was off work for over a week. And I was far from the only one. So the place was a bit of a mish-mash, we were struggling to cope and let's just say, the higher-ups thought the best way to manage the caseload was to shout louder – at whoever happened to be closest. But because we had nothing to go on, no one to talk to, no hard evidence, the De Luca killing gradually slid down the pecking order.'

'That other murder,' I say, 'What can you remember about it? Was it related?'

'You know, I'd forgotten about it completely. It only popped into my head while I was talking a minute ago.' He scratches his chin. 'A man in his early twenties, if memory serves.'

If memory serves? Well, there's something wrong with that picture. 'So how long did you stay involved in the De Luca case?'

'I was a beat copper for three years, so I was only called upon when needed. But when I transferred into CID as a DC, my boss Fraser Anderson had the case on his list so every now and again we'd take another crack at it. But still, nothing.'

'Ah, yes,' I say. 'Fraser Anderson. Tell me about him.'

'Anderson? He was the real deal. Worked hard, tough, fair, and honest as the day is long. I was devastated when he died, he was only forty-four.' Hugo reflected on that for a moment then continued. 'So, going back to your question, yes I do believe it was investigated properly but there was nothing. Not a spark. So trying to convince our bosses that we should keep the case alive was a lost cause and they shut it down.'

'Okay,' says Jeff. 'A minute ago your view was that any police corruption was small fry. Are you sure? I know *Operation Countryman* was thoroughly discredited, but that was more about the way the initiative was managed and the results it produced.'

'Or didn't.'

Jeff smiles. 'As you say, but what I'm getting at is the corruption was there, it just wasn't uncovered properly. And bent coppers, apart from one or two, weren't caught and punished.'

Well before my time, naturally, but what Jeff's talking about here is, back in 1978, allegations emerged that enormous sums of money – bungs – had been paid to over a hundred officers from the City of London Police, and from Scotland Yard's Flying Squad. Some ranked as high as Commander. These officers were accused of taking bribes, planting and concealing evidence, conspiring with bank robbers and improperly facilitating bail. The then Home Secretary, Merlyn Rees, brought in officers from different jurisdictions including Hampshire and Dorset police forces to investigate under the banner, *Operation Countryman*. As a result of, allegedly again, "high level obstruction from senior police officers and leading figures in the criminal justice system", the operation became hopelessly compromised and was wound down four years later. Despite costing a reported £4m – an enormous wedge of cash at the time – only two successful prosecutions were secured. The remaining officers were acquitted. A right royal waste of time and money.

'Honestly, Jeff,' says Hugo. 'Apart from bottles of booze and the odd free lunch, I didn't witness anything worth bothering about.'

'So no one ever passed you a brown envelope, or what was the term, offered you "a drink"?'

Hugo squirms, blushes. 'Well, yes. They tried that on with most coppers. But you asked about my boss, Fraser Anderson. I told you he was honest, and he was. Scrupulously. He was an elder in the church, and he made it explicitly clear he wouldn't countenance dishonesty. So if he found out anyone had taken a backhander, their feet wouldn't have touched. Criminals shied away from bribing officers in his team, they knew we wouldn't bite.'

I butt in at that point. 'Are you sure he was honest, Hugo?'

163

'That's not up for question, why?'

'I spoke to the PC you told us about, Theresa Green. She went with you to visit the De Luca family that day. She told me, and I quote, "He was definitely on the take".'

Hugo's eyes practically pop out. 'And you'd accept the word of some wee lassie who was only in the job for five minutes versus that of a highly respected DI?'

'No, I would not. But I've had Theresa's statement corroborated by another PC, a woman who told me your boss sexually assaulted her and transferred her out to keep her quiet. And you know what? I believe her.' I stare him down. Challenge him to come back at me. He stays quiet.

Jeff picks up again. 'Anderson died aged forty-four. What of?'

'He took his own life.'

'Know why?'

'He left a note. It just said, "Sorry, please forgive me". But when a person commits suicide, who can possibly understand their state of mind?'

'Nothing to do with him being bent?' Jeff leans forward. 'Was he bent, Hugo?'

Hugo jams his hands in his jacket pocket. 'I won't dignify that with an answer.'

Jeff raises his eyebrows at such a pompous reply, then says, 'If Fraser Anderson didn't deliberately suppress it, who else could it have been?'

Hugo leans forward, glares at him. 'You've got a real bee in your bonnet about this. Why are you so bloody sure that happened?'

'Because Stevenson said it did. Years afterwards, someone tipped him the wink.'

Hugo taps his fingernail forcefully on the table. 'Well, it certainly wasn't Fraser Anderson, I can tell you that for nothing.'

'Theresa also mentioned a detective who was close with Anderson, either a DI or a DS. Apparently everyone used his nickname, but we don't know what it was, or his real name. Do you remember him?'

Hugo blinks a couple of times; his gaze skitters round the room before halting at a point somewhere off to our left. 'No.

164

Sorry. Doesn't ring a bell.' He opens his mouth as if to say more but stops. Dead.

'What?' says Jeff.

'Oh, nothing. Just thinking back, that's all.'

'Are you honestly trying to tell me you can't remember your colleagues' names?'

'That's right. I can't. Well, not all of them, anyway.'

Well, I'll find out later what Jeff thinks about that. But, not to put too fine a point on it, our man Hugo is lying his arse off.

* * *

Jeff's mobile had buzzed a couple of times towards the end of our chat with Hugo. He'd glanced at it, turned his nose up. But Hugo's gone now, so Jeff asks me to hold on while he makes a call. He listens. I recognise a colleague DI's voice. He's a good man to have around but when the chips are down he can come over a bit whiny. And he's full-on nasal now.

'I need to tidy up here,' Jeff tells him. 'Then I'll be right over. I'll ring you from the car.' He taps his screen, drops his phone into his pocket and turns to me. 'I need to go but I'll be here in time for the next call. In the meantime, can you confirm the chain of command above and at the same level as Fraser Anderson. Judging by Hugo's reaction right at the end of that interview, I'd say he's hiding something.'

I shoot him a look. 'You and me both, Jeff.'

I hear light footsteps approaching, fast.

Ella appears in the doorframe. 'Boss. The feed's down again.'

Chapter 44

Wednesday 20:30

Natasha's primary focus was the inlet, and the water pouring down. 'I have to block it. But how? It's too high.'

She considered the possibilities. 'Even if I could reach it, what would I do? Jam something in? But what, and how do I make it stay put? Stick my thumb in like that Dutch boy did with the dam?' She shook her head. Grimaced. Clenched her fists. She wasn't giving up, not by a long shot. But right then, she had no idea what to do.

Bizarrely, it occurred to her that once the water rose to a certain level, she'd be able to swim up to it. She pictured herself treading water, using only her legs to hold her position while she tried to seal the pipe.

She knew she was no more than relatively fit. Sure, she walked plenty; name a student who didn't? But she didn't go to the gym, wasn't a runner, didn't play sports. When she'd been climbing on that indoor wall, her shoulder and thigh muscles had burned after only a couple of ascents. All she had was a fairly average nineteen-year-old's natural fitness, she'd never worked at it. And as far as swimming was concerned, on holiday she'd played with the other kids in the pool, threw herself down the slides, stuff like that. So, she'd always been confident in water but would never have described herself as any more than competent.

* * *

Gazing up at the end of the pipe, holding a damp towel, mentally she smacked into a wall. All along, the table had been her castle, her stronghold against the constantly rising water level. But not now. Even with the extra height the table afforded her, the water was still at her knees. She buried her face in the towel and sobbed. Over and over and over. This time, mantra or no mantra, it took her an age to recover her composure.

'Okay, Tash. Getting out of here is down to you. No one else. Just you.' She draped the towel over the box in an attempt to let it dry but realised it would be easier to paint over a shadow.

She'd resigned herself to staying on her feet, for a while at least, so had thrown the bucket into the water to give her space on the table. It was too dangerous to stand on. That was a last resort.

Inexorably, she was drawn again to the inlet. 'If I was three or four inches taller, I could reach it. Pity I'm Scottish, not Dutch.'

She performed the calculations one more time. She'd discovered she was so exhausted that if she did the sums once, then counted again after even a brief pause, she came up with a different answer. She concentrated. Hard. 'Five foot nine, which is the height I need to be. Minus five foot three, which is what I am. Leaves six inches. And six inches is about fifteen centimetres.' She worked it through a second time and confirmed the answer. 'Yes. Fifteen centimetres. And that's handy. Because you, my little box, are about that high.'

She studied it. Earlier, she'd needed extra space to keep her hoodie and shorts dry and had reasoned that some items in her survival kit wouldn't come to any harm if they were wet. So, she'd rearranged the contents to leave only the facecloths and towels inside, while the packets, cleansing bottles, and the remaining apples jostled for space in the bucket. But when the box began to float away, she had to put a few of the heavier items back to keep it anchored.

The laws of physics dictated the box must float, so she positioned it beneath the inlet and pushed it down into the water till it bumped against the tabletop. Then she tried to stand on it. She slipped off a few times before she got it right. She could touch the pipe with her fingertips but only because she was stretching one arm. As soon as she brought the other arm into play, her stance evened off and she was short by a couple of centimetres.

She swore. Loud. Long. And repeatedly. Then she thumped her forehead with the heel of her hand. 'You complete idiot, Tash.' She glared at the box through the water.

'Flat. I've been fixated on it lying flat. Why on earth didn't I stand it on its end?'

She couldn't believe the idea hadn't occurred to her but stopped short of beating herself up. Between the stress and the exhaustion it was hardly surprising she wasn't thinking clearly.

She gathered herself, refocussed, and decided it would be more stable, and easier, if she stood the box on its long side. She judged it to be about twenty-five centimetres wide, so that would give her about a ten-centimetre boost compared to it lying flat. So she turned it, adjusted the placement, and stepped confidently onto the box.

Chapter 45

'What gives you the bloody right to hound my mother? In her own home.' Marlon Stevenson's tone is remarkably calm. Hard. Chilled. 'An old woman with terminal cancer? You sick bastards.' He leans forward, a light bounces off the ever-present sunglasses. 'To quote your own words from earlier, "We have no intention of speaking to your mother or your sister again". Just proves I can't trust a word you say.'

That's a bit rich, I think. Neither Jeff nor I respond. We're stuck between a rock and a hard place. We can't allow Stevenson to dictate terms, but we need to keep him onside. And most of all we can't afford to put Natasha's life in more danger than it currently is.

That's twice we've spoken to Isobel Stevenson and still she's given us sweet FA. We were convinced that when Marlon found out, he'd retaliate by switching the flow to high. So, as soon as we'd finished with the redoubtable Mrs Stevenson, we left her alone with Florence.

That was nearly four hours ago and clearly Marlon didn't hear straight away that we'd visited his mother again. Reason is, I'd taken a chance and asked Florence if she was willing to help us. When she said she was, I told her to stick to her mother like glue to make sure she didn't phone him. That was until half an hour ago when Florence was primed to leave Isobel to her own devices. Now I'm reasonably certain Florence doesn't know how to contact her brother, but Isobel does. And the elder sister, Denise, is in the same boat as Florence. These are only assumptions, but they're all we have.

Jeff doesn't let on that we know Marlon has been talking to his mother because it suits us if we look a bit dim. So, all Jeff says is, 'We had no choice but to speak to your mother, and she was in the care of your sister when we left her.' Then we collectively hold our breath in case he says he's turning the water up.

We're lined up as we were earlier, with our resident body language expert observing Stevenson, and our sound techs patched in. Jeff follows the script. 'Before we discuss what we have for you, Mr Stevenson, may I ask if you'll consider releasing Natasha Emerson to save her from further distress?'

'You may. But the answer will be no,' says Marlon, without missing a beat.

Damn.

I study him to try to work out how tired he is. Clearly, I've never kidnapped and threatened to kill anyone, but he must be feeling the strain. Having said that, while we're running about at his beck and call, for all I know he's been relaxing with his feet up between calls. We, on the other hand, are becoming exhausted; fast approaching breaking point. If the timeline we're working to stays as it is, our next conversation will be at 03:35. I dread to think what state I'll be in by then.

Jeff holds his hand up. I know what's coming. 'The live feed has dropped out. Is this down to you?' Stevenson doesn't answer immediately, which gives Jeff the opportunity to follow up. 'You will remember I asked you the same question during this afternoon's call.'

'And did it come back up?'

'You know it did, after we signed off.'

Stevenson simply shrugs and moves straight on. 'While we're on the subject of further distress to Miss Emerson, DCI Hunter, how about you convince me you're making progress.'

'I have secured extra resource: officers working in conjunction with our Area Control Room, and a team of detectives.' He neglects to mention it's a team of two. Let's call that a sin of omission.

'But Cooper and her team are not working solely on my grandfather's case, are they? Oh no, they're chasing shadows and wasting time, like I told her not to.'

Jeff doesn't react, all part of the plan. He carries on as if Stevenson hadn't spoken. 'You want to know why the case was closed. I'll give you the bald facts first.'

'Oh, not that old crap regurgitated. Let me guess. No evidence, no suspects, no witnesses. Is that the best you can do? Because if it is, you'll end up with a body on your hands.'

'No matter what you think, Mr Stevenson, those points are germane to the case, and I can't ignore them. But what I can say is we're re-examining them all. At the same time, we're checking closely to see if the actions of corrupt police officers could be at the heart of it.'

Stevenson is stopped in his tracks. Jeff has used the "C" word. Part of our strategy with these calls is to use direct, straightforward terms – no weasel words. It seems to be having the desired effect.

He leans in, his posture tense. 'Have you identified anyone yet?'

'Thus far, we've identified two officers to study further.'

'And their names?'

'No, Mr Stevenson. Whether I like it or not, I am mandated to follow policy at all times. And that policy clearly states that I cannot and will not name any officers we are investigating, even if I believe they were corrupt. Neither will I destroy the reputations of individuals who may be deceased thereby causing their families undue distress. Whether they are police officers or not, we still operate to the maxim, innocent until proven guilty.'

'Detective –'

'And I will not budge on that, Mr Stevenson. Not one inch. If I conduct this investigation in a manner that puts people's backs up, I stand no chance of achieving the outcome you crave.'

I'm studying our kidnapper closely on another monitor. That's twice Jeff's hit him like that, and he hasn't retaliated. He's stretching his body in the chair, leaning to left and right, massaging his side. It's obvious he's suddenly become extremely uncomfortable. I wonder briefly what the body language guy will be making of this. I glance over at Andrew, who's typing furiously. He bangs down on one last key then jabs his finger in the direction of my monitor.

An instant message pops up: "*Tangible signs of discomfort displayed as per earlier call (upper abdomen). Stretching, massaging above kidneys, less likely to be tension. Suggests cause is health related but not my field. Discuss medic ASAP*".

I read Andrew's message for a second time, recalling the chest and abdominal pains Stevenson had reported to his doctor. I wonder if he's beginning to suffer from the strain and might be willing to negotiate when I hear his voice rising. 'The next contact will be at 03:35. Get me a name, DCI Hunter. And if you don't, Miss Emerson's situation will deteriorate. Rapidly.'

Shit!

Jeff stretches. Maybe for effect, I don't know. But he genuinely does surprise me when he stands up, walks behind his chair, and rests his hands on the frame. He doesn't swivel it from side to side, he holds it perfectly still. 'Mr Stevenson, I am tired. My team, who in recent times have been working far longer hours than I have, are also tired. If you make us work through the night, and expect us to produce results, we will inevitably hit a wall. Your demands on us will mean we'll run out of energy, at a time you need us to be fresh.' Stevenson moves to speak, but Jeff holds his hand up – an enormous risk. 'Our judgement will be impaired, and we will make mistakes. I don't want that. Neither do you. And certainly, neither does Natasha Emerson especially as we are over 12 hours into the 48 you have imposed. Those are simply statements of fact.'

I'm tempted to stand up and cheer, but stay welded to my seat, eyes fixed on Stevenson. Then, blow me down, Jeff kicks off again. 'Also, people we need to talk to do not work nights. So we will, through no fault of our own, hit roadblocks wherever we turn.'

'And tell me,' says Stevenson, his lip curling up more than a little, 'was that another statement of fact?'

My boss doesn't sigh extravagantly but I bet he'd love to. Instead, he stares directly at the camera and says, 'It was.'

Stevenson leans forward. 'Well, here's another one, Detective Chief Inspector Hunter. Despite your promises not to question my family, you have interrogated my terminally ill mother, who's never done anyone a bad turn in her life. And for that, you will pay. Or, rather, Natasha Emerson will pay.'

Someone connects a high voltage battery to my nervous system and before I can shout at the screen, he says, 'I've changed my mind about increasing the water to the higher flow for an extra hour because you're clearly not taking me seriously, so, this time ...' He flashes a malevolent smile. 'It will be three hours. The water will stay at high flow until 00:50, meaning you will only have ... 29 hours before the room fills up.'

He stretches out a hand. 'Next call 03:35, Hunter. Get me that name, or I'm switching the water back to high. And that's where it will stay.'

He pauses. 'Are we clear?'

We're not given any time to answer. The screen goes blank.

Chapter 46

'Boss.'

Ella is speaking to me from her desk. Her voice is hushed, almost apologetic, as if she's not certain she wants it to travel this far. Her expression is set, meaning she's about to tell me something I don't really want to hear. Like when you're expecting a visitor, while at the same time hoping they don't show up. 'The feed's coming through again,' she says, still quiet.

There's more. I know there's more. I give her a prod. 'And?'

'And the flow rate is at high.'

Naïve perhaps, maybe even ridiculous, but I had been praying that Stevenson was bluffing. However, hope has given me the middle finger and disappeared over the horizon. 'What's Natasha doing?'

'Still trying to reach up to the inlet, but for the life of me I can't imagine what she plans to do if she reaches it.'

I turn to Jeff. He's on his mobile, offering advice to another DI. My colleagues all know he's tied up with me and they're doing their best not to disturb him, so this is obviously an emergency. The door creaks as Steph walks in. Her hair is darker than usual, still damp from the shower.

There are only four of us here: Jeff, Ella, Steph and me. I sent Andrew home a few minutes ago. The poor lad was absolutely shattered, clearly in more pain than he was letting on. Tom 1 is driving him; he's taking some downtime too. His twin disappeared in the direction of the kitchen about half an hour ago and hasn't been seen since. I'm struggling to get upset about that; the two of them have hardly lifted their heads all day and have got through a power of research. Crissi went off duty a couple of hours ago, there was nothing more she could do at Hugo's house. She'll contact them at 07:00 to ask if they need her. If not, she'll come in to spell Ella. And Tobias had exhausted all options to find the VW, so I'd sent him packing too.

If Stevenson carries out his threat to keep the flow on the higher rate till 00:50, and as sure as eggs is eggs he will, it won't be three hours we'll lose off our deadline, it'll be six. He told us that by the time the water slowed, we'd be down to 29 hours remaining and when Ella confirmed his calculations, I felt like I'd been kicked in the stomach. In my head, that 30 hours' barrier was significant, and it's been shattered.

I sense Jeff's winding up his call, so I give myself a shake, perk myself up. I'd rather not sound like the Grim Reaper when I tell him the latest.

But he's ahead of me. 'A similar pattern to earlier, isn't it? He takes the feed down, comes on the call with us, then once we've signed off he reinstates it. Why? What's he playing at?'

Ah. The six-million-dollar question. We've all been trying to figure that out, but we end up talking in circles. Does the feed drop out itself? Maybe. Is there a technical reason it has to be refreshed? Maybe. Does he go somewhere? Maybe. To wherever he's holding Natasha? Maybe. All those and more. And each one has the same answer. *Maybe.*

Twice we've asked him why the feed went down, but he dodged the question both times.

My eyelids head south, and I experience that faint buzzing sensation behind my eyes; a sure sign I'm about to drop off. I would stand up and move around but I cannot be bothered.

We have two deadlines looming. The first at 00:50 when Stevenson should turn the water down. I'm looking forward to that. The second one I'm not. Our next call is at 03:35 and we're no closer to finding out who was responsible for pulling the De Luca investigation all those years ago.

But for the moment, I give up. I am beyond being able to rationalise. I need to sleep.

Chapter 47

Wednesday 22:00

Natasha hadn't expected the box to collapse and, arms flailing wildly, only just managed to stop herself toppling backwards into the water. When she stood on it, the box and its lid had separated and everything she'd been keeping dry had fallen out. The towels and facecloths sank at once, the other items drifted away.

But she had no time to recover from the shock before she noticed a different sound; one she hadn't heard for ages. 'Shit! The water.'

She didn't have to look up at the inlet, the splashing in front of her indicated clearly that the flow had increased to the higher rate. She was within a hair's breadth of losing it; only a gargantuan effort stopped her. She clenched her fists, knocked them gently against each other three times, then resorted to her mantra, pulling her shattered self-discipline back from the brink.

'Okay, Tash. Good recovery. Now, stop. And think!'

She stripped off her shorts and slipped down into the water, now almost at her waist. After a few failed attempts she managed to fish the towels and facecloths off the floor using her toes. Her automatic reaction was to wring them out but rejected it as an utterly futile gesture, so she threw them in the box.

She studied the rim of the box and its lid. All that had been holding them together was a pair of blue plastic clips, one on each end. She studied them critically. 'Cheap crap. Hardly surprising it collapsed. But how the hell do I make it stronger, so it'll take my weight?'

As things stood, she had absolutely no idea but before her morale plummeted again, she dragged herself into a positive frame of mind. 'Thing is, *Natasha*, you'll just have to figure it out. So get cracking, yeah?'

'Yeah.'

Chapter 48

Marlon Stevenson was pissed off.

Seriously pissed off.

When I went on that call tonight, I had absolutely no intention of turning the water to high. Okay, maybe I would have, but only for an hour. No way on earth was I planning to make it three.

But, at the end there, I flipped. And all because bloody DI bloody Cooper hassled my mother. Again.

Then I found out Mum couldn't ring me for ages after Cooper and her sidekick left the house because Florence wouldn't leave her on her own. So the bastards have turned my own sister against me too. Well, I couldn't care. They can't change what's going to happen.

And the annoying thing, the really *annoying thing, is although I regret putting the water back on high, I can't go back on my word. They'll think I'm a soft touch, and I can't have that. So, the police have three hours less, and so does the Emerson woman.*

Maybe that'll teach them. Or maybe it won't. Whichever way, it's not my problem.

Marlon sat down. Slugged from his bottle of water. Shut his eyes. The stress was building. Not quite overwhelming, but his composure was definitely beginning to fray at the edges. Earlier, he'd cut it fine returning to the house after putting what he termed his "belt 'n braces" plan in place. Something he'd needed to do, just in case.

Forget "just in case", Marlon. Best not go there. Anyhow, it won't change the outcome.

"Marlon". He'd always detested his name but there was nothing he could do about it. Strangely, some of the kids at school thought "Marlon" was dead cool, so he played on it for a while. But then came the "Mar-*lyn*" brigade, the piss-takers who delighted in changing the second syllable. He'd have liked to punch their lights out, but he was a timid lad, so that wasn't an option.

Later, as a young adult, "Marlon" provided some ironic entertainment. "Marlon? After Marlon Brando? Wow!" But it didn't last, and he reverted to being "That boring guy with the weird name". *Thanks for nothing, Mother.*

Calmer now, his recollections drifted back to earlier. *I expect they've twigged why I drop the feed before the call then reinstate it afterwards. Hunter isn't stupid. Cooper must be on the call too, but she's staying out of sight. Wonder why? Could be he's deliberately keeping her quiet. She boobed early on, didn't she? Cost them an hour. Still, it won't do any harm if the top man's running the show. He's direct, straight talking. I like that; he won't take any crap from anyone working the case.*

But is he actually getting anywhere? Does he really have names in the frame? On the next call, if there's even a suggestion he's stalling, I'll be cranking things up. Big time.

Marlon had considered cutting the gap between calls but was forced to admit Hunter was right. *What on earth can they do during the night? Fair point, I suppose, but who said anything about fair. Not my problem.*

He snorted. "Not my problem". *That'll be on my gravestone.*

He yawned, his eyes watering. He was desperate to sleep. He'd been living on his nerves all day Tuesday, wondering which of the many components of his plan might go awry. Waiting to find out if Natasha and her friends followed their normal pattern of a few drinks down at The Shore. Then lying in ambush on Commercial Street, and the con with the box of recycling. Finally, grabbing her before driving to the site via his well-rehearsed route through Trinity.

"The site". He never referred to it by its name or location in case he slipped up in the intervening months. If he ever needed an excuse to slip away, he'd say, "I'm working at the site". Or "I'm going down to the site". Normal industrial language and nobody batted an eyelid.

So yes, he needed sleep. He'd managed to stay relatively calm during the three calls but handling Hunter and Cooper had elevated his stress levels. And now? *Jeez, what a crashing comedown. Never mind, a couple of hours kip, that'll do me. Shower, eat and get myself geared up in plenty time.*

He set the alarm on his mobile for 00:30, went through to the bedroom and stripped off. He lifted a pair of red pyjama bottoms off the bed before having a wash and brushing his teeth.

Wish I'd brought slippers, this place is manky. Three bloody great Retrievers in a house this size. Hairs on every surface. How can anybody live like this?

Still, only one more night, and then …

And then, what?

He didn't have the answer. But, by the end of the following day, it would all be over.

One way or the other.

Chapter 49

1966
Friday 4th February
19:55

The young man dodged the traffic as he splashed his way across the road, collar up, coat tails flapping, leather soles slapping on the tarmac. He had a peculiar gait, as if both his knees were encased in splints.

Edward Tweed climbed into the passenger side of a wine-coloured Ford Zephyr. It gleamed under the streetlights, with angular tail fins that could slice an apple. He ran his fingers through his hair and stared straight ahead. The windscreen wipers squeaked back and forth but were making little headway against the deluge. He trailed his fingertips along the walnut fascia, briefly wondering if it was fake. 'The polis must be paying pretty well these days. Or have you got yourself a part in *Z-Cars*?'

The driver ignored the jibe. On this foul February evening, humour wasn't high on his agenda. He pulled away from the kerb and accelerated smoothly into a gap, ignoring the angry parp from the double-decker bus that filled his rear view mirror.

They drove in silence for a couple of minutes before Edward hitched sideways on the bench seat to study the driver. He was only five or six years older than his passenger, but his dress and his demeanour suggested the gap should be wider. He kept his eyes fixed on the road. Clearly, he knew he was being observed but if it bothered him it didn't show.

'So what does Carlo want to talk to me about?' said Edward. 'Because I can't say I'm desperate to meet him.'

The driver tutted as he was forced to pull out to pass a black cab that was half in and half out of a parking space. 'I wouldn't address him by his first name if I was you. He'll view it as disrespectful. And, he hasn't told me why he wants to meet you, I'm only the driver. But I don't think you have much choice in the matter. If you don't go to him, he'll come to you. And trust me, you want that like you want an extra hole in your arse.'

'So I've to call him Mister Ferrara? That's a bit old-fashioned isn't it?'

The driver passed a set of traffic lights and pulled in. He yanked on the handbrake and twisted sideways. 'Eddie, I know we've never seen eye to eye, but you need to listen to me. I'm on your side here.'

Tweed guffawed at that. 'My side? Since when have you ever been on my side? I mean, you might be screwing my sister but –'

Edward jerked away as the other man lunged at him across the seat. 'Shut it, you jumped up little fucker. Don't you dare use language like that when you're referring to her.'

'Or what?' The tone was aggressive, and deliberate.

'Or the next time you get yourself in deep shit I won't arrange for you to be lifted and stuck in a cell for your own safety. I'll leave you out there to get your head kicked in.'

Edward's lip curled up in a malevolent sneer. 'Do whatever you like. I can handle myself. I don't need some interfering tosser stepping in for me. Especially a *polis* tosser.'

The driver shook his head. 'Which is precisely what I'm talking about. You say you can handle yourself, but you haven't a bloody clue who or what you're up against. Ferrara doesn't just run restaurants, he's a hard-nosed ruthless bastard if you push him too far. Now, one of his favourite sayings is,

179

"These things have a way of working themselves out". So my guess is he's going to offer you an olive branch, a way out of this mess so everybody can move on. And, Eddie, you need to accept it.'

Edward stayed silent. The driver kept talking. 'I know you don't like me; call me a pig and stuff like that. Well, guess what? I ain't losing any sleep over that. But why don't you try putting other people first for a change?'

'Like who?'

'Like your mother. Do you know that every time you step out the door, she's petrified it'll be the last time she sees you in one piece?' He paused for a second, hoped that had sunk in. 'Now, I hear you've got yourself a wee gang of hangers on. Let me tell you something, Eddie, they're not even second division compared to some of the guys you've upset. And I hope you've already figured out, that when the going gets tough they'll disappear like shit off a shovel. In fact, I happen to know they're already wetting themselves because people are looking for them.

'So, please, Eddie. If you only ever listen to me once, make it now.' He didn't wait for a response, he moved off again. He drove straight ahead onto Leith Walk, passed three or four openings on the left then, opposite the bus depot, he slowed before making a sharp right into a tight street with high tenements looming on both sides.

As they turned, Edward glanced through the passenger window. He caught a brief sight of the illuminated sign hanging over the Italian restaurant's doors, about 30 or 40 yards further up The Walk, while light from the double-fronted windows spilled out across the broad pavement. Puzzled, he confirmed the street sign up to his left. *Springfield Street*.

'The Khyber Pass?' he said. 'Why the hell are we going down here?'

At that time, Leith had two main immigrant communities: Italians and Sikhs. The latter had emigrated from the Punjab in the late 50s and their families settled in various areas of the city. When Springfield Street became home to a small enclave, it was immediately christened "The Khyber Pass" by irreverent

180

Leithers. That was an era when the term politically correct was no more than a gleam in the lexicon's eye.

'Ferrara said I was to drop you at the back door then drive round to the front and wait there. It's probably so you're not spotted going in. Keeps everything private.'

Edward fidgeted in his seat and chewed at his nails as the Zephyr's tyres swished across the wet cobblestones, before turning first left up a lane that ran parallel to Leith Walk. No sooner had the driver straightened up when he hit the brakes, bringing the car to a slithering halt. Directly in front was a delivery van, its rear doors open revealing drums of olive oil, large sacks of pasta and crates of fresh fruit and vegetables. A man in overalls had just finished loading a trolley with cardboard boxes marked *Valpolicella Classico*. He manoeuvred it past the side of the van towards double doors that opened into the restaurant's kitchen.

'I'm not sure about this,' said Edward, all his senses on high alert.

'Don't be daft. It's a Friday night, the place will be mobbed. Nothing's going to happen to you in a restaurant full of diners. Go in, listen to whatever he's got to say then do the full, yes sir, no sir, three bags full sir routine.' Edward nodded, perhaps more to reassure himself, and opened the car door. The driver laid a hand on his arm. 'And remember, it's *Mister* Ferrara.'

Once Edward was squeezing past the van, the Zephyr reversed along the lane into Springfield Street and headed back in the direction of The Walk.

The driver was searching for a parking space in front of the restaurant when realisation struck. Something was wrong. Decidedly wrong. All the lights in Carlo's had been switched off, the sign above the door was in darkness, and the blinds were down.

Without making sure the road behind was clear of traffic, he jammed on the anchors, leapt out, and sprinted across the street. He spotted the handwritten sign stuck on the inside of the glass, long before he was able to read it.

Closed due to family bereavement.

Reopening Saturday.

Chapter 50

Natasha didn't need to check around the room to know there was nothing else she could use to make the box more stable. Briefly, she considered tying the lid on with the sleeves of the hoodie but then realised there was a drawstring in her tennis shorts. It took her a while to untie the damp knot before it pulled free of the waistband, and while she was doing that, it dawned on her the hood also had a drawstring. It was much thicker but once she freed them both, she joined them together with a reef knot. 'Right over left, then left over right.' She grinned. 'Thanks, Grandad.' A few seconds later she dragged her sleeve across her eyes, blinking till her vision cleared. Another train of thought to be hounded out of sight.

So hopefully she had a method of securing the box, but nowhere to work. All she could do was lean into the wall, press her body against the box, and have a stab at tying the lid on. She started with the traditional parcelling technique, round the long sides then the short sides, but even tied together the drawstrings weren't long enough. She resorted to a single loop but either it slid off the plastic or the lid pinged off when she tested it, even by simply pressing the ends of the box together.

Again, she considered the problem. 'There must be something else I can use. Ah-hah! The baseplate.'

This time when she pulled the drawstrings round the box, she held the ends in her left hand. She took the baseplate, threaded the drawstrings through the two outside rivet holes and tied a knot as close as she could to the metal. It was still far too loose, but she wasn't finished yet. She twisted the baseplate round and round in ever-tightening circles. Now the drawstrings were as taut as she could make them. She was about to congratulate herself when the baseplate began to spin in reverse. She stopped it, but as soon as she let it go it continued to unravel.

Undeterred, she untied the knot once more then rethreaded it using two diagonally opposite holes in the baseplate. She repeated the twisting process and this time, she secured the drawstring by running a loop through the other two holes, then round on itself using the only other knot she'd ever mastered, a bowline. 'Chalk another one up for Grandad.' And no tears this time as she remembered the rhyme he'd taught her: "Up through the rabbit hole, round the big tree; down through the rabbit hole and off goes he".

The bowline prevented it unravelling but it was still too loose. When she tested the lid, she didn't believe it would withstand her weight, although it was much more secure than it had been earlier. Now she had the bit between her teeth. 'I'm definitely on the right lines, it just needs fine tuning. A spot of finessing.' So, she dismantled her knot but this time she concentrated on tying the drawstrings as tight as her fingers could manage and making sure she didn't allow it to unravel at all. She kept everything in place, threaded it immediately and retied her bowline knot. She tested the lid again but still wasn't satisfied. She turned again to her survival kit.

'The facecloths.' She opened the box, squeezed water out of one of the cloths, rolled it up and jammed it beneath the drawstring at the edge of the box. She did the same with another cloth at the opposite end. She plucked the drawstring like a guitar. 'Happy with that. Don't think Jimmy Page could do much with it but there you go.' It was time to put it to the test.

As before, she pushed the box down into the water and stood on it. Now the inlet was within reach, but her balance was precarious until she adjusted her stance. Then she was more secure. If or when she needed more height, she could turn the box the other way, but at this point that was far too risky.

She recalled her final trip before eventually realising she'd never be a climber. Clinging to a greasy rock slab, fingers numb with the cold, driving rain bouncing off her helmet, and praying her courage wouldn't fly off with the wind.

Different circumstances entirely. But that was precisely how she was feeling right then.

Chapter 51

The Following Day
Thursday 01:10

Whispering voices bring me back to life. I don't have the luxury of surfacing at my leisure because the horrible events of recent hours barge straight into my brain and shove everything else aside.

The sound techs had been prompt with their report but all it did was confirm the residential location theory. A door slammed, could be in the same house, possibly an adjoining building. Stevenson hasn't given away any clues he's in cahoots with a third party, and that they're in the same house. But nothing's impossible. A faint siren, there's a fire somewhere. And definite sounds from a TV: dramatic music and high-pitched voices. Sadly, we're no further forward.

Immediately after the call, Jeff and I discussed the signs of discomfort Stevenson had displayed, and agreed it was worth contacting his GP. Regrettably, the doctor clearly possesses a first-class honours degree in noncommittal. "Yes, those symptoms might be related, but equally they might not be". Thanks a bunch, doc.

I feel like shit but have no choice; I drag my eyes open. Jeff and Steph are standing, staring over Ella's shoulder at her screen. Tom 2 is beside her. The tension is palpable, and the whispers only enhance it.

I haul myself upright, pick up a drinks bottle and stagger over to join them. I may have just surfaced but I know better than to look at the screen, so I move to the other side and face my colleagues. 'What's up?'

It's Tom 2 who speaks first, although it wasn't much of a race. The others all look at me as if I'm the last person they want to speak to. 'The flow should have reduced …' He checks his wrist. 'Nearly twenty minutes ago. It's still at the higher rate.'

The questions come charging in, but the answers sprint off in the opposite direction.

'Fuck,' I say. 'What about Natasha? How is she? What's she been doing?

'It doesn't seem to have fazed her at all,' says Ella. 'In fact, I reckon it's spurred her on. She's been trying to stand on the plastic box, but it kept collapsing under her weight. She managed to beef it up, tied it together with drawstrings from her clothes and manufactured some locking contraption with one of those baseplates.'

This is incredible. I'm not sure how it's possible to be so proud of someone I've never met. Even the thought brings me close to losing it. I can't fail this young woman. It's that simple. I just can't.

Jeff is standing with his arms folded, plucking at his lower lip with thumb and forefinger. 'What are you thinking, Boss?' I say.

'We've been discussing the feed; it's gone down twice. And both times it coincided with the calls. This afternoon and this evening. About one hour ahead of each call.'

'And?'

'And it can't be coincidence. We can only imagine it's because he does something in relation to Natasha, or to the room. He doesn't want us to see what that is, so he takes the feed down.'

'Maybe he goes into the room.'

'Possibly,' says Jeff. 'But, if he did, you'd think Natasha's behaviour might have changed. But it hasn't. We can see she's still highly motivated to escape, not just sitting on her hands waiting to see what happens.'

'Is there anything different about the room? Something not there that was before. Or the other way round?'

'No,' says Steph. 'We thought about that, and I've been back through the footage. Nothing missing, nothing extra.'

I imagine all five of us saying, "Hmmm" in unison. We don't, but I for one am thinking it.

After a lengthy pause, I say, 'Ella. If the water doesn't go back to normal …' I hesitate to ask the rest of my question but professionalism kicks in just in time. 'At what point will the room fill up?'

She scribbles a quick calculation on a log that's been running and looks up at me. There are tears in her eyes. 'Sometime between 14:00 and 15:00 today.'

I do my own calculation. 'So, a maximum of 14 hours from now.'

Again, I swear. With venom. And repeatedly.

Chapter 52

Thursday 01:20

From her new position standing on the long side of the box, Natasha was able to examine the inlet more closely. 'Looks like the opening's a similar width to the neck of the sports bottle. I wonder if I can jam that over the pipe.' Carefully, she climbed down, picked up the bottle and clambered back up. She wobbled for a second but managed to steady herself.

She unscrewed the cap and held it between her teeth. She knew she was about to lose her drinking water, so she took a healthy slug before pushing the bottle onto the inlet. A second or two later, she yelped when water squirted out the sides and hit her in the face, making her lose her grip on the bottle. It hit her on the shoulder on its way down. Trying to catch it, she almost followed, but slapped both hands on the wall to stop herself.

Keeping her hands flat on the vinyl, she dropped down into the water. When she wiped her hand across her face to clear the spray, she realised the droplets were fresh water, not stale. She thought about that. *It's warm. So does it pass through a hot water tank? Or maybe it's mains water through a boiler, therefore it should be drinkable.* She tipped the contents out, let the flow run over the outside before rinsing it thoroughly. She cupped her hand beneath the flow and took a mouthful. Then she allowed some to run into the bottle and tasted it again. *Warm, not unpalatable, but I'll drink it.* She tapped her knuckle on her temple. *Yet another example of you not thinking clearly, Tash.*

Every time she overcame one of these setbacks, she felt a little better about herself. *What doesn't kill you makes you stronger, as they say.* She had no idea who *they* were but was beginning to recognise the truth in the saying. *Apart from the kill part. I'm not keen on that.*

She made two more attempts to fit the bottle over the inlet but gained nothing apart from another soaking. Plus, holding it above her head and manoeuvring it was exhausting; her arms were nowhere near strong enough. Reluctantly, she dropped back onto the table, let more water flow into the bottle and replaced the cap.

* * *

The broken ceiling light in the adjacent corner was only a few feet away and something about it registered with her. The fitting was like a kitchen downlighter, but instead of being flush, the centre of the fitting appeared to be raised as if a small glass marble was partly embedded in it.

Moving around had become significantly more difficult. Standing on the floor, the water was up to her waist. She hadn't worn the shorts for a while and even with the hoodie rolled up, she was struggling to prevent it from getting wet. She didn't like it, but once more, pragmatism won the day. 'This top's going to have to come off.' Like earlier, she didn't hesitate. She pulled it over her head and stuck it in the box with her shorts.

Then she towed the table nearer to the light. She peered at it for only a few seconds, took half a step back and stuck her hands on her hips. 'Is that a camera?'

She'd assumed all along that The Effer must be watching her but decided that was insignificant compared to everything else she'd had to deal with. She realised that since she'd been incarcerated, most of the time she'd either ignored or forgotten about him watching.

So, is that really a camera or simply a different type of bulb? After all, this isn't exactly a show home, is it? She checked the other two, and it definitely was different. *The marble sphere, is that the lens? Some sort of 360-degree fisheye thing?* It was foreign to her, so she didn't know for sure and actually, she realised she didn't care. At least her family would know she was still alive.

And to demonstrate how little she did care, she glared at the downlighter and gave it the finger.

Chapter 53

Thursday 03:00

Natasha had tried everything to stop the water coming in. She'd reached the end of her tether. Given up.

No matter what position she adopted, the depth of the water had become a major problem. It was deep enough to swim in. Standing on the table it was at her waist and perched on her platform, above her knees. She'd stood the table on its end but as soon as she put any weight on the legs, they'd threatened to break away from their fixings. And without the table, all was lost. Another idea killed off.

She'd begun to lose sensation in her feet, so standing up on the box left her feeling incredibly insecure. That, and she had no strength left in her arms. In combination with everything else, her motivation had been diluted by every litre of water that flowed in.

The only point she thought might turn out to be positive was the two-centimetre plastic pipe hadn't been finished off neatly. A short length was left sticking out. She'd jammed a facecloth in, but the material was too thick. Then an apple core, but it flew out. She'd used her teeth to tear the pocket lining off her shorts, pushed it in but it wouldn't stay put unless she held a hand over the end. Frustratingly, she couldn't maintain the pressure. Not when she was at full stretch and tiring fast.

A glimmer of hope had arisen when she covered the pipe with the cap from the sports bottle but that also resulted in failure. Although the cap was threaded, the pipe was not.

Unlike before, the flow hadn't reduced over time. The level was rising steadily. Her morale had plummeted further, and she had nothing to exercise her mind. Just four walls, the ceiling, and the water level. And her family. As before, when she began to think about what they were doing and how they'd be faring, she had to forcibly shut her mind down.

She may have been struggling mentally but her poor physical state was contributing to her stupor. She was dog-tired. She had no idea how long she'd slept in total, or how much time had passed since she'd waved her friends off at The Shore.

Desperate to sleep, she hauled the broken bucket up onto the table, jammed the box inside to make a rough platform and slumped down on it. She knew it could easily split and cause her serious injury but couldn't summon up the energy to care. The water was halfway up the bucket, but still she crashed out.

Chapter 54

Jeff and I are waiting for the next call. There is no other suitable phrase; we are bricking it.

It's due in quarter of an hour, at 03:35, and the flow is still at the higher rate. I hate to admit it, if only to myself, but Natasha Emerson's survival prognosis is bleak. We're losing time at a rate of knots: down to 23 hours. Another significant milestone – one full day – obliterated.

We still don't have a name, and one isn't going to magically materialise out of thin air. All we have is Hugh's old boss, Fraser Anderson, and he's dead. Jeff and I discussed whether we might temporarily put the blame on Anderson, but it was a hypothetical proposal that bombed before it drew its first breath. The man's wife died not long ago. We know this because we checked. But in checking, we discovered the couple had four daughters. If we told Stevenson that Anderson was responsible, and he broadcasted it to the nation, we'd be well and truly screwed.

We even discussed the possibility of contacting them – yes, at three in the morning – to ask if we could use their father's name until Natasha was safe. But that bombed even faster. Mud sticks, and all that.

So, we wait for Stevenson to send us a link. Jeff will have to play it by ear and deal with whatever shit Stevenson dishes out.

At 03:44, Jeff scrolls through his phone. The link always comes directly to him.

But 03:45 arrives, then departs. No contact.

03:50. Still nothing.

04:00. When eight bells toll, if you're in the Royal Navy.

Jeff is pacing about. 'What the hell's going on? Has he forgotten? Or slept in? Or has something terrible happened to Natasha?'

'Or he's released her, and he hasn't told us yet?' I say, ever hopeful.

Ella calls over. 'Strike that last one, Boss. She's still on live feed.'

'Where's the water level?'

Ella's under strict instructions to ignore questions like that from me and manages it with aplomb. One of these days I'll remind her who's boss around here.

Jeff slumps into a chair. Is practically consumed by several yawns stitched together. 'Or perhaps we're worrying unnecessarily, and he's just late.'

'Whatever it is, we're goosed,' I say. 'We can't contact him. There's nothing we can do.'

'Any chance he might have spoken to Hugo directly? Bypassed us?'

'Eh? Why on earth would he do that?'

'I could counter that by asking why on earth would he kidnap Hugo's granddaughter and threaten to drown her?'

Accepted, he's my boss, but I glower at him anyway. 'It's just gone twenty past four. I'll ring Hugo.'

But Hugo doesn't answer. I keep trying and after ten minutes, I give up. 'I'm going over there to kick his door down.'

Instead, I give it one more crack. I'm on the point of cancelling the call when he picks up. His voice is clear. 'I thought you'd call. I'll come to you, the family's asleep.'

That catches me out. 'You don't need to do that, Hugo, I was just phoning to—'

'I *said*, I'll come to you. I'll be there in ten.' And the line cuts off.

I look at my phone, then at Jeff. 'Something wrong?' he says.

'It most certainly is. And before you ask, I have no idea. But I dare say we'll find out in ten.'

* * *

I'm waiting for Hugo at the front desk when the doors slam open. As he walks towards me, he blows his nose. His eyes are bloodshot. Could be exhaustion, but somehow I don't think it is.

We climb one flight to Jeff's office.' Hugo marches straight in, and slumps down in a chair without being asked. He doesn't take his coat off and the collar bunches up around his ears.

My boss's tie is ever so slightly askew. Barring the odd nap, we've both been awake all night, but he was definitely the last to fall by the tiredness wayside. Me? I'm shattered beyond the point of reason.

Then Jeff says, 'Clearly something's wrong, Hugo. So why don't you tell us.'

It's obvious the man's struggling to find the right words, so we wait. After a couple of false starts, he says, 'I've done something really stupid. And I don't know if I'll ever be able to forgive myself.'

Jeff and I lock eyes. Definitely unexpected.

My boss straightens his tie. 'Well, I guess you'd better spit it out.'

Chapter 55

The Previous Night
Wednesday 22:30

It was half an hour to closing time when the man walked up to Hugo, who was loitering at the corner of the bar. He hadn't been there longer than a few seconds.

'Mister Emerson,' said Kenny, grinning. 'Ha! Don't need to call you Detective Inspector now, do I? Just plain old *Mister* Emerson.' He leans forward, invading Hugo's space. 'Well, I'm here, now what do you want? Because clearly you do want something, otherwise why would you be here, talking to a lowlife like me, in a shithole like this?'

The barman raised an eyebrow but didn't take his attention off the pint of Guinness he was pouring. 'Now, Kenny. Be nice. You don't want me to bar you again, do you?'

Kenny snorted. 'I should be so lucky. So, buying me a drink, Hugo? Lovely, isn't it? First name terms after all these years.'

Hugo signalled the barman. 'A diet Coke, please, and whatever he's having.'

Kenny rested his hands flat on the bar top and scanned the gallery. 'Oh, a large Lagavulin, I think.' He looked Hugo up and down. 'Diet bloody Coke?' He motioned to the barman. 'Hate drinking on my own. Give him one too.' The two men took a couple of sips each. 'Whatever you've got to say, spit it out, Hugo. I'm a busy man.'

Hugo wondered how Kenny could be busy at half ten at night but would never have dreamt of asking. So he started talking. Kenny listened. And so did the barman. But that was okay, he was Kenny's eyes and ears.

When Hugo had finished, Kenny ordered two more large single malts from the Isle of Islay, but his hand didn't stray anywhere near his pocket. He asked Hugo two questions and once he had the answers, said, 'Hope your piggy bank's got plenty in it because this is going to cost you.' Then he told Hugo how much, and that it was a cash-only deal.

Hugo didn't react. There wasn't any point. Kenny wasn't the bartering type. Kenny lifted a beermat. 'Write your number on there, and I'll be in touch.' He drained his glass, slipped off the barstool and wandered across the sticky carpet to the toilet. Hugo was about to follow, but the barman shot him a look, so he stayed where he was. He settled the bill but took his time finishing his whisky. He was tempted to have one for the road, but he knew damn fine he'd never stop at one. He didn't notice Kenny leaving, but when he eventually headed for the loo the barman paid him no attention.

He walked off home. He hadn't brought the car; there wasn't a chance he'd have stuck to diet Coke. He'd been shitting himself the whole time he'd been in there and whisky was the only answer.

Now all he could do was wait.

Chapter 56

The Following Day
Thursday 00:05

'Threaten me all you like,' said Isobel Stevenson from her bed in her living room. 'I'm on the way out. So life's pretty shit at the moment, and whether I shuffle tonight or in a few months' time, matters not a fuckin' jot to me. So, go on, knock me around, see where that gets you.'

The man she'd been mouthing off at was called Magowan. No one knew his first name, and few had dared to ask. Kenny had risked it once, but the younger man had simply repeated, "Magowan". His expression made it clear the matter was closed.

Magowan made a sad face. 'You might think you're being brave, you foul-mouthed old crone, but you're actually pretty stupid.'

'Your opinion, son. And you're entitled to it.' She folded her spindly arms and stared at the wall.

He sighed at that. 'I rarely use violence against octogenarians, Mrs Stevenson. But that's not a hard and fast rule. So, I'll ask you one more time, where is your son hiding? I need to talk to him. And I need to talk to him. Tonight.'

'Magowan,' said the hulking thug standing to his left. Known as Spud, his features resembled a miniature Stonehenge that had been deposited in the centre of his pudgy face. 'It's actually just past twelve, so technically it's already morning.'

'Don't be a smartarse, Spud,' said Magowan. 'It doesn't suit you. Well, the smart bit doesn't but the arse does.' They both laughed at that. Then, abruptly, Magowan fell silent, dropped the grin, and eyeballed Isobel. 'Now, here's the thing, Mrs Stevenson, Spud's another one who can be stupid. But I didn't bring him along with me tonight for his intellect. No, Spud is here partly because he possesses the moral compass of a starving crocodile.'

Isobel glared at him. 'Partly?'

'Aye, partly. The main reason he's here is, since he was about fourteen, he's earned himself a reputation. A reputation that means there is not one single woman in Leith, nor anywhere else he's been for that matter, who's had sex with Spud and would even dream of repeating that particular mistake. And that includes the trashiest wee junkie slag down at the docks. And the reason is, Spud has certain … tastes.' He stretched up and clapped a hand on the younger man's shoulder. 'Isn't that right, Spud?'

'Definitely, Magowan. Bang on.' If Spud had been strolling down The Kirkgate in his Sunday best at that moment, heads would have swivelled to admire his swagger.

Magowan turned back to Isobel. 'Actually, Mrs S, please allow me to be more specific. Spud has sex with women. He doesn't make love to them. He doesn't sleep with them. There is zero affection involved. Those concepts don't enter his tiny mind when Spud is, how can I put it, in the zone.' He paused. 'Get my drift, Isobel?'

The old woman made a vain attempt to swallow. She couldn't have spoken if her life had depended upon it. Now she'd been introduced, she realised she'd heard all about Spud, and his notorious reputation.

Magowan moved to the door, pulled it open, shouted. 'Bring her through.'

A third man dragged Florence into the room. When she began shouting and bawling at them, Magowan took a step towards her. The sharp crack of his open palm, closely followed by Florence collapsing like she'd been shot, silenced the room. Then, as if nothing had happened, he pirouetted and waved his arm around theatrically. 'Cables Wynd House, Spud, but christened "the Banana Flats" by irreverent Leithers. Of the Brutalist architectural style, I'm told. Completed in 1965 and conferred with "A" listed status by Historic Environment Scotland in 2017. Concrete, therefore practically soundproof. I expect you'll remember this, Mrs Stevenson, the first families who moved in here, in early '66, were mainly decent law-abiding citizens who were only too delighted to escape the slums they were brought up in. I expect they polished their brasses, cleaned the stairs, kept the place neat and tidy. Behaved themselves. But times changed in this lovely carbuncle of a building, didn't they, Spud?'

Spud preened again. 'Aye, that's right. Round about the time *Trainspotting* came out. Ewan McGregor and his pals ran this place.' A puzzled look crossed his face. 'Magowan, did the punters have to move out during the filming?'

His boss held up one finger. 'Actually, my boy, that is a popular misconception. Although *Trainspotting* was meant to depict life in 1980s Edinburgh, most of the locations were in Glasgow. Or at least the Scottish ones were.'

His sidekick appeared momentarily put out at that but moved on quickly to the point of his story. 'Anyway, I'm called after one of them. Spud. He was a total radge. And there was Sick Boy, and Tommy. And that wee bird, the one that turned out to be a school-lassie. What was her name? Cos she was a wee shag. Still is, mind.' He jammed his hand down the front of his trackie bottoms while he lusted over Kelly Macdonald, or the teenaged character she'd portrayed at any rate. 'And there was that bampot Begbie, he was a mad —'

'Now, now, Spud. Language. There's ladies present.' Magowan adopted an exaggerated contemplative pose; index finger touching his chin, eyes up to the nicotine-stained ceiling. 'Where was I going with that? Oh, yes – times have changed. Most of those decent law-abiding citizens are long gone. Instead, not all I hasten to add, but most of your fellow residents are crackheads, hookers, nasty bastards. In fact, my old man told me that a few years ago, a bunch of office workers had to be locked inside their building over the road because some arsehole in here was taking pot shots at people walking up and down the street with a .22 rifle. So that gives you an idea about the calibre – no pun intended – of the citizens who occupy this place. But I'm sure you know that damn fine. Now, despite the lateness of the hour, I called in to have a chat with the reprobate who lives next door to explain that if he heard anything, let's say, untoward, he should simply turn the telly up. Assuming he hasn't sold it to feed his habit, that is.'

Magowan gazed down at Florence. Then at Isobel. Smiled. Instantly, his hand shot out, grabbed Florence's nightgown at the throat and ripped it down the middle. Buttons pinged off in all directions. 'Spud. Haul old Mrs Terminal Cancer off her bed and stick her in that chair. Give her a grandstand view of you having fun with her daughter.'

'Don't you fuckin' touch her, you ugly bastard,' screamed Isobel.

Magowan waited till Spud had dumped the hysterical old woman in the armchair before leaning right into her face. 'A word to the wise. Once my colleague gets into the groove, nobody, not even me, will be able to stop him.'

He paused. 'So, Isobel. Last chance.'

196

Chapter 57

Magowan's call was answered on the first ring. 'Kenny. I've got an address for your man, Stevenson.' He read it out. 'We're on our way there now.'

* * *

Hugo stabbed at his screen before the ringtone sounded. 'Hi—'

'Don't use names,' said Kenny. 'We've got him. Meet me on the corner of Crewe Terrace and Pilton Place.'

'But I've been drinking—'

'I don't give a fart. Just get there.'

'Okay. What's the address?'

'No address. Not yet.'

* * *

It was nearly one in the morning when Hugo pulled up. Kenny climbed out of his car and signalled him over. They walked for a few minutes, cutting through a series of lanes, across a couple of streets and through a ramshackle gate into an overgrown back garden. A rough line of broken flagstones led directly to the rear of the house. Kenny checked for security but there wasn't even an outside light. Off to the left, a moped leaned against the wall, below a window. The door was ajar, the inside in darkness. Kenny walked straight in, let Hugo pass him and clicked the door shut. He led Hugo through the kitchen and into a tiny hall. A one-foot-square frosted glass pane in the front door allowed just enough light to see where they were going.

'Up here,' said Magowan, shining his mobile phone to direct them to the first-floor landing. 'And mind your feet when you get to the top.'

Kenny was still a few steps shy of the landing when the soles of a pair of bare feet appeared at his eye level. He stopped and Hugo's chest bumped into his backside. Hugo was about to ask Kenny what he was playing at when he too noticed the feet. Then the red tartan pyjama bottoms. Followed by the body of Marlon Stevenson. Flat on his back. Arms akimbo. Face like old dough. Glassy eyes staring. At nothing.

And not a mark on him.

Kenny didn't shout. In fact, his demeanour was more like an indulgent father who'd discovered his kids elbow deep in the cookie jar. Or biscuit tin; they were in Leith after all. 'Care to explain, Magowan?'

Magowan folded his arms and gazed down at the body. 'It's the most bizarre thing, Kenny. We'd come in the back door, uninvited you might say, and were nearly at the top of the stairs when the boy in the tartan breeks came at us with that.' He indicated a claw hammer that dangled from Spud's fingers. 'Not exactly armed to the teeth, but still. Anyway, I suggested to Spud that it would be beneficial to all concerned if he took it off him. So Spud performed the old mock charge act and roared straight into the guy's face. To discombobulate him, you know?'

Kenny knew exactly what Magowan was talking about. Animals, soldiers, streetfighters, cops on a dawn raid; they all employ similar tactics. Make lots of noise to throw the assailant, or victim, out of kilter. 'But,' said Magowan, 'and this is gospel. The boy froze, Spud relieved him of the hardware, and he went down like a sack of tatties. Nobody touched him.'

Kenny turned to Spud. He knew the man was as thick as four posts tied together and if Magowan was lying, his sidekick's face would give the game away. 'Spud?'

But Spud looked him straight in the eye. 'Totally weird, Kenny. Never seen anything like it in my puff.'

Kenny didn't ask stupid questions that included the word "ambulance". He knelt down and lifted Marlon's wrist. Pressed it with two fingers for a few seconds then dropped it and did the same on the side of Marlon's throat. He turned to Hugo, shook his head.

Hugo let out a wail. 'Oh, Jesus. What am I going to do now?'

Kenny rose to his feet and eyeballed the older man. 'You, Hugo, are going to do nothing. You go home, mention this to nobody, not even your missus, and forget what you've seen tonight.' He pointed at Stevenson. 'We'll deal with him.' Then he walked right into Hugo's space. 'Oh, and Hugo …'

'What?'

'You don't go near the cops. You keep schtum. Got it?' He waited for an answer, but Hugo just stared at him.

'But Kenny. My granddaughter. He kidnapped her. And no one else knows where she is.'

'I know that. I'm not stupid.'

'So I have to find her. You've got to help me.'

'Do I?' said Kenny.

Chapter 58

Kenny followed Hugo to the kitchen door, pulled him back by his sleeve. 'A word, Hugo. Forget everything that's happened but don't forget this. A minute ago I was mildly tempted to tell Spud to smack you with that hammer, so take this as a clear warning. Keep your mouth shut!'

Upstairs, Magowan was waiting. 'I checked again to make sure nobody was hiding. But come through here a minute.' He led Kenny into a small bedroom. A single bed had been stood on its end behind the door. Stacked into a corner next to it was a chest of drawers, a bedside cabinet and a lamp. A high-backed dining chair stood sentry in the middle of the floor, behind it was a blank wall; a laptop with its lid open sat on a card table. A reading lamp like you would find behind your favourite armchair was angled down at the table. An array of pictures and photos were leaning against the skirting board, clearly they'd been taken down off the wall. Scrapes, pinholes and dust lines were testament to that. Across the floor ran an extension lead with a four-gang socket; a charging cable ran from it to the laptop along with an unoccupied cable that was possibly for a phone. 'It's like a wee recording studio,' said Magowan.

Kenny nodded. From what Hugo had told him he could guess the purpose of the setup but saw no need to enlighten the younger man. He shrugged. 'Who knows?' He jerked his thumb in the direction of the landing. 'You definitely didn't touch him?'

'I've told you once, Kenny. And you know I don't like repeating myself.'

The other man accepted the rebuke but didn't bother acknowledging it. They understood and respected each other, and neither would give an inch. Having said that, Kenny would never dream of crossing Magowan, who could go from crack-a-joke to Krakatoa in the blink of an eye, so Kenny remained the epitome of calm. 'Likely to be prints anywhere?'

Magowan held up both hands. 'Spud's got gloves on too.'

'Did you have to break in.'

'No need. The lock's rubbish.'

Kenny glanced down at Magowan's shoes. Expensive trainers. He thought for a few seconds. 'Stevenson's probably had a heart attack or a stroke, so when they find him they'll assume natural causes. Leave everything as it is, lock the door behind you, and dump the hammer. It's dry outside but we should all get rid of our shoes. Stay in your car and watch the house until the kids are away to school, then shoot off home. Meet me in the pub tonight, on your own, and we'll settle up. Alright?'

'Alright.'

* * *

Hugo crept into his house, hoping not to waken the family but he'd no sooner put the kettle on when his wife appeared in the kitchen doorway. She asked him where he'd been and if there was any news. He trotted out his rehearsed lie. 'I got a call from the station, but it was a false alarm.'

Outside, the security light above their patio doors clicked on. He peered through the venetian blind at their next door neighbour's tabby cat perched on the garden wall. The cat lifted a paw and began licking it. Hugo let the slat ping back into place. 'There's no chance I'll sleep now so I'm staying up. Do you want a coffee?'

His wife stepped forward and tapped him on the chest. 'How many coffees have you had in the last twenty-four hours?'

He shrugged. 'Two or three. Four at the most.'

She hit him with a sad expression. 'Fibber.' Then, she moved closer. 'Whisky, Hugo? And driving?' He blushed as she turned away. 'I guess when you're good and ready you'll tell me where you really were.'

Hugo didn't respond to that. There really wasn't any point.

Chapter 59

No one would ever describe me as a woman of few words, but right at this moment, I can't conjure up any that are remotely suitable. After what Hugo's just told us, in relation to the search for his granddaughter, we might as well all go home to bed.

Like me, Jeff is stunned. Not only into silence but immobility too. When I turn to gawp at my boss, it's the first move either of us has made since Hugo stopped speaking, which feels like about a month ago.

It's our visitor who shatters the atmosphere. 'You could say something.'

I'm trying to figure out what I can possibly say that isn't entirely comprised of profanities, but I don't have to. Metaphorically speaking, Jeff flings open the window and kicks propriety's arse out into the street. 'You're an ex-copper, Hugo. You know how these things work. What on God's green earth possessed you to do something so … so bloody idiotic, you stupid pig-headed old —' He leans forward over his desk. 'You haven't just, and I quote, "done something really stupid". You have fucked up. Royally.'

Hugo's eyes are boring into his thighs, the tears follow suit. He tries to speak, fails, then pulls his arms into a tight hug. It appears as though he's about to fold in on himself.

Jeff's back on an even keel. 'The house where you found Stevenson. You said you left there at ten past one.'

The old man nods, he knows where this is going.

'So what the hell have you been doing for, what is it, almost four hours since you discovered he was dead?' I do wonder if Jeff had been going to point out that with Stevenson gone, no one knows where Natasha is being held.

'I couldn't get my head round it,' said Hugo. 'I panicked. Didn't know what to do for the best. I needed time …'

Neither of us mentions that as far as time is concerned, he's wasted a good chunk of it. I don't have to calculate; we only have ten hours left.

I can't take much more of this. Sitting, and waiting, and worrying. I stand up, walk over to the wall facing Hugo, lean on it. I want to yell. I want to scream. I want to march across the floor and slap him about the head till my hand stings. But instead I say, in the calmest voice I can muster, 'I'm going to ask you questions, Hugo, and for most of them, the best possible answer will either be yes or no.'

He gazes at me, drags the back of his hand across his eyes, and nods. Because he knows everything has changed for him. He's admitted to being aware of a deceased person, whose cause of death is as yet undetermined. However, major problem alert: we don't know if Hugo was the cause. After all, he certainly had the motive, and he was in the house, so he had the opportunity too. And finally, as far as the search for Natasha is concerned, he's forfeited any right to be kept informed of our progress.

Progress? He could have killed the chances of that stone dead.

Time for my first question. 'Are you sure it was Marlon Stevenson?'

'Yes.'

'And he was definitely dead?'

'Yes.'

'The house. Do you know the address?'

'No.'

'But you could take us there?'

'Yes.'

'Will you give us the name of the man who managed to find Stevenson?'

A shake of the head this time. No words.

'Or how you happen to know him?'

Another shake. Not unexpected.

'Is that because you're scared of him?' I say.

'Yes.'

'Who else was in the house apart from this man?'

A hesitation. 'No one.'

'Like to try again, Hugo?'

'No one.' With more confidence, but he's still lying.

'Do you know how they found Stevenson?'

'No.'

I lock on eye contact. 'I asked you how *they* found him, Hugo. That's plural.'

He flushes but stays silent.

I move on. 'Did they threaten Stevenson's family?'

'I'm not answering that.'

I'll ask Isobel about it later. I doubt she'll give up a name either, but it's hardly important right now. I don't know what I'll be charging Hugo with but if we don't find Natasha in time, the poor man will rot in a hell of his own making.

'Jeff,' I say. 'I'm going to speak to the team. Catch me up?'

'Two minutes, and I'll be right with you.

Chapter 60

'That was Steph on the phone,' I say. 'They didn't find any keys.'

Andrew and Tom 2 are back with us, while Tobias and Crissi are en-route. Hugo had led Steph, Dave, and a couple of PCs to a house where they'd broken in and found Stevenson's body, as Hugo had described. I explain to the others that, based on stills from the video, Steph had more or less confirmed it was him, but we still need formal identification. She's called an ambulance, a doctor, Greg Brodie our Crime Scene manager, and our friendly Polish pathologist, Dr Klaudia Grześkiewicz.

Steph had been under strict instruction that as soon as Greg gave the go ahead, they were to ransack the place for keys that might belong to another property – one that might be holding Natasha. They did find some, of course; what house doesn't possess a collection of orphan keys? And although the keys we're looking for might be in amongst them, Steph couldn't find any that were marked in any way. They'll keep searching but we might already have yet another dead end. More interestingly, she found keys on a VW fob but, unsurprisingly, the fob didn't have a vehicle registration number. One of the PCs drove round the surrounding streets, blipping the key all over the shop, but struck out.

Hugo has been brought back here. His clothes and shoes were taken earlier and he's waiting to be examined forensically because he's admitted being at a crime scene. But I've not cautioned or charged him.

The doctor confirmed that Stevenson's death was almost certainly down to natural causes, and Klaudia believes it's likely he died an hour or so either side of midnight. By nature, pathologists are cautious creatures, and Klaudia's at the "Z" end of the scale, so I'm not in the least surprised she won't commit herself until she's carried out an autopsy.

Greg and his team ran the crime scene and found no signs of forced entry. They did suggest the kitchen door might have been tampered with, but added the caveat that the lock was so old and worn it would struggle to resist a kid poking at it with a lollipop stick. He said he'd find it difficult to argue that any marks on the internal mechanism weren't simply fair wear and tear.

As a forensic scene, Greg admitted it was far from the easiest he'd worked. To use his word, the house was "manky". The owner either didn't own a vacuum cleaner or the thing was bust, a spring clean was about a decade overdue, and the kitchen flooring and the carpets in the hall, stairs and landing were a few stages past threadbare. Finally, there was dog hair on every surface, most probably from one or more Golden Retrievers. Without a sample from intruders, it's impossible to conclude that someone other than Hugo had been present.

Steph sent us images from what was clearly a spare bedroom that had been temporarily dismantled. Andrew compared them with the video and confirmed Stevenson had made his calls from there. Steph also discovered a laptop that was password protected; she'll hand it over to Bob.

Unopened mail on the kitchen table established the owner's name. She's not present on any of our systems and at this stage we don't know the relationship between her and Stevenson. I'll ask Isobel.

Steph then made herself exceedingly unpopular by knocking on the neighbours' doors at what was a fairly ungodly hour but, shock-horror, no one had heard anything during the night. And although the area is far from the worst we encounter, domestic CCTV is conspicuous by its absence.

The question is, do I believe Hugo's tale where, against all his training and experience, he'd hired a hard man to put the frighteners on old Mrs Stevenson and her family, and that Marlon dropped down dead with fright? It does sound stupidly plausible. The autopsy should prove it one way or the other, but unfortunately Hugo refuses point-blank to disclose who this third party was. Considering the bigger picture, if Stevenson did die of natural causes it will matter not a jot, but I'll have to hand Hugo off to another CID team while we continue to search for his granddaughter.

Greg has a second team of Scene Examiners at Stevenson's own house and he'll correlate results between the two and report back more formally later. Our deceased kidnapper's been meticulous in his preparations thus far, so I doubt his house or car will turn up anything new.

But I live in hope.

Chapter 61

Thursday 06:00

Drifting fitfully in and out of sleep, Natasha was beginning to succumb. As the water level continued to creep up her body, it seemed to constrict her. Discomfort had translated into pain. She'd descended into a morose state of mind, her morale at an all-time low.

As another fit of despair bubbled up she called up her mantra. *Be calm, Natasha. There are worse things …*

But then, she thought, *Are there? No, there bloody aren't. Nothing in the world could possibly be worse than this.* This *is the absolute pits, and I—*

She stopped. Brooded. Swore she would not cry. Not this time. She hauled herself, one more time, to her feet.

'Right, Tash. You can't sit here and do nothing. You can't give up. Not yet. There must be a solution, there just must be.'

She raised her eyes to the inlet and immediately became light-headed and nearly lost her balance. Once she recovered, her mind raced into overdrive. *What if I become ill? Or collapse*? She braced herself against the walls as if these events were inevitable. And imminent. Words flew in and out of her brain at lightning speed.

Water. Health. Pollution. Toxic. Illness. Death. Chicago.

It was as if she'd been hit by a jolt of electricity. Several muscles jumped, like she experienced sometimes at that about-to-fall-asleep moment.

'Chicago.' She grinned. 'That's the answer.' She tried it on again for size. 'Chicago!'

Her mind flew back to first year. She'd attended an evening talk that was supplementary to her course. The subject was engineering miracles. It featured an amazing story about Chicago in the nineteenth century. She recalled the facts, tossed them around in her head, made some adjustments. 'You know, it might just work!'

She felt like cheering. For the first time in she didn't know how long, she was positive, back in control. 'That's it. That's how I can stop the water coming in. As long as I haven't drowned before I manage it.'

She half-swam, half-waded around the room to gather the items she needed. The sports bottle, the other half of the snapped bucket handle, and a facecloth. Then she stood on the table and turned the box on its short end to give her as high a platform as possible. It was risky, her balance wasn't perfect, but she had absolutely no choice.

On the table, with the water up to her waist, she set to work.

Chapter 62

Magowan would later tell Kenny that he wasn't particularly surprised when, getting on for six that morning, a police vehicle and a blindingly obvious unmarked car screeched to a halt outside the house. 'Yer man was always going to cave,' he'd said.

Kenny made a *Don't care* face but there was no doubt he did, and he'd be sending Magowan to pass a blunt and unambiguous message to the Emerson family before the day was out.

Magowan had been parked about 60 or 70 metres up the road, with a direct line of sight to the front door. When the police trotted up the side of the house he slid down in his seat and reached for the ignition key, but his hand remained poised in midair while an ambulance and three other cars arrived in quick succession. They'd managed to completely block the street, so he decided to wait. See how events panned out.

A bloke wearing a high-vis jacket, carrying a toolbox and a long yellow spirit level appeared from a house opposite. He stopped on the pavement to watch what was going on then jumped into his car, performed a tight three-point turn and drove off. In the following ten minutes, two of the man's neighbours performed similar manoeuvres. Not long after that, Magowan told Spud to lie down below the window line before he too made a three-point turn. As he indicated left at the top of the street and hit the accelerator, he said, 'Okay. The coast is clear. Time for a well-earned kip.'

Spud was glad to hear it, but sleep would have to wait until he worked out how much he could score from the refurbished Samsung Galaxy he'd filched from the dead guy, while Kenny and Magowan had been in that wee bedroom.

By pub opening time he'd checked for data he could sell on but found none. He had spotted the flow control app on the home screen, but he hadn't a clue what it was, so he went ahead, and factory reset the device. He sold the phone within half an hour for the equivalent of a couple of pints.

But he could never have known that, if he hadn't taken the Samsung, by six o'clock that morning Steph would have found it. And she could have stopped the flow of water into Natasha's prison.

Chapter 63
Thursday 07:00

'Dammit!'

For the umpteenth time, the water had forced the cap from Natasha's sports bottle off the end of the pipe. However, the Leith motto is "Persevere", drummed into every schoolkid as "Try, Try, Try Again". She was proud of it, always had been, so that's what she'd been doing. Persevering.

Every time an idea didn't work, she modified it. A couple of times she thought she'd succeeded, but after short spells on the pipe, the cap pinged off. As before, constantly working above her head was exhausting and debilitating. It was all she could do to lift her arms.

With each attempt, she'd become adept at anticipating when it was about to fly off and was ready to catch it. But eventually it caught her unawares. With the last modification, it had stayed on for so long she thought she'd cracked it, but the pressure built up and the cap hit her on the cheek. Attempting to react, her foot slipped off the box, across the surface of the table, and off the edge, cracking her shin on the way down. Arms windmilling, her world froze for the briefest instant before she plunged backwards into the water. She was completely submerged, but kicked herself to the surface, shook her head to clear her eyes and, as if it would make a difference, stood upright on the table as quickly as she could. Horror-struck, she spotted the box lid sliding below the surface and further down, the empty box. The hoodie and shorts billowed nearby. Her last chance of staying dry had gone.

'Shit. Shit. Shit!' She stared down at the sinking garments then burst into tears and screamed till her throat burned hot. She had no energy to recover the box and simply leant into the corner and stayed there. She didn't care that the water was at shoulder level.

But what Natasha couldn't possibly have noticed was her fall had generated a wave that hit the wall, splashed up onto the ceiling and washed over the light fitting that did indeed contain a camera.

Chapter 64

Steph's still tied up, so I take Ella with me to visit the Stevensons for the third time. Despite my opinion of her, I feel dreadful informing Isobel of her son's death and do my level best to soften the blow by explaining it was likely the result of natural causes.

She and her daughter exchange glances, but when I ask if that registered with them, true to form, Isobel barks at me. 'Mind your own effin' business.'

I don't respond to that, but I do explain I will need someone to identify it's Marlon.

Florence immediately says she'll do it but Isobel snaps at her. 'I'm not an invalid, so phone me a taxi. I want to see my son.'

Florence lifts her mobile. 'I should ring Denise —'

Isobel slaps her hand on the bed. It only makes a whumph, but she gets her point across. 'You'll do no such bloody thing.' Florence's eyes spark open but, surprisingly, her mother softens her tone. 'I'll phone Denise. Once we know for sure.'

'Isobel,' I say. 'I can arrange a car for you.'

She hits me with yet another glare, it's a wonder there's any skin left on my face. 'I want nothing from you. You hear me? Nothing.' She's struggling to get down off her bed and Florence pushes past me, supports her mother till she's steady on her feet.

Ella steps back to let her pass then bends down and picks something up off the carpet. No, not one thing, two. She holds out her hand to show me. Two small white buttons, from a blouse or a shirt. One has a tiny piece of material attached.

Now that Florence has changed positions, I spot the bruise on her cheek and take the opportunity while it's there. 'Did someone come here last night? Put pressure on you to find out where your brother was?'

Florence won't meet my eye. Ella and I both know the real answer is *Yes, they did, but I'm not talking. Not now, not ever.*

So I try another tack. I tell her the address where Marlon was found. 'Florence, do you know whose house it is?'

Isobel answers me instead. 'That's my niece's place although I couldn't tell you the last time I saw her except for weddings and funerals. I do know she travels with her dogs a lot. Shows them, I think.' She fixes me with another look but there's no energy in this one. 'I'm being honest with you here; I didn't know Marlon was in touch with her. Or that he was at her house.'

As we're leaving, I murmur to Ella, 'Funny, isn't it? Whenever someone says they're being honest with me, I know they're lying to their back teeth.'

'Too right,' she says. 'But at least she didn't swear on her life.'

She earns herself a sharp dig in the ribs for that one.

Chapter 65

I've only been back in the incident room a few minutes when Tobias says, 'Theresa Green is on the line.' It's obvious my colleague didn't shave while he was home last night; by my reckoning he'll be sporting a full beard before the day's out.

'Typical,' says Theresa. 'I couldn't remember what we called that guy until I stopped thinking about it and of course it jumped straight into my mind as soon as I woke up this morning. As you would expect, people only used it behind his back, but his nickname was "Tetley".'

I get it. Tetley. As in tea. As in leaf. Tea leaf. Rhyming slang for thief.

'But I'm really sorry,' she says, 'I can't remember his real name and, being upfront with you, I'm not going to. It's just not there.'

I end the call. Stare at my desk, phone in hand. I'm tempted to swear but I desist. What's the point? Is discovering this man's name still important, especially now that Marlon Stevenson is dead? But it's yet another lead that's fizzled out. Another avenue closed down. Another piece of the jigsaw I have failed to slot into place.

A couple of my team have been listening in. They're waiting for me to tell them what Theresa said. But I don't trust my voice. I turn away, fuss around trying to find a tissue in my bag. Pretend to blow my nose.

I don't imagine I'm fooling anyone.

* * *

A glam redhead, who I know is the wrong side of sixty but looks and behaves like fifty is years in the future, sashays in and makes a beeline directly for Andrew. Despite the circumstances. this brings a smile to the face of everyone else here, apart from the aforementioned bold hero. His demeanour suggests he's been waiting for the hangman, who's turned up for work ten minutes early.

'Andrew. Luvvie,' Bob coos, stretching out an arm and fluttering her fingers like Cathy running up that hill. 'It has reached my ears that you are suffering from a tender derrière. Is there anything I can do to help? No? Oh well, never mind.' Then she veers sharp left and heads for my desk. Stopping halfway, she turns. 'Oh, and just to say, you can pop round and light my bulbs any time you like.' She hits me with a wink that would flap a curtain.

She plonks herself down in front of my desk. 'Darling Melissa. The laptop. The one that little Steph brought to me. I have news.'

I blink. 'Have you broken into it already? I'd assumed it would have a high level of protection.'

Bob waves a hand in the air. 'Pah! I've seen tighter security in a nurses' accommodation block.' She affects a glum countenance. 'And that, my dear, is the extent of the good news.' She drops the high drama act and switches into reporting speak. 'Sorry, but there were no emails or other messages stored anywhere. The links were untraceable, and the hard drive offered up nothing apart from the video file.'

'Bugger. But to be fair, I didn't expect anything else.' I snap my fingers. 'Did you solve the mystery of why we couldn't pause or stop the video.'

She sits back. 'Would you like the grown-up's explanation or the dummies' guide, as per usual?'

I make a face. She knows perfectly well where to pitch it.

'You've heard of Denial of Service attacks that can bring an organisation's network down. Well, this is a primitive version called Parallel Data Swamp Streaming or PDSS. When you pressed *Play*, a second file streamed in parallel for the duration of the video. This second file, the swamp file, broadcasted masses of data in a constant stream, so dense it occupied all the spare memory capacity on the device that was playing it, meaning you couldn't break in. If you'd known what to do you could have disabled it through *Task Manager*, but it's so off the wall probably only an IT specialist, like yours truly, would have considered checking there.'

I nod. Let that float around for a while. 'But how did he manage to view us through the laptop's camera?'

'Ah. Fairly standard hacking procedure he probably found on the good old interweb. He embedded a script in the video file that activated as soon as you pressed *Play*. It gave him access to your camera and microphone.'

I scowl at her. 'You're all the same you IT bods, sneaky buggers.'

She laughs as she stands up. 'Lucky I'm on your side then, isn't it?'

I'm bidding her goodbye when Ella strides across the room. I don't need to ask. Her expression tells me something terrible has happened. 'Boss. The feed's dropped out. But this time we know why.'

* * *

I stand behind Andrew while he cues up the feed to a point just before it had cut off. This time I must watch it; wild horses couldn't stop me. I have a death grip on his chair, and I don't intend letting go anytime soon. Bob's by my side, her hand making soothing motions in the small of my back.

The view of Natasha is highly distorted because she's so close to the camera. But it's still obvious how close the water is to the ceiling. She's standing on everything she has at her disposal and the level is at her waist.

'Was she still trying to stop the water?' I say.

'Yes,' says Andrew. 'She's tried all sorts of things to cap it. Nothing's worked.'

'And it's been at the higher flow rate all night,' says Ella. 'So everything's been much tougher for her.'

'Andrew,' I say. 'Have you calculated how long she has left before …'

'Yes.'

'Tell me.'

So he does. And, between Ella and Bob, they get me into a chair before I collapse.

Chapter 66

I pull everybody together in the incident room. 'I don't like to use the word "hopeless", but Marlon Stevenson's death is a gamechanger. We have fewer than seven hours left to find Natasha, meaning the situation is desperate and we have to shortcut everything. We need inspired thinking to figure out where she's imprisoned because, no question, we're up against it. So, a short timeout is in order to reassess everything we've got so far.'

* * *

I scan the exhausted faces round the table and summon my gee-up-the-troops voice. 'Right, where are we?'

'Jeez, Boss,' says Ella. 'For a second there, I thought you were going to clap.'

Shows you how knackered we all are, that hardly raises a titter.

We'd placed police notices on Commercial Street. "Did you witness any suspicious activity? Or this woman, or this man, or a silver VW van? If you drove along this route, please check your dashcams". Zero response. We even put out Instagram posts for the teenagers wearing hoodies. But that was a punt, and we knew it.

Stevenson's demise means we've been free to blast stuff out on all our social media channels, while the Chief Super has authorised television and radio appeals on local and national stations.

I spoke to Ronnie Cockburn in the Control. As part of his remit, to deal with the fallout from our appeals, he can pull in resources from all across the city and from other jurisdictions if necessary. They will gatekeep calls and messages, and filter promising information through to us.

I was surprised when we got a hit more or less immediately, before the usual cranks and nutters dreamed up their fairytales. A call from the male half of the lovey-dovey couple who walked along the street ahead of Natasha. "Aye. That van did pass us. We couldn't fail to notice it. Just thought, white van man acting like a tit, with the music belting out and all that. But I'm sorry, we didn't notice where it went".

I take a deep breath. 'Folks. I believe the probability that Natasha is being held somewhere in Trinity is heading for nil. Last night, Tobias was right. Transferring her from the van to a house would have been too risky. Always the chance of bumping into a late night jogger or a dog walker dragging Fido round the block before bedtime. So, on the balance of probability, there's no point in continuing to search there. We simply don't have the time. We have to move on.'

There are murmurs of assent, but no one likes it. It's not the way we normally work. Regrettably, we don't have a choice.

I continue. 'So how did he get clear of the area without being picked up on camera? He could have moved her into a second vehicle, but I'd say it's far more likely he changed the plates again.'

'We did check for reports of VW plates being nicked,' says Steph. 'But nothing came up.'

'It could be he didn't change the plates,' says Andrew. 'Maybe he was ready with bits of tape and all he did was alter a couple of digits. Might have been enough to fool a camera.'

'It might, indeed,' I say. 'If he'd swapped vehicles we'd have found the VW by now. That means he didn't. Therefore, Tobias, we keep searching for it.' I clamp my eyes shut, try to concentrate. 'So, if she's not in Trinity, where else could she be?' I grab a laser pointer. 'Steph, I need that map on the board again.'

The map shows the areas that border Trinity to its south and west, while the Firth of Forth forms a barrier to the north. We also have the main arteries leading out of the city and on those, we've highlighted important junctions with cameras. I bounce the green dot around. 'If he drove along any of these, ANPR would have picked him up.'

We review all the routes he could possibly have taken, ruling out dead ends, lanes that wouldn't accommodate a vehicle, and apartment blocks and industrial units with no through roads. The options left open to us are fairly clear cut. I draw tight circles with the green dot, highlighting the only part of the map that contains both residential and commercial buildings. Granton. A larger area to the west of Trinity that butts right up against it.

'My money says she's in there,' I say.

We're all silent for a few moments then Jeff says. 'Are we ruling out that he doubled back and drove east, in the opposite direction?'

'We have to. Because if he did, the game's up the pole.'

Tobias glances at Steph, his translator in these situations. 'We're buggered,' she says, out of the side of her mouth.

'Before we move on, any joy finding a head-on image of Stevenson in the VW?' says Jeff.

Tobias's expression makes the answer to that abundantly clear.

As I scan the map, I notice there's no reference to scale. The area we'll have to search is expanding, and the magnitude of the task facing us already felt overwhelming. Especially with the ever present deadline looming – in hours that are now down to single digits.

Jeff summarises things for us. 'In the absence of facts, we have to use our judgement: Trinity's a dead duck. We've no footage of the van anywhere, which could mean he's switched vehicles. But if he'd done that, we'd have found the VW. Next, if he'd tried to drive to a different part of the city, or leave Edinburgh entirely, we'd catch him on film. Plus, that means he'd be holding her miles away from his base at the cousin's house, so again, our judgement says that's unlikely. We've no evidence to prove it, but with Granton being adjacent, that's our best bet. She must be in a building, we don't know if it's residential or commercial, but Granton has plenty of both.'

He checks with us all, nobody disagrees. He jerks his thumb in the direction of a monitor. 'If she's in a house, that can't be a normal room. It would be virtually impossible to make it waterproof, plus the weight would pull the house down. A basement, or a cellar is more realistic.'

'What about an outhouse?' says Tobias. 'Or a garage?'

'They're both options because if they were of brick or concrete construction it would be easy enough to fill in the doors and windows.'

Steph leans forward, elbows on her knees. 'If he did that, unless the building was totally secluded, surely somebody, either a neighbour or a passer-by, would ask him what he was up to. Because that would be more than a bit weird, wouldn't it?'

'I have to agree,' I say. 'I can't imagine Stevenson taking the chance of drawing unwanted attention.'

'Fair point,' says Jeff. 'I'll make sure we ask that on any appeals we make. Just in case. But going back to the garage idea, an adjoining garage is a possibility but unless it had roof space, gaining access would cause issues. But that leads me to the idea of an integral garage. The complication with them is the internal construction needs to comply with fire regs to prevent any blaze that starts in the garage from spreading to the rest of the house. When my folks extended, they added rooms above an integral garage. The internal walls were blockwork but the ceiling, and therefore the floor above, was a timber construction that just had to be fire resistant for a period of time. Sixty minutes, if memory serves.'

I lean back, pluck at my bottom lip. 'If it is an integral garage, sealing the whole kit and caboodle would have been relatively straightforward. Plus, he could have created a hatch from the room above. And, added bonus: all the work would have been behind closed doors.'

I glance around. Everyone's either nodding or making positive noises.

'Just for completeness,' says Andrew, 'are we ruling out a lockup or a self-storage facility?'

'Definitely,' says Jeff. 'They're not a good fit for many of the reasons we've already discussed.'

Now it's Ella's turn. 'The main problem I see is if he's done all this work, whose house could it be?'

'Are we certain he doesn't own a second house that he's kept secret from his family?' says Jeff.

'His sister says no chance,' I say. 'According to her, he practically bankrupted himself to buy his own place. A two-bedroom terraced. He's a blacksmith, on a decent wage, but not enough to splash out on another property.' I scan the list on the board. 'Having said that, can I double-check he isn't making payments on a second mortgage, and we've run searches on the Land Registry for Scotland.'

'I've gone over them twice, Boss,' says Tobias. 'There's nothing.'

I'm ticking items off so quickly it's making me dizzy. 'What about a long term let he's modified without the owner's knowledge?'

'Leasing companies are supposed to check properties regularly,' says Andrew. 'My agent was in last month.'

Steph snorts. 'Ha! We rent our house. The agent's never been within a mile of the place, and we've been in more than a year.'

'So a long term let is possible, but not all that likely,' I say. 'Right, before we move on, what are our best bets on the residential front?'

'Integral garage. Basement or cellar. Adjoining garage,' says Jeff. 'In that order.'

Everyone gives me space to mull over all these points. Yes, Natasha might be in a house, but it would need to be a decent size, probably detached, most likely with an integral garage. The VW can't be sitting outside on the street, so either the house would need to be on a sizeable plot of land or have lots of privacy. And, for me, the one aspect that says a residential property does not fit the bill, is proximity to other humans.

I explain my thoughts, nobody disagrees. Reluctantly, we set aside the possibility of Natasha being held in a house. Once again, we move on.

'Next, industrial premises,' says Jeff. 'It is possible he's rented a place, and modified it with running water, electricity supply, maybe even heating. And definitely a mobile internet router because of the live feed.'

'If he leased a property through legitimate sources, that would be risky,' I say. 'But how would he find a suitable place otherwise?'

'It could be derelict,' says Ella.

'I think that's as risky as the other options we've discounted,' says Andrew. 'Even derelict properties are owned by someone, so how could he be sure the owners wouldn't show up one day and discover he's made major alterations?'

I gaze at the map. It's not so long ago that Granton, and the harbour, were teeming with light industry. But that sector was tied into the significantly larger docks at Leith. So, in 1983, when Henry Robb's shipyard finally shut up shop after 600 years of shipbuilding, many of the related service industries also went to the wall. Years later, with the boom in housing and construction in Leith spawned by the Scottish Office relocating, plus Ocean Terminal and the Royal Yacht *Britannia*, everything turned full circle. Light industry and retail commerce have mushroomed. Including the revitalisation of Granton, which forms a sizeable chunk on our map.

'So we talk to commercial leasing companies, and to the ESPC.' I'm talking about the Edinburgh Solicitors' Property Centre. Their website has a commercial section.

This is a far more straightforward discussion because all the options – a unit, a large garage, or a small warehouse – would be suitable. Natasha could be in any of them. So, our money is now placed fairly and squarely on a commercial property. And one that belongs, even temporarily, to him.

We talk for a few minutes longer, but I for one have had enough chat. I'm champing at the bit to get on.

But I can't escape the nagging doubt that none of the options we've considered are a perfect fit. Every single one is flawed, one way or another.

* * *

I rub at my eyes. Whoever dripped chilli oil in them must have done it while I wasn't paying attention. 'I'm just thinking, Stevenson reacted there and then to things that were said on the calls. For example, he was able to adjust the water flow at a minute's notice. So, he must have been able to do that remotely because he wouldn't have risked travelling between his cousin's house and wherever he's holding her, more often than absolutely necessary.

'But if he went from the house to the location where he's holding her, it can't be far away, can it?' We look at each other. The ELPN. The *Edinburgh Lanes and Paths Network*. An extensive spider's web of cycling and walking paths that serves the north of the city. Most of these paths run along disused railway lines that once transported freight trains. We had a case last year where the bad guy zoomed around the city on an ebike, doing bad guy stuff. CCTV cameras on the ELPN are scarcer than Shergar shit, and we had the devil's own job tracking his movements.

I sigh. 'Steph. Ella. Can you plot all the possible routes between the cousin's house and Granton. Start with footage from cameras closest to the house and see if you can pick him up.'

* * *

We're in the incident room, phones going off like church bells on Easter Sunday, but there's one area of relative tranquillity and that's the space currently occupied by my injured lieutenant. Andrew appears to be disregarding his obvious discomfort and is working in his own bubble, alternating his attention between his notes, his PC, and an A4 pad that he scribbles on. It looks for all the world like he's sketching. He mutters to Ella, rakes about in his desk drawer and pulls something out. They walk, actually he limps, over to the nearest wall. He indicates a point high up on the wall with whatever he has in his hand. Ah, it's a measuring tape. She stretches her arm up as high as she can, on her tiptoes, and he measures the height from the floor to her fingertips. He shows her his hand. He's holding it like he's screwing in a lightbulb over his head. She stretches up, mimicking his action. Andrew measures again. This time the high point is a touch lower.

As I'm watching I realise the others are doing likewise. Steph's on the phone but her eyes are on them. Jeff is leaning back in his chair, head tilted to the side. Tobias had been heading for the kitchen, but he's stopped in the middle of the floor, stained coffee mug dangling from a finger.

Once Andrew has measured to the second point that Ella can reach, he marks it with a blob of Blu Tack. He studies the tape, pulls it out further. Ella leans in, taps her finger at a point on the tape. He nods, and they return to his desk. He jots something down, then picks up the phone.

Andrew and I have worked together for years. Like most working partners, I spend more time with him than with my other half. And the signs are clearer than a Harvest Moon. Jeff catches my eye, makes a face, goes back to what he was doing. I don't. I spin my chair across the floor to Andrew's desk and wait till he hangs up. 'Spill, my boy. What are you up to?'

He stays perfectly still for a few seconds, pondering. I don't interrupt him. I glance at Ella, who throws me a couple of tiny nods. She knows but won't steal her colleague's thunder. Finally, he says, 'The space she's being held captive, I know what it is. Or at least I'm pretty sure I do. Give me ten, fifteen minutes and I'll be able to confirm.'

He explains what he's thinking and it's crystal clear he's bang on the money. But I keep that to myself until he can prove it. I do not want to create a false dawn.

* * *

Ten minutes later we're all gathered around the whiteboard while Andrew puts the finishing touches to what he plans to show us. We've all taken a short comfort break and Ella's nipped across the road to our favourite Italian café and brought us a cardboard box packed with drinks and breakfast pastries.

Once he's ready Andrew limps to the front. He's using a walking pole to keep the weight off his knee. He binned the crutches hours ago. 'Remember when we first watched Natasha on the film?' he says. 'She was stretching up towards the inlet but was well short of the ceiling. Ella's about five foot four, similar height to Natasha. So with her help I've replicated what Natasha was doing and from that I've been able to gauge the height of the space with a reasonable degree of accuracy. I make it about 2.4 metres, almost eight feet.'

'So, similar to a room in a modern house?' I say.

'Yes.'

'Or your average flat-roofed garage?' says Steph.

'Again, yes.' He pulls up an image of the end wall of the room; the wall facing the camera. He taps his iPad, and a vertical line appears on the right hand side of the image. It runs from floor to ceiling, and he's annotated the measurement, 2.4 metres, next to the line. Once more he taps the iPad and now a horizontal line runs along the top of the wall from corner to corner. 'I sent the image to a media tech, asked if she could analyse it and calculate the width of the space based on the height.'

'I'm guessing she could,' says Jeff.

'Yes. And without going into the geometry and other complicated stuff I didn't understand, she reckons the height of the room and the width are both 2.4 metres.' Another tap on the iPad and that measurement also appears.

I steeple my fingers beneath my chin. 'Andrew. How are you going to measure the length of the space accurately because the fisheye lens, or whatever it is, makes the image look a bit skewed?'

He smiles. 'I don't have to, I know for certain it's 5.9 metres, or 19 feet.'

'That is extremely precise.' says Tobias. 'How can you be so sure?'

'Because Stevenson made a mistake. When he spoke to us that first time, he told us, and I quote, "the room that holds Natasha Emerson has a capacity of 33 cubic metres".

'Ah, so you've worked out the height and the width, and calculated those against the cubic capacity.' I'm sporting a puzzled expression; it's matched by my tone. 'Sorry, but how does that tell you where she is?'

'It doesn't. But it does tell me what she's inside. Those measurements could be a garage, could be a basement, but I'd put my last pound on her being inside a steel shipping container.'

'Your last pound? Wow!' says Steph, grinning.

Jeff groans. 'A shipping container. He was a blacksmith, so to make it waterproof all he had to do was weld the doors shut.'

'Indeed,' says Andrew. 'Cut a few holes for lights, vents, the water inlet. And remember yesterday morning when she was screaming at the ceiling? I'll bet he built a hatch to lower her in, but we can't see it because it's flush with the ceiling.'

Like the others, I'd never considered a container. I'd always imagined they were mainly for storage or transport, moving stuff around the world. I didn't know people cut holes in them. Andrew goes on to explain that it's big business worldwide. They've become multi-purpose, converted into home offices, garden rooms, holiday properties, offshore accommodation modules. Companies bolt them together, stack them up and make budget hotels and low price housing. Who knew?

'This could be the breakthrough we need, Andrew,' I say. 'That was smart thinking. Kudos.' He and Ella touch hands as they pass each other, like tennis doubles partners do.

'Right, Tobias,' I say. 'Find out if there are companies in or around Edinburgh who carry out these alterations. Ask them if by any chance they did this one, but also confirm if an experienced blacksmith could've done it himself.'

'Will do,' he says.

'Next. Where would he source a shipping container? And where is it?'

Ella pipes up. 'While our resident genius was getting organised for his big reveal, I had a look at that, so I can give you some contacts, Tobias. I don't know about altering them, but they're not cheap to hire long-term. I've spoken to a few suppliers and although they do rent them out to the public, the delivery space issue rules out most inner-city households. So I'm beginning to wonder if he's using one that's already on a site.'

'Delivery space issue? Tell me more about that,' I say.

'You've all seen skips being delivered; they use chains and a hoist to lift them off the lorry and drop them into position. These things are much longer, and heavier, so they use a different method. The container arrives on the back of a transporter. The driver needs a straight line to reverse into the space where the container's going, tilts it off the back then drives away, again in a straight line, leaving the container in the space.' She demonstrates with two books on her desk, starts off with one on top of the other before sliding the lower one, the transporter, out from under the container. She points at the two books that are in a straight line. 'Andrew believes it's a twenty-foot container, not a forty. They're huge. But even for a twenty-footer, they need sixty feet in a straight line to drop it off. A forty-footer needs a hundred feet.'

Amazing what I learn in this job. But now I can appreciate what she means about the space that's required, and how unlikely it would be to deliver one to an average semi-detached in a tight street with cars parked all over the place. 'So, what you're saying, Ella, is we can't state definitely it's not on a residential property but commercial makes much more sense. Yes?'

She nods enthusiastically and I carry on. 'Andrew, another job for your council woman. Is there such a thing as a commercial properties' register? If so, can it be filtered to show those that are either on short term let or empty? And, while I'm on that, with the services he's using – water, electricity, blah

blah blah – I doubt the container's out in the middle of a yard. That means it's most probably inside or directly adjacent to a building.'

Steph holds a hand up. 'Thinking about where it's located, it could be Stevenson was at a client's premises surveying a job or delivering materials and spotted what he was after.'

'That's a great idea, Steph. Talk to his boss. Ask if Marlon had been in the habit of visiting clients. If so, get a list of places he's been in the last two years.' She nods, grabs her coat, and trots towards the door.

Next, I say to Ella, 'The map you and Steph were plotting the cameras on, how's that coming along?'

'Nearly finished. Maybe fifteen minutes and I'll be done.'

'Good. Because like we discussed earlier, if he's visited the container since he put Natasha inside, we need to know how he got there because his car's been on his driveway all this time. So, method of transport, route, and how often he made the journey. I imagine the distance between the house and the container will be relatively short and straightforward. It'll be typical if he's using the ELPN, the council should shut that bloody thing down.'

Ella heads for her desk, and I turn to Andrew and Jeff. 'Right. What else is there? Have I missed anything obvious?'

They both tell me I haven't.

That's encouraging because we're fast running out of options.

Chapter 67

Thursday 09:00

Standing there wearing only saturated underwear, Natasha was cold and uncomfortable. Under any other circumstances she'd take wet clothes off, but not today. Everything else was soaked so she had nothing to dry herself with. She pulled her forearms tight against her chest and kept them there, giving her at least the delusion of warmth. She leaned into the wall, let her chin drop and closed her eyes.

She had done her best to stem the flow. Tried everything she could think of. And had failed. No more cards to play. She was hungry. Exhausted. Miserable.

The Effer had won. She had lost.

She became aware her bra was cutting into her, beneath the cup on the left side. She slid her fingers in behind the material, eased it away from her skin, then let it settle back into a slightly different position. She crossed her arms again. Then paused.

A few months previously, she'd been on the point of throwing out an old bra because the underwire was exposed; it had come adrift from the stitching. Through simple curiosity she'd poked about at it, and discovered the wire was a thin metal strip sheathed in nylon.

Without giving it a second's thought, she unclipped her bra and held it by one of the cups. She flexed the curved underwire back and forth while she worked through what was in her mind.

Then she glowered up at the end of the pipe.

'I'm not finished with you yet,' she said.

Chapter 68

'I'm sorry to break the news about Marlon, Mr Wallace. Are you okay? Can I get you a drink of water?'

'No. You're all right, dear. But I need a seat.'

While the old man was getting himself sorted, Steph glanced around. Wallace Fabrication was a small unit in a lane behind a row of older houses in Granton. They were in a cluttered cubbyhole at the front of the building. A door to the rear was half open, and through the gap she could see haphazard piles of raw materials and what appeared to be half-finished jobs. Gates and short lengths of fencing were stacked up against each other; a few looked like they'd been there since the place was built.

'Do you have other employees apart from Marlon, Mr Wallace?'

He shook his head. 'No, there's only the two of us. I used to take on apprentices but I'm seventy-four and I'm not up to it these days. I asked Marlon a few times if he wanted to take over the business, but he wouldn't commit because of his mother. She seemed to monopolise his time, you know?' He gazed around, shuffled a couple of sheets of paper on his desk, gave out a huge long sigh. 'He did most of the work here. Has done for ages. I paid him a decent wage to make sure I kept him, but I only take out of the business what it can stand.' He waves an arm. 'This is my pension plan, dear, but that depends on me selling it as a going concern.' The old man seemed to be bearing a significantly heavier burden than when Steph had first walked in.

When she asked about clients Marlon might have visited, Wallace hunched up his shoulders before letting them drop. 'I'm a blacksmith, dear. Been on the tools my whole life. I don't do admin. So, yes, Marlon would have gone out to clients' premises but there's nothing written down. I have a lassie who comes in once a month to keep the books up to date.' He smiled. 'Well, when I say *lassie*, she must be pushing sixty. She makes up invoices from the job sheets so if you phone her, she'll send you a list. I don't keep much in the way of paperwork on the premises. Too many break-ins.'

Steph called the number Wallace gave her and spoke to the "lassie". She was brusque, efficient, and not a woman for small talk. Within five minutes, she'd emailed Steph a list of nearly forty clients that Marlon could have visited, to quote for a job or to carry out work during the previous two years. She'd included descriptions of the work; everything from fixing a garden gate to larger jobs on commercial premises.

Wallace scanned the list. He explained that all bar two were repeat business, and they were both domestic jobs. They scored off another half-a-dozen that were domestic, a similar number that were well outside the city, and two that were across the water in Fife. But when Steph started to ask about others they could rule out because the premises might be too small to hold a shipping container, he stopped her. 'Marlon did all of those, so I wouldn't know.'

'Okay, Mr Wallace. Thank you. Now, I'd like to ask you if Marlon could have made alterations to a container. Like welding the doors shut, cutting holes for services, installing a hatch in the ceiling.'

He stared at her as if she'd asked him for his inside leg measurement, then said, 'Standing on his head. I've actually no idea why he stuck with me all these years. He's talented, a hard worker, good at what he does. Sorry, did.' He rubbed his eyes, all of a sudden looking much older than his age.

'What about lights? Or plumbing?'

'Don't see why not. Most tradesmen have a working knowledge of other trades. Probably wouldn't have known about latest regulations and stuff like that. And it might have been a bit rough and ready, but decent enough. Why are you asking about all this anyway? Why on earth would Marlon have been modifying a shipping container?'

Steph smiled down at the old man. 'I'm sorry, Mr Wallace. I'm afraid I'm not at liberty to say.'

Wallace took a breath as if he was going to push for more, but instead slumped back in his chair. He stared off into middle distance. 'Marlon worked here for all those years, and

I never met his mother. But I know she's not well. If you're talking to her, please pass on my condolences.'

Just at that, the phone rang.

Steph glanced at it, but Wallace didn't turn round. 'I'm not answering that. No real point, is there?'

Chapter 69

I'm wandering about the incident room, searching for inspiration whilst trying to keep my body from seizing up, when I hear Tobias ending a call. He catches my eye, so I go over to his desk.

'I've spoken to three companies in Scotland who specialise in shipping container modifications,' he says. 'Two in Aberdeen, one in Invergordon, and they all said the same. Larger jobs like full conversions are always carried out at their yards, and they don't work with private customers because they're governed by a strict certification standard which precludes that. But they did confirm what Mr Wallace told Steph; the modifications I described would all be within the capability of a competent blacksmith or welder.'

I sigh. 'So, he's managed to find a container nobody's using, and modified it himself. But where?'

* * *

With the feed no longer coming through I find myself moving from one team member to another, trying to keep my spirits up as much as theirs. I'm chivvying them along, helping where I can, but the mood is flat. We're no longer watching the clock, we moved into single figures ages ago. I'll never admit it, but I sense we're all waiting for the inevitable. I talk to each of them in turn, but as the hours pass by, their updates become less positive, and contain fewer details.

I sit with Andrew as he takes a call from the commercial properties department at the council. He says, 'Yes. It's just arrived,' and clicks on an email at the top of his inbox. He scrolls up and down in a PDF while the chap explains it contains information relating to company names and addresses, all with the Granton postcode: EH5. After a couple of minutes, Andrew thanks him and hangs up. 'You were right.' He points at the screen. 'This is their register of commercial properties, but they've stressed it's only as accurate as the info provided by the property owners. If they don't notify a change to a unit's status, which could be the unit is sublet, to lease or sell, mothballed or whatever, the council have no way of knowing if the status is accurate.'

'And let me guess, they don't have the resources to go through them.'

Andrew treats that as rhetorical: smart lad. 'In the Granton area, with a decent tolerance round the outside, there are over thirty properties that, according to the register, are not in current use. A sign of the times I'm afraid; harsh economic trading conditions in the city. If units are sublet we can check them by phoning or visiting. If they're to lease or sell we can call the agencies. And if they're mothballed we'll have to find the owners. It can all be done.' He glances up at the clock. 'But it'll be time consuming.' He leaves the rest unsaid.

He clicks the *Print* icon. 'I'll get started on it.'

I stand up, lay my hand on his shoulder. 'I'll pull it off the printer for you.'

'Thanks. But I need to move.' He points at his stomach. 'And I'm hungry.'

* * *

I feel like I'm a spare part.

Steph and Ella have finished plotting out their map with routes and cameras, and Tobias is helping them to sift through CCTV footage. Although they're all working at their desks, a blown-up version of the map is on the whiteboard, so I go over to take a look. Dozens of red dots signify cameras in our target area; the board appears to be suffering from an outbreak of terminal acne.

I gaze at the map, wondering what the hell else we can do to find Natasha. But I'm all out. No more ideas.

Jeff's gone to speak with the Chief Super and our media advisors. By now they'll have pressed the button on an agreed programme of broadcasts.

This is the media equivalent of carpet bombing. We're targeting local and national TV, radio and newspaper websites, backed up by more social media appeals. The messages are consistent and aimed at the Granton area. Have you seen this woman or this man? Have you seen a van like this one, bearing this registration plate? If you own a vehicle, particularly a VW van, please check your number plates haven't been stolen. Have you noticed any unusual activity like a neighbour making alterations to a garage or an outhouse, sealing it up, blocking up doors or windows? If you own or lease commercial premises, and have an unused shipping container on site, have you checked it recently? Have you witnessed or heard of anyone modifying a shipping container?

Ronnie and the Control teams are bracing themselves for the onslaught that, leaving the loonies and the numpties aside, we hope will throw up the one nugget that will help us find Natasha Emerson. So I head off down there. Might as well get abuse from him as anyone else.

I hope and pray we're not already too late.

Chapter 70

'And you're certain?' says Jeff. 'No possibility she's still alive?'

We both check the clock. 16:10. And it doesn't lie.

'Andrew's done the maths,' I say. 'I've gone over his calculations, and so has Tobias.'

'If the circumstances weren't so dreadful, I'd take your word for it every day of the week.'

Before he says "But", I start reeling off the facts. We have an estimate of the water level when we last saw Natasha on the feed, erring on the side of caution. We've calculated the flow rate of water through the inlet, based on the initial specifications provided by Marlon Stevenson, again with some caution. And we've included the time that has passed since the feed went down.

Jeff has been taking notes as I've been speaking. He's studying them now. I keep silent. This is his decision, and there's a better than even chance it's one of the most difficult he's ever had to take. Eventually he pushes pen and notepad towards the centre of his desk. 'We'll give it forty-five minutes more, till five o'clock. At that point I need to call this for everyone's sake, not least Natasha's parents and the rest of her family.' He glances up. 'But also for your team. You've been under tremendous strain.' I note he avoided mentioning Hugo by name. 'As far as our investigation is concerned, at five o'clock we'll be altering our focus from rescue to the recovery of Natasha Emerson's body.'

Chapter 71

I'm sitting with my team when at five o'clock, bang on the button, Jeff walks in. 'Has anything changed?' he says.

Nobody speaks.

'In which case, time's up.' He turns to me. 'Do you want to come with me to speak to the Emersons?'

No, it's the last thing on earth I want to do ... 'Yes, of course. Crissi is already over there. I'll meet you in the car park in five minutes.'

Crissi calls to say the whole family are at Hugo's place, about halfway between here and Granton. We'd released him under caution as soon as his forensic checks were complete. Crissi's done her best to prepare them, but when Jeff and I walk in they all fall to pieces.

Employing a blend of words and tone that is a combination of respect, kindness, sincerity and plain speaking, Jeff explains what's happened in the last few hours and that we no longer expect their daughter and granddaughter still to be alive. He is careful to state, 'The investigation has now moved from rescue to recovery.'

'Have you found her?' says Natasha's father, Iain.

'No. We're still searching. And we'll keep searching until we do.'

'So there's still hope?' This time Iain addresses me, as if I might offer a more positive prognosis.

I don't give him a direct answer. I don't have any right to tell them not to hope, even if the facts demonstrate there can be none. So I repeat Jeff's statement about recovery, not rescue.

Hugo stays silent. His wife is beside him on the sofa, clamped to his left arm while his daughter is on his right. They're holding hands down by their sides. But his son-in-law, Iain, is in an armchair, isolated from the others. His arms are stretched out, gripping the leading edge of the seat so tightly the cushion is practically flat.

Hugo doesn't appear to be angry, or at least not with us. Being fair, he can't be. But today, no one is talking about fairness. He knows what he did. As, it seems, do his family.

Since we arrived, Iain has been blatantly disassociating himself from Hugo. He addresses Jeff directly. 'Have you found the man who was responsible for that bastard Stevenson dying? Because he's the one who stopped you finding her. You could have worked on Stevenson, made him tell you.'

'No, we haven't found him,' says Jeff, his eyes fixed on Iain. 'The responsibility for finding Natasha and this person has been passed on to another team. The DI leading that team will stand DC Banerjee down and bring in their own Family Liaison Officer.'

Iain jerks a thumb in Hugo's direction. 'In that case, make *him* tell you.'

No one answers him. If anyone is going to, it should be Hugo, but he's already made it clear he will not reveal names, and never will. Even if it means he goes to jail. We know through Crissi that the family have already made several attempts to persuade him, but in his words, "We can't mess with these people. If I did give out a name, I'd put all of you in danger. So, no dice. I'm saying nothing".

I ask them if they'd like me to stay, along with Crissi, but they say they don't. So we explain what will happen next, then shake everyone's hands and leave.

Jeff and I drove over there in separate cars. We agree to meet the day after tomorrow and he heads back to Queen Charlotte Street. I've already told the rest of the team to prepare a handover, tidy up, and go home. I made it clear I didn't want to see them in the office until Monday morning.

I drive off and as soon as I'm out of sight of the house, I pull over. I dial my husband's number; he picks up on the second ring. 'Callum. I'm coming home. Please be there for me.'

I leave it there. I couldn't get another word out if my life depended on it.

Chapter 72

I'm less than a mile from pulling up the drawbridge and releasing the piranhas into the moat when my phone goes off. "Ronnie Cockburn – Control".

'Where are you, Mel?' he says.

'Heading home. You'll have heard we've been stood down. Jeff's passing the investigation on, I won't be back in for a couple of days.'

'Yeah, I heard. Tough break for you.'

Then, silence. Never a good thing. 'What do you want, Ronnie?' *Damn. That was a stupid thing to say.*

'Our social media posts are throwing up all sorts of crap, as usual. Took a call a wee while ago from a journalist, wanting to talk to you. But I'm guessing I already know the answer to that.'

'Got it in one, Ronnie.' I pause, hesitate, but I can't stop myself. 'How are things going?'

'Oh, as you'd expect. We're all over the place, swamped, trying to check everything.'

I feel for him. I know first-hand how these situations can explode. 'I'm sorry. But I'm shattered. I need a break.'

'Quite right, Mel. Go and spend time with your family. You deserve it.'

I pull into a bus stop. Switch the engine off. 'I don't really, Ronnie. I failed that poor girl.'

'You did nothing of the sort. You gave it your best shot like you always do. Wasn't meant to be, that's all.'

I smile. Not one of my better ones. 'Thanks, Ronnie. You always know the right thing to say. I appreciate it.'

He chuckles. 'Yeah, that's me. Mother Theresa all over.' He waits a couple of beats. 'Do you still live out near Davidson's Mains?'

I close my eyes, shake my head. 'I do, yes.' I sigh, and I bloody well make sure he hears it. 'I have a hunch, just a little one mind you, that you want me to do something that happens to be on my way home.'

He gives me an address where he's had a report about a generator, or genny, that's been running constantly "for days". And it so happens I'm only three minutes away, whereas his next available patrol will be at least twelve to fifteen.

'You've no idea how many times we get complaints about gennies,' he says. 'The numpties out there don't seem to realise there's a reason why they run overnight. That's their purpose in life. It'll only take you a couple of minutes, Mel. And nothing surer, it'll be a false alarm.'

Chapter 73

As soon as Jeff walked into the incident room after visiting the Emerson family, he immediately noticed – or rather sensed – the atmosphere was markedly different.

Andrew, Steph, Tobias and Ella were all hunched over their monitors, flicking their mouses around and jotting notes. He stood behind Andrew, who registered Jeff's presence by raising his left hand. But he didn't shift his gaze from the screen.

'What's up?' said Jeff. 'Last I heard you were all going home.'

Ella's desk was on the other side of the low divider. She spoke across the top of her monitor. 'We were, but then Andrew had an idea.'

Jeff pulled a chair over and was moving it in next to Andrew when a yell came from a few desks away. It was Steph. 'Got you. You sneaky bastard.' Four heads twisted in her direction, but she didn't look up for a second or two. And when she did, she glared at them all. 'Are you lot coming to see, or what?' Then she realised Jeff was one of the four and a grin flashed across her face. 'Oops! Sorry about that, Boss. But you're going to want to see this.'

And once she had taken them through the sequence of events displayed on her screen, Jeff said, 'Right. You three get over there. Andrew, find out where Mel is, then contact Ronnie. He'll know who to pull in.'

Chapter 74

From the pavement, looking through a chain link fence across a concrete forecourt, I can hear the genny buzzing away. Driving here, my thought processes went like this. *Stevenson could have been using mains electricity to power the lighting, heat the water, and drive a mobile internet router or whatever setup he'd put in place. But he could also have been using a generator, probably diesel.* Several times I had to wipe my palms on my trousers.

I arrive and scan the building, an industrial unit with no signage to indicate who owns it, or the purpose of the building. Looks like it's all closed up, shutters down, no vehicles on the forecourt, Volkswagen or otherwise. *Why, then, is there a genny on site?*

I peer at a notice on a wooden door that was blue at one time. It sits next to a steel roller door that is definitely wide enough and high enough to take a container. And remembering what Ella said about the space that the transporter would need in front of the doors, my eyes tells me it's long enough.

The notice has a mobile number, but I can't read it from here. I take a photo and when I zoom in, the writing is clear enough.

After the briefest hesitation, I key in the number. A man answers.

I explain who I am, and where I am, and ask what the generator is powering.

He says, 'I rented that unit, then subcontracted it. I provide emergency storage for companies who've had, for example, fires or floods, and need somewhere to store their goods, or whatever, until they either get back into their own building or they find a new place. I've got units all over Edinburgh. They're going for a song because, as you can imagine, there's a glut in the market. The genny you can hear is running refrigerated units for a company whose warehouse roof was declared unsafe and they had to evacuate. In fact, I've not long left the place, I was replenishing the diesel tank. Why are you asking?'

He sounds pleasant enough and I'm on the point of telling him "Thanks, it doesn't matter", when I realise I can't do that. He might be innocent enough. But there might be a container in there. And it *might* be full of water … *Stop, Mel. Just stop.* My heart is thumping, it's a wonder he can't hear it. I speak with authority, slowly and more calmly than I feel. 'You'll need to come here right away, sir. I've got police officers standing by, ready to check inside.' If he is an associate of Marlon, there's no harm in him being under the impression I'm mob handed.

'You're kidding, right? I'm at the hospital. I've got an appointment with an orthopaedic consultant. I've waited nearly a year for it.'

Since Covid, times have changed in the medical world. I'm no longer surprised when I hear about appointments at strange times. 'I'm sorry about that, sir. But no, I'm not kidding. I'm deadly serious. I promise I'll do what I can to get you a new appointment.' I have absolutely no idea if I can wield that power, but I need him here. Now.

And then I call Ronnie and demand he sends backup. Like, yesterday.

Chapter 75

'Mel. Where are you?'

I give my phone a filthy look, as if it's to blame. 'What's this, Andrew? Are you and Ronnie running a *Where's Mel?* competition?'

There's a beat of silence on the line, before, 'Where are you, Mel. I need to know.'

That catches my attention. He said, "Mel". Not boss. And he said it twice. 'What's wrong, Andrew?'

Seconds later, I'm running for my car. I haul open the door, jump in, hit the pedal and hammer into a U-turn. A lamppost looms into view, but I don't stop. Not sure how much I missed it by.

* * *

I've followed Andrew's directions and driven to a street less than half a mile away. I've kept the line open. 'Andrew. I'm here. What am I looking for?'

I scan rows of industrial units on both sides. Similar in design, the same developer must have built them. Same colours, same sizes, same frontages. They all have chain link fences but one or two don't have gates. There are a few vehicles on the forecourts but clearly some of these units are empty.

'You want the left side of the street, Boss. About three or four units down.'

I start the car rolling forwards. 'Be more precise, Andrew. There are three in a row, all with *For Lease* signs. Which one is it? Give me something!'

'There's a lane running between two units, it's the unit to the left of the lane.'

'Yes. Got it.' I pull to a stop and jump out, phone in hand. 'I'm outside. But the gates are padlocked.'

'Ronnie's got backup on the way, including Fire and Rescue.'

'Damn! On the way is no bloody use. I need assistance, and I need it this minute.' I glance up and down the road. Tumbleweed City.

I don't have time to wait. I stare at the gates. They're hanging a bit off-centre, on posts that are heavily rusted where they enter the ground. I look at my car. At the gates. *Sorry, Callum.*

Just as I'm about to plough through them, I realise a seatbelt would have been a good idea. I straighten my arms, angle my face to the side, and when the airbag hits me I jam my foot on the brakes. Before my head has stopped spinning I'm out and running.

The front of the building is much the same as the storage facility I left a few minutes ago. Double metal roller doors, and a wooden one to the side. I sprint to that door and grab the handle, but it doesn't turn. There's a glass panel in the top half, but it's reinforced with wire. So I run to the side of the building away from the roller door.

Please God, let there be a window on this side.

Yesss! And this one doesn't have wire in the glass.

I glance around. There are lumps of concrete paving at my feet, so I grab one and throw it at the window. The concrete bounces off; my son would have described that as a "girlie" throw. I spot a heavier piece, lift it with both hands, line myself up, and scream as I hurl it at the glass. I gawp at the opening. Most of the panel has fallen out; only a few shards left, stuck into the bottom of the frame. I pick up another smaller chunk, knock out the rest of the glass, then realise I'll never get my leg over the sill. Not in a million years.

I scout around, hoping for a box to stand on. A crate, an old pallet. Anything.

Nothing.

So I reverse a couple of steps, take a run at it and launch my arms and upper body at the opening. And when I eventually land face first in a pile of shattered glass on a concrete floor, my immediate concern is my front teeth. After I've stood up, shaken myself down, I run my tongue across the top and bottom. Good. No metallic taste.

But when I pat my pockets for my phone, they're empty. I search the floor around my feet. Nothing there. Outside the window? Yes! And the screen's still on. I yell. 'I'm inside, Andrew. But I've dropped my mobile.' I hear a tinny voice, so I suppose he heard me.

And now I hear it. The distinctive sound of a diesel generator chugging away. The space is lit by Perspex panels set in the sloping roof. To my right is a silver VW van. I move towards it, the sliding door in the side is open.

And next to the van, parallel to the unit's external wall, is what looks like an enormous block of insulation. But, as I move closer, I realise it's a latticework of single boards, wedged up against a rust-red shipping container. I walk towards it. Slowly. I rip lengths of insulation aside, and several others fall away naturally to reveal the container. It's obvious the doors have been welded shut from the outside.

I hear a gurgling sound coming from beneath it and bend down for a closer look. Attached to the underside is a white plastic box about one foot square. On the face is a dial, similar to an old-fashioned manual oven timer. I still have one somewhere; you twist the dial to set the amount of time. The dial has the numbers zero to 23 in black. It's sitting at zero. But what does that mean? Was it set to a certain time and that time's elapsed? Or was it never set at all? No way of knowing. Therefore, ignore it.

Running out of the base of the box is a short length of concertinaed hose connected directly to a drain that disappears beneath the smooth concrete floor. This is definitely where the gurgling is coming from, but I don't know what it means, and I don't have the time to find out.

I move closer and stop at the foot of a mobile wooden staircase. A miniature version of those things they wheel up to the side of a plane. But this has no canopy at the top, and no handrail.

I touch the side of the container. Droplets of water are wending their way down the metal grooves, falling the last few centimetres to the dusty concrete floor. They've created a long straight line of tiny pools, marking the bottom edge of the container. I have to get on top of this thing, but I'm terrified by what I might find.

I have no choice. So I put one foot on the bottom step, keep my hand on the wall, and move steadily upwards. The condensation stops short of the top.

I climb till I'm level with the container and, after a brief pause to gather what's left of my courage, I step sideways onto the roof. I only feel secure when I have two feet on the flat surface, and I've moved away from the edge. We've always known there was a hatch and it's at my feet. It's fastened down by two wooden battens that fit into metal slots. Even I can tell they too have been welded on.

But my first thought is the water inlet. I know where it is in relation to the hatch and scuttle over to that corner. The inlet is there: a grey plastic plumbing pipe that fits into a connection on the roof. I try to twist it but it's rock solid. There's no way it'll move, not without a wrench.

I look back. Electrical cables run to the light fittings and three vents are set into the top. We hadn't noticed these before, probably because they were flush with the ceiling and invisible to the camera. I hear the faintest of whirring noises and notice the vents are fitted with small electrical fans, only one of which is spinning.

I scuttle over to the hatch. Again I hesitate. I persuade myself into action, kneel down and grab one of the wooden battens. It won't move. So I use two hands. It gives, a little, but that's all. So I stand up and kick the bloody thing. It doesn't move on the first kick, but it squeaks over when I boot it a second time. I haul at it, and it slides out of the slot. I move to the other batten on the opposite side of the hatch. It offers no resistance.

On the other edge, equidistant from the two battens, is a handle. Also welded on, and wide enough to get two hands round. I grab hold and pull it up. The hinges move smoothly. The hatch isn't particularly heavy, but I fumble and have to use my hip to steady it. Once it's past the point of no return I let it fall away. It makes one hell of a racket.

A brief surge of moist air slaps me in the face. I take an involuntary half step back to regain my balance then gaze down, into a cool blue light. Like a gigantic hot tub.

I drop to my knees. Lean down as far as I dare. And call out for Natasha.

Chapter 76

Events were now out of Andrew's control and there was nothing else he could do until he heard from Mel, or one of the team, or Ronnie. A few minutes earlier, Jeff had slung his jacket over the back of his chair and left the room.

Andrew stood up, kept the weight on his good leg, and stretched out his spine. He looked down at his desk; the top was awash with paperwork. He thought about a coffee but decided he'd tidy up first and wait for Jeff to come back. Someone needed to be available to answer calls.

As if on cue Jeff's mobile rang, so Andrew hobbled over and hit the green icon. It was a DI from one of the other MITs. When Andrew told him Jeff wouldn't be gone long, the DI said he couldn't wait and asked Andrew to take down a number and pass it on. He touched his shirt pocket, realised he didn't have a pen and quickly scanned Jeff's desk. There wasn't one there either, but he simply couldn't be bothered hirpling all the way over to his own desk. Then he spotted Jeff's pen, clipped into his inside jacket pocket.

He made a move towards it, stopped, then said, 'Oh, bugger it. He's not going to mind, is he?' He wrote down the number and ended the call.

'Detective Sergeant Young, I hope you're not nicking my posh pen. Theft is a crime, you know,' Jeff joked, when he spotted the heat shooting up from Andrew's throat to his hairline. 'Mind you, if you were, even I might be quick enough to catch you.'

Andrew smiled. His DCI was a top bloke, they all knew how lucky they were to work on his teams. He twirled the *Mont Blanc* in his fingertips, hefted the weight, read the inscription on the barrel: "DJH". Andrew wasn't surprised about the "J" being the middle initial, he'd seen Jeff's signature every day for years. 'It's beautiful. Did I hear you saying it was a gift?'

Jeff nodded. 'From my aunt when I became a DI. Said if I was going to be a pen pusher, I might as well have a decent pen to push.'

'Are you not scared you lose it? Thieving Detective Sergeants notwithstanding.'

Jeff shrugged. 'I suppose. But if I didn't use it for work, it would only lie about in a drawer at home, wouldn't it?'

'I guess,' said Andrew turning towards the door. 'I'm going for a coffee; can I get you one?'

'Please. Black, one sugar.'

Chapter 77

'Natasha!'

I pray she can respond.

Silence.

I lean further in. So far down, my arm muscles begin to tremble.

I try again.

'Natasha! Can you hear me?'

All I can hear are the condensation drips falling into their little pools on the concrete floor below.

'Natasha! I'm a police officer. Can you hear me?'

I lean down once more, brace myself against the sides of the hatch. But it's no use. I can't support myself for long. A few more seconds and I'm sure I'll topple in.

I sit back on my heels. I'm too late. Way too late. Logic supported by maths told us the container would be full hours ago. I don't know what to do. Wait for the fire service? I should go down and open the rolling door. Move my car. Will they say anything about me totalling it? And what about Callum? Ah well, he's been talking about a new one anyway.

But I'm disgusted with myself. Comparing the loss of a crappy car with the life of a young woman who's been murdered in the cruellest, most barbaric way imaginable.

I make to move but my muscles ignore me. Stare down into the water. I can hear a trickle. Water from the inlet, I suppose. An apple core appears from my left. It bobs past, spinning slowly as it moves. A piece of fruit, floating about in a shipping container full of water.

Full of water?

'Hang on!'

I look down at the surface. Examine it closely this time. I drop onto one knee and reach down towards the apple; it's still twirling around. I have to stretch to get my fingertips wet. I snatch them away as if the water was scalding.

The container's not full. Why not? Did the water stop flowing in? Did Natasha manage to stop it? Or slow it down?

I don't understand. The rate of flow compared to the hours that have passed means it should be full.

I blink. *What was that?* The water. It moved. It's still moving. A ripple. A tiny wavelet. A second one, bigger this time. Then a sound. A voice? Natasha's voice?

'Oh, my God.' I shoot my legs backwards, lie flat on my stomach, push my head right down and twist my neck. A light shines in my face. I bring my arm down which tilts me alarmingly towards the surface. I grab the side of the opening with my right hand and shield my eyes with my left, squinting into the corner where Natasha was, last time we saw her.

The strain of leaning, the glare, and the warm moisture in such an enclosed space makes me feel like vomiting. I shut my eyes, tight. Concentrate. Force the sensation to pass.

I focus on the corner. 'Yes!'

She's slumped in the corner, leaning on the wall, her head lolling to one side. The water is lapping in the crook of her neck. Her right arm is horizontal, waving just below the surface, but with no strength. A sports bottle is tied to her front and, apart from a towel hanging off one shoulder, the poor girl appears to be naked. *Did that bastard strip her?* Now I spot items of clothing that have sunk to the floor.

She's speaking, repeating a phrase over and over. But her voice is low. Barely a whisper. I can't make it out. Apart from her name, "Natasha", every few words.

I try again, much louder this time. 'Natasha. Listen. Can you hear me?'

She doesn't open her eyes. But when I scream, 'Natasha!' her eyelids spark open.

We lock eyes. Again, she waves her arm.

I beckon her. 'Swim over here, Natasha. I'll pull you out.'

She shakes her head. 'Can't. Too tired.'

This time I use both hands to entice her towards me. I almost overbalance and again I have to grab at the hatch. 'Come on, honey. You can do it. Just a few strokes and you'll be safe.'

She's facing in my direction, but her eyes are glazed. She stretches her arm out till it's practically straight.

And flops forward into the water.

She floats there. Her other arm rises to the surface. The sports bottle bobs up at her side and drifts away on the end of a length of cord.

She is face down in the water. Red hair like a halo on the surface. And she stays that way.

She doesn't swim.

She doesn't move.

She doesn't do anything.

* * *

I'm stunned. Scream, 'Noooo!'

I'm up on my knees. What do I do? I'd done the maths earlier. Height of container, 2.4 metres. So therefore, depth of water 2.4 metres minus my arm's length. That's easily two metres. And I'm nowhere near as tall as that.

I glance up at the harness, attached to the chain, driven by a motor that's operated by controls. I have no idea how they work. And even if I did, I don't know how to put a harness on.

How long does it take for a person to drown?

And it's not just that I can't swim, I'm petrified.

All this flashes through my mind in the beat of a hummingbird's wing.

247

Then, a memory of my mother speaking to me. "Melissa, you can swim perfectly well. There's nothing to be afraid of." She smiles a mum's comforting smile, sprinkled with confidence and encouragement. She's in a pool, somewhere warm and sunny, and standing only a couple of metres away. The water is halfway up her body, deep enough for me to swim in, and shallow enough to put my feet down if I need to. "Just push yourself away from the side, darling. You'll be fine. I'm here to catch you".

I kick my shoes off. Sling my legs over the edge of the hatch. Slide in.

Then I choke when the water goes up my nose and before I can react I'm in a silent, pale blue world, my vision obscured by a swirling stream of bubbles.

Chapter 78

Andrew had stayed behind in the incident room to hold the fort, and Jeff was there too in case decisions were needed. The two men were firmly in waiting mode. Waiting for Steph, Tobias, Ella, and the emergency services to arrive at the location. Waiting to hear from Mel. Waiting to be told if Natasha Emerson was still alive.

Waiting.

Jeff stifled a yawn. 'Talk me through how you found the container.'

Andrew took a deep breath and spilled out his tale.

It had all begun just after 17:00 when the team were supposed to be going home. But they were dithering, not really wanting to leave. Steph was going round shutting down PCs and monitors and came across a paused image of Natasha from the early hours of that morning. A fresh pair of eyes, she'd spotted what she thought was a stain on the hem of Natasha's hoodie. Curious, she stepped the recording back in thirty-minute segments till she eventually found a point where the hoodie was clean. That was around the time Marlon had pulled the feed before the 15:45 call.

Steph fast-forwarded and when the feed was reinstated, the stain had appeared. Andrew and Ella were annoyed and embarrassed they missed it, as was Steph. She'd examined the footage, looking for anything about Natasha or the room that had changed while the feed had been down. Being fair, the mark was only the size of a pound coin. At first they wondered if it was a splash mark, but they asked Bob to enhance the image, which revealed it had a dark pigment. They discounted blood because no one had noticed Natasha incurring injuries apart from minor abrasions. She hadn't eaten any chocolate, so the most obvious source was tea, coffee, or even soup. But if it was liquid, Stevenson must have brought it to her.

More than once during day, there had been comments that Natasha didn't seem as panic-struck as perhaps she should have. If Stevenson did visit her that probably explained it. Knowing what your monster looks like is actually less terrifying than never meeting him.

Thus far it had all been guesswork, but then Greg Brodie's report arrived. It contained a full inventory of items discovered at the house where Stevenson's body was found. The list included a moped parked in the garden outside the kitchen window, and in a cupboard under the stairs they found a Deliveroo bag, along with a bike helmet and waterproof gear. The woman who owned the house, Marlon's cousin, also owned the moped. But neither the moped, the bag nor the gear had fingerprints on them. Greg didn't consider that to be unusual. It would be a hardy driver who would zoom around the streets of Edinburgh at that time of year without gloves.

Andrew traced the owner's phone number through her council tax records. Transpired she'd left Edinburgh the previous weekend to visit her sister in Wales, before moving on to show her dogs at a prestigious event at the National Exhibition Centre near Birmingham. Yes, she did know Marlon was staying at her house. She explained they'd reconnected after the rift that had kicked off between their families back in the 90s. When pushed, she explained it was Marlon who'd made the first contact. Then, only a week or so earlier, he'd asked if he could possibly stay at her place while he was "having new central heating installed". She'd been only too happy to help him out.

Now Andrew was gradually putting a theory together. He figured Stevenson had taken the feed down prior to the afternoon call. Then, with the camera off, he'd driven to the container undetected, disguised as a takeaway driver. At that point, the stain appeared on Natasha's hoodie, so Andrew reasoned Stevenson had brought his prisoner a drink, passed it down to her through the hatch, and she'd spilled some.

Then, prior to the evening call, he'd taken the feed down again. Andrew supposed the kidnapper had gone to the container a second time but couldn't work out why. He could only assume Stevenson had used the moped again, similarly disguised.

But now they had two relatively precise windows where they could search for him, during the times the camera wasn't running. Andrew reminded Jeff that he'd asked Stevenson twice if he'd taken the feed down and he'd body swerved the question both times. In their discussions throughout the day, the whole team was convinced that at those times, Stevenson had been up to something he needed to keep secret.

When Jeff and Mel had set off to tell Hugo's family it was highly likely Natasha was dead, the others had been expected to follow instructions and go off duty. But they were all sitting around, staving off the inevitable, when Steph noticed the stain. When Andrew began putting everything together, it was all hands to the pump, searching for Marlon driving his cousin's moped between her house and an unknown address in Granton at two different times of the day.

It was Ella who eventually hit motherlode. She uncovered footage of a rider travelling towards the house in the afternoon, so she reversed the route and, twenty-five minutes earlier, she picked up the same rider heading in the opposite direction: to Granton. Not long afterwards, Tobias found the same moped rider during the evening window, driving the same route.

Andrew was virtually certain it was Marlon riding the moped. But he still didn't know where Marlon had begun his journey because he was already heading back towards the house when he first appeared on film. Everyone was convinced that his starting point and the container's location had to be one and the same.

So Andrew contacted Ronnie to ask if the Control had received any social media alerts from nearby. He wondered why the sergeant sighed when he confirmed a report which stated: "A genny has been running all hours". Ronnie's teams had been swamped with calls, some well-meaning, but most utterly bogus, and a complaint about a noisy generator was well down his priority list. He gave Andrew the street name and unit number.

Being a belt 'n braces guy, Andrew asked Steph to check the Wallace Fabrication client list for that address. She couldn't find one, so she called Mr Wallace.

"Not one of ours, dear," came the devastating response.

Mr Wallace had chuckled when Steph said, "Shit!"

But then he said, "Ah, but wait a minute. This is ringing a bell." There followed a profound period of silence that lasted so long Steph imagined heading round there to give him a good shake. Then Wallace came back on the line. "You're in luck. We did do a job at that address. I was helping a mate out, so it's not on our books. Marlon went round and priced it up. He did the work later that week as I recall".

Andrew was just about to say *And then we knew we had him* when the phone rang. He picked up and listened for a few moments, asked a couple of quick questions, then said, 'We'll be right there.'

* * *

Andrew eventually tracked down Tobias and Ella standing by a pillar opposite the nurses' station. Steph was a few metres away, talking to Hugo, who had his arm around his daughter. She was in a terrible state: red eyes, blotchy cheeks, dabbing at her nose with a tissue. His wife and son-in-law were a similar distance further on.

Ella glanced past Andrew at the sound of leather soles slapping on the vinyl flooring, heading rapidly towards them. It was Jeff. Breathless. 'How is she?'

Ella blinked furiously before she could speak. 'They're working on Natasha now.' She gestured behind her. 'Hugo and his family are waiting to hear. It's been about twenty minutes.'

'And Mel,' said Andrew. 'How is she?'

'Mel's fine.'

The voice came from behind Andrew, and from a lower level. He spun round, stared down at a pale-faced woman sitting in a wheelchair, dressed in a hospital robe with a blanket draped across her shoulders. A tall chap stood behind the chair, beaming. 'Mel's fine,' said the woman, again. 'Apart from looking like a drowned rat, feeling like shit warmed over, and wondering if she can make a claim on police insurance for a new car.'

At that, a commotion broke out further up the corridor: cries and high pitched squeals. As one, they swivelled to see Hugo pumping a man's hand. But the two men were forced to break their grip when Hugo's daughter shoved him out of the way and flung her arms round the man's neck. He just managed to snare his stethoscope before it slithered to the floor.

'Husband!' Mel craned her neck to look up and behind her at Callum, holding tight onto the wheelchair handles. 'I require carbohydrates, preferably fish and chips, with lashings of tea.' She flapped a hand as if she was surveying her dominion. 'As do these fine people. And, on our way home, a detour to the fire station if you would be so kind. There are a couple of rather hunky firemen I'd like to thank for pulling yours truly and the incredibly amazing Natasha from a watery grave.'

'Watery grave?' Jeff shook his head. 'Drama queen.'

But the DCI was perfectly well aware that if the rescue services had arrived even five minutes later he'd probably have had not one fatality on his hands, but two.

Chapter 79

Three Days Later
Monday Morning

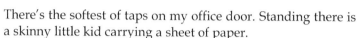

There's the softest of taps on my office door. Standing there is a skinny little kid carrying a sheet of paper.

Except she isn't a kid. This is Dr Klaudia Grześkiewicz who, true to form when we meet, is wearing a smile that if she gave it a bit of oomph, might reach the dizzy heights of faltering. She's lucky if she's seven stone soaking wet. Bar staff have been known to offer her a box to stand on.

Unlike some of my colleagues, Klaudia and I don't go way back. We first met on a murder case a year or so ago. We didn't gel particularly well, but we both worked at it and now we have a perfectly amiable professional and personal relationship, if a touch on the formal side on her part.

On her way in she breaks step and gawps at the wall outside the door. She raises an eyebrow then hurries forward to my desk.

'Klaudia.' I indicate she should take a seat.

'Detective Insp—' She clamps her hand over her mouth. 'Oops, sorry, I forgot. Melissa.'

This is what I mean by formal. Took me several meetings before I eventually persuaded her she didn't need to use my full bifta title. But we've come a long way since then and maybe, one day, she'll be comfortable with just "Mel".

She's studying me across the desk. Brows down, lips in a straight line. Can't possibly miss the scrapes and bashes about my face and hairline. 'I would say I have seen you looking better,' she says.

I laugh. 'Gee thanks, Klaudia. Thursday was an unusual day in the life and times of Mel Cooper.'

'I understand you saved the kidnapped woman from drowning. I must offer you my most sincere congratulations.' She glances over her shoulder, blinks, and smiles once she's facing me again.

Appreciate that, Klaudia.' I'm not sure what's going on with her, but I point at the sheet of paper she's still holding. 'Is that the autopsy report on Marlon Stevenson?'

'It is. Let me confirm what I've written.'

This is another Klaudia-ism. This woman is an expert in her field, we're lucky to have her. But it wouldn't matter if she'd finished the autopsy ten minutes ago and her report was one sentence long, she would still read it before telling me what it contained. But I've learned not to push her, and, after all, what killed him is likely to be irrelevant. So I relax and give her space.

'Marlon Stevenson,' she says, 'died from an abdominal aortic aneurysm.' She looks up, transmits a do-you-need-me-to-explain blink, and I reply in kind. 'The aortic artery supplies blood to the body. We have an ascending aorta, and a descending aorta.' She uses her own body as a living diagram, running the point of her index finger up and down her front. 'The descending aorta travels down from the heart, through the chest and the stomach. An aneurysm is where the artery dilates – or bulges – to a point where the wall becomes compromised. The normal diameter of a descending aorta is in the order of 1.5 centimetres. My measurements suggest that Mr Stevenson's aorta had dilated to approximately *six* centimetres in diameter.'

I try to imagine a blood vessel that's two and a half inches wide, about the length of my thumb. 'That doesn't sound good.'

'It does not. I discussed it with his doctor, who told me Mr Stevenson had issues relating to high cholesterol and high blood pressure, plus he was a heavy smoker until recently.' She blinks again but stops short of "tsk tsk". The doctor had suggested arranging a scan, but I understand Mr Stevenson declined. That would have been at least nine months ago.'

This sounds familiar. I remember when my dad turned sixty-five, he went for a routine scan, part of a programme for all males of his age. 'If the artery was enlarged to that degree, would a scan have picked it up?'

She nods. 'That is most likely. But his doctor is of the opinion that even if they had performed a scan and found the artery was enlarged, his patient would not have accepted any further treatment.'

'Why, Klaudia?'

She lays the paper down on my desk. 'If, nine months ago, the artery had measured one centimetre less, at, for example, five centimetres in diameter, the treatment options would have included surgery. But the operation to treat a large aneurysm has a considerably high degree of risk that sometimes results in serious complications that the patient may not survive. The alternative is to do nothing but the risk of rupture while living your life varies from person to person and, on that basis, some people decline the surgery and leave the aneurysm untreated.'

'So they gamble? Decide to take their chances?'

'They do. Now, even if they do ask about the surgical option, it might not be feasible and there may be no other appropriate treatments.'

'Would he have had symptoms?'

She smiles. 'I am not an expert in these matters, but I was expecting you to ask so I have conducted some research. It's entirely possible Mr Stevenson was asymptomatic, but he may have experienced discomfort or pain in the chest, abdomen, lower back, or here.' She points to her side. 'Over the kidneys.'

'Ah.' I explain to Klaudia that we'd reviewed the videos of Stevenson and confirmed he did massage his upper abdomen and his sides during the second and third calls. 'So, the artery burst—'

'Ruptured.'

I smile. 'Ruptured. And he bled out?'

'Correct. As the wall of the aorta stretches, it becomes weaker, meaning it can rupture. If it does so, it can cause life-threatening internal bleeding that requires immediate medical intervention. Statistics show that approximately seventy per cent of people either die before they reach hospital, or they do not survive emergency surgery.'

I puff out a breath. 'So Stevenson was a ticking time bomb, but he didn't know it.'

Klaudia rocks her head from side to side. 'He was, but whether he knew or not is conjecture.'

'So, was it coincidence that it ruptured that night, or could something specific have triggered it?'

'In these circumstances, coincidence is always a possibility. But equally it could have been brought on by stress, exercise, or perhaps a rush of adrenaline caused by sudden trauma or excitement. Anything that would rapidly accelerate the heart rate.'

I ponder everything we've spoken about. Did he Google his symptoms and make the leap to aortic aneurysm? Did his state of health mean the possibility of a long sentence didn't concern him? Did he think he was already on borrowed time? I guess we'll never know.

I stand up. 'Thank you for coming over to explain all that, Klaudia, but you could have phoned. Saved yourself a journey.'

She nods. 'Yes. But I wanted to meet with you in person, to tell you that what you did to save that young woman was exceptionally brave.'

I'm taken aback. More than a little embarrassed. Then she says, 'Especially as you suffer from aquaphobia.'

Is it possible to be taken further aback? But before I can respond she sticks her hand out, and we bid each other good day.

She's just passed through the doorway when she glances, yet again, at the wall. As she reaches Andrew's desk she pauses for an instant, then laughs lightly, jams her hand over her mouth, and rushes away. I sigh. Like many women, she has a thing for Andrew. But still …

Steph is at her desk. She leans sideways towards Andrew. They obviously exchange some sort of joke but when they catch me eyeballing them they whip round to whatever they're pretending to be doing. Andrew's shoulders are shaking.

I march out into the room. 'Right, you pair. What the hell's going on?'

But it's Tobias who gives the game away because his eyes are not on me. I swivel to follow his gaze.

Some cheeky bugger – there are two obvious suspects – has Photoshopped my nameplate. The two O's in Cooper have been replaced by lifebelts, and images of The Little Mermaid have been stuck on either end.

I can't even pretend to be annoyed.

Chapter 80

Later That Afternoon

The sliding glass door swishes open. A mouth-watering waft of freshly baked baguettes assaults me; at least a hundred calories a sniff, I reckon.

I step to the side to let a couple leave. He smiles and thanks me, she marches straight past. I expect it's not the done thing to beat someone to death with a two-foot stick of French bread, even if she is an ignorant peasant. Still, I'd be able to eat the evidence.

I glance up at the sign as I walk in. *Al's on McDonald*. Right next to the library. Natasha heaves herself out of a fat couch near the door, gives me a hug and a kiss on the cheek. 'Thanks for meeting me,' she says. 'I've been looking forward to seeing you again.'

I smile. 'Me too.' This is the first chance we've had to talk properly. I take in the bruising on her face and neck, and the splint taped round two of her fingers. 'How are the hands?'

'They're okay, still ache a bit.' She holds up her right hand. 'Broken pinkie. Didn't even know I'd done it. And my nails will never be the same again.'

I chuckle at that.

'And you?' she says.

'Oh, I'm fine, thanks.' And it's true, I am. Seeing Natasha here today would brighten the spirits of a corpse.

We place our order and carry our coffees to a window table. A tram heading up town glides silently past the end of the street. A young lad with blond hair and dressed all in black deposits croissants, butter, jam and cutlery in front of us. 'Let me know if there's anything else I can get you,' he says, smiling. He goes straight to the next table and begins clearing up a mess of crumbs that suggests a dozen four-year-olds did battle on the site.

I wait till our early chat dies down, then pick my moment. 'I need to say this, Natasha, you are an unbelievably determined and brave young woman. I don't know how on earth you managed to keep going, not to let him beat you.'

She blushes a fabulous shade of pink. 'You know, I've been thinking about it a lot. I was in there for nearly two days and if I'd given up straight away, I can't begin to imagine the state I'd have been in by the time you rescued me.' She blinks, doesn't quite prevent the tears from forming. She gathers herself. 'I know I thanked you in the hospital, but I imagine I was babbling on, so I wanted to say it properly now.'

I shush her. Now we have matching pink faces. But she presses on. 'And I heard you're terrified of water.'

I smile. 'Funnily enough, not any more. My husband took me swimming. "Kill or cure", he said. Fortunately, it was cure. Anyway, lots of people helped me find that container, but it was the fire service who pulled us both out.'

We fall silent for a few seconds. I ask, 'How are you coping? Are you having counselling?'

'No.' She taps her temple. 'The Effer messed enough with my head. I don't need anyone else tinkering about in there. Not at the moment. I'm confident I can sort myself out but if it turns out I can't, I'll definitely speak to someone. But all good so far.' She makes a face. 'I won't be joining you in the pool anytime soon, though.'

Laughing, I say, 'That was your name for him. The Effer?'

'That's right. It helped me focus.' She hesitates, goes for it. 'Tell me more about him.'

'Has Hugo not explained?'

Natasha shuffles in her seat. 'Grandad feels terrible. Responsible, you know? So we all agreed it would be better for everyone if we didn't talk about Stevenson, put him firmly in the past.'

I raise an eyebrow at that. The eyebrow is saying, *yet here we are and you're asking questions.*

She smiles. 'Mum and I had our fingers crossed behind our backs.'

I settle in and tell her the whole story, or at least the parts I'm authorised to. About Sandro De Luca, Hugo, Isobel, Marlon …

'Marlon?' she says. 'As in Brando? That's his real name? Shit, no wonder he was fucked up.' That gives us both a fit of the giggles.

We chat away about inconsequential nonsense for a while. Then, 'My grandad. I know it was a few hours before he told you about finding the guy. Is he in trouble?'

I was hoping to get out of here without being asked that question, one of the few I can't answer honestly. So I tell her I can't comment, which is probably what she expected.

She moves on. 'I'm curious about the building and the container. Who owned them, and how did he manage to keep the whole thing a secret?'

'We discovered the chap who owned the building died early last year. His children are bickering about his will, which is also being contested by both his ex-wife and his new one. So everything is tied up in legalities. The building was more or less mothballed, but it still has electricity and water for maintenance purposes. All the infighting means the building's designation is unchanged; the council's database still has it listed as fully operational. And the container was already in there. We think Stevenson knew about it because he worked on the site, but he had to take the risk that none of the family would turn up out of the blue – to check the building after a storm, or whatever. I guess he figured it was justifiable.'

'But lining the inside with heavy duty vinyl, why would he go to all that bother?'

'We've been wondering about that too. At first we thought it was to insulate the space, to keep the water as warm as possible. He'd stacked insulation panels against the outside but that could simply have been to disguise it was a shipping container. If he'd left the inside bare, a blind man could have told us what it was and it would have been easier to find you.'

'And the water flowing in, why did that keep changing?'

I make a face. 'Do you really want to go there?'

She nods. 'I need to know so I can put it to bed.' So I talk for a while in vague terms about Stevenson's demands, the flow rates, and the interim deadlines he set. She's already figured out he was using an app to control the water, but she doesn't know about the forty-eight hours, and I steer her well away from that. 'Did you find his phone?'

'No. Nor yours.'

She points at an iPhone on the table. 'Mum bought me a new one. Every cloud, and all that.' She hesitates. 'Were you watching me on live stream?'

'I wasn't, but my team were rooting for you all the way. Or at least until you fell in and knocked the camera out.' It's my turn to hesitate. 'Can I ask you a question now?

'Sure.'

'They were watching you trying everything you could to block the inlet but then we lost the feed. It appeared to us that somehow you managed to exert enough pressure to spring a leak further back, at a connection on a pipe that he'd run across the floor. When our crime scene guys drained the container they found various bits of material and plastic. They logged them all, but they couldn't put the picture together. So, tell me, how did you do it?'

She's sporting a grin that's practically round the back of her head. 'Ever been to Chicago?'

Well, that came in from left field and it must be written all over my face.

She tells me an amazing story that dates from the mid nineteenth century. Beginning in 1855, Chicago created one of the United States' first comprehensive sewer systems. As a result, enormous quantities of concentrated sewage, combined with the Chicago River's industrial and animal waste, all emptied into Lake Michigan. Problem was, the lake was the city's source of fresh drinking water. The citizens were poisoning themselves and a radical solution was needed. Incredibly, they hit on the idea of reversing the flow of the river to redirect the water inland, along with its effluent, where eventually it would connect with the Mississippi.

This was no small river system: 156 miles in length, and at its widest point it would accommodate twenty London buses, end to end. But through the construction of a network of canals and lock gates, by 1900 the Chicagoans had completed one of the greatest ever American feats of civil engineering. They turned their river round; it flowed in the opposite direction.

'Wow,' I say. 'That's amazing. But how did it help you?'

She leans forward on her elbows. 'As you've already said, I was trying to block up the inlet, but nothing worked. When I remembered that story, I realised it wasn't just about stopping the water coming in because the pressure would keep building. I needed something much stronger to reverse the flow, push the pressure back along the pipework. I was hoping it would find a weak point, a loose connection maybe, that would cause a leak outside the container.'

She explains how she used the bucket handle to score the outside of the pipe, bore two holes through the end, and through the cap of the sports bottle. She picked her bra apart, pulled out an underwire and used that to fashion a thread on the outside of the pipe. She jammed the cap on top and eventually managed to thread it onto the wire. She used the other underwire to tie the whole lot together and fashion her home-made compression joint.

'It stayed on for a good while,' she says. 'But eventually I tightened it once too often and sheared the thread on the inside of the cap. The whole thing fell to bits in my hand. I had no idea if it had worked or not. Perhaps it was wishful thinking on my part, but it seemed the flow wasn't as strong as before.'

I lean over the table, take hold of her uninjured hand and squeeze it gently. 'Your idea was genius, Natasha, and it most certainly did work. Our crime scene techs found a leak at an elbow joint. The water was still flowing in, but the level had stopped rising.'

That catches her attention. 'If water was still flowing in, why did the level stop rising? That doesn't make sense.'

I laugh. 'Before I reveal that little secret, tell me about when he brought you the coffee.'

Her jaw drops. 'You knew about the coffee?'

'Yes. When did you spill it on the hoodie?'

'I'd no idea how long I'd been in there when he opened the hatch and lowered a thermos mug. It was locked onto a chain, and he told me I'd have to drink it there and then.' She grimaces. 'I don't even like the stuff, but I took it anyway. I was so nervous I spilled some while I was opening the lid. I tried to talk to him, pleaded with him to let me go but he told me to shut up and if I didn't, he'd take it away. But him turning up like that gave me confidence. If he was going to let me drown, why the hell would he bring me coffee. And that sustained me most of the way through, until the water was way high up.' She doesn't qualify what "way high up" means, and I don't push it. 'But you spotted it? The coffee stain.'

I feel guilty when I confess we only noticed it late on. I explain that we'd worked out when it first appeared and tied that into the feed going down. About how we thought he must have visited the container, otherwise where did the stain come from. I went on to tell her about the feed going down again, maybe a second visit, finding the moped and the Deliveroo bag, and tracking him on CCTV.

'We proved he made a second visit at about half eight in the evening. We suspect he manually set a timer to open a drain at a specific time. Our techs measured the flow, it was designed to let out slightly more than was coming in. We can't be absolutely certain, but the level had probably been falling for a while before I happened along. It's a dreadful thing, but even if you hadn't managed to burst that connection, the container was never going to fill up.'

She raises both hands to her head, grips her hair on both sides. 'But I don't understand, why didn't he set the app to turn the water off?'

That's a tricky one to answer and my conscience has been wrestling with it for days. Do I tell her Stevenson increased the water flow for three hours because we pushed him too far by hassling his mother? Or how he would probably have reduced it again at about one o'clock that morning if he hadn't died? Or that the reason he was dead can be laid fairly and squarely at her grandfather's door?

I've discussed all these ad nauseum with Jeff and the answer is, no. I don't say any of these things. What would be the point? What would she gain? So here's what I do say. 'I don't know why he didn't set the app. Perhaps he was concerned it might have failed because signals and Wi-Fi are never 100% reliable. Or he was worried about a power cut. Sadly, we'll never know.' I don't float my theory that he was feeling a bit off that day and was scared his aorta would explode. I'd tested that one out on the team; they didn't exactly laugh me out of court, but it was close.

Natasha's shaking her head, big time. 'So he was never going to kill me. He was always going to let me go.' She thumps her fist into the palm of her other hand. 'The bastard.'

And that's where we leave it. We chat for a while longer, more inconsequential nonsense. Despite her protestations I pay the bill. As we're putting our coats on, I say, 'What are you up to for the rest of the day?'

'I've got a hot date. With a fireman.'

'Really?'

She laughs out loud. 'I wish.' She checks her phone. 'A lecture on steam turbines at three o'clock.'

Chapter 81

The Following Day
Tuesday Morning

DS Andrew Young possessed many talents but the one he was displaying at that moment was what Steph mockingly referred to as his "superpower": a mystical ability to create order and calm from any chaotic administrative situation imaginable. Efficiently and methodically he was archiving the case files, making a mountain of paperwork disappear like garden party guests during a cloudburst.

He was fast approaching the finishing line when he opened a box file containing the organisation charts that he and the Thompson Twins had been sifting through. Truth was, in the search for the officer who'd been known as *Tetley*, they'd struck out. If Andrew had been working with first names instead of initials it would have helped a lot, but it wasn't until the early 80s that, in documents such as these, the police first began to use names in a more informal fashion. Tracking down the individuals from over forty years earlier had been a real drudge -- everybody was retired, some had died, a few were still around but not in the best of health.

They'd hoped the names Wilma Knight had given them would throw up the answer as to who shut down the case and why. But the officers working it would have been in their thirties and forties and, as Steph had quipped, they were all firmly in the pushing-up-the-daisies category now. A police officer's lifestyle was often not the healthiest.

Andrew decided to take another quick look before he filed the charts. He worked through them, page by page, running his finger down the names. He was well through the file and had just turned a page when he paused and thought for a second before flicking the page back.

About two rows from the bottom was a name. A Detective Inspector, who would most probably have been male. The surname was unusual, but that wasn't what had caught his eye. 'Jeez. What are the chances?' More out of curiosity than anything else, he ran a search. It pulled him down a deep rabbit hole and it took him the guts of an hour to find his way back to the surface.

About ten minutes in, he stopped to look for a phone number in the case notes. 'Theresa,' he said. 'This is DS Andrew Young from Leith police. Do you have a minute?'

Theresa gave him the answer he needed, which encouraged him to keep searching. Eventually, he pushed his mouse away. He stretched and glanced over at Mel's office. He could see her staring blankly at her monitor, elbow on the desk, chin in hand. *Looks like a good time to interrupt her.*

His ankle was much improved, but he was still wearing the airboot. Although the team had stopped calling him "Hopalong", he was still limping slightly as he crossed the floor. He tapped on the glass panel in the open door. 'Boss. I've found something. You'll want to see it.'

Chapter 82

Later That Afternoon

Retired Detective Chief Inspector Douglas Harmiston, who some had only ever referred to as *Tetley*, gazes down at me from the doorstep of his detached sandstone villa overlooking the Forth Estuary and says, 'Don't bother introducing yourself. I know who you are and why you're here.' He half turns away. 'You'd better come in.' He'd been a tall man, but his bearing is no longer what it was, and he walks with a stick.

At first glance the house is tidy enough, but it could do with a dust and a deeper clean than either he or his cleaners are in the mood for. Sadly, I happen to know the lady of the house passed away a few years ago.

Sitting in an armchair he rests the stick against his thigh and gazes out of the generously proportioned bay window. 'I'd always known about my nickname.' He smiles to himself, and I wonder if he's talking to himself too. 'Funny, isn't it, people use it behind your back and think you don't know. "Tetley". But what they don't know is, I'm not a thief. Never have been.' He interprets my expression correctly. 'You don't believe me. And why should you? I only heard about Hugo Emerson's granddaughter yesterday. I meet up with some old cronies for tea and a scone, and they told me she'd been found alive. Used to be we went out for beers and a curry. How things change with age. You're young, years yet before you get to that stage.' He muses on that for a few seconds, decides not to delve any deeper. 'I'm so glad you found her. People tell me she's remarkable. I've never met the lassie, but she's obviously made of stern stuff. And the guy who kidnapped her is dead? Good.' With not a trace of malice, simply a statement.

I gaze around. High ceilings, intricate cornices, double skirting boards and a wide fireplace in the same lush golden wood. And beautiful pieces of art. Grand, that's how I'd describe this room. He waits till I'm back on him. 'My second wife inherited all this from her folks. They died way before their time, and we moved in. She was an only child, you see. That was back in '73 and we've been here ever since.' He glances up at the mantelpiece, there's a photo in a silver frame of an elderly woman relaxing on a garden bench. 'I'm eighty-three so the day I move out of here it'll be in a box. We never had kids but I've got a niece and a nephew so the house will be passed down. But you know about them too, don't you?'

He coughs, hacks, takes a few seconds to settle down. Then jokes, 'Better get that box ordered, I think.'

* * *

He asks if I'd like tea or coffee, but I decline. It remains to be seen if we'll still be on civil terms by the end of our little chat.

'I've heard great things about you and your team,' says Harmiston. 'And ever since I was told you were working on the Emerson kidnapping, I've been expecting you to show up at my door. So, how did you find me in the end?'

I rearrange my legs; make myself more comfortable. 'We knew you existed, but we didn't have a name. My boss and I both asked Hugo but he pretended he didn't remember you. He was lying, and we knew it. We pushed him but he clammed up. Then one of my colleagues was doing the hard graft, trawling through old organisation charts for anything that might jump out. He spotted your name. Or rather, your initials.' A smile plays around his mouth when I say that.

'Andrew was curious, no more. But he followed his instincts and contacted one of your old colleagues. She hadn't been able to remember your name but when he gave her the initials, it clicked, and she confirmed you were the man they called Tetley. But she threw us a curveball because she thought you were dead.' I watch his eyebrows rise at that one. 'Which led Andrew to search for you in the newspaper death notices' archive. While he was searching, he came across a name that rang a bell with him, so he clicked into the notice. Imagine his surprise when in the list of the deceased person's relatives, he discovered a woman with the same name as you. Harmiston. Neither Andrew nor I had ever heard that name before, and now we had two.'

My host runs his tongue along his top lip. I'd say that shook him up a bit, but he recovers quickly. He leans forward, elbows on his knees. 'If you think that was my starter for ten, and now I'm going to spill out the whole sorry tale, you've got another think coming.' I suspect he was going to add "young lady" on the end of that. He has that look about him.

He sits back, folds one long leg over the other, rests his elbow on the arm of his chair, and attempts to affect an air of nonchalance. But he misses by the length of Leith Walk. So before he can get too comfortable, it's time I dragged him back to a place he won't want to visit. 'Did you know Sandro De Luca personally?'

His brows drop. He doesn't answer immediately, but when he does, his voice is higher by half an octave. 'Can't say I did, no.'

'You sure?'

He nods. Clearly he doesn't trust his voice, but no matter. By remaining silent he's answered my question, and he knows it.

Douglas Harmiston's problem here, is he can't be sure I'm not chancing my arm. So I smack the ball firmly back across to his side of the net. 'You've got a story to tell, so why don't you cut the crap and spit it out.'

He opens his mouth as if he's about to deny it, but his face falls. He lifts a dark green aluminium flask from down by the side of his chair and takes a sip. Then he begins to speak.

* * *

'I was still in my first year as a copper. I was young, gung-ho, and not half as smart as I thought I was.' His voice is gathering strength already. 'One day, a chap I know asked me to do a favour for a friend. Nothing illegal but certainly unethical. Big mistake. I didn't ask who the favour was for. Big mistake number two. Had I known, I'd have run a mile.' Nods to himself. 'At least I'm pretty sure I would. But the recipient, guy called Carlo Ferrara, was keen to express his gratitude. Nothing major, a slap-up meal for me and a girl I was trying to impress in an Italian restaurant halfway down The Walk. I was told Carlo knew the owner, which turned out to be true because the name on the licence was his missus. Anyway, instead of impressing my date, I drank far too much and behaved like an arse. So much so, she walked out. The staff looked after me, sent me home in a taxi. The next day I was like death warmed up, and completely mortified. But my mother told me to drag my sorry carcass out of bed and get round there to apologise.

'I had the hangover from hell. The barman persuaded me to try his famous cure. A hideous concoction made from Drambuie, cream and some other ingredients. Spices or herbs, I can't remember. Looked and smelled absolutely foul but tasted like nectar. After a couple of those I was in a jolly old mood, happy as a little sandman. Then a waitress – or whatever they're called these days – sat down beside me. Absolutely gorgeous, Italian, and not a waitress. Obviously. She told me she'd finished her shift, they brought us food, carafe after carafe of red wine with that straw stuff wrapped round the jug. She came on to me and before I know it, we're in a flat upstairs and she's doing stuff I couldn't have dreamed about. I was only nineteen, sheltered life.

'We went on so-called dates. Always to the local Italian restaurants, never paid a penny. She told me I should keep that to myself, joked they didn't want the place flooded with cops hoping to score a free meal. One day, I turned up to meet her and was told Carlo wanted to see me in his office. I strolled in all smiles. "Hi, Carlo", but he launched himself at me, grabbed me by the throat, screaming that she was his daughter and I'd got her pregnant. He threatened all sorts. I was shitting myself. I'd heard through the grapevine who he actually was, and what he was involved in, but my brain was in my pants, and I'd found many ways to convince myself the stories about him were all bullshit. He told me I'd never see her again, that he'd sent her back to Italy, which probably meant he'd transferred her to one of the family's other restaurants. Then he calmed down, told me he wasn't going to kill me, but I owed him, and I'd have to do him a few more favours. I was still crapping myself but when he told me what these favours were, I refused. He said something to the effect, "Fair enough, you're a brave man, I like that, off you go". I managed to stand up somehow, but he said, before you leave, I have this for you. It was an envelope. Told me to open it so I did. It was a photo of my sister. She was younger than me, a sweet girl. Then, from nowhere it seemed, he produced a flick knife. Pressed the button and the blade shot out.

'DI Cooper. Every penny I got from him, I gave away. Charities, the church, people down at heel, you name it. Somehow I got away with it, was never challenged. A couple of years later, Carlo dropped dead of a heart attack and, an oversight I suppose, he hadn't told anyone about me. Seems I was his own pet stooge.'

* * *

'So you were free and clear,' I say.

'Maybe not completely, but with Carlo being dead, I hoped I'd managed to sneak out from under.'

He stops talking and looks at me as if to say, *And that's that*.

Sadly, he's mistaken. I have no intention of letting him off the hook that easily.

'Sandro De Luca.' My change of direction makes him blink. 'The investigation into his murder was going nowhere. Your colleagues had literally nothing to go on. Then, less than a week later, another murder pushed it down the pecking order. The body of a young man was discovered on the foreshore at Newhaven.' I twist the thumbscrews by half a turn. 'Do you remember it?'

While I've been working this investigation, I've been glared at by a world champion, and what Harmiston slings in my direction isn't a patch on Isobel Stevenson's. For the second time, he and his voice take a vow of silence.

I smile. It's my best killer smile, I work on it every day. 'Let me help you with that,' I say. 'The Harmiston listed on the death notice that Andrew found – remember I mentioned it earlier? It was Karen Harmiston, your ex-wife. And the subject of said notice was the same young man whose body was found at Newhaven, five days after Sandro was murdered. I suppose I could ask if you're able to recall his name, but let's not bother. The dead man was Edward Tweed. Karen's brother. And, therefore, your brother-in-law.'

At that point, if I'd strolled across the carpet and planted a kiss on the end of his nose, he couldn't have been more stunned.

'So, Douglas. Tell me all about Edward.'

He takes another sip from the flask. 'How much do you know already?'

I shrug. 'Most of it. I just need you to fill in a few blanks.' I gaze at him.

He stares back. 'Bullshit.'

He hauls himself upright, not without effort, and wanders over to the window. There's a gull somewhere, up on the roof probably, screeching its head off. A shadow flits across the glass and the room falls silent again. I wait. I'm in no hurry.

* * *

'Edward,' he says. 'Or Eddie. I often wonder what would have become of him if he hadn't …'

'What? Killed Sandro De Luca?'

He's still facing away but I spot him tensing up. He doesn't turn. He intends to tell this story to the window, the dunes, and the blue water beyond. 'He'd have been seventy-seven now, and if he hadn't taken it into his stupid head to kill Sandro he might still be alive. And I … well, who knows how my life might've panned out.

'Eddie was my brother-in-law, but we existed on opposite sides of the tracks. I was six years older, I started going out with Karen in '63. That was the year of the terrible winter, snow up to the car roofs. I was about twenty-three, so he was sixteen, seventeen, and that's when it all started to go wrong for him. His dad died, he began acting up, his mum was in a helluva state herself and couldn't control him. Stayed out all night, got in a few scrapes; you know the sort of stuff. We were married the year after their dad died, and she pleaded with me to keep Eddie out of trouble. He was her kid brother after all. So, a couple of times when things were threatening to get seriously out of hand, I *arranged* for him to be lifted. Stuck him in a cell for his own good. But it didn't work. He was getting money from somewhere, started acting the big man, built himself a wee gang of hangers-on. Everybody thought he'd grow out of it, come to his senses. But no. I tried talking to him, more than once, but I was a copper, and he didn't trust the cops. Especially me. Truth is, we'd never really got on so me being a copper was a handy excuse for him.'

'When did you find out he'd killed Sandro?'

'Two days after. The investigation was still at its height and there was a lot of pressure on us to find the killer, so we were rattling cages like there was no tomorrow. Leith might've been a rowdy place at the time with the docks and everything, but the majority of people were good hardworking folks, and family was still important. One day, Karen's sister phoned, said Eddie was behaving strangely. He was drunk. Strutting around the house, running his mouth off, making grandiose statements about how Leith was his town now. She ignored him at first, thought it was idle bragging. But she eventually asked him what he was on about, told him if he knew anything about who might have killed Sandro he should speak to me. But he laughed her off. "I'm not talking to that pig", or words to that effect. But later on he slipped up, said something he didn't mean to, then back-pedalled and became aggressive with her when she called him on it. And that was definitely out of character. He and his sister were only a year or so apart.' He crossed two fingers on his right hand. 'They were like that.

'But I did speak to him, and I knew, just knew, that somehow he'd fucked up. I tracked down the guys he'd been hanging about with and paid them a visit. Their reaction told me what I needed to know. Sandro had lots of friends and they were rampaging about, trying to find out who'd killed their man. So Eddie's boys were crapping themselves too. In fact, I always wondered if they knew beforehand that Sandro was the target. Or if Eddie sprung it on them.'

'Did he ever admit it to you?'

'He didn't have to.'

'And you didn't report it?'

'Carlo pulled me in. Told me I was to leave it. Said something like, "These things have a way of working themselves out". Heavy on the Italian accent.' He smiles ruefully, eyes drifting away. 'When *The Godfather* came out I wondered if they'd done their character research down in Leith. These guys were way ahead of their time.'

He clams up. I expect he knows what's coming next.

'Edward was murdered a week after Sandro,' I say. 'I suspect Ferrara put out the order. Do you know why?'

'Although he was angry because Eddie had killed Sandro, that wasn't the whole story. Carlo's view was that *business* in Leith operated to a fine balance, and Eddie had upset it. It wasn't until long afterwards that I put two and two together – in Carlo's world, taking Eddie out of the equation was simply to restore the balance. Crazy, but that's the way his mind worked.'

I shake my head at the sheer waste of a young life. 'So what happened?'

He hesitates, puffs out a breath. 'Carlo told me he just wanted to speak to him. Oil over troubled waters and all that shit. I was to bring him into the restaurant. Public place, he'd be safe. Carlo said he wanted to keep things private, and I was to drop Eddie off in the back lane. But there was a delivery van in the way, so I told him to get out and walk the rest. It was only a few yards. I was to park up and wait for him but when I got round to the front door it was closed and all the lights were off. Sign on the window said it was due to a family bereavement. That's when it clicked. I'd been well and truly stitched up.'

'At any point, did you not suspect something like that might happen?'

Harmiston doesn't answer. He goes back to staring out of the bay window.

* * *

'After his body was found,' I say, 'you kept your relationship a secret. Why?'

He thinks for a few seconds. 'The way things stood, Eddie was a victim. But if the wider world knew we were related, they'd have started poking about and there was a better than even chance they'd have discovered he was a murderer too. I know it's a terrible way to put it, but that would have killed his mother. So I kept a close eye on the De Luca case, and every time it looked as though it was going anywhere, I undermined the investigation. Made sure evidence was lost or altered, dropped words in a few ears, kept Carlo informed. And when I was promoted to DCI – Carlo was long dead by that time – I obviously had more clout, and I was able to shut it down.'

'So Carlo was dead, but you continued to protect Edward's reputation?'

He nods. 'And the family's. The truth is, at heart he wasn't a bad lad. Misguided, yes. Stupid, yes. Ideas above his station, definitely. But if the concept of killing Sandro and becoming so-called top dog in Leith hadn't entered his head, eventually he'd have come to his senses, and we wouldn't be sitting here today.'

I drum my fingers on the arm of the sofa. 'But Karen found out.'

He drops his head. A tear falls silently onto his shirt. 'It didn't take her long to figure out something was up. I hated lying to her and it was getting to me. She went on and on at me, wouldn't let up. Eventually I had to tell her.'

'But she kept it to herself?'

'She did, but only because it would have come out that her brother was a murderer.'

'She divorced you.'

'Threw me out on my ear and started proceedings the next day.'

'And Hugo?'

The look on his face suggests he'd been praying we were done and dusted. 'And Hugo, what?'

'He also knew?'

Harmiston sighs. 'Hugo was always a loyal friend. A brilliant detective. One of the best. Every time I was promoted, starting when I became a DS, I managed to convince him to tag along with me. He'd done his level best with the De Luca investigation, but he never figured out why he couldn't crack it. Unfortunately, one day I spoke out of turn, mentioned a name I shouldn't have known, and he caught me out. I was completely screwed, had nowhere to go. He went absolutely radio.'

I blink. 'Radio?'

He smiles, first time in a while. 'Radio rental. Mental.' He flaps a hand. 'It's an old saying, before your time. Anyway, I had no choice, I told him everything.'

'I'm assuming the two of you are no longer on speaking terms.'

There's a gap before he says, 'Not really. No.'

We both fall silent, then he says, 'What happens now? What will you do with all that?'

I eyeball him. 'In the end, that's not up to me. I have enough to refer the matter up the line for further investigation. But I'd be surprised if it would be in the public interest to pursue a case against you especially as I suspect that privately, you've suffered enough over the years.'

I gather my things and push myself up from the sofa. 'Just before you go,' he says.

I'm fairly sure I know what's coming. 'Yes?'

'My ... em ... nephew. Will you tell him about all this?'

I fish my car keys from the depths of my bag. Lock eyes with him. 'What do you think, Douglas?'

Epilogue

Chapter 83

Two Days Later

Thursday Morning

'DI Cooper? I have a journalist down at the front desk asking if she can have a word.'

I'm racking my brains for a plausible excuse, when the officer follows up quickly with, 'She says she has information relating to the De Luca case, and I've to stress she's not looking for anything from you.'

I hesitate. It's amazing what journalists will dream up to get their foot in the door. But if it's to do with Sandro De Luca, I'm intrigued. 'Tell her I'll be down in a couple of minutes.'

* * *

Susan Mitchell isn't what I expected. A cheerful woman with a strong Edinburgh accent, she's wearing a mid-length camel coloured raincoat, and I guess from the stains around the left shoulder that she's a granny to at least one toddler. She rises out of her seat to introduce herself and as she sits down, she prods a white A5 envelope into the middle of the table.

'I imagine you're busy,' she says. 'So I'll get straight to the point.' She loosens the belt on her coat and unfastens the buttons. 'Jeez, it's warm in here.' She flaps the collar. Smiles ruefully. 'Hot flushes. I could see them far enough.'

I like this woman. But she's right, I am busy. I'm going to visit Hugo Emerson in about an hour and I need to make damn sure I'm ready for him. 'You wanted to talk to me about Alessandro De Luca.' I point at the envelope. 'You've brought me something?'

Susan lifts the envelope by the corner and a black hardcover notebook slides out. The edges of the pages look as dry as a stick; this wasn't purchased any time recently.

'My uncle,' she says, 'sadly no longer with us, was called Paul Taylor. I doubt the name will mean anything to you ...' She pauses long enough for my reaction to tell her she's got that right, then carries on. 'Back in 1966, he was a young lad of thirteen. But he had a job, off the books. He was a night watchman, a watchie, at Leith Docks. The night Alessandro De Luca died; it was Uncle Paul who found him.'

That catches my attention. 'Paul Taylor? Doesn't ring a bell. Was he interviewed, do you know?'

'I don't think he was. He told me he was really spooked, took fright, and ran off home. He was only thirteen after all. He had thought De Luca was dead, but he couldn't be sure, so his mother persuaded him to go back and check. His aunt went with him, but then they couldn't find a body, so they assumed De Luca wasn't dead after all.'

I lean forward on my elbows, dredge around in my memory for Hugo's testimony. "A night watchman found him ... An old man, long past retirement age, died while we were still investigating ... Sandro was still alive ... Night shift workers called an ambulance, but Sandro died before they could get him to hospital".

I throw these snippets around, drop Susan's uncle into the mix. The first person to find Sandro wasn't the night watchman, it was Paul Taylor, who promptly scarpered off home. Then the old man happened along, and Sandro was whisked off in an ambulance. Taylor came back, didn't find a body, so thought Sandro had survived.

I lift the notebook. 'At what point did your uncle Paul find this?'

'I think he told me that although De Luca was gone, his coat was still lying on the ground. Uncle Paul picked it up and the book fell out of the pocket. Then, of course, De Luca really was dead, and my uncle never went anywhere near the docks again, so he still had the book. It was years later before he gave it to me, not long after I became a journalist. Told me it belonged to "*Mister* De Luca". He'd never read it, but he knew it was really important. He said De Luca carried it everywhere and wrote stuff in it all the time.' Her expression reflects memories from years ago. 'So Uncle Paul thought that because I was a journalist, I could do something with it.'

'Couldn't you?'

She smiles again. I notice a small blemish on her front tooth, not unlike a freckle. 'I'm a sports journalist, DI Cooper. I cover women's hockey, golf and tennis. When I explained that to him he was disappointed, but I said I'd show it to some colleagues who might be interested.'

'I'm guessing they weren't.'

'Nah. They pooh-poohed it. Ancient history, they said.'

I nod. Wonder what I should do. *Am I in the mood to see what's inside Pandora's box?*

Apparently I am. I take my time, scan each page as I flick from one to the next. Spidery handwriting with a pencil that was clearly blunt most of the time. I imagine Sandro licking the point before he jotted down each entry. He was clearly a man who liked order and detail, each double page refers to a person or an establishment. The entries are itemised with dates, names, and always, amounts. In pounds, shillings and pence, naturally. Most mean nothing to me apart from The King's Wharf, a pub on The Shore with a history that can be traced back to the fifteenth century. But then, I turn a page and the name at the top leaps out and dances on my eyeballs. "D. Harmiston".

I scan down, a page and a half of entries, find none where the dates are more than ten days apart, with amounts appended that in today's terms appear trifling but by my reckoning they were probably substantial at the time. I reread the details and I tell you what, if Douglas Harmiston gave all that money away, I'm surprised he hasn't been canonised.

I replace the notebook in the envelope, hand it to Susan. Smile. 'I do appreciate you bringing this in, but I doubt I can use it after all this time. Statute of limitations, you see.'

That last part was bullshit. We don't have statute of limitations in the UK but I'm hoping a sports journalist won't call me on it.

Chapter 84

That Same Afternoon

'I wasn't expecting you today, DI Cooper,' says Hugo over his shoulder. He walks ahead of Steph and me into his conservatory. He settles himself in one of three two-seater sofas, there's one under each window. I didn't have him down as a chintz kind of guy. 'No Jeff?'

'He's taking a wee break,' I tell him. That's more or less the truth, but he doesn't need to know that. He appears undecided whether my boss's absence is good news or not. He'll find out soon enough. 'How's Natasha?'

Having met with her the other day, I know exactly how his granddaughter is. I'm only asking because he'd have expected me to.

'Oh, she's getting there, thanks. Or at least she says she is. She'd been staying with her parents since ... you know. But she moved back to the flat in Commercial Street and started classes again this week. 'We'd all prefer she took things a bit slower.' He throws his arms out wide. 'But what can you do?'

He gives me a look. 'Thanks for asking. But you didn't come here to ask about my granddaughter. What do you want, Mel?'

I swerve the blunt question. 'When we interviewed you the day after Natasha was kidnapped, we asked if you remembered a detective from that time who was known by his nickname. You said you didn't.'

He affects an over-exaggerated pose that's meant to be relaxed. Truth is, he's anything but. 'That's right. I didn't remember. Besides, loads of people had nicknames, and some of them weren't too complimentary.'

'Last week, I had a long chat with one of your old colleagues. Douglas Harmiston.'

'Did you now? I'm afraid I haven't spoken to him in a long time.'

'Turns out Douglas Harmiston had a nickname. It was Tetley.' I glare at him. 'But you knew that. Didn't you, Hugo?'

Now he comes flying forward. The index finger of each hand jabbing at me. 'Now you listen to me. After what I found out about that man, I wanted nothing whatsoever to do with him. A bent copper? Undermining all the efforts of brave and honest policemen, and women, up and down the land. He can rot in hell as far as I'm concerned.'

'Even although his brother-in-law had been murdered? The case you told us you'd mysteriously forgotten about. The one that just – how did you put it? Oh yes, it "popped back into your head" while we were talking. Thing is, I checked it out. And you were right, it was a man in his early twenties. And you also know that case was unsolved.' I glance at my notes. 'Two full fingerprints on the murder weapon but they never traced the killer.' I throw him my most sardonic expression. 'Now, Hugo. Tell me this. Has there ever been a copper who's forgotten an unsolved murder case, especially one they worked on?' He doesn't answer that. I suppose it was rhetorical. 'There but for the grace of God go you.'

That catches him by surprise. 'Meaning?'

I don't need to read up on this one. I have my script memorised, and I do not plan to miss and hit the window behind him. 'We were desperate to find the man who deliberately suppressed the De Luca case. We asked you to help us find a copper who had a nickname. It turned out to be Tetley, and that copper was Douglas Harmiston. You could have given us his name, but for some reason only you can comprehend, you chose not to. That was at 20:46 on the Wednesday evening. At 21:52, during our second call with

279

Marlon Stevenson, we were not in a position to give him the name he was looking for, so he increased the water flow in the container where your granddaughter was imprisoned. Then, by your actions, you caused the death, intentionally or unintentionally, of Marlon Stevenson. That meant the water flow remained set to high for the rest of the time she was held captive. When she was finally pulled out of there by Fire and Rescue, Natasha was within minutes, maybe even seconds, of dying. But let's leave your granddaughter out of it. Because you wanted, and I'll paraphrase your words here, "nothing whatsoever to do with Douglas Harmiston", your stubbornness, no, make that your downright stupidity, nearly cost me my life.'

I move forward till I'm perched on the edge of the sofa. Glare at him. 'So you were right. I didn't come here to ask about Natasha. I came here to inform you it's time you paid the consequences for your decisions that night.'

I turn to Steph. 'Over to you to do the honours.'

When we landed on his doorstep, I doubt Hugo Emerson was expecting to be charged with attempting to defeat the ends of justice in relation to the three and a half hours during which he did not inform us that he knew Marlon Stevenson was dead.

But it only goes to show, not everything that happens in life is what you expect.

Chapter 85

The Following Day
Friday 15:00

Jeff Hunter watched his mother as she fussed around, making a pot of tea for two.

The best bone china clinked as she placed delicate cups in flowery saucers. While the tea was brewing she filled a matching plate with five types of biscuit, two of each, all of them chocolate. Jeff was perfectly sure she wouldn't eat any of them, and he wasn't desperately keen on chocolate himself.

He carried the tray out into the conservatory and spotted his father pottering in his greenhouse. They were both in good nick for eighty-five, he mused. His dad had waved when Jeff arrived, pointed at his wrist and held up both hands with his fingers outspread. Jeff stuck up his thumb; it would help if he had his mum to himself for the next few minutes.

He let her twitter lightly away while he munched his biscuit and sipped his tea. He wasn't ignoring her, he just needed to bide his time before he asked his questions.

'So you're having a couple of days off, are you, Jeffrey?' She peered at him across the biscuits. 'I'm pleased about that. You were looking a bit peaky when you came in.'

Jeff smiled. "Peaky". He could hardly remember an occasion when she'd thought him anything other than peaky.

'Anyway, Son, you've obviously got something on your mind, so you'd better spit it out. I know your dad told you ten minutes, but he'll be ages yet.' She smirked. 'Time doesn't register in a greenhouse, apparently.'

Jeff reached into his inside pocket, lifted out his *Mont Blanc* pen and held it in the fingertips of two hands. He twirled it round, mesmerised by the sunshine glinting off the silver detail. He stopped when the initials faced up at him.

'My goodness,' she said. 'Is that the pen your Auntie Karen gave you. Oh, she would be so chuffed to know you're still using it. But are you not worried you might lose it?

Because it wasn't cheap. I was there when she bought it. Gray's of George Street, you know. It was a fancy shop, back in the day.'

'Coincidentally,' said Jeff, 'a colleague asked me the same question a few days ago. I said, who'd take it. After all, my initials are on it.'

She stretched for his empty cup, spun it round so she could lift it and the saucer together. But Jeff placed his finger on the saucer and applied enough resistance to prevent her taking it away. 'When was the day, Mum? When did Auntie Karen buy it?' He gently took her hand, stroked the back with his thumb. 'I know it wouldn't have been cheap. And I'll wager it was pre-decimal.'

He smiled. He loved his mother. She was such a lovely gentle woman, and he knew the concept of not telling him the truth was utterly beyond her.

'Ah,' was all she said.

Jeff glanced out of the window. If anything, his father was deeper inside his greenhouse than he'd been when he waved.

His mother pointed at the pen, still lying on the tea tray. 'Karen bought it for her husband before … well, just before. But of course, after the divorce, there was no way she was giving it to him. She probably stuck it in a drawer and forgot all about it.

'Then, when you came along, and we chose your name, we didn't realise what we'd done. With your initials, I mean. Not at the time. But, as you know I was in hospital for several days after you were born, so your father had to go to the Registry Office.' She shook her head at the memory. 'Silly old fool.' She stopped, chuckled. 'He was a silly young fool back then, I suppose. But some things never change. Anyway, off he tootled down to Leith Town Hall to register your birth. One job. One simple job. And he got it wrong. Your *father* registered your names the wrong way round. Should have been Jeffrey Daniel Hunter, but he got himself all in a dither, and registered Daniel *Jeffrey* Hunter instead. So you were "DJH" instead of "JDH". It happens more often than you would imagine. I should know, my mother wanted my name to be Valerie, but something went wrong there too.'

She paused. 'But when I told Karen what we were calling you, she flipped. Shouting and screaming and everything. Most unlike her. I couldn't understand what we'd done wrong. Till she spelled it out, literally. But your birth certificate had been issued and there was nothing we could do about it. Then we found a solution. Your grandfather was Daniel, as you know, so we told everyone we'd given you his name, but to avoid any confusion, you'd go by your middle name.'

She grinned, as if in triumph. 'Jeffrey, you were. And Jeffrey you will always be. That made me happy …' She jerked her thumb in the direction of the greenhouse. 'If we *had* called you Daniel, *he* would have been insufferable. His son with the same name as his father.'

Jeff picked up his pen. 'After she divorced Douglas Harmiston, why did Auntie Karen never remarry?'

His mother had clearly been expecting Jeff to mention Harmiston because she didn't bat an eyelid. 'Well, he left his own brother-in-law at the mercy of those gangsters. Absolutely unforgiveable. From that point she wouldn't trust any man. I did suggest she could become a lesbian but that didn't go down too well.'

Jeff fought the urge to laugh out loud. When he recovered, he said, 'But how come I've never heard any of this before, Mum? Why did no one ever tell me I nearly had an uncle who shared the same initials as me?'

'As far Karen was concerned, it was, "And we shall never speak of this again" or whatever the saying is. Is it theatrical?'

Jeff shrugged. He'd never heard it before.

He knew that wasn't quite the end of it but needed to pick the right time. It arrived while he was helping her tidy up. 'Karen's long gone,' she said. 'But I need to know. How did you eventually find out?'

Jeff hesitated. This needed to come from him because sometime in the few days, one of his colleagues would be contacting her. He moved in closer. 'Mum, we've recently solved a murder that happened in 1966, and I'm sorry to say a member of our family was involved.'

Instantly, Jeff regretted his choice of words, and his gaze dropped to the floor. He'd intended to be straight with her, but he'd chickened out. Instead of "a member of our family" he'd intended to say "your brother".

But when he looked up, he was surprised to see her wearing a calm, benign expression. Bright eyes, and a serene smile. She'd been way ahead of him.

'Edward killed this person?' she said.

Jeff swallowed. Said, 'Yes,' and they took their seats again. Before his nerve failed him, he explained about Sandro De Luca, his grandson Marlon Stevenson, Hugo Emerson and his granddaughter, Natasha. And how events dating back almost sixty years connected those four people, and eventually led Mel to a sandstone villa on the coast, a few miles east of Edinburgh.

'That's where Douglas lives,' she said.

Jeff nodded, and they both fell silent.

Fortuitously, Jeff's dad chose that moment to burst through the kitchen door. 'My word,' he said. 'I've been working like a Trojan today.' His wife rolled her eyes at that one. 'Any chance of a cuppa?'

Chapter 86

Later That Evening

My boss swallows an enormous slug of his beer. A Leith IPA, with frost all the way down the outside of the glass.

'Oi, steady on,' I say. 'I'm out to play tonight, you know. Can't have you plastered before we even get started.' I take a decent sip of my Chardonnay. I've heard there are weirdos out there who don't like it. Personally, I could drink the stuff to a band playing.

'Imagine you having the same initials as Douglas Harmiston,' I say, taking a sneaky peek at my palm. 'Did you know, if I had three letters written on my hand, the odds of you guessing them correctly are only one in 17,576?'

Jeff blinks. 'Did Andrew work that out for you?'

I slap my hand flat on my chest. 'Jeffrey. I'm shocked you think I'm so shallow.'

'Ah. So he did, then?' Another quaff of IPA.

I smirk. 'Busted. Right, tell me. How did it go with your mum this afternoon?'

'All good.' And he leaves it at that.

Or he tries to, but I'm not having it. 'And did you mention what you were talking to me about earlier?'

Another slug. A delaying tactic. 'About me possibly resigning?' He studies me across the table. 'I did not.'

'Okay,' I say. 'Before we have too much to drink, let's you and me discuss it.'

His eyebrows pop up. 'Should that not be you and I?'

'No. Me is talking, you is listening. Now, where was I? Oh, yes, why on earth would you even consider resigning?' He makes to speak but I karate chop the air in front of him. 'Because a man you never met, who happened to be your mother's brother, committed a murder? Eight years before you were born.'

He opens his mouth again but this time I only have to threaten violence to stop him butting in. I continue. 'Or is it that you have a tenuous relationship, through a marriage that didn't even happen, with a bent copper who was on the take while you were still in nappies, and retired a full five years before you became a police officer?'

This time he doesn't try to speak but he does hold my gaze. However, I do that little kid thing where I open my eyes wide, waggle my head from side to side and keep him on lock-solid eye contact. He smiles, breaks off, shakes his head and reaches for his beer.

'Because,' I say, 'those would be two utterly ridiculous reasons for a top, top police officer, like yourself, to resign. Detective Chief Inspector Jeffrey Hunter, tell me you agree with me.'

He stays silent. Wipes frost off his glass with his forefinger. Still silent. He's wavering. Time for the *coup-de-grace*. 'Okay. One final point, and you'd better listen.' His glass is in midair. Once he puts it down, I lean over the table, give him my best Paddington hard stare. 'If you do resign, I'll drive past your house every morning on my way to work and give you serious evil eye.'

'You don't go anywhere near my house on your way to work. It would be miles out of your way.'

I flap my hand. Pick up my Chardonnay. 'A minor technicality. So when I get in on Monday morning, you'd better be there. Got it?'

He laughs. A huge uproarious belly laugh. Heads turn in the pub to see what's going on.

He raises his glass and clinks mine. 'Got it, Mel.' Then he pauses. Says, 'Oh. One more thing.'

I glower at him. 'Oh, what now?'

'It's your round.'

THE END

Acknowledgements

Some will say that writing is a solitary pastime, but my experience is that's far from the case. So many people have read my books – a few whom I know but many I don't – they've encouraged me, offered unsolicited and positive feedback, and been wholeheartedly supportive. Every single time this happens it brightens up my day, makes me feel part of a community, and for that I feel incredibly privileged.

Many kind and generous individuals have helped to bring this latest work to life by giving freely of their time, expertise, advice and opinion. I can only apologise if I've forgotten anyone, but these include: my niece Dr Anna Wight, Brian Gallacher, Debbie Mitchell, Ellie Heffernan, Eve Nicholson, Kenny Mair, Lesley Crerar, Linda Gerrie and Susie Spence. Thank you also to the *Deen Divas* who acted as a focus group and helped me figure out how this story was going to pan out.

48 Hours, Then She Dies is a work of fiction, but I've tried to make it as accurate and realistic as possible, particularly in relation to Police Scotland activities and procedures. Without tremendous help and advice from Duncan Smith and Stuart Murray, that would have been extraordinarily difficult so thank you, gentlemen. Any errors or inconsistencies that remain are entirely down to me.

One of the stars of this story is Leith itself. People who are familiar with the areas I've described may have noticed I've taken a few liberties with the geography and invented a few places and settings to make the story fit better.

An enormous thank you to my friend, Chris Livingston and to my cousin, Joyce Nisbet, who have worked with me on all my books. They read and critique the later drafts, highlight inconsistencies in my writing (both technical and creative) and offer guidance and solutions to fix them. This leads to huge amounts of editing and rewriting but neither is a chore. Okay, being honest it's a total pain, but the outcome is a significantly better book than before they got their hands on it. I am incredibly grateful to both of you for your invaluable contributions.

And finally – as ever – THANK YOU to my wonderful wife, Shiona, for the hundred-and-one unseen roles you played to help me get this book out there. Creator, reader, editor, sounding board, designer, motivator, supporter, polisher, publisher – the list could go on … and on … and on. I've said this before, and I'll say it again; I couldn't have done it without you. I love you. HTM.

About Harry Fisher

Harry Fisher is a native of Leith (the port for Edinburgh) so, mainly, that's where his stories are set. Write about what you know, and all that.

Prior to self-publishing his debut, Harry had never written a word of fiction, so he just launched in. Cold turkey for authors, as he called it.

Now he's written and published four crime thrillers in the Detective Mel Cooper series. At the time of writing (31/08/24) his first three books all rated 4.4 Amazon stars from over 2,500 ratings – 60% of which are 5-star. This is book four in the series and was released in October 2024.

Harry loves chatting about crime writing, especially meeting people face to face. He lives in Aberdeen with his wife, Shiona. They share their home with their crazy Hungarian Vizsla – his job is to stop them seizing up completely. So far, it appears to be working. They are into travel, the outdoors, wine and food, and if all four can be combined then so much the better.

Way Beyond A Lie

Introducing Detective Melissa (Mel) Cooper and her team.

"Betrayal. Has Consequences. Deadly Consequences"

Your wife goes missing. She leaves no trace.
Would *you* try to find her?
Damn right you would.

"Ross McKinlay's wife vanishes during a seemingly ordinary shopping trip. Reeling from grief and confusion, he's determined to find out where she's gone. But soon Ross discovers something chilling – he's not the only one looking for Carla ..."

A taut psychological crime thriller set in Edinburgh and Prague, involving an organised criminal gang who deal in identity theft and cybercrime. During a free book promotion in October '22, *Way Beyond A Lie* was downloaded over 38,000 times in five days and reached #1 in the Kindle Free Chart, worldwide.

It's been a while since I've been so engrossed in a book that I couldn't put it down. Well written and a great storyline. A refreshing change. *Goodreads Reviewer* ☆ ☆ ☆ ☆ ☆

Be Sure Your Sins

Detective Melissa (Mel) Cooper series – Book Two

"Six People ... Six Events ... Six Lives Destroyed"

You know they are guilty. So, how far would you go to make sure they suffer?

Edinburgh detective Mel Cooper is mystified by six strange cases, where six disastrous events destroy the lives of six individuals and their families. In parallel, she's investigating a particularly nasty serial blackmailer, who kidnaps a vulnerable young woman in a desperate attempt to evade capture.

Meanwhile, two unrelated people are monitoring Mel's progress closely. One has been manipulating Mel throughout, while the other waits - certain they will eventually be caught.

But as Mel edges nearer to linking the two cases, her bosses order her to back off.

Why are they interfering with her investigations?
Who are they trying to protect?
And how far are they prepared to go to stop her?

I loved this story from the beginning to the end. I devoured it (there is no other word to describe it) in two days.
Goodreads Reviewer ☆ ☆ ☆ ☆ ☆

Also by Harry Fisher

Yes, I Killed Her

Detective Melissa (Mel) Cooper Series – Book Three

"You kill your wife. You get away with it. So, why isn't that enough?"

"In the 21st century, is the perfect murder remotely possible?

Edwin Fuller is convinced it is. He's cunning, calculating, and chilling. He makes a plan. He carries it out. And he kills his wife.

Fuller's plan has worked; he's got away with murder. Case closed.

Until he makes a big mistake."

Endorsed by James Oswald, best-selling Scottish crime author. "I'd recommend this to anyone".

In January 2023, *Yes, I Killed Her* was awarded Crime Book of the Year 2022 by the indie website www.chillwithabook.com

Great storyline, strongly written characters and a nail biting ending - just my kind of book.
Amazon Reader ☆ ☆ ☆ ☆ ☆

Printed in Great Britain
by Amazon